Dad Jokes & Pine Cones

C.J. BANKS

ISBN 978-1-7779937-1-9

Land Acknowledgment

This book was written on the traditional lands of the Anishnabek, Haudenosaunee, Attawandaron, Wendat and Lenape people, in the territory of the Upper Canada Treaties. As a settler to this area, I acknowledge the importance of the Indigenous people and their contributions to my region, nation, and culture, as well as their unfair treatment by the government of Canada and settlers past and present. I support the fight for Truth and Reconciliation, justice for the missing and murdered women and girls, and healing for those affected by the horrors of residential schools, the '60s scoop, and current injustices.

CONTENT WARNING

- This book was written by a **Canadian** and edited by Canadian editors. It includes Canadian spelling, slang, and culture. Canadian spelling is a weird mash-up of UK and US spelling, a dash of French, and our own flair. If you see an extra "u", "l", or "re" instead of "er", it's supposed to be there.

- While this is an adorable, steamy (sex on-page), and hilarious book, it touches on some **difficult topics** that you may need to step away from. That's okay. I still love you. Some of those topics are; mental health issues, grief, abuse (historical and in flashbacks), homophobia, transphobia, suicide (flashbacks), drunk driving, addictions (historical), and on-page panic and trauma triggered attacks. There are also incidences of vomiting, fire, and vandalism.

- There is also **swearing**. This book is no stranger to the F-bomb.

I want you to love this book as much as I do, and I want you to take care of yourself first. If you are struggling with your mental health, I urge you to reach out to a professional. Be it a doctor, crisis line, or a therapist. You've got this.

DEDICATIONS

To my spouse. I love you more than words can say. Thank you for putting up with my tears and self-doubt, late nights, and for being my #1 supporter. Tee hee!

To Vicki, Mercedes, and Amurlee, who pushed me to keep going, be a better writer and a better person.

To my amazing FaeBaes. You all have helped me through tough times. Even if you had no idea you did. You rekindled my love of reading, pushed me outside of my comfort zone and inspired me to write this book. Thank you.

To my Rainbow Community, who needs to know that mental health issues do not make you any less lovable and amazing. The world needs you to be who you are, someone needs you to be their person, and I need you to be your awesome self.

CHAPTER ONE

"Shhhhugar." I held back a swear word as I entered the already dark auditorium ... gymnasium ... What did they call this? Gym with a stage. It smelled like old gym mats and dodgeballs. Gross.

I scanned the audience for a seat, and my heart fell when I thought I saw Alex in the front. But no, it wasn't him. Of course it wasn't. He was dead. A lump formed in my throat as I forced myself to look for a place to sit.

There were a couple of empty, grey, metal, fold-out chairs nearby, and I slumped into the closest one. Shedding my jacket off, I pretended I had been there the whole time and wasn't out of breath. Man, I was out of shape.

On the stage, there were kids wiggling about in mittens and hats. One picked his nose, another cried, and most followed their teacher's funny dance moves and sang wildly off-key. One girl channelled the spirit of Aretha Franklin and gave it. There was one every year, and I lived for it. When their song about snowflakes ended, they waddled off. The teacher looked beat. God bless teachers. Not a job I could manage.

"Now the grade ones will sing about a mysterious man who brings children gifts. I wonder who that could be." Principal Davis read deadpan off a cue card. Who picked her to be the MC?

1

At least she wore an ugly sweater with blinking lights to be somewhat interesting.

"It's Santa!" a kid yelled.

"We'll see." Her mouth froze in a fake tight grin.

"No! It's Santa!" the kid argued.

The will to live visibly drained from the principal.

The gymnatorium door opened and in slipped a beautiful man. At least I thought he was. The dark made it difficult to see. What I could see was long, dark hair, sharp, elegant features, and he was tall. Real tall.

He searched for a place to sit; I moved over and gestured to the empty chair. Accepting my offer, he glided into the squeaky seat.

"Thanks," he whispered, out of breath. His legs folded so much to fit in that chair, his knees were well above his waist.

"No problem. Welcome to the running-late father's club." Stupid attempt at a joke. Socializing was not my forte.

"Thank you. Is there a membership fee?"

He was witty. My shoulders relaxed.

"Being here is paying enough dues. Although you missed the kindergartens, so you're hosting the next potluck meeting."

"Well noted." He tucked a strand of long hair in behind his ear as he eyed the stage and slipped off his coat. His attire was a nice, black, tailored peacoat, black dress pants, a deep blue shirt, and a burgundy vest that fit his shape rather well. I hoped it was dark enough that he couldn't tell I blushed.

My slovenly appearance of old ratty jeans and an ugly Christmas sweater made me look like a swamp monster next to him. I tried my best to not shrink away into nonexistence.

"Have the grade twos gone yet?" His breath was sweet, like he'd also shovelled a supper of granola bars into his mouth while running out the door.

"No, they should be next."

Energetic grade ones pranced around. The kid dressed like Santa had a costume malfunction. His bum pillow popped out, and he almost lost his pants. He laughed hysterically as the teacher struggled to fatten him up again.

"Don't you hate when your butt falls off?" the other father whispered.

"They have a cure for that now." I grinned. Oh no, I could not say what I wanted to at an elementary school Christmas show. A butt plug. Thank you, lady in front who shushed us. We both stifled laughter.

With phone in hand, I waited impatiently as the grade ones exited stage left and pressed record. Emma sashayed onto the stage in the red, poufy dress … and her snow boots. Frig. Her red Mary Janes were still in the front hall where I forgot them. The curls in her hair that I had fought diligently with had fallen flat. One ribbon had slid halfway down her long, black hair. There was a large run in her tights. I thought I had bested those bastards, but they fought back and won. I think Emma picked at it and made the run bigger. But she still worked the look.

God, I loved that kid.

I surveyed the kids on stage. Some I knew from pickup and drop-off, but most I had no clue who they were. Still, moving to this neighbourhood was a good choice. I hoped. The class was more diverse than her last school.

Several Korean families attended this school. And none of them cared that Emma's Korean was broken nor that the only dad of hers they'd met was a pale ginger. Alex would have loved having a Korean community nearby. I had worried that marrying me separated him from his community. He said his family and K-dramas were all he needed to be connected, but I still felt guilty.

Mr. Pretty hit record on his phone. With his lips pursed tight, he held his breath. Did parents have stage jitters for their kids? Should I have had stage jitters? Was I a terrible parent? The kids started singing the song I rehearsed with Emma all week. She sang louder than most of her class, and fairly on key. Very proud of her.

"Which one's yours?" I leaned over and asked Mr. Pretty. The light scent of vanilla and chai wafted off him.

He sighed and lowered his phone. "The one who just bit the little girl in the red dress. Which one's yours?"

On stage, Emma's mouth froze open in shock. I shrugged. "The little girl in the red dress."

"I'm so sorry," he said.

"Don't be." I raised my hand. "Wait for it." Almost on cue, my daughter slugged his son in the face. Gasps and murmurs waved throughout the audience. I wondered how many noticed he bit her first. "Shall we retire to the backstage and deal with this?"

"I suppose we should," he muttered. With drooping shoulders, he shuffled towards the door. For such a tall man, his deflated stoop made him look so short.

Mr. Pretty and I headed out of the gymnasium into the mint green foyer covered in kid's artwork. We didn't get far down the hallway before my daughter ran to me in tears. I scooped her into my arms and rubbed her back.

The music teacher, Ms. Kruger, marched towards us with Mr. Pretty's son in tow. His cries echoed against the concrete walls. He broke free from the music teacher and clung to his dad's leg. Leaving trails of snot and tears on Mr. Pretty's pants. Gross.

"Mr. ...?" The teacher looked between my red hair and pasty, freckled complexion self and my beautiful Korean daughter. She knew Emma was mine; we'd had meetings before. But Emma and I didn't share a last name. I hoped to change it one day, or at least hyphenate her last name. Alex didn't like hyphenated names, so we didn't add mine when she was born.

"O'Connor," I said.

"Mr. O'Connor, your daughter's behaviour is unacceptable. We have a zero-tolerance policy here." She scolded me.

"You saw he bit her first, right?" I asked.

"Does not matter, she should not have punched this young man."

Oh. The rage. He got to be "young man" while my daughter was "unacceptable." I struggled to keep my voice calm. "So, you're telling me you want me to teach my girl if a boy assaults her, she shouldn't defend herself, she should let him do it?"

"Mr. ...." She forgot my name already. Ignoramus.

"O'Connor," Mr. Pretty answered for me.

"Mr. O'Connor, that was not what I said."

"Really? Because it sounds like it to me too." Mr. Pretty defended my statement. "We should ask why my son bit her."

Ms. Kruger shook her head at Mr. Pretty. "Mr. Decker, your son's behaviour has been increasingly poorer. Where is his mother?"

Mr. Decker blanched. "Why does it matter? I'm his father."

The teacher stared at me and gestured to Emma. "And where is her mother?"

"Father," I snapped. Lava flowed in my veins. "My husband passed away last year. And if you paid attention, you would know that. We had a parent-teacher conference specifically to talk about that." My voice cracked, and I ruffled my hair.

Coming out of the gay-widow closet over and over made me want to crawl into bed and sleep forever. Worst thing was, I think she remembered our conversation, but ignored it. Nausea built in my stomach. It was hard enough for Alex to be dead, but to have to defend his existence hurt so much. Our family was real and valid and fuck her for not respecting us.

Now I worried I was in the wrong here. Should Emma have let it slide? Should I not have taught her to stand up for herself? Any kid with two dads needed to fight for themselves more than most kids. *Am I a shit dad?*

"Well, someone gave birth to her." Ms. Kruger muttered as she turned red.

"Whose vagina I came out of is none of your business," Emma said.

Yeah, that comment was one hundred percent on me. I said a variation of that sentence often, and I was lucky she left out the swear words I usually added. Ms. Kruger's eyes widened, and Mr. Decker bit back a laugh.

Should I scold Emma for saying that or be proud of her? The desire to phone Alex's mom for advice grew.

Emma's tears got bigger, and I tried to soothe her while I figured out how to proceed. Hoping Mr. Decker had suggestions, I turned to him, but he gave me an uncertain lopsided shrug. I guess we were lost in this together.

His son still clung to his leg awkwardly. Did kids know where they were grabbing and how uncomfortable it was? The son looked up at me with wild, blue, panic-filled eyes and clung harder. Mr. Decker muffled a grunt. I knew that look on the kid's face; I'd felt that look. This wasn't a kid who was out to be mean; this was a kid who felt scared and overwhelmed.

I knelt to face him and ignored how close to eye level Dad Decker's crotch was. "Hi," I greeted the boy. He looked like his father, but round and scruffy. Like he was the kid who was hard on his clothes and tried to brush his hair and wash his face on his own but missed the mark. "My name is Aloysius. You can call me Wishes. I know, it's a weird name. What's your name?"

"Reese," he whispered.

"Now that is a name people can read and spell," I smiled. "Emma speaks highly of you. So, Reese, I'm curious why you bit her?"

He shook his head.

I examined Emma's arm. There were teeth marks but no broken skin. "Well, you have an excellent set of teeth. Your dentist must be proud."

Reese's lips curved upwards at the corners, revealing holes in his smile that awaited adult teeth.

"It's more common than you realize for people to bite others when upset or excited." That did not sound right. Oh no. My face caught on fire.

"Are you a biter?" Mr. Decker's voice dripped with amusement. "I mean, when you were a kid?"

Maintaining eye contact with Reese, I ignored his father's comment and told Reese my story. "Vincent McDonald. When I was seven, I took piano lessons. My teacher and parents were convinced I was the next Mozart. They registered me for all the local competitions and recitals. And guess what? Vincent

6

McDonald's family also believed he was a protégé and put him in the same competitions. He won every one of them."

"All of them?" Reese asked.

"Yup, all of them."

"I guess you weren't the next Mozart," Reese said innocently.

Thanks, kid. "I suppose you're right. Now Vincent and I, outside of the vicious piano competition circuit, were best friends. I used to spend hours at his house. One time, we were both enrolled in this competition I had practiced an insane amount for, and I swear my performance was perfect. But guess who had higher marks than me?"

Reese looked at me with curiosity. "Vincent McDonald?"

"That's right, Vincent McDonald. So backstage, I bit his hand so hard his fingers swelled, and he couldn't play the next round. He dropped out of the competition and didn't snitch on me. With him out of the running, I won."

"Did you leave teeth marks?" Reese asked.

"Deep ones."

"Did his fingers turn colours?"

"They did. It was gross. They started as dark purple, then turned green. I was worried his fingers would fall off." Reese's eyes widened and he looked at Emma's bite marks. "But they didn't. He was fine. Emma's fine."

He bit his lip.

I continued my story. "Apparently, there was a talent scout at the competition, and Vincent was trying to win a scholarship to a music camp. One his family couldn't afford. He lost the chance to go to camp because of me. And, I lost my best friend." Reese looked at the ground. "That's the story of why I bit Vincent McDonald. What's your story of biting Emma?"

Reese's big, wet eyes looked at me. "The lights were really bright, and it was loud."

"Makes sense," I said. "Bright lights and noise bother you?"

He nodded.

"And Emma sang the loudest. That's my fault. We sing a lot of karaoke at home, and we don't hold back. You should hear her sing eighties ballads. She's good."

Emma, who was still in my arms and getting heavier by the second, smiled as she wiped her tears dry.

"I also get stressed with weird lighting, or if there's too many people, or it's loud, and sometimes textures get to me," I said. Reese tugged at the collar of his worn sweatshirt. "But, biting people will not help. Trust me. You still have those big feelings, and now someone is in pain." It seemed my years of being in therapy were paying off with nuggets of advice.

"I'm sorry I bit you," Reese said to Emma.

Emma slid out of my arms. "It's okay. I understand. Sometimes I help Daddy when things get too big for him." Didn't want people to know that, kiddo. Thanks. "Sorry I punched you. Can I hug you?"

Reese nodded, and Emma gave him a big hug. They were giggles and adorable in seconds. I stood and tipped my head to Mr. Decker. The teacher was nowhere in sight; she must have wandered off. Good.

"Thank you for understanding," Mr. Decker said, wide-eyed.

I smiled awkwardly. I was such a dweeb. Did people still say dweeb?

"Most people assume he's a jerk, but he's not. He's a sweet kid. He just ...."

"Gets overwhelmed?" I offered. "Life can get overwhelming. And he might need ice on that bruise. Although some people find bruises rugged. Take Batman, for instance. His name is even Bruise Wayne." It took great effort to keep a straight face.

"Did you ...?" He paused. "Seriously?" Mr. Decker had a beautiful smile. Perfect teeth. "Ronan," he held out his hand.

My stomach fluttered. Why was he so pretty? And named Ronan? Wasn't that some kind of hero's name? Wait, I was supposed to do something? "Aloysius, or Wishes." I shook his hand, and the hairs stood up on my arms the moment we touched, causing me to drop his hand abruptly. Leave it to me to take the awkward handshake a step further. We stood uncomfortably as our kids chatted and tittered.

"Sorry about your husband," he offered.

That was sweet of him. "Thank you."

More awkward silence while I tugged at my sleeves.

"Daddy, I'm hungry," Emma whined.

"What would you like?" I brushed her bedraggled hair out of her eyes.

"Pizza!" Emma said too enthusiastically. Reese winced, and I reminded her to lower her voice. She whispered, "Pizzaaaaaaaa."

It was unbearable how adorable she was. "Sounds like a good idea." Before I realized what was coming out of my mouth, I asked, "Would you two like to join us?"

"I'm lactose intolerant," Reese stated.

"Well, are there restaurants that have both pizza and lactose-free options?" I asked Reese.

"I know a place nearby," Ronan said with a smile that made his cheeks go round and pink.

He had a deep poetic voice that I could have listened to all day. Hell, I'd be enthralled if he read the phone book to me. Imagining him reading Hamlet left me momentarily transfixed in a strange daydream. "Lead the way."

After we bundled the kids in their snow gear, we strolled down the road. The children raced each other to the trees and back, while Ronan and I made cringeworthy small talk. Well, he talked, and I rambled and stuttered.

The houses were lit with Christmas lights, the street lamps donned the city's festive bows and banners, and a light dusting of snow fell. The kind that twinkled like a million stars. Smoke from the chimneys of houses with woodstoves gave the air that warm and cozy by-the-fire sensation.

Emma flopped in the snow and made snow angels. Part of me wanted to scold her for getting wet, and the other part wished I could join in. She jumped up and ran to me. "Daddy, do you think *Appa* would have liked my dress?"

Oh, my heart. "Yes, bug-a-boo. He would have loved your gown so much he would have bought one for himself to look like you."

She laughed and ran off to catch Reese. A tear escaped. Damn.

"You okay?" Ronan asked.

"I'll be fine; we always are." I smiled, but I hurt.

Snow landed in Ronan's hair, and with the light, it looked like the sky covered him in diamonds. I stared at him while he yelled for the kids to stop at the corner and wait for us. Yeah, my heart still ached. But maybe Christmas wouldn't be as hard this year with a new friend.

CHAPTER TWO

The restaurant wasn't fancy. It was the kind of restaurant where it didn't matter if your kid spilled something or talked too loud, and the red gingham tables came pre-sticky. It smelled of a mix of bread, pizza, and floor cleaner.

Emma and I shared a small pineapple-and-bacon pizza. With a rumbling stomach, I regretted not ordering a medium. The sweet pineapple left me salivating. When did I last eat an actual meal? Was it today? The tang of the pizza sauce immediately reminded me to take an antacid when I got home. When did I get this old?

Reese ordered a kid-sized cheeseless pizza. And Ronan only ordered tea, claiming he wasn't hungry. I tried not to be suspicious, but I used to skip meals to afford a treat for Emma.

As the children talked, I offered Ronan a slice of pizza. When he tried to refuse, I channelled my Korean mother-in-law and insisted. Shoulders softening, he licked his lips when I slid the plate across the table. Then he picked the pineapple off. Well. There went any chance of friendship.

"I don't have a mom," Emma stated. "I had two daddies. But Appa died last year."

She talked about this often, even with strangers. Her therapist said it was her way of processing her grief. But this conversation

11

made my stomach churn. With lips pulled tight into a thin line, I stared at a stain on the table.

"I have one daddy," Reese said. "Mom is alive but doesn't live near here. But I don't care about her, anyway."

"Where is she?" Emma asked with her mouth full. Gross.

"Pen-a-tang-wa-sheen," Reese attempted to say. "It's far away."

My eyes flashed to Ronan as he shifted in his seat, avoiding eye contact. A subtle nod confirmed what I heard but stated, I'm not talking about it.

As difficult as it was for Reese to say, Penetanguishene was polite code for prison in our province. The Central North Correctional Centre was in the town of Penetanguishene. And judging from Ronan's expression, Reese did not mean she lived in the town.

"I hated visiting her. Daddy said we don't have to go anymore, so we don't. But I miss road trips with Dad," Reese told Emma.

"Reese," Ronan said in the stern "stop talking" tone. The kiddo shrunk into himself. Ronan closed his eyes and clenched his jaw.

Yikes. Desperate to change the subject, I opened my mouth to tell a bad and poorly timed joke. Luckily, Emma cut me off.

"Know what I hate?" Emma asked. My lungs sucked in air, and I braced for the tact of an outspoken seven-year-old. "Rudolph the Red-Nosed Reindeer."

Bless this kid. Somehow, she knew when people needed a laugh. She went off on a rant about how the story of Rudolph the Red-Nosed Reindeer supported emotional abuse, the patriarchy, and capitalism. This was one of the many reasons why I loved her, and why I needed to be aware of what drunken conversations she heard.

"— Really. What the fuck is with that?" she asked. Loudly.

Oh fuck. The dirty looks from other tables made me want to run from the restaurant.

The urge to cover her mouth was strong. "Hunny, that word is an at-home-only word, remember?" Did I say she could swear freely at home? I was a shit parent. "And an adult-only word. Right? Appa would not be happy about you swearing. And he would be mad at me for accidentally teaching it to you." Couldn't believe I pulled the dead-father, guilt-trip card. Real great idea there, Wishes. I envisioned the look of disapproval her therapist would give me.

"Sorry, Daddy." She bowed her head and picked at the crust of her pizza.

Crap. "I'm not upset, bug-a-boo. Just a reminder." What would other parents have said?

I worried people judged me harsher than other parents. I'm a young(ish), gay, widowed dad, whose kid was not the same ethnicity as me. A veritable checklist of identities society deemed as atypical. Far from the perfect, white, heteronormative, nuclear family.

I constantly needed to explain myself and apologize for minor mistakes typical families got away with. House a mess? Typical families were "hard-working people whose priorities are their kids and not the dishes." Me? "A slob who neglects the environment his poor kid lives in." At least, that was how it felt. Jerks longed to point a self-righteous finger and say, "Those people shouldn't have children."

On top of worrying about what others thought, I worried I was ruining my daughter's life. The universe dealt her several traumatic events in her brief time on Earth, and I couldn't get my act together enough to make it all better. Some of those traumatic events were my fault, and that guilt would haunt me until the day I died.

"I love you, love-bug," I said and kissed her forehead. "Are you enjoying the pizza?" That was the third time I asked, but I was desperate for a conversation change.

"Mmm!" She sparked a debate with Reese about weird, bug science facts.

I stared out the window into the dark, inky sky and noticed the snow had picked up since we arrived. I wondered if I should cry or laugh at my seven-year-old daughter swearing in front of another kid and classroom parent.

Internally I groaned, as I dug myself deeper into the pit of social outcast. No longer would people purchase our brownies at bake sales, which by the way, were the best. Switching schools again was the only option to save face. Perhaps we should change cities. Ronan would forbid Reese from playing with the loud, swearing, little feminist girl. People would exile us from neighbourhood parties. I really needed to stop fucking swearing around Emma.

Alex would be disappointed.

Ronan leaned in and caught my eye. I braced myself for the reprimanding. To be told I'm a failure and they should take away my kid.

Instead, he grinned and raised his cup to me. "To being a single dad."

A wave of relief crashed down onto me, and I raised my glass of water. "To single dads." The clink of our glasses rang loud, and we burst out laughing, catching more dirty looks from other customers.

He lowered his voice. "A few months ago, Reese stubbed his toe and said the M-F word. I was so grateful we were at home. I'd like to say I don't know where he learned it from, but it was me."

Yay, I wasn't the only one. "I've tried not swearing, but it's hard."

"I hear ya," he said. "Have you met all the parents in our class?"

"No, it's difficult to attend parent nights when my babysitter is my mother-in-law who doesn't like to drive in the dark. Plus, I hate people, and my mother-in-law can drive at night fine, and I have other babysitters. But it's my excuse."

Ronan chuckled. "That is an impressive excuse. I made it to one once, and it was a nightmare. They gossiped so much you'd think they were in high school." He fidgeted with his mug. "Well, they talked about you. Guessing why you're single and took bets on who seduces you first."

"What?" I sputtered. Why did this discussion take place? It was offensive. And yet, I leaned forward for more.

Ronan mirrored my lean. "The top bet is Amber, single mom of Everest. And in second place is Tracy, not-so-happily married mother of Jaxeon."

"I wouldn't date Tracy even if I were straight. She's a hot mess. Always giggling and touching me while we wait for the kids after school." My brain took a moment to put together the puzzle pieces. "And now I understand why. I assumed I was entertaining, but I'm only fresh meat. Way to burst my bubble," I said. "Who'd you bet on?"

"Gambling isn't my thing."

"Who would you bet on?"

He shrugged, turned red, sipped his tea, and busied himself with moving Reese's coat around. Suspicious.

I let it drop. "What outlandish theories do they have about me?"

With a glance at the kids, he pressed his lips shut. "Can ... Okay, this is going to sound weird, but can I have your number? I'll text you." He slid his phone over to me.

Was I making a friend? Or was this a trap? "S-sure." I saved my number in his contacts.

"Aloysius. That's how you spell your name?"

"No. I want to make my life extra difficult. Life is too easy as a gay, red-haired, introverted weirdo. Making my name impossible to spell by the average person spices things up."

The side-eye he gave me was the perfect balance of "that was funny" and "STFU."

Ronan

Apparently Samantha, who lives near you and is a stay at home mom and lead gossiper

She said "various characters of different social standings" come and go from your house during school hours

And she thinks you ...

Run a business from your home

I read the text over and over. Wondering why we hid this conversation from the children.

Aloysius

I do run a business from home

15

He nearly spat out his tea. "Seriously?"

"Yeah. I want to be available for Emma. Daycare is stupidly expensive, as is renting a workspace, and everything I need is at home. Flexible hours means I can work when Emma is at school or asleep and be there for her when she's at home." This wasn't gossip worthy, what was I missing? The sensation of being bullied in grade school crept in.

"What is your … profession?"

"Musician and audio engineer. I have a sound studio at home, so musicians come over when they want a recording session." How was this taboo?

"Musician," Ronan said.

"Yeah, in an overly simplified way. I produce albums, or demos; sometimes I help people with compositions, or I'll play accompaniment. And I write and record my own music." I read the texts again. "Why is this gossip?"

His thumbs moved across the phone screen.

Ronan
She thinks you're a prostitute

There was the joke I was missing. How did I not see that? Probably because I didn't think sex work was a bad thing.

Aloysius
I would never do that
At home
Not with Emma there
I would rent a dungeon and that can get expensive
And I prefer the term "sex worker"

I gave a small coy smile over the top of my glass and took a long sip of water while his mouth gaped open.

Ronan
Are you messing with me?

Aloysius
I don't know you well enough to answer that :)

With fingers laced together, I set my elbows on the table and cradled my chin in the hand hammock. Blinking innocently, I watched him look between my texts, me, and the kids. Mouth opening and closing like a fish.

I needed to stop this conversation before he believed I actually was a sex worker and called Children's Aid Society. "I used to work in an orange juice factory, but I couldn't concentrate. So, I got canned."

His face morphed from confusion to realization and ended in deep laughter, showing off his dimples. "You're one of those dad-joke dads, aren't you?"

I gave my best wacky-dad grin.

"Daddy?" Emma grabbed my attention. "I'm full."

The plate sat pizza free, and my last slice was mysteriously missing. Sneaky kiddo. "Okay, ready to head home?"

She yawned and said yes. If we didn't get home soon, she would have an epic overtired meltdown. Which would trigger my dad-failure meltdown.

The server brought me my bill, and I threw some cash down before I helped Emma get ready to leave. Poufy dresses and snowsuits did not mix. Ronan watched the server take the money and asked where his bill was.

"I'm sorry, I assumed you were … on one bill. Let me go change it," the server offered.

"Don't bother," I said.

"But —" Ronan protested.

"You owe me a coffee." I hoisted Emma into the air and pretended she wasn't too heavy for me to carry.

"You shouldn't have done that."

"Truth be told, I wasn't aware I paid for yours. I saw a number and paid it. So, you owe me coffee." Without waiting for his rebuttal, I headed out the door.

The cold air slapped me, and Emma's tired haze lifted enough that she could walk on her own. Thank god. What was I supposed to do? Did I start walking home? Did I wait for them to say goodbye? How did this work? The door opened and Reese ran to Emma to babble about Pokémon.

"Do you live close enough to walk?" Ronan asked.

"Yeah, I'm a few minutes down the road." An enormous pink Victorian-style house sat on the corner of this street and the one I gestured to.

"We'll walk with you. We live that way too."

The lamplight lit his cheekbones and reflected the snow settling onto his coat. He looked as if he were in an ad for a cheesy Christmas movie. The lamplight probably made me look like a ghost or a vampire. Blue light was not my friend.

"Cool," I said. My brain forgot how to hold a conversation.

At the corner of the street, Emma took Reese's hand as we crossed the road. My heart soared. She could be loud and snarky, but also caring and compassionate.

Ronan elbowed me and pointed at them with a sweet, heartwarming smile. When the kids were out of earshot, he leaned into me. "Thank you. People think Reese is a strange kid and he often gets into trouble. He doesn't have friends, and he gets sad easily. Doesn't help that I work long hours, and he's stuck in a shitty afterschool care program."

"He's a sensitive soul, isn't he?" I asked.

"He is. Perhaps too much."

I chewed my lip and wondered how much of my own mental health I wanted to divulge. There were things about Reese I saw in myself. "Does he often struggle with loud noises and bright lights?"

"Yeah. I had him tested for many medical conditions, but there's no diagnosis. Doctors think his brain is struggling to process — stuff he's been through. He never meant to hurt Emma, promise. Sometimes his brain glitches, and he reacts the only way he can think. He's bitten me many times." Ronan rubbed his arm.

I waited for him to continue and chewed my cheek to stop myself from interrupting.

"He's talked about Emma before and how she's often his reading buddy or plays with him at recess. So, thanks for raising a good kid, and for understanding that he didn't mean to hurt Emma."

I felt this thick and goopy heaviness overflow from his chest. My feet stopped in their tracks. "We understand tough experiences. They may differ from yours, and you don't need to tell me what happened. But we know what it's like to have major life-changing experiences and glitchy brains. Maybe that's why Emma is okay with his quirks? She acts out and struggles too. If she had better emotional regulation, she wouldn't have punched Reese. It's only the start of December and I have already had many parent-teacher interviews."

His tight lips curled in a sad smile. There was an unspoken understanding and appreciation between us. We strolled after the kids, who bickered over who was the best Pokémon. "So, Penetanguishene, eh? You okay?"

"Yeah, we'll be fine." He echoed my answer from earlier. "We always are."

"That's not what I asked. I asked if *you* are okay."

His lip turned red from being chewed on. "Okay, enough."

"If you need to talk, hang out, or arrange a playdate. You have my number."

"Thank you," he said in a tight voice.

Light reflected the dampness in his eyes. Poor guy. Hugging him would be weird, right? *Yeah, no. Don't do that. Don't be weirder than you already are.* "Plus, you owe me coffee."

He laughed a velvety, rolling laugh.

"This is me," I said in front of my house. A modest, two-storey, white house with a concrete paver pathway and a single-car driveway. Smaller than our last house but still a decent size.

Emma requested we paint the shutters hot pink in the summer. I might let her.

Emma banged at the door, trying to break in.

"Ah, you're the one with the Santa flamingos. Reese loves the weird garden stuff you do."

"Emma's doing," I said. "She loves gardening, it's a big dill for her and she loves her thyme outdoors. It's her way to sage against the machine. And her work is absolutely raddishing. When spring comes, going to the flower nursery is her favourite thing to do, because you can't plant plants if you haven't botany." How I said this with a straight face, I did not know. I was proud of myself.

Ronan blinked a few times before laughing. "You really are *that* dad."

My cheeks burned, and I looked towards the house. Emma was seconds from hulking out and smashing the door open. "Well, it was nice to meet you. Have a good evening."

"You too."

Awkward pause. How did these moments work? Hug? High-five? Handshake?

"Night!" I squeaked louder than expected and hurried to the front door. As I let Emma in, I glanced over my shoulder and caught Ronan watching us. He ducked his head and sped off to catch up with Reese.

Was he making sure I made it into my house? That was nice.

CHAPTER THREE

V inny sprawled on my old, oversized, grey couch and listened to me play a solo piece I had been working on for a few months, making notes as I went. It was depressing. Both the piece itself and the amount of effort I had spent, and I still had yet to complete it. It was full of angst and grief. This was the first day in many moons I had touched it. The ending faded out pathetically. I hadn't finished that part yet. How did you end a piece when you still hadn't sorted out those feelings?

"Well?" I raised an eyebrow at Vinny.

"Genius. You touched the depths of my soul and made me long to scream in anguish. There are a few technical suggestions, but you nailed that melancholy."

He ran his hand through his slicked-back, dark brown hair. I loved him but hated how much product he used. Mind you, he tried to get me to use more product, so my curls weren't so "floopy," as he called it.

Vinny was always a handsome man, even in high school. With his soulful, brown, puppy eyes and square features, he switched between rugged and distinguished, depending on how he dressed. Put him in a tank top and cargos, he was the guy you'd go hiking with. In a tux, he was the guy you'd have dry martinis with. But the real Vinny was the guy who wore whatever was clean, and you had pizza and boxed wine with while watching trashy movies.

Vinny eyed my hands, tightening and tugging at the cuffs of my shirt. "You okay?"

The floodgates opened, and I sobbed. Vinny opened his arms wide. "Oh buddy, come here."

I slinked to the couch and curled into his bear hug. Vinny didn't believe in toxic masculinity BS; he knew I needed a crying cuddle. And he was a good cuddler. Lifting weights was one of his pastimes, which led to him giving amazing hugs. We'd always been touchy-feely friends. And yeah, as teens we were more touchy and feely than just friends. But he stayed with me after we ended whatever that awkward relationship was.

He had been with me for almost my entire life. Well, minus the few years it took him to forgive me for biting him when we were kids. Forgiving me was the greatest gift he'd ever given me because I couldn't have asked for a better friend.

After Alex died, I struggled through serious depression. Only a handful of people stuck with us, and he and his wife, Katherine, were my heroes. Katherine took care of Emma, while Vinny took care of me.

I breathed in his earthy-and-citrus cologne. Its familiarity grounded me and stopped me from floating away in a thought spiral.

"What's up?" he asked.

"It was so weird at Emma's winter concert to not have him there. Usually, he's front and centre, cheering the loudest of everyone. His absence was immense. And frig Vinny, it hurt. And Emma got bit, and she punched a kid, she and the kid had meltdowns, and I barely hung on."

"Wait. Someone bit Emma? Give me names and I'll take the motherfucker out." Vinny sat straight, making me pull away from him.

"No, we're good. I don't think the courts would be in your favour if you attacked a seven-year-old." I chuckled and wiped my eyes. "Besides, she gave him a black eye, and I think he was reacting to a panic attack or overstimulated. We had a chat about it, and I told him the story about me biting you."

"Great, I'm glad my childhood trauma came in handy." He gave a half smile, half sneer.

A tinge of guilt dripped in my stomach. "Aww come here." I roped him back into a hug. "I love you."

"I love you too." He patted my head. "Emma's okay?"

"About the bite? Yeah. Everything else? I'm not sure. I hear her crying at night sometimes. She misses Alex, and I don't know if I'm doing things right."

"She knows you love her and you're doing your best. You both go to therapy, communicate fairly well, and you are as open as a parent can be without being disturbing." He rubbed my back. "I look forward to when you see yourself as the amazing parent I see you as."

"Thank you." I pulled out of his arms and sat back on the plush couch. "Hey, guess what? I think I made a friend. After the concert fiasco, Emma and I went out for pizza, and I invited the boy who bit her and his father. It was nice to talk to another parent."

Vinny grinned, making his brown eyes sparkle. "This is excellent. Socializing beyond us and other musicians is good. I'm proud of you."

I bowed my head and my mouth pulled into a tight grin. Alex was the social butterfly while I was the "nod, smile, and hide in the corner with the cat" kind of person. Vinny's acknowledgment of my efforts to talk to new people made my chest warm.

"So, tell me about this new buddy," Vinny asked.

"I didn't learn much about him, honestly. But he seemed nice. He's raising his kid on his own, so it's nice to know another single dad whose kid can be a handful." Mentioning the wife in prison thing might not be the best idea. Vinny could be overprotective of me and Emma.

Loud giggling and footsteps thumped overhead. Vinny and I beamed at each other. Katherine, Vinny's wife, played with Emma every moment she could. She and Vinny wanted kids, but they had not had success getting pregnant yet. Having Emma to pamper and mother helped her feel better, and it helped Emma and me immensely.

"We should focus on work while we have Emma-free time," I said.

Vinny huffed and pulled out a folder of music we were working on together, and I opened my laptop. Releasing a collaborative album had been a dream of ours for years. Piano solos, duets on one piano, two piano duets, and I'd throw in guitar for a few pieces. I wanted to bring in some of our friends for more instruments, but I was self-conscious writing music for instruments I don't play. Vinny insisted I try.

It felt nice to get back into my music. To me, it was a sign I was healing and becoming myself again. Both exciting and scary. I looked forward to it. I think.

Waking up was hard to do. Monday morning came too fast after a busy weekend with Vinny and Katherine. Vinny and I worked together on the beginnings of amazing music. It gave me a familiar electric buzz that once was consistent in my life. Katherine made waffles for Sunday brunch, then took Emma out for a girls' afternoon. It was amazing to have friends like them. While it was primarily a work weekend, this was one of their ways of monitoring me. It warmed my heart to have them in my life.

But it also meant I had little time to relax and reset my brain to get ready for another week.

I shuffled to Emma's room and knocked gently before stepping in. "Hey bug-a-boo," I said and gave her a light shake until her eyes opened. "Do you want me to read to you?" I didn't remember when we'd started this tradition, but I read to her before bed and when she woke up. It meant we had to start our day earlier, but it helped put her in a good mood.

Lately, we'd been reading one chapter per morning of *The Lion, the Witch, and the Wardrobe* by C. S. Lewis. Last week I caught her looking in the back of her closet for Narnia, which I did as a kid too. The idea of sparking magic in her life tempted me to leave a pine cone in there, but I hadn't yet.

Unfortunately, the difficulty with reading in the morning was that neither of us wanted to stop, and we were late for school several times because of this. The Fates tempted me to keep reading this morning, but my phone buzzed and interrupted.

Ronan. The notification preview read: *Hey, I know this is …*

"Okay, bug-a-boo, you get ready," I said. "I've got to respond to this."

She complained but got out of bed while I closed myself in my bedroom. My palms were sweating. Gross. Why would he text me this early? Why would he text me at all? That flash of "something's wrong" hit me.

Ronan
Hey, I know this is awkward since we just met

But I got a call this morning from Reese's afterschool care. There's a major flu outbreak and they need to shut down for a few days to clean everything

Apparently it's barfageddon. Including staff

Would you be willing to take Reese after school until his afterschool care opens back up? If you're busy and can't, I understand. But I remembered you said you have flexible hours so you can be available to take care of Emma. I know you work from home, and I don't want you to think I'm not respecting that. Because it's valid and I'm jealous. So if you can't and you're busy, I get it. But, if you can, I'd be very thankful

Reese is showing no symptoms of the flu

I can pay

Aloysius
Absolutely, I can watch Reese
And no need to pay. Single dads need to support each other

Ronan
Thank you so much. Really appreciate it
I'll send a note telling the school you're picking him up
I can get him from your place around 5:30. Is that too late?

Aloysius
Not a problem
Any dietary or medical needs I should know about?

Ronan sent me several long texts about Reese's lactose issues and what milk alternatives were his favourite. If he acted out, how I could best help him. How not to get bitten. What his viewing restrictions were. And so on. It was both overboard and endearing.

Ronan
Okay. I'll see you at 5:30
I'll bring you that coffee

Aloysius
Uh–uh. No. You're taking me out for coffee
I work from home. I need out of the house
... not a date
Just to clarify
Cause it totally looks like I asked you ... told you ... but no.
Not a date

Ronan
XD Got it. This weekend, I'll take you out for not date coffee

CHAPTER FOUR

Afterschool pickup rolled around, and I was already spent. Most of my day was cleaning any space Ronan might see. Meaning, I shoved junk into my bedroom. Outside the old, two-storey, red-brick school, I shivered and made small talk with Tracy about the kids' schoolwork. Science class was a unit on insects, so I told her you could tell the sex of an ant by putting them in water.

"Girl ants swim away," I said, "but a boy ant floats. Get it? A boy ant floats? Buoyant means to float."

She appeared not to understand and now I had guilt for not including nonbinary ants.

Emma bounded out with Reese in tow, and I released a giant, internal squee of delight. Their teacher peeked out the door and waved to make sure I had Reese. Tracy gave me a curious look as I offered Reese a snack, but she grinned when I offered her one. I meant it for her kid, but she ate it, which was fine too.

Out of fear of the hangries, I always brought food for Emma. Today, Emma was too excited to show her friend her house to waste time with things like eating. I had jogged to keep up, and I was not the type of man who jogged. Sweat trickled along my spine. Gross.

"Boots!" I hollered as they bounded into the house. "Emma, come here." I squished her cheeks in my hands when she thumped back to me. "I know you're excited, but you need to take it down half a notch. Show him where we hang our coats, put your lunch bag, agenda, and homework on the table. *Then* you can give him a tour."

She switched into her impression of the butler Alfred from *Batman*. She put on a bad, exaggerated, posh, British accent and became the impeccable host. She helped Reese hang his wet outerwear in the bat-closet, calling him "sir" and bowing ridiculously deep as she led him into the bat-kitchen. She got her manners from me. And her dramatics.

By the time I made it to the kitchen, both of their belongings were laid out on the table, and the youngsters were nowhere in sight. Their giggles echoing from upstairs made me grin as I cleaned out both lunch bags and returned the clean containers to Reese's bag.

Then I got nosey.

I flipped through Reese's agenda and saw many notes from the teacher. We typically got three a week. He was getting one a day. Notes about his low grades, crying in class, biting his arm, hitting himself in the head, hiding under tables, covering his ears, refusing to talk.

A rock sank in my gut.

This poor kid was not doing well. Today's note said he and another student were disruptive and talkative. I glanced at Emma's agenda. Her note was the same but added she helped another student.

Reese's math book looked like an art book with many red marks from the teacher, and Reese's scribbles over his work. He pressed so hard in spots the pencil must have broken. Ronan's handwriting scrolled across several pages; Reese got the questions right whenever Ronan helped.

His literacy books were at the lower end of the expected range for his age. Stuff Emma read in kindergarten. Flipping through his journal, I found an entry about his mom.

"My mom is bad. She is in jale."

Reese's story about Ronan was sweet. "My dad is my sooperhero. He luvs me and I luv him. He works too much, but he *illegible* smile." There was a drawing of Ronan in a superhero suit, flying through the air.

I put the books away and flopped into a wooden kitchen chair, wondering if I could help. A lot of traumas were displayed on those pages. His acting out, his grades, his emotional rollercoasters hit home with me. If it hadn't been for Katherine and Alex's mom, Emma would be like Reese. Whatever Reese's mom did, it did a number on his mental health. Dread bubbled in my esophagus as I imagined the horrible things that might have happened.

My foot bounced against the white floor tiles. This adorable munchkin needed more support. Did Ronan and Reese have anyone helping them? Would I be overstepping my boundaries if I tried? I called the kids to do their homework; at least today I could do something.

It was subtraction in the tens. I pulled a bunch of dried macaroni shells from the pantry cupboard and, as a team, we worked on their homework. Emma realized what I was doing and didn't rush or blurt out the answers.

After a few questions together, I watched Emma and Reese use the pasta shells to visualize the questions without my help. Reese's shoulders drew back, and he answered several questions without help from either of us.

My spirit lifted as he laughed at Emma repeatedly saying, "What in the shell?"

He mimicked her and said things like, "What the shell is twenty-five, take away ten?" Their giggles were contagious.

"You guys did great. I'm super proud of how you worked together," I said as I read over their work and drew stars in their books. "Okay, do your reading, then you can play." They grabbed books and ran into the living room. I heard Emma help Reese sound out the bigger words.

I glanced at the analogue clock I got to teach Emma to read time, hauled out my large stainless-steel pot, and started supper. Ready to impress, I pulled out my fancy Japanese knife set I used on special occasions. Strong fragrances filled the air as I minced garlic, chopped onions, and mixed my special blend of Indian spices. For years, cooking was not my forte. The more I learned and tried, it became meditative and an expression of love. Now it was one of my favourite hobbies. Knowing what I fed my daughter was important to me.

At 5:30 p.m. on the dot, Ronan knocked on the door. "Hey." He grinned when I opened the door. He was red-cheeked and dusted in snow, and a frigid wind blew around him.

"Hi." My heart jumped into my throat, and I broke into a sweat. No idea why I was freaking out. My palms dampened as I awaited my evaluation to assess if I was capable enough to be around his son.

"I still brought you coffee." He handed me a cup from a local coffee shop.

It smelled sweet and bitter, with a hint of caramel. I clasped it and took a deep breath. Caramel latte. Excellent. My shoulders instantly relaxed. "You didn't have to but thank you." I stepped out of the way. "Come in."

He closed the door behind him and stood on the mat as he glanced around, staring momentarily at the giant photo of Alex next to him staring back. From the entranceway, he peered into the lived-in living room. The kids lounged on the couch, still reading. Emma was reading *The Lion, the Witch, and the Wardrobe* to Reese.

A smile curled on Ronan's pretty, pink lips. "Hey, Reese."

"Daddy!" Reese slid off the couch and gave Ronan an enormous hug.

"Okay, buddy, time to get ready for home," Ronan said.

"Oh, I —" I gulped air. "I made a large pot for supper if you two want to stay." I knew it was sneaky to ask in front of the kids. It elated Emma to have a friend visit, and I chose to be sneaky to make it last longer. Sure enough, the kids begged to have supper together.

Ronan relented. Although, I think it relieved him he didn't have to go home and cook. I hung his coat for him. My hands shook. I had someone over besides Vinny or Katherine, or a work-related person. This was nuts. I tugged at the cuffs of my sleeves.

"Okay bug-a-boo, can you set the table?" I kissed the top of Emma's head. She took Reese by the hand, and they galloped away. While Ronan and I wandered further into the house.

"Wow, nice piano." He gestured at my black baby grand in the corner. "You play?"

I stared at him and blinked. Handwritten sheet music littered every surface of the piano, and my tablet of sheet music sat waiting to be used on the stand. "No. I just like the way it looks."

"Right, you're a musician. Sorry." He blushed and ran his fingers through his long, dark, flowing hair. "I was, I dunno, picturing guitars."

"I have those." My acoustic guitar sat in the corner. "There's more in my studio."

"That's cool." His eyes brightened. "I wouldn't have taken you for a rock star."

I struggled not to take offence at the fact he sounded more interested that I played guitar over the fact I have a freaking baby grand in my freaking house.

"Oh no? What would you have taken me for?" I shifted as he gave me a slow once-over. My baggy sweater and black jeans felt inadequate. I had put thought into what I wore, knowing I'd have company. But I looked bedraggled next to him.

Clearly, his job had a dress code. He wore charcoal dress slacks, a short-sleeved button-up shirt with polka dots, and a dark blue vest. I sensed vests were his thing, and I could live with that. They hugged his curves.

"For dinner. Kidding." He turned redder than a boiled lobster. "I don't know. Something quiet. Maybe a librarian? Or working in a flower shop?"

"Really? Why would you say that?"

He shrugged. "You seem the quiet and awkward type."

Now I turned red. "Good guess. I am not a rock star, and I am quiet and awkward." My hackles went up, and I needed to prove that we quiet, awkward types were just as awesome as rock stars and that my piano was fucking amazing. I strode to the piano and sat with a huff. Beethoven's "Moonlight Sonata," third movement, poured from my fingers.

The piece was complex, fast, and required to be played with passion. It demanded a sacrifice of sweat and tears for any shred of mediocrity. But I was aiming for higher than mediocre. So, there was a lot of sweat and hair flopping. Yes, I was showing off. It was a risk to play this piece, but my soul needed to play it. I played it at least once a week.

Ronan sat on the chair next to me with lips parted in awe. His entire demeanour sparkled while Emma and Reese danced around the room. I enjoyed the adoration of my music.

"Holy f— cow," Ronan said immediately after the last note stopped ringing. "How is it possible for someone's hands to move like that? Your fingers were everywhere in a blur. I didn't think humans moved like that. I'm lucky to type forty words per minute. Play me something else."

"Any requests?" I panted and pushed my hair back. What was this? Self-confidence? Ego? God, I missed this feeling.

His brow furrowed in thought, and a wrinkle between his eyebrows creased. I resisted poking it. A grin broke out on his face. "'The Waltz of the Flowers.'"

"Oh, you're a Tchaikovsky man, I see."

"Yes, I'm a Tchaikovsky man, and Debussy." He looked deep into my eyes and smirked.

My ears went pink. Did he tell me he's bisexual? Tchaikovsky was gay and historians said Debussy was straight. Did he know this, or was he making small talk? Why would he know that? I cleared my throat. "You have a multitude of tastes. Impressive."

"I like a wide range of music."

The familiar white tablet was cool in my hands as I searched for the sheet music. "It's been a long time since I've played this, so bear with me."

He leaned forward with his elbows on his knees as I played. The kids floated and danced like goofballs. I swayed with the music as I played. I was always a physical player and put my entire body and soul into it. Alex said I looked like I was having sex with my piano.

During an uncomfortable, drunken conversation, Vinny admitted watching me play sometimes turned him on. He described my face as on the cusp of an orgasm. Alex said I was embarrassing. It made me self-conscious while playing for a while, but I couldn't hide my emotions. I couldn't change who I was, no matter how hard I tried.

When done, Ronan stood and gave me a standing ovation. "That was phenomenal. You're very"— he flourished his hand — "involved when you play."

My cheeks burned and my ego retreated while my negative self-talk whispered bad things. *He's being nice because he feels bad for you.* I needed to change focus before the voice got too loud.

"Supper should be ready. I made lactose-free lentils and curry. There are some spices in it, but since I don't know about your spice tolerance, I didn't add much. There are plenty of options if you want to jazz it up some." I led the way and the aroma of curry and cumin wafted through the air with the steam as I lifted the lid off the pot.

"It smells divine. I'm salivating," Ronan said. "Dinner and a show? You're spoiling us." He slid an elastic off his wrist and tied his hair into a messy bun.

The meal went off without a hitch. The children led the conversations; I spent most of the time avoiding Ronan's beautiful blue eyes and pretending I was red due to how warm the kitchen was, and not my introverted anxiety.

Which worked, because Ronan blamed the globs of hot curry sauce he added for his blush. He fanned himself and sucked in air sharply. The kids and I teased him.

"I cayennot believe you added that much curry," I said.

"He was not peppered for how strong it was," Emma said.

"After ignoring our advice, he had this cumin," I said.

"Dad's a spicy nugget," Reese said. I needed to teach him the way of the pun.

After supper, we gave the kids video game time while I cleaned.

"Let me." Ronan touched my hand as I reached to gather the dishes. I felt a slight buzz of energy in my stomach. "You cooked; I'll clean."

"I don't mind, I've got this, Spicy Nugget." I interjected.

He rolled his eyes at me and grinned. "You need to reheat that coffee I got you and let me take care of this."

Oh dear. That was a pretty smile.

"S-sure," I stuttered. I microwaved the coffee, leaned against the counter, and watched him load the dishwasher.

He turned to me, smirking. "Were you checking out my ass?"

"What? No." Yes. "I was making sure you loaded the dishwasher right."

"Sure. Your reflection said otherwise." He pointed at my shiny mixing bowl on the counter. Et tu, Brute?

"It's true." Both reasons were correct.

"Did I pass your test?"

I hummed. "Not bad." Dishwasher was six out of ten, but that ass was a ten.

"Next time, I'll watch you load the dishwasher." Ronan raised an eyebrow and started the machine. "So I can see your preferred method of loading your machine."

He watched me sip my latte, and I ignored him, but the longer he watched me, the more I wanted to run shrieking from the room. I caved and looked at him. His eyes were big and sorrowful. Silence dragged on too long for my comfort. I tugged at my sleeves.

"Thank you," he said. Voice barely audible over the dishwasher. "Thank you for welcoming Reese into your home and making supper. I wasn't expecting that."

I bobbed my head. "It's no problem. I haven't seen Emma this ecstatic in ages. She and Reese get along now. I guess the trick to making friends is to bite people. And making friends for her is ...." I gave a lopsided shrug.

"Same for Reese." He stared at me for one more second before continuing, "Well. I suppose we should go do homework."

"It's done. Unless you have your own homework. And I washed the lunch containers. Tonight is for you and Reese to do your thing."

Poor guy looked like he was going to cry. He bundled Reese into his winter coat and looked giddy about spending father-son time. Reese protested until I promised him he could play video games with Emma tomorrow.

CHAPTER FIVE

I couldn't sleep. I had one too many nightmares of Alex dying, and I couldn't face another minute of it. I woke before the sun and decided to get some work in before Emma had to get ready for school.

With a large tea, I sat at my desk in my small, in-home recording studio. My current job was editing a demo song for a ghastly garage band. The singer was off-pitch and sounded like a dying seagull. It was my job to improve the recording. Why did I accept this job? Oh, right. Money.

I didn't abhor jobs from online request sites. Sometimes they were fun, and musicians listened to my advice to develop their skills. I lived for those projects. And sometimes, it was know-it-all teens screeching in my ear. This was one of those times.

As I listened to the singer bray, a slight crackle under the song grew irritating. I checked the audio file and my equipment to discover the noise came from my old faithful headphones. Fuck.

They were showing their age. Most people wouldn't be able to hear the crackle, but I could. They sufficed for this low-paying job, but if I were producing one of my own pieces, a beautiful classical work, or supporting a superb artist, these were no longer adequate.

My jaw clenched, and I swallowed my disappointment.

Alex had given me these when I started my recording label. They were bright, glossy, stinking orange, and I loved them. They became an icon of who I was. Photos of me wearing them were all over my website and social media. The day Alex surprised me with them, I cried like a baby. He was proud of my music career. He was proud of me.

Frig, we were happy back then.

My newer, higher-end headphones sat on the cluttered desk beside me. In the spring, I had found them hidden in the bedroom closet with a tag that read "To: Wishes - From: Santa." I had ogled them for months before Christmas but couldn't bring myself to spend that much money. Even as a business write-off. Of course, Alex, the sweetheart he was, splurged and purchased them.

Alex never had the chance to give them to me.

My gut clenched and turned. Even after death, Alex made me feel special. It took me months after finding them to gather the courage to open the package.

To open my final gift from Alex.

They were too precious for this screechy foolishness. These headphones were suited for decent compositions. Maybe it was silly but tainting them with this crap would hurt my soul. All the emotions tugged at the core of my being. Grief sucked. But it inspired some splendid music. So that was ... something.

I held back tears and hit "play" and the angsty band moaned. Through my audio editing software, I adjusted the recording until I had something not completely horrid and sent the file off to the band to await their complaints. I was a music producer, not a miracle worker. The vocals sounded awful because they were awful.

I stood and stretched. My studio was small, but it was mine. This house spoke to me, specifically for this room. There were no windows, so no outside noise interrupted recordings. I covered the white walls with colourful soundproofing squares, posters of my concerts and album covers, photos of Emma and Alex, and a modest collection of guitars.

It was big enough for recording equipment, writing space, keyboard, and a mic setup. Another musician and I fit comfortably with elbow room to play. Any more, and we had to squeeze together awkwardly. Once I somehow fit myself and two cellists in here. After all, there's always room for cello.

Swinging my arms around, I tried to get energized before settling back into the chair. I had forty minutes before I had to wake Emma. I opened my own files. A file full of dreams and hopes. I hauled out my notebooks and slid on the newer headphones. With closed eyes, I touched the cool, white plastic and thought of Alex. His bright smile, cute dimples, and the crinkles around his deep brown eyes when he laughed.

He was a goofball and obsessed with K-pop; he sang them incessantly. He used to step into the bathroom while I showered and sing loud and off-key at me. Trapping me to listen to him being obnoxious. I revelled in those hilarious and perfect moments.

My heart both swelled and stung, remembering his ludicrous personality and warm, rolling laugh.

I missed him. I missed raising Emma with him; I missed cooking with him; I missed putting up with scary movies with him, because I loved it when he held me to protect me. Now our little family was broken. I was broken.

Pressing "play," I became lost in my own piano melody. With pen in hand, my fingers flew across the notebook. Things to add, change, consider, and what I wanted Vinny's opinion on.

Time slipped sometimes when I worked on my own compositions. Either more passed than I thought or a second stretched for hours. While working on others' projects, I had an internal clock to signal the end of the day. Perhaps it was an internal metronome. With my music, time became abstract.

Movement on the monitor mounted to the wall caught my eye. Emma stood in the hallway, waving her arms at the security camera. Mouth moving, but the soundproofing silenced her yells. My eyes flicked to the clock, and I cursed. There I went, time slipping and winning the father-of-the-year award again. Yanking off the headphones, I flung open the door.

"Daddy! You didn't wake me up," Emma whined.

"Sorry. We'll be fine. We still have fifteen minutes before school starts. Don't worry. Go brush your teeth." I shooed her upstairs and followed. A pit in my stomach ached. I was not sure if I'd ever get a handle on single-father life.

"Daddy, I want to wear my blue dress," Emma was brushing her teeth in the dingy yellow bathroom I never got around to repainting.

"Hunny, we're running late. I think jeans and sweater are the best idea."

"It's our winter class party." She gave me big, brown, puppy-dog eyes.

Damn. I couldn't win. I ran into her room and pulled out her blue dress with rhinestones. Between spits of toothpaste, I shoved the gown over her head. No gracefulness here. Her long, silky, black hair tangled in my fingers; she almost punched me in the jaw as we wrestled the dress into submission.

She gasped and exclaimed in my face. "I need my tights!"

Motherfucking tights. I consistently put holes in them. "Love-bug, we don't have time."

"But they have snowflakes on them, and I'll be cold without them."

Like hell I'd let my baby girl freeze. "Okay," I said. "You brush your hair, and I'll grab them." I dashed into her room, ripped apart her dresser, and then noticed they sat on top. A mess of clothes littered the floor at my feet. No time for remorse.

Back in the narrow yellow bathroom, I closed the toilet lid and set her on it. "Okay, legs out." She stuck her legs straight out for me to put on her tights. "Why did the opera singer wear flip-flops on stage?" Emma rolled her eyes. She had Alex's eyes. And attitude. "Because she was an all-toe singer."

"Dad," she groaned.

The tights fought back, but with brute force and determination, they relented and I managed to not tear a hole. Success.

We ran downstairs; and I squished her into her snowsuit. I jogged into the kitchen, threw way too many muffins into a bag for her breakfast, and shoved her lunch bag into her bookbag. Why were there so many bags? I grabbed her agenda to pack when it opened to her class calendar.

"Emma," I called out. She waddled like a marshmallow man into the kitchen.

"Yeah?"

"The winter party isn't until next week."

Emma batted her eyelashes at me. Brat.

"I look amazing," she said and took her bookbag as she toddled to the door. "I want to say bye to Appa."

I hoisted her into the air to kiss Alex's photo by the door.

"Bye Appa," she said.

My insides shattered. I kissed the portrait too. "Bye, love."

We rushed outside and hoofed it down the street.

Late.

After school, I taught Reese to play "Hot Cross Buns" on piano. His pre-dinner concert for his dad was a raging success. I made bibimbap, and Ronan brought cupcakes. On the third day, Ronan couldn't stay for supper, so I filled containers and sent them home with white-people tacos. Ronan beamed when I handed him the bag. I enjoyed helping. I had been the dad who needed support but was too afraid to ask. Fuck, I was still that dad.

The fourth day Ronan texted me partway through the day. Reese was returning to the afterschool care program, and an empty pit opened in my stomach. It was nice to have him play with Emma. It was even nicer to have him and Ronan for supper.

Having another adult to talk with gave me an inkling of sanity. I had planned to make homemade pizza, and I already made apple cobbler. It had been over a year since I made a nice dessert like that.

Emma had a meltdown because she wanted her friend over. She yelled vile things at me. Like I was a failure as a father, and she hated me. We both needed a cooldown period, so I left her crying on her bed. With Alex's photo clutched in my hands, I sobbed on my own bed until I had no more tears. I wished I could ask Alex to help with Emma.

When we both calmed down, and we had a long chat about her behaviour and her thoughts. It took four chapters of our book before she relaxed enough to fall asleep.

I flopped onto the couch and ignored the dishes and the work I should be doing. My fuel tank was empty, and there was no energy left in me. I grabbed my phone.

Aloysius
Hey, you awake?

Ronan
Barely. Long day
What's up?

Aloysius
Nothing really
Emma had a rough time accepting Reese wasn't coming over
Epic meltdown
Screaming, crying, saying mean things to me
How was Reese?

Ronan
I got bit. He broke skin
He hates his afterschool care. I think some kids bully him

The three dots of writing flickered on and off, and I waited for the text.

Night

Aloysius
Good night

CHAPTER SIX

F riday afternoon, I found a black mailbox that read "Decker" four houses down and left half a cobbler on the front steps. The house was a modest, two-storey, off-white house. The venetian blinds in the windows were bent. No flowers or bushes out front. A "Unit B" sign stuck to the siding and a pathway led to a side door. I hoped I left the cobbler on the right stoop.

After supper, Emma and I lounged on a pile of pillows on the floor, working on a puzzle and watching the new She-Ra cartoon. I loved that show.

My phone buzzed.

Ronan
Thank you. It was delicious

Aloysius
I don't know what you're talking about ;p

Ronan
Tomorrow, 2 pm, Beanado?
No kids?
For coffee, that is ...

Aloysius
Sure!
I'll see if my friend can take Emma

Ronan
Cool. See you later

I smiled. Nay, I beamed. I had a new friend, and we were hanging out. Without kids. This is a new pinnacle in my life post-Alex. That was bizarre to think. Life post-Alex. It was easy to categorize life as pre-trauma and post-trauma.

Alex would be happy I was making friends. It thrilled him when I made friends without his help.

Aloysius
Hey, can you do me a big favour and watch Emma tomorrow afternoon?
I'm meeting a friend at 2

Sex Goddess Katherine
Sure, I can use her as an excuse to see this kid's movie I've been wanting to see.
Wait … you don't have other friends.
This a friend, or a *friend*?

Aloysius
Thank you. Can you get her around 1:30?

Sex Goddess Katherine
Yes. And you're avoiding the question.

Aloysius
Friend. Not *friend*
Straight friend

Vinny the Great
Oh, is this the dad of the boy who bit Emma?

Sex Goddess Katherine
Someone bit Emma?

I spent the next ten minutes telling Katherine about the concert drama and arguing it was not a date. I was not at the dating stage. The conversation had put me on edge, so I lied and said Emma needed me and shut my screen.

Even joking about dating made me nauseous. It had only been in the last month or so that I could go a week without crying over Alex. I was not ready to move on. I didn't know if I'd ever be ready. He was my world for years. Him and Emma.

Alex had this magical power and made me feel unstoppable. His support helped me start my music label. We laughed so much and loved doing dumb shit to make Emma giggle. Well, usually we laughed and were content. He wasn't always the best husband. All couples have rough patches, right?

He was good with Emma. I was the academic and creative dad, while Alex was the run-around-and-do-crazy-stuff dad. The King of Pillow Forts and Kicking Soccer Balls. They acted out plays of knights battling dragons with costumes and cardboard swords. I was the Foley artist, making the sounds and playing live soundtrack music.

Fuck. My heart tore thread by thread inside.

Emma curled in my arms, hugging me. I didn't notice I was crying. This kid. This kid taught me I was stronger than I knew.

"Love you, Daddy," she said.

I kissed the top of her head. "I love you too, love-bug."

It was 2:08 p.m. by the time I reached Beanado. I loved their logo. A tornado of coffee beans. They must have named it around the "Sharknado" movie fad. Guilt bubbled in me for running late, but I had a hit of inspiration for one of my compositions and time slipped. But dang, it was a good few notes.

After rushing to get ready, I couldn't stop checking myself out in the mirror. Emma had picked my outfit. A light blue sweater she said showed off my red hair and green eyes, brown corduroy pants, and a plastic necklace she made for me at school. I hoped I looked okay. I was more coiffed than at Emma's concert, and he had seen me running around in a stained apron, baggy sweaters. Why was I so nervous?

I breathed in chilled air and soaked in the sun on my cheeks before I opened the door. I could do this. Maybe. Oh god.

I found him sitting in one of the comfy chairs by the fire. "H-hey," I greeted and draped my coat over the back of the chair before sitting. The smell of freshly roasted coffee was strong in the café. Quiet jazz played loud enough to hear but quiet enough for a conversation.

His hair was down and wavy from being snow damp, and his cheeks were pink. He had the perfect point to his nose. Angular and strong. He wore a deep purple dress shirt, a charcoal grey vest, and black dress pants. Fashionable even on his days off.

I tripped over awkward small talk before he got us drinks. He said I looked like a gingerbread latte person, and I asked what a gingerbread latte person looked like. "Like a pumpkin-spice latte person." He was right. I hated he was right. I was a basic bitch.

"What do you do for a job?" I asked when he returned. I inhaled the scent of ginger and nutmeg in my latte.

"Nothing fancy. Office assistant at a tech R&D company. It's alright." He avoided my eyes as he shrugged with indifference but didn't elaborate. I didn't press for more information.

I pictured him dressed in well-fitted clothes with his snappy vests, standing behind a counter and greeting people. He would smile and page someone, announcing their guest through an intercom. Or perhaps he was the assistant for the VP or CEO and ran ragged with fetching files, arranging meetings, and spilling coffee on a VIP as if he were in a rom-com. The VIP would scold him but then ask him to pretend to be his date for a fancy company event to make their ex jealous, and they'd fall in love.

I wondered if he chewed on pens or stuck them in his hair?

I watched him track someone walking across the street. He went stiff.

"Everything okay?"

He stared a moment longer then shook his head to pull himself away. "Yeah, yeah. I thought I saw someone I knew, but I think I'm wrong." He sipped his coffee. "Tell me more about your music." He smiled brightly.

I blathered about the music I produced for clients and how I loved helping musicians improve their compositions. I rambled about classical music and how I loathed Pachelbel's "Canon in D" because every wedding gig requested it.

"Composing gives me life," I said. "I wish I had more time for it. My friend Vinny and I are working on a new album together, and I'm stoked. We're planning on doing a concert too, which we haven't done for well over a year."

"Vinny? The boy you bit?"

"Yeah. We rekindled our friendship in high school, and I let him bite me back." I did my best not to turn red, but I failed at hiding a shy smile. Vinny bit me back, but not out of revenge. "We blurred the line of BFFs and BFs as teens." Why was I telling him this? *Shut it, Aloysius.*

Ronan's eyebrows shot up. "Oh."

Ronan had an enchanting smile as he listened to me ramble. It was nice to have someone new to talk with. Not once did he give me the impression he thought I was a weird music nerd that no one liked. He made me feel like a star in my own way.

He bit his lip. "Do you have any of your work on you?"

"I forgot my piano at home." My half smirk elicited a rolling chuckle and a headshake from him. I pulled my phone out of my pocket, dismissed the texts from Katherine, pestering me for up*dates*, and opened my recording files. My thumb hesitated to press play. My chest tightened and my lips pressed together.

"I won't make fun of you. I want to hear, but it's okay if you don't want to share." Ronan's voice softened.

I blinked rapidly. This was my soul, and sharing my soul was so intimate. It was a part of me. Sure, complete strangers listened to my albums, but it was different when it was someone I was trying to get to know. "No, it's fine. I left my headphones at home, so the sound won't be perfect." I hit play, handed him my phone. The bitter coffee scent wafted with his breath as I leaned in towards him.

My heart pounded. I sipped my latte, awaiting judgement. I picked a piece inspired by Emma's fifth birthday. It was an upbeat, joyful, and fairly complicated piece. We had gallivanted around a splash-pad park and a carnival. Emma got jacked on sugar. Alex won me a stuffed bear, and Emma a giant unicorn. I had to wash sticky cotton candy out of the stuffed unicorn. Emma did not sleep well that night. It was worth it.

Ronan held my phone closer to his ear to listen. "You wrote this?" His eyes were open and bright.

I chewed my lip and nodded.

"And it's only you playing? It sounds like two people."

"Nope. Just me." My voice was timid. My shoulders curved forward, and I tugged at my sleeves.

His expression shifted between happy and wonder. He watched me watching him. I didn't even notice I was staring until I became uncomfortable and I turned away. He listened to the whole six minutes and forty-eight seconds. I worried he'd listen to a few seconds, feign interest, and hand me back the phone. But he soaked it in.

At the end, he exited out of the app and his eyes lingered on my screen. My wallpaper was a photo of Alex, me, and baby Emma. Ronan's honey-thick pity oozed out of him.

"You look young," he said.

"Twenty-two."

"I thought I was too young when we had Reese, and I was twenty-four. He was an oops, which led to a shitty, oops marriage." His eyes flickered to me. "Don't tell him."

"Obviously," I scoffed. "Emma was an oops too."

Ronan straightened in his chair. "How? Did Alex ...? Or you ...?" He danced around the implications of adultery.

"Alex's sister got pregnant at sixteen. At our wedding, with my cousin. While we wanted kids, we didn't plan to start a family that early. But this was an opportunity to have a baby who was blood related to both of us. Which we clearly never dreamed would happen. And now we..." I cleared my throat. "I have the most wonderful child in the world."

"Next to Reese." He raised an eyebrow, with a one-sided smirk.

I shrugged, sipped my latte, and returned his raised eyebrow. Daring him to challenge me.

He pursed his lips into a tight, puckering seam. "Can we exchange awkward questions? The proverbial elephants in the room. You tell me what happened to Alex, and I give you the Cole's Notes on Reese's mom."

I shifted in my seat. I hated talking about Alex's death. But I wanted to know Ronan's story. "S-sure." I tugged at my sleeves. "S-so. To put it simply, he was killed in a car accident. He went to the bar and never came home." A rock formed in my throat. My hands shook, and I put the latte on the coffee table in front of us.

"It was his drunk, dumb ass that got himself killed," I continued. "He died on impact. It was a single-vehicle accident. Thank god." Fuck. I scrubbed my hands over my face, then tugged at my sleeves.

I paused before describing the marks on the concrete pole he had wrapped our car around. "The police said in order to mangle the car the way he did, he must have been way over the speed limit. Shrapnel littered the street. A few days later, I laid flowers at the sight and found one of Emma's toys in the ditch. And the question 'what if she was in the car' has plagued me since." I tugged harder at my sleeves.

"Emma and I had to drive by that pole almost every day on our way to and from her school. One reason why we moved." My voice was hollow and flat, but if I didn't go numb, it would hurt as if someone slowly skinned my body.

I started to tell him how I had to identify his body, but my voice caught in a hiccup. Ronan touched my arm and told me I didn't need to say any more. But I pressed on and revealed sometimes Alex's mangled face haunted my sleep. Except he looked more like special effects makeup. Everything was surreal, a movie played underwater.

My mouth was dry, and I tried to swallow. Ronan's grip tightened on my arm, and I looked at him. His lips curved in a soft, soulful smile.

"I'm so sorry. It sounds terrifying." He withdrew his hand and sat back.

I didn't know what to say. I didn't want to retreat into my dark place, so I took a deep breath, smelled my latte, faked a smile, and tugged at my sleeves. He regarded me with damp eyes, as if he were trying to take away my pain. To help me shoulder my burden.

"What happened to your wife?" I asked, wanting the attention off me.

"Ex-wife. We're divorced. The judge found her guilty of possession and distribution of narcotics. Among other things." He fidgeted with the tips of his hair.

"Woah. She was a drug dealer?" I tried to rein in my surprise, but I was shook. Drug dealer never came to mind when I imagined what she did.

"Yeah." He crossed his arms, making him seem small. "One of her friends made meth, and she sold it."

What did one say here? "Did she do drugs too?"

He chewed his nails. "She's done drugs for years. We both did." He closed his eyes for a moment. "I quit when she got pregnant, besides cannabis occasionally. She was sober while pregnant, but postpartum kicked her ass and she started doing more and harder stuff. It was a nightmare. We tried. We really did. AA, NA, outpatient rehab, inpatient rehab, therapy, couples therapy." He tapped his foot on the floor.

"But she lied about everything. She lied about attending meetings. She gaslit me in front of our couples therapist. She snuck drugs into the inpatient rehab and got half her peers high. They were all kicked out. I watched her lose herself, and there was nothing I could do. Protecting Reese became my primary job. I couldn't help her anymore."

"How was she with Reese?" I hated this question, but I had to know. Reese's behaviour issues started to make sense.

"Sometimes she was great. But sometimes she ..." His voice trailed off. "A Children's Aid social worker checked in often."

"I'm so sorry Ronan. I'm glad you two are safe now." This was one of those times where "I'm so sorry" sounded meagre compared to what I felt.

"Thank you."

He told me he came home to find a stranger strung out in Reese's room, with Reese asleep in it. I gasped, held my breath, and broke out in a cold sweat. Vanessa, his ex, was clueless and passed out on the couch. Reese said he didn't think the man hurt him. Ronan had asked several times if he remembered something new since, as did Children's Aid, as did Reese's therapist.

Ronan told me he had to use naloxone to revive his wife or her friends several times. Reese even administered it once on his mom. He would have been five.

My fingers turned numb while I imagined his little hands fumbling with a needle to save his mom's life.

Ronan tried to take Reese and run, but she threatened to call the cops on him for kidnapping. When he finally bolted, she stayed true to her word. The police issued an amber alert, and they arrested him. Their social worker intervened and helped. The police arrested Vanessa and Ronan told them everything, including where to find all the evidence. The police charged her with domestic violence and child endangerment on top of the drug crimes.

At some moment, during his story of epic proportions, I mindlessly touched his arm. It shocked me I had the balls to touch him. He patted my hand and slumped back into the chair. I mirrored him and crossed my arms.

"That's fucked up" was my eloquent response to his tale of woe.

He laughed. "Just a little." Ronan sipped his coffee. We sat in silence. Bonding over trauma was a weird thing humans did.

"I have a question." He broke the silence. "And you can say no. Reese loved being at your house. And this had been the best week at school this whole year. The afterschool program he goes to is garbage and expensive. I can barely afford the trash. Could ... Would you ...?"

"Are you asking me to babysit Reese after school every day?" I sat straight and gasped. My insides exploded with glee, and the sun grew brighter.

"Yeah."

"Yes," I said above the socially acceptable volume. "I'd love to watch Reese. He is an awesome kid and Emma adores him. It's good for her to have someone to play with."

"Seriously? You'll do it? I'll pay you."

"No. Maybe pitch in for groceries every once in a while, but besides that? No. Single dads need to support each other. I'm already taking care of Emma. I can handle another munchkin for a couple hours a day."

"What if in the mornings, I walked both kids to school?"

"That would be great," I said. Again, above the socially acceptable volume. Emma got her volume control from me. "I suck at getting her to school on time. I'm *that* parent. After school, no problem. But before school? My brain doesn't want to function right." I gasped. "I could nap after she left."

We clinked coffee mugs in agreement, and his dimples deepened with his smile.

My near-finished mug stared at me. "I shouldn't have drunk all that. It'll keep me awake all night." Then I remembered. "Tomorrow, Emma and I are doing gingerbread houses. You and Reese should come. Vinny and Katherine will stop in, and I think you'd get along with them. Emma would appreciate someone her age."

"He'd enjoy that. I'll check with him."

"Awesome. But I cannot do what I did last year. I ate three gingerbread houses and got so sick. The doctor diagnosed me with munch-houses-syndrome." I cackled at my dad joke.

Ronan winced and groaned.

CHAPTER SEVEN

The gingerbread smelled incredible. Cloves, vanilla, cinnamon, sugar, and ginger. I woke early to get started, so we'd have plenty of panels, backup panels, and in a variety of shapes to make different architectural ginger wonders.

Emma helped me dump the ingredients in the large, stainless-steel mixing bowl. And outside the bowl. And on the floor. I worried about how much of what ingredients made it into the batter. Thankfully, she helped me with the backup panels and not the main panels.

I loved that she enjoyed helping me in the kitchen. My little sous-chef. And what were gingerbread houses for if not for making a mess?

Ronan and Reese joined us in the early afternoon. Reese wore an adorable snowman shirt. Ronan, wisely, did not dress business casual. He wore a tight, long-sleeved shirt that said, "ho ho ho" and equally tight jeans. I was glad I was already hot and flushed because that ass looked astounding.

"Is your shirt an advertisement?" I tried not to giggle.

"One-hundred percent." He winked. I died.

Meanwhile, a pink terrycloth headband pushed my hair out of my eyes and in all other directions. My stained, oversized sweatshirt I stole from Alex years ago kept falling off my shoulder.

Butter slicked my apron. And there were tiny flour handprints on my butt.

Emma had batter in her eyebrows, and I didn't know how she managed that. Thankfully, her clothes came pre-stained. It was an old shirt of mine with a picture of Frederic Chopin in a box and read "Chopin," then next to it was him outside of the box and read "Chopout."

Ronan eyed it. "That was your shirt, wasn't it?"

I grinned. "Yes. Yes, it was."

He rolled his eyes. But I saw the effort it took for him to keep his lips from curling. Both he and Reese marvelled at the kitchen full of gingerbread house parts. Gingerbread besieged our limited counter space.

"Is it called gingerbread because it's made by a ginger?" Ronan asked.

"I don't know. When you make bread do they call it ..." I looked at him, searching for a comeback and failed. If this were a diving competition, I'd be the guy who belly-flopped. "... blue-eyed bread?" Fuck, that was pathetic. My stomach knotted. "I'm about to make the icing. Reese, you want to help me?"

Swift topic change. Not noticeable at all.

I eyed his tight shirt that did not hide his pecs. Ho-bread! I could have said ho-bread. And now it was too late. Wait, would that have been super rude? God, I was shit at friend-making. I blushed harder and wanted to crawl in a cupboard and die. He'd been here less than ten minutes, and I already made an idiot of myself.

Reese nodded eagerly. I pulled over a second wooden chair for him so both he and Emma could reach the mixer. I measured everything out using Emma's pink-kitten measuring cups and gave them step-by-step directions.

Everyone picked out their pieces, while I loaded the piping bags. Emma was determined to do her own house. Team Decker worked together. Neither had ever made gingerbread houses and were excited.

"Alright Emma, show me your pipes," I said.

She gave me her best muscle flex and roar, and I flexed my noodly soft arms and roared right back at her. I should have been embarrassed having Ronan witness this, but Emma's smile was bright, and it filled me with a powerful burst of sun in my chest. Reese joined in, squeaking more than roaring.

"Alright, pipe on three." I attempted to sound like I knew about sports.

"One, two, three, pipe," Emma and I barked at the same time.

She went to town with piping her icing to hold the panels together.

I demoed for Reese and Ronan. Reese had difficulty holding the bag, and icing kept slopping out the back over his hands. Ronan struggled to make a straight line, and his hair flopped in his face. He stuck his tongue out while he concentrated.

Ronan looked through strands of dishevelled hair and smirked at me.

"What?"

"Enjoying the show?" His smirk deepened.

"What?" I had been staring at him and hadn't realized. "I'm seeing if you need help."

"Any tips?" He blew out the side of his mouth to try to blow the hair out of his eyes, but to no avail. The strand flopped back and into his mouth. This cycle repeated itself so much I worried he'd hyperventilate.

"You're doing great," I said. "I think if you need advice, Reese can help. He's kicking butt."

Ronan preened with pride for his son. "He is."

Reese gave me a giant grin with icing-stained cheeks. His gingerbread house was a disaster, but that was not the point of the compliment.

I dashed upstairs and grabbed an elastic from Emma's stash and an orange terrycloth hairband for Ronan to choose from. He selected the hairband. I was pleased to have a hairband buddy.

Once our houses were "glued" together, it was time for the fun part. I dumped the candy in the centre of the table. The kids went nuts. I'm sure they ate more than they used to decorate.

It bemused me to see Reese's chaotic tackiness and globular part of their house, versus Ronan's well-thought-out attempts at details and relatively tidy side. Emma strived for seven-year-old chic, while I attempted ornate multicoloured stained-glass windows. Not the best job, but not horrible.

"Hey, Daddy?" Emma asked. "Why did the gingerbread person go to the doctors?"

I taught her this one, but I refused to ruin her dad joke. "I don't know, love-bug."

"Because he was feeling crumb-y," Emma cackled. I loved this kid. I howled with laughter.

"Emma, you have something right"— I stuck a glob of icing on her nose — "there."

She squealed. And thus started our traditional leftover icing fight. She smeared icing across my cheeks. I let her so I could hear her giggle. Reese joined instantly by wiping his palms on Emma's arms.

Emma stuck her fist in the leftover icing sugar, and hell broke loose. Icing sugar everywhere. I had so much in my hair that I looked at least twenty years older. Emma looked like a creepy child from a horror movie. Reese smeared icing sugar across Emma's forehead. I was positive I saw him snorting the sugar off the table. Gross. And a red flag from his trauma.

Emma and I hadn't laughed this hard since Alex died. I didn't care the kitchen was going to take forever to clean. Her laugh was the best thing to me.

I heard a sound and looked to find Ronan taking photos and chuckling in the corner of the kitchen. Here were me and the kids, covered in white powder and sticky glaze, and there stood Ronan. Spotless. Thinking he was exempt from this madness. Emma and I exchanged quick glances that spoke thousands of words of mischief. She knew what to do. I grabbed her waist, hoisted her into the air, and charged towards Ronan. He barely had a moment to object before small sticky hands smeared his cheeks.

Reese was quick to enlist in the attack on his father. Ronan found himself covered with powdered handprints. I stepped aside to give the goblins more room for their massacre. He was defenceless, no arsenal of food stuff within reach. It was at this moment Reese revealed Ronan's Achilles' heel. He was ticklish. Damn right I took photos.

He escaped the wretched, tiny fingers and gasped for air between laughs. His devious blue eyes met mine. We both reached for handfuls of icing sugar. But alas, he was quicker than me. His powdered hands mussed my hair. I protested and turned to run, but his arms enclosed around me into a bear hug from behind. Pinning my arms to my waist.

His laughter vibrated against my back, and his breath warmed my neck.

The tiny goblins betrayed me and attacked. I couldn't evade or defend myself. I was screwed. The goblins unleashed into full assault mode. Ronan directed them where to find more ammunition. Bastard. But Emma hadn't laughed this much in ages, and my chest couldn't handle how marvellous this was. My lungs struggled to breathe because I was laughing so much and screaming for mercy.

And holy crap, either Ronan was strong, or I was incredibly weak. Or both. I could not break free, no matter how much I struggled. And damn, I did not realize how tall he was. He had to fold over me to get a secure a good grip.

He smelled like vanilla.

"What on Earth is going on?" Katherine exclaimed as she waltzed into the kitchen with Vinny.

Vinny observed our state of disrepair. White powder on the floor counters, cabinet, my no-longer-blue walls, us, and how did we get it on the ceiling? His eyes fell to the arms surrounding me. I noted a quirk of an eyebrow before Emma turned and yelled, "Uncle Vinny." And ran after him with thick-icing fingers.

"Shit." Vinny bolted down the hall.

"Language," I called out. "Emma, don't touch anything that isn't Vinny." Reese squealed with laughter and ran after Emma. I heard

Vinny shouting for help and a thumping noise that sounded an awful lot like him being tackled to the floor.

Katherine had a cat-got-the-cream grin. Ronan still had his arms around me. Fuck. My body tensed, and my back became cold as Ronan took an enormous step away.

"So, my name's Katherine," she said. "I assume you are Ronan? I'd shake your hand, but …." She gestured to his dirty hands.

"Nice to meet you." Ronan inclined his head. Slightly out of breath.

Katherine inspected our gingerbread houses. "These look wonderful." She looked over my shoulder. "I see there're enough panels for Vinny and me?"

"Have at it." I swept my arm over the counter.

Katherine leaned into the hallway and hollered, "Monkey, come help me with my gingerbread house."

"Coming," Emma shouted back, followed by galloping footsteps.

Reese dragged Vinny along by the hand into the kitchen. He did not come out unscathed. He slunk into the kitchen behind his new master, winded and unkempt. His typically dark, slicked-back hair stood on end. A porcupine with white frosted tips.

"Hey, I'm Vinny," he said to Ronan with a slight pant. "I'm Wishes' overly protective best friend who would either die for him or help him bury a body. Just saying."

"Good to know." Ronan stiffened. "I'm Ronan. I'm merely a neighbour whose kid is in Emma's class. No need for murder."

Vinny grinned. "Good." Emma kicked him under the table. "Point taken. I'll be nice. Hey." He turned to me. "No Christmas decorations yet? You need help?"

"No, not yet. I think this year I may enlist the help of Reese?" I looked at Reese, who nodded vigorously. "We're going all out this year."

"We're making up for last year," Emma said. She looked at Reese. "We didn't do Christmas last year."

"We don't have big Christmases since it's only the two of us. Why didn't you have Christmas?" Reese asked. I sensed Ronan tensing next to me.

"Daddy was in the hospital," Emma stated as a matter of fact. "After Appa died. I spent Christmas with my *halmoni*. That's Korean for grandmother."

Reese tried saying halmoni a few times.

I felt a hot flash of discomfort. I tugged at my sleeves. What is with kids blabbing things we didn't want to share?

Katherine gave me a sympathetic smile and saved me by asking Emma to show her how to glue the walls together. I leaned against the counter, curved my back, and crossed my arms.

Ronan leaned next to me and assessed my facial expression. "You okay?" His voice was quiet.

I nodded. My tongue felt like a ball of muscles that was too big for my mouth. I knew I wasn't able to hide the fact that my smile had dropped into a tight line that dipped on the edges.

He pressed his foot against mine. "You wanna talk?"

I shook my head. "Maybe later." It was exhausting to have these marvellous, hilarious moments, then be slapped with a reminder that my life was a mess. I plunged into those shadows in my mind again. I didn't deserve these moments of joy.

A hand settled on my shoulder. I looked to Ronan, who jutted his chin towards the living room. Glancing at the kids laughing, I realized I should leave the room. Or the house. I didn't want to sully their day with my mood swings.

I stood in the middle of the living room, afraid to sit on the furniture with my dirty clothes. Our furniture wasn't anything special; nevertheless, cleaning my kitchen *and* living room was the last thing I needed to do tonight. I turned in circles, hugging myself, trying to figure out what to do.

"Hey." Ronan grabbed my attention. "Christmas is tough for us too. If you need anything, ask."

"Thank you. I appreciate that." I chewed on my lip in thought. "What does your Christmas look like?" I asked. Both because I was curious, and I wanted to change the subject.

"It's quiet. My parents visit my sister in Montreal, and my uncle Tim likes to go somewhere warm, so there're no relatives to see. I'm not much of a cook, so we have our traditional chilli in a slow cooker. We read stories and watch movies. It's never been a day to remember."

It sounded both sweet and sad. "What if you came here for Christmas dinner?" My mouth morphed into an elastic grin, the kind that was so big it reached your eyes. "It would be great. Emma could use a friend her age. The rest of us are adults. Vinny and Katherine will be there. And my in-laws. I could use a friend who's not knee-deep in grief for Alex."

Ronan made the "I don't know" expression and opened his mouth to talk, but I cut him off.

"My father-in-law is making the turkey. But I'm making everything else. Apple pie, cookies, two or three types of potatoes, baked asparagus, veggies, salad, mulled apple cider, mulled red wine. I'll have a charcuterie spread for appetizers. Oh, and I'm making fresh bread." I bubbled and hopped a bit before I grabbed his hand without thinking. A curse of having Vinny as my best friend — I didn't always remember other people's views on touch differed from ours. We believed in platonic cuddles. Most people didn't, it seemed.

"After food, we play games and sing carols, get drunk. Please come. If it's not your thing, you're only a few houses down and you can leave. And you can bring your chilli if you want to. Please?"

Ronan's mouth opened and closed, trying to say something, but all that came out was a goofy grin. "Okay, okay. Stop bouncing." His hand tightened around mine.

A hot tingle ran along the length of my neck. I pulled my hand away and clapped. "Thank you."

He ran his hand through his icing-tangled hair. "Wait, you make your own bread? How?"

"I love making bread. Fresh bread tastes better and smells amazing. It's not as hard as people make it sound. You take the path of yeast resistance." I did the laughing dog meme pose.

Ronan facepalmed and grimaced. "Seriously?"

CHAPTER EIGHT

The weeks leading to Christmas moved too fast for me. I wanted to savour them. I missed everything last year, and that made my first Christmas without Alex even more unbearable. But it was done. All the firsts were over now. Father's Day, Alex's birthday, Emma's birthday, and, of course, the anniversary of Alex's death. Each passing marker without Alex was rough, but they would never be as horrible as the firsts. I hoped.

This year, I wanted to give Emma a wondrous Christmas, a big celebration of getting our shit together and moving forward. New house, new school, new projects for me, and new friends. We weren't forgetting Alex. I didn't think I'd be capable of that; rather, we were creating a new normal, and I hoped it could help us heal. It was difficult being stuck in a family of three, with only two people. Now, we were finding balance.

Reese came home with me after school again, and I loved it. I enjoyed taking Reese to swim class. Emma and I watched, cheered him on, and read to each other when we got bored. I texted Ronan pics and videos of Reese in class. Emma insisted we send an annoying number of selfies with goofy filters. He didn't mind. On swim nights, he brought us take-out for supper. I liked swim nights.

I didn't care that I needed to set aside work early to take Reese to therapy. It was convenient that his therapist was Emma's as well. So, we booked the kids' sessions back-to-back. I loved that Reese was getting support, and I got the kids treats afterwards. I gave us space for any necessary post-therapy conversations.

Reese was usually quiet after sessions, but he gladly accepted hugs.

When cleaning out Reese's lunch bag one day, I noticed remnants of a bland, basic lunch. Nutritious enough, but not exciting. I suspected cooking wasn't Ronan's forte. Emma confided in me they shared lunches because he enjoyed what I gave her.

Thus, I started making lunches for Reese. And Ronan. One morning Ronan came to get Emma, and I handed him one brown paper bag with Reese's name elaborately drawn on it by Emma. And I handed him another brown paper bag with his name elaborately drawn on it by me. I tried to tone down my grin, but I couldn't.

"What's this?" Ronan asked. He looked baffled.

"I made you lunch. And Reese."

"Why?" His smile was lopsided, and his eyebrows quirked.

"You mentioned that sometimes you forget your lunch, and you didn't always have the time to grab something on your break. So, I thought I'd make you something." I bounced. I tried not to bounce. But it didn't work. "And since I was making two lunches, I made one for Reese, too. And myself. Now I hopefully won't time slip and forget to eat."

"Time slip?"

"Sometimes when I'm working, I lose all sense of time. I have multiple phone alarms to make sure I get the kids in time."

Emma burst by us and ran outside to play with Reese.

"Th-thank you for this." He held the bag like a Fabergé egg. His blue eyes sparkled, and his rosy cheeks pinked more. "You didn't have to."

I shrugged. "I wanted to."

He smoothed back his hair, which was pulled into a springy ponytail. A tight smile formed on his lips, and he bowed his head in thanks. His eyes flickered between me and the bag. His mouth opened and closed, but instead of talking, he ducked out the door to usher the kids to school. I stood in the doorway and waved bye. The kids didn't see me. They were already running off with hands full of snowballs. But Ronan waved back. Then was hit in the back by a snowball.

Around 1 p.m., my phone buzzed, pulling me out of my work hyperfocus.

Ronan
Did you remember to eat?

Aloysius
Oops. No.
Thank you kindly for the reminder
I lost track of time

My chest warmed to think I had a new friend to spoil and who checked in on me.

Emma and Reese plowed through the door after school. They inspected the gingerbread houses to see if any had fallen. They took bets that Vinny's would fall over first. Before they ran off to play video games, they dumped their schoolwork on the table. Emma powered on the game console before I could take my coat off.

Boots and winter clothing were strewn across the entryway. Against my better judgement, I put them away. My parenting mind said they needed to do this themselves. But my empathetic side said, they're having fun, don't interrupt that. I was a softy. Alex was the disciplinarian.

I looked through their agendas. They both had notes reporting they talked too much. I should have scolded them, but instead, I smiled. There were also notes about Emma helping a friend, and Reese's success in math today. My chest filled with the warm and fuzzies.

Reese's laughter exploded from the living room. While it was only for a couple hours, our little family grew bigger. And I liked it.

I wanted two kids, but Alex didn't think he could handle it. He was right. I took care of Emma the most. Still, there were days I wished Emma had a sibling to play with. My imagination flickered: What would life be like if Reese was my kid too? What I saw, I longed for. A happy, laughing, goofy family.

I had the rice cooker going, vegetables boiling, and curried chicken in our one-pot by the time Ronan arrived. I had given him a key so he could let himself in. There was a fleeting moment of my brain playing house, and he was my husband coming home to me and the kids. "Hello, sweetheart" was on the tip of my tongue. But my beautiful husband was dead. A hollow ache crept through my stomach. These mood swings left me disoriented.

I peeked around the corner and welcomed Ronan with a wave and smile.

Ronan kissed the top of Reese's head, and they told each other about their days. It was too cute. I wandered back into the kitchen to check on dinner and my reality. Ronan meandered my way but stopped in the hallway. I peered out to find him staring at my wedding photo. It was a group shot of me, Alex, Vinny, Katherine, and Alex's groomsmen. Who dropped off the face of the earth after Alex died. Not once did they check on us. Bastards.

"You looked amazing. So happy," he said.

"It was a pretty great day. I mean, it was seven years ago when I slept more and weighed less." I wrapped my arms around my stomach and shifted on my feet.

Ronan raised an eyebrow at me. "You don't take compliments well, do you?"

I shook my head.

"Well, Wishes. You were gorgeous then, but you're better looking now." He held my gaze.

"I-I disagree." I shrank away. Alex would have made fun of me for how much weight I gained since his death.

"I'm being honest, Wishes. Yes, you were young and dressed up here. But...." He fiddled with the tips of his hair. "I dunno. You're a great dad, your baby face matured, I really like your hair, you have an established career, and you're a good person, and"— he chewed on his nails — "to me, this makes you more gorgeous now." He looked at the floor and rubbed his neck.

My brain didn't know how to process this. It took a few mental reboots to think of a response. "Thank you, I guess. It's nice to know a straight man thinks I'm attractive." Well Wishes, that was rude and dismissive. Way to go.

Ronan's mouth paused open. "Um. I'm not —"

"Dad!" Emma yelled from the kitchen. "Water's boiling over!"

I bolted into the kitchen to save the veggies.

I had Reese over for a few extra hours one evening to let Ronan go Christmas shopping. As a thank you, he took Emma for the entire weekend, and it was glorious. I took a Saturday afternoon nap! I hadn't had that much time to myself in ages.

Ronan sent me photos. He took them to the winter festival, and they went on the sleigh rides, did carol singing, and drank hot chocolate.

Vinny and Katherine came over Saturday evening and helped me sort through my Christmas decorations. Picking Alex's Christmas decorations we could use and what would be difficult for Emma and me to see every day. This hurt. And while it made me bawl, I insisted on putting up the photo of me, toddler Emma, and Alex dressed as Santa.

My phone buzzed, and there was a photo of Emma and Reese tangled in Christmas lights standing in Ronan's living room and laughing.

"That is so cute," Katherine said as she took my phone and cooed. Vinny looked at it over her shoulder. And then … they scrolled through my messages with Ronan. Bastards.

"Wow, you two talk a lot." Vinny nodded with a grin.

I snatched the phone away and glared. "My business. And yeah, we coordinate about the kids often."

"A long conversation about why the *Muppet's Christmas Carol* is the best Christmas movie of all time isn't coordinating things for the kids." Vinny gave me a knowing look that I hated.

"It is too. We are planning a Christmas movie night tomorrow. And don't you dare say anything bad about the *Muppet's Christmas Carol*." I crossed my arms.

"Everyone knows *Elf* is superior." Vinny crossed his arms.

Katherine raided my wine rack. "I'm not dealing with this again."

One day after supper, Ronan helped me put together our new fake Christmas tree. The old one did not survive the move. Emma insisted on a six-foot, bubble-gum pink tree with built-in, colour-changing lights. I wholeheartedly agreed. Alex would never have allowed a pink tree. Never. Ronan admitted it looked "interesting" after being wrapped in tinsel garlands.

"I think it's beautiful." I beamed and stepped back to admire the tree. My foot caught on a box, and I found myself falling backwards into the coffee table full of glass bobbles. This was going to hurt.

I didn't see it happen, but an arm reached out and grabbed me. I found myself in Ronan's arms, pressed against him. Everything in my body went rigid as I processed what happened. The scent of chai tea wafted from his sweater. We lingered there a second longer than what proper social decorum deemed acceptable.

"You good?" He let me go.

I was both thankful and sad when he released me.

"Yes. Thank you. You're my hero." A nervous laugh escaped my throat. I glanced at the box I had tripped over and saw a photo of Alex peeking out of the top. Watching me. Judging me. "That would have ruined Christmas for sure. Smashing all the bobbles."

"And cutting yourself." Ronan looked aghast. "Priorities, dude."

"That too." My lips pressed tight, thinking of the disaster of last year. I tugged at my sleeves. I took a deep breath and smiled. Yeah. I was burying my thoughts and emotions. Yeah. I was pretty sure he could tell.

His mouth wavered as if he were trying to say something. The dullness in his eyes told me I didn't want this conversation.

"Would you like some tea? I have chai?" My cheeks burned red hot. I thought of how nice he smelled.

Blue eyes searched me for answers to a silent question, but he said, "Yeah. Sure."

"Great," I said. "I have to warn you though, last week I burned it. But I remind myself if at first you don't succeed, chai chai —"

"No." He put a finger on my lips.

I spoke around it. "— Chai again."

Ronan chuckled as I flounced out of the room.

CHAPTER NINE

When Emma woke, I knew it would be a rough day. She stomped around the house and snipped whenever I asked her to do something. I knew better than to engage her when she was huffy. It was best to keep your head down and let her ride it out. Her appa was the same.

Her teacher phoned me later that day, telling me Emma had recess detention because she called the teacher a nitwit. A note was being sent home that I'd need to sign. Ugh.

It was the one-year anniversary of my hospitalization. I assumed Emma wouldn't remember the specific date. But apparently, she did. Shame held me back from telling her teacher that it was an anniversary of a terrible event. I couldn't bear it if she asked me what had happened.

With extra snacks at the ready, I met the kids at the school for the home-time bell. Emma came pounding out, scowling, while Reese walked behind her with his head hung. A kid jogged by Emma, whispered something, and ran off before she shoved him.

"Stuff it, Joey!" she yelled. That got me a few shocked looks from parents.

I offered the kids granola bars and headed home. The tension in the house was thick and uncomfortable. Emma's anger was a copy of Alex's. I flinched every time she banged a cupboard or glowered at me. Reese hid behind me, clinging to my pants while I prepped for supper. I was making spaghetti with my homemade pasta sauce. One of Emma's favourites. I hoped it would put her in a better mood.

I told the kids to go play for a bit before they started homework. I needed alone time to read the note from the teacher. Emma stalked into the living room while Reese cautiously slunk behind her.

The note in Emma's agenda explained that she grew agitated during family studies. The teacher said "mummy and daddy" too often. Emma asked her to say "parents" or "caregivers" because families were diverse. Her teacher said "mummy and daddy" again, so Emma called her a "frigging nitwit."

I empathized with Emma's rant and rage. And I was proud of her for defending our family, and others, and I was beyond proud she managed to not say "fucking nitwit." But I'd have to chat with her about not insulting the teacher.

I found a pen and wrote, "I apologize for her insult and outburst. I will talk to her. Our single-dad, formerly two-dad, family has been through a lot lately. Please be patient with her. She's dealt with terrible events a seven-year-old should never deal with."

I noted there was no apology from the teacher. It took effort to not write "fix your fucking language."

I gave the kids a few more minutes to play, while I collected myself and did more supper prep, before I called out, "Hey, kids? It's time to do your homework."

Reese obediently sat at the table and started without a word. Emma snarled but turned off the TV and joined Reese.

It wasn't long before Reese huffed over a math problem. Emma's patience with him waned, and she rolled her eyes. I asked if I could help, but he snapped at me, which made Emma snap at him for being surly to me.

He growled. Legit, deep, back of the throat, animistic growl.

This was turning into a massive meltdown if I didn't step in.

"Hey, do you want a drink?" I offered to Reese. "I have apple juice."

"No," he shouted.

"You've got this. Do you want me to help?" I remained serene and bright.

"No, I don't. I'm an idiot. Joey's right. I'm stupid and retarded." Reese's tone was a strained, not-quite yell.

My insides turned to ice. The r-word was a filthy word, and I hated that someone used it against Reese.

"Look at me, Reese." I waited for him to meet my eyes. His chest heaved. "You are not stupid. You hear me? You are far from stupid. I've seen you ace these problems. When I was your age, I struggled with math too. Heck, I still struggle with math. I worked harder than my peers, and yeah, I felt stupid. But feeling stupid and being stupid are two different things. You are not stupid. I'm sorry he used the r-word. That's not nice, and it's not true."

I wasn't getting through to him. Tears streamed along his pudgy cheeks.

He grabbed his math book, and in a roar of frustration, he threw it. I didn't think he intended to throw it at me. I really didn't. But it flew through the air and knocked over my pot of fresh, puréed tomatoes. Sauce splashed on my arms as I tried to grab the pot in vain. It made a deafening crash as it struck the floor and red sauce splattered my white floor tiles and cupboards. The crimson liquid pooled by my feet. My kitchen looked like a horror movie. Acidic tomato tang filled the air.

I froze.

Emma froze.

We simultaneously had flashbacks.

Reese cried and repeated, "I'm sorry."

Emma went white.

"Sweetheart," I said. I pulled her attention to me. "It's tomato sauce. See?" I licked the purée that dripped from my fingers. "Yummy tomato sauce."

"Why did you do it?" Her lip quivered when she looked at me. "Why did you do it?" she screamed.

This wasn't a conversation for Reese to witness. If I had been thinking, I would have pulled Emma aside and had a heart-to-heart with her. But my brain froze, and no words came out.

"Really? Nothing to say? Appa was right, you are pathetic."

"Emma," I yelled. "That was mean."

"I don't care. You're not my real dad," she screamed. "Appa wasn't my real dad, and he left me. You almost left me. My real dad didn't even want to meet me. You all suck! I hate you!"

She threw everything in her reach at me. I evaded the bigger stuff, but I let some of it hit me. I deserved it. A novel hit Reese on the forehead and he wailed. I don't think she hit him on purpose. I hoped.

"You grow a spine too!" Emma shouted at him. "I'm always taking care of you. Stand up for yourself sometime, will you?"

Reese hit himself in the head over and over while making loud whirring noises. I slipped an oven mitt between his hand and temple. But putting myself that close to Emma put me in hitting range. And she did it. She punched me in the arm.

She struck me. I froze. I couldn't drop the oven mitts and move aside, or Reese would hurt himself. Panic spun my mind, and I lost all words. My daughter hit me. My seven-year-old child hit me. I winced as she pulled back her fist to strike again.

"Emma!" Ronan seethed. He panted with his coat still on, dripping melted snow onto the floor. He glared at Emma. "Stop. What are you doing?"

Reese freaked out at his dad's resounding voice and bit me. He mostly got a mouth full of sweater. But he got actual arm too, and he wasn't letting go.

Emma yelled, "You can't tell me what to do. You're not my dad either." She flipped Ronan the bird and ran upstairs.

Ronan managed to get Reese to let me go. I backed away and slid down the cupboards to the floor. *I am pathetic.* Ronan knelt beside me and smoothed my hair out of my eyes. "You rest. I've got this." He handed me paper towels before returning to Reese.

My arm hurt, and my soul had shattered. How did everything explode like that in less than a couple of minutes?

I dissociated and missed how Ronan calmed Reese and moved him to the living room. But I snapped out of it with a start when Ronan carefully lifted the paper towel from my hands and, with a gentle touch, wiped tomato sauce off my cheeks. He reached for my red-stained sleeve to pull it back, and I cringed. I snatched my arm to my chest, spreading the tomato gore onto my torso. My shirt was ruined, but knowing me, I'd still wear it.

"No," I said, "it's okay."

"I should check the bite marks. If he broke skin, you'll need to clean it."

I took the paper towel from him and cleaned myself off. "I'm fine." The idea of him touching me made me sick. The secrets I hid under my sweatshirt flooded me with shame.

"Okay, sorry. I didn't realize it was an issue." He sat on the floor beside me, pulling his knees to his chest. "Sounds like you've had a shit time." There were fresh teeth marks on his hand.

I nodded and fidgeted with the paper towel.

"What was that all about? I know Reese explodes easily, but Emma said some harsh things."

"What did you hear?"

"She feels abandoned by Alex and bio-dad and is pissed at you for almost leaving her."

I looked away in silence. My throat tightened, and I retreated inside myself.

"Wishes, you can talk with me." Ronan waited for me to say something, but when I didn't, he continued. "This single dad thing is complicated. And it's so hard when it's only you. We're responsible for this little human who sometimes is incredible, and occasionally, an unmitigated monster."

I tugged on my sleeves and stared at the red pool staining my kitchen floor.

"You can't let her talk to you like that or hit you. That's not cool."

"I deserved it. I did something shitty."

Again, he waited. Again, I didn't go on.

"Jesus, Wishes, you don't deserve to be hit by your kid. Even if you did something shitty. It's called communication and we need to teach our kids how to do it. Whoever made you think you deserved to be hit was a fucking asshole. You can't let her get away with this. It's teaching her she's allowed to be an asshole when she's upset. What if she grows up to beat her loved ones when she's pissed off? What if she hauls off and hits Reese when they are arguing? She already gave him a black eye once."

I was going to be sick. Bile hit the back of my throat, and I steadied my head between my knees.

His warm hand drew circles on my back.

"You have to do something about it."

"I know." My voice was subdued and raspy.

I turned to him and watched him rest his head back against the tomato-massacre–free cupboards and stare at the ceiling.

"I'm not perfect either. Lord knows I'm not. I'm fucking up left, right, and centre. It was my responsibility to save him from his abusive mom, and I took too long. I'll never forgive myself for that."

He held his breath for a moment while he played with the tips of his hair. Part of me wanted to tell him it wasn't his fault. That abusive relationships are scary, and he did better than I could. But none of that came out. My throat closed.

"I borrowed money from my parents last week so we didn't get our gas cut off," he said. "I'm not proud of it. But I haven't been able to stay on top of the bills." He looked at me with fatigued eyes. "Parenting is so hard." He was giving me an opening to speak, but I pressed my lips tight instead.

"I used to bank serious coin," he continued. "I was a civil engineer, but I lost my job because Vanessa kept fucking me over. I didn't trust her with Reese, and I had to bring him into work one too many times. My boss was usually understanding. But when Reese peed himself in the middle of a crucial meeting and started screaming, she couldn't let it slide anymore.

"On top of it all, the divorce was messy. Because Vanessa was in jail, she couldn't get a lot from me, but she made me spend all my money on lawyers' fees. I fell from sports cars and a fancy house to renting from my uncle, an old beater Corolla, and struggling to give Reese decent Christmas presents. And she still makes up bullshit things to call my lawyer over. And that costs money every time. She just pulled some bogus shit that cost me over two hundred dollars in lawyers' fees. Right before Christmas. She'll never let me move on."

"Wow" was my intelligent response.

"How do you afford this?" He gestured around us. I realized I must seem well off compared to what he's dealing with. I do love my Kitchen-Aid appliances. "No offence. I didn't think classical musicians made enough money to buy a house like this."

My insides knotted. "Okay." My voice was rough. "First, that is offensive. I make a comfortable sum of money. Second, sure, Alex was the breadwinner. He was a dentist. But I worked hard too. Third, you want to know how I can afford this house? Alex died. That's how." I was spitting venom now. "He had really good life insurance, and I made money selling our old house. So yeah. That's how I won my lotto to pay for my house. This pathetic musician's husband died so I can live here."

I tugged at my sleeves and shook with anger. I wanted to stand and leave, but the exhaustion from my emotional rollercoaster held me to the floor.

"Oh fuck. I'm so sorry, Wishes. I am the asshole here."

"Yeah, you are."

He grunted. "I deserved that."

"Why do people assume I'm poor? I make money. I pay the bills and put money away for savings. I don't have parents to help me with my bills. It's just me. I am so sick of people making me feel like I'm less than. My career is centuries old, and the world would be bleak without classical music. I don't need you, my friends, or Alex, to make me feel like a pathetic loser. Not everyone can do what I do. I started training when I was five. How many careers demand that of you? Not engineering."

He clenched his jaw. I might have pushed a bit too far, but I was on a roll.

"I did four years of university, and then completed my masters while raising Emma, and dealing with — other stuff. I did one of my practical exams playing Bach with baby Emma crying in her carrier on the floor next to me. One of my classmates had to take her out of the room. I've worked so hard, and I'm not a freeloader."

"That's not what I said."

"No? But you said I couldn't afford this house. Clearly, you don't think much of my job." The feeling of inferiority was strong. Good old rejection sensitivity dysphoria.

"I never said that," he snapped. "I love your music. You are extremely talented, and it's an honour to hear your music. I'm sorry I took out my frustrations on you. Especially since the kids put you through hell. I'm a dick." He rested his head on my shoulder, and the tension washed out of my body. "I'm so sorry. I really am." There was a pregnant pause. "Why is this so hard?" I heard him sniffle against me. "You don't have parents?"

"I have my in-laws and Vinny's parents. But they live in Ottawa now," I said. "My parents kicked me out during my last year of high school. I lived with Vinny and his folks until university."

Didn't tell him how I slept in Vinny's room and didn't always sleep on my mattress on the floor. Sometimes we cuddled and talked, and sometimes we fooled around. We were horny teenagers sharing the same bed after all.

Ronan looked at me, wide-eyed. "They kicked you out? You were a kid. Why?"

I shrugged and made the international, flopped-wrist sign for "gay."

He stiffened. "For real?"

"Haven't talked to them since. It wasn't a blowout fight. They calmly informed me I no longer lived there. They were cold. Vinny's parents tried to fix things for us, but it didn't work. They don't know about Emma."

Ronan scooped me into a hug. It caught me off guard, but it was exactly what I needed. He muttered something into my shoulder about being sorry and my heart warmed.

When he pulled away, we sat silent, staring at the wall across from us and processing the whirlwind that was the past few minutes.

With care and caution, I took his hand and inspected the bite marks. Several red dents but no broken skin. I raised his hand to my lips, and I kissed his boo-boo. "There. All better."

We burst out laughing.

CHAPTER TEN

I had been awake for hours before Emma, doing last-minute Santa stuff, and getting started on food prep. My dough for the breads was rising while I stared at my colour-coordinated cook-time schedule Emma and I had taped to the fridge. I had everything planned to the minute. Lord help anyone who caused my schedule to be off because I didn't think I could handle it. I needed everything to be ready on time. I needed this to be perfect for Emma. For me.

Emma came bounding downstairs in the new llama pyjamas I gave her as her Christmas-Eve gift. "Hurry daddy!" she yelled as she ran by the kitchen.

"Don't start without me," I called after her.

I set my Santa-suit apron on the flour-covered counter and jogged after her. This was my first time being Santa on my own, and I had to see her reaction. Many tears had been shed last night while I set out the presents, but I hoped I did okay. Alex was amazing at displaying gifts. He rivalled fancy store displays. If it weren't for those high standards, I would have heaped them on the couch and called it acceptable.

She checked to make sure Santa ate the cookies she left out. That was always my job, so I didn't forget. She skipped to Alex's portrait by the door, and I lifted her so she could kiss it.

"Merry Christmas, Appa," she whispered.

Don't cry. Don't cry. Don't cry. I did not want to cry this morning.

We opened presents and played with her new toys. I got a few books and gift cards for more books, and fancy notebook with sections of blank staff paper and my initials embossed in gold on the cover. I was a lucky boy. Emma gave me a miniature crystal piano. Gaudy, but sparkly.

"I got it when Ronan took me to the winter festival," she said.

I gave her a giant bear hug. "It's beautiful." I turned it around in my hand and saw the Swarovski label. Now I wondered how much I owed Ronan. This had to cost more than the $20 I gave her for my present.

I stood and placed it atop my baby grand piano. Emma clapped. I *never* put anything on my piano. No cards, no knickknacks, no flowers, and certainly no drinks on my piano. This was a big deal, and she knew it.

After I made waffles for breakfast, and we dressed in our new Christmas clothes, Emma took to her toys, and I took to the kitchen. Vinny and Katherine were first to arrive. They came bearing gifts and copious amounts of alcohol. I started mulling wine and cider right away.

"This smells amazing," Katherine said, as she and Vinny sat at the kitchen table. She dug into the leftover waffles, as was our tradition. "Do you have the bread in?"

"I have dinner and pre-dinner bread in, because I know you."

"You're a saint," Katherine said and drowned her waffle in strawberries. "So, Ronan is coming, huh?"

"Yup." I blushed.

"Is this friend thing turning into a thing thing?" Katherine asked.

I turned bright red. "No. He's straight, and I'm not ready to date."

"Judging by the way he looks at you, he ain't straight. Just because he had a wife doesn't mean he's straight," Katherine said. "You have firsthand experience with Vinny's bi-ness."

A few puzzle pieces of hints I had ignored clicked into place. Oh fuck. "What do you mean by the way he looks at me?"

"It's the same way Vinny looks at you sometimes," Katherine joked. She used to joke that me and Vinny were married, as we were prone to cuddle and knew everything about each other. But she hadn't called us husbands since Alex died. That joke no longer sat right.

Vinny gave her a nudge and stole a handful of strawberries from her. "Seriously, I'm not getting 'I just want to be friends' vibes from him. Nor you," he said.

I didn't want to talk about this or hear it. This was not happening. I decided I needed to purée strawberries. In my very loud, green blender. I threw the strawberries in and hit a high setting. Vinny and Katherine exchanged looks and took their waffles into the living room. I let the blender growl to a stop. I needed whole strawberries, not puréed. Fuck.

My apple pie was almost ready for the oven when Ronan and Reese arrived. I asked Reese if he wanted to help me put on the top crust, but he played with Emma instead. Couldn't blame him.

Ronan offered to help. He peered into a pot of boiling water on the stove. "What are you making?"

"That one? That's a Christmas necessity."

"There's nothing in it." He squinted into the steam, looking for food.

"Yes, there is. It's holy water. I'm boiling the hell out of it." I smirked before I dumped in the cut-up potato that sat next to the pot.

"Ass." Ronan scoffed and failed at not smiling at my ridiculous dad joke.

"Have you ever made pie?" I asked.

"Nope. Not even from frozen."

"Well, let's change that." I handed him an apron. It wasn't until he unfolded it that I realized it was the rainbow-striped apron that said "Sounds Gay, I'm in." He didn't bat an eye as he put it on. I taught him how to roll out the crust and how to not let it stick to the wooden rolling pin. Originally, I planned on a lattice top but decided it was too complex for his first pie. I showed him how to crimp the edges shut. We got into each other's personal space bubbles. Our legs bumped into each other, and our arms pressed together. We shared a *Ghost* moment when I moved his fingers to help him seal and crimp the edges.

Of course, Katherine walked in to get two tumblers of mulled wine at that exact moment. She gave me a knowing look, as if she knew my thoughts and feelings better than I did. I hated she made being friends with Ronan into something more than it was. I stepped away from Ronan, like standing close to him was wrong. I was touchy-feely with Vinny, and we were only friends. Why couldn't I be close with Ronan without being accused of having a thing with him? Fuck off, Katherine. My muscles tightened and my shoulders raised.

Katherine took her wine, smirked, and left the kitchen.

Ronan turned to me. "Did I miss something?"

"No," I said as I tugged on my sleeves.

"Clearly I did, because you're tense and acting weird."

"It's nothing," I said. I drew a deep breath, pushed my emotions to the back of my brain, and smiled. "Do you want to help me make the lemon meringue pie?"

"You're not fooling me when you change subjects and smile as if nothing is upsetting you. I've been letting it go. And since it's Christmas, I'll let it go today. But one day, I'm not going to let you pretend things are fine. Okay?"

I chewed on my lip. "Yeah, one day." There was an uncomfortable silence.

"Yes, I'd love to help you make a lemon meringue pie."

"Excellent, but first," I said. I ripped a piece of bread from the fresh pre-dinner bread, slapped some butter on it, and shoved it in Ronan's mouth.

The groan he made caused me all sorts of pants-region issues. His shoulders slackened and eyes fluttered and rolled back into his head. "Fuck yeah." Melted butter dripped down his chin, and I wanted to lick it off or run screaming from the room. "You're right, fresh homemade bread is amazing. That was orgasmic."

"Glad you liked it," I said. And rather than continue to watch him eat more and cause myself a mischief, I dove back into baking.

Ronan's baking skills were on par with his son's. I told him what to do step by step and how to do every single thing. Luckily, I did the pie crust yesterday.

"Like this?" Ronan asked for the fiftieth time. His efforts to meet my standards of perfection were admirable. That ass was admirable.

"You're doing great." I flashed an encouraging smile, and his demeanour burst into beams of sunshine. It was adorable. His tongue stuck out of the corner of his mouth as he tapped the measuring cup, releasing the sugar grain by grain into the bowl. Painfully slow. And yet, he still spilled.

I did the meringue myself. Too complicated for a newbie.

"Hey, so, um," Ronan said. He wiped his hands off onto his apron and pulled a small package out of his pocket. "I got you something. Merry Christmas." He thrust the box towards me as if it were a bomb.

Little lightning bolts lit my brain. "You didn't have to." I protested, but I still yanked the box out of his hand with enthusiasm. He wrapped in last week's newspaper, which I thought was smart. Better for the environment and frugal. "Your present is under the tree." I didn't want him to think I forgot about him. I opened the small box and found two items. One, a Beanado gift card. He wrote on the back, "We need to do coffee more often – R." Why was my heart racing? Was I having a panic attack?

The second item was a coffee cozy that read "Basic PSL Bitch." I laughed so hard I almost peed myself. "It's funny 'cause it's true." I was a Basic Pumpkin Spice Latte Bitch. No shame. Well, some shame. I snorted, which caused him to laugh hard. "I love it. Thank you." I wanted to hug him but didn't know if I should. Instead, I looked at the clock and gasped. "We're behind schedule. Let's pick up the pace." As we baked away, I glance into the living room to see the kids playing and most likely couldn't hear us. "How much do I owe you for Emma's gift?" I asked.

"Nothing."

I gave him the "yeah, sure" look.

"Honest. The market vendor had a sale. Plus, it's missing the stool and there's a tiny chip, so it's no good to collectors. Emma got the cute kid discount. Plus the handsome father discount. And yes, I pretended to be her father and flirted to get a better deal."

"I'm flattered you flirted on my behalf."

"Do you want the personal phone number of an antique dealer?"

"Nah, I'm good, thanks. I have a friend who deals in antique musical instruments. Last month some creeps robbed her," I said. "Damn luters. Get it? Like people who play the lute? L-u-t-e-r-s."

"Someone robbed your friend? That's horrible."

"No, it's a joke."

"Why is that funny?" Ronan was aghast. "My friend's photography store was robbed last year. They caught the guy, but he said he was framed." His deadpan was on point.

I blinked. "Did you make a dad joke?"

He chuckled.

"I'm so proud of you."

My in-laws' late arrival time made me fret over my perfectly calculated cooking timing. Vinny and Ronan helped me make sure nothing burned.

"Breathe, buddy." Vinny rubbed my back. "We got this." He stopped me from checking the veggies for the hundredth time. Ronan peeked for me when Vinny turned his back and gave me the thumbs-up. Nothing burned. Thank god.

The sound of the front door opening filled me with excitement and nervous energy. Once I saw my mother-in-law, all worry drained from me. She hugged Emma first. Then introduced herself to Reese, who she hugged right away. Finally, she made her way to me, standing outside the kitchen.

"Hi Mom," I said as I hugged Hyunji. Her rose-scented perfume covered me with a sense of peace and love.

"Hello, my boy," she said. "The house smells amazing." She pulled back and grasped my shoulders. "Thank you for doing this. I know this is difficult, but you're doing amazing. Alex would be impressed with you."

And there I went. Crying. She held me for a few moments before procuring a tissue from her pocket, and she patted away my tears. I hoped it was clean.

Her face was red and blotchy as she took my hands. "It's okay, son. We can hold him in our hearts, but today is a day for celebration. No more tears today. Okay?"

I sniffled and nodded. When she was around, I became a child. My relationship with my mother was nonexistent, so having Hyunji around me, I played the role of the son. And I loved it. I loved her.

"Who is this?" my mother-in-law asked.

Ronan stood in the kitchen. Trapped and unable to escape from witnessing our little cry.

"This is my friend, Ronan. Reese's dad." My voice trembled. "Ronan, this is my mom, well, Alex's mom, Hyunji."

"I'm your mom too." She squeezed my arm.

Ronan reached out and shook her hand. "Nice to meet you."

My father-in-law, Jung Ki, came bursting through. "Make way for the turkey!"

Hannah, my sister-in-law and Emma's birth mother, stumbled into the living room, loaded with gifts. She and Emma chatted. Emma adored Hannah, but Hannah always seemed distant. I imagined it was difficult to watch the child she birthed be raised by someone else. Especially now that she was an adult and could handle a kid. We always tried to include her in Emma's life. I reached out again after Alex died. But Hannah seemed to prefer to love Emma from a distance. I respected that. At least she knew she was always welcomed.

Introductions were made, and food was served. The feast was giant. We would have leftovers for a week, and I couldn't have been happier. It filled me with joy to feed my people and have everyone visit like we used to do before Alex's death. A tiny cloud of grief floated off in the corner, chilling. A significant improvement from the suffocating thick fog it was last year. Fog that was so humid and clung to your skin. That thick fog hadn't been around for weeks.

Emma insisted on sitting between Hannah and Hyunji, and Hyunji insisted Reese sit on the other side of her. She helped cut their food into smaller pieces. I sat between Ronan and Vinny. Jung Ki sat at the head of the table. I was thankful. That was Alex's spot, and I didn't think I'd ever be able to sit there for holidays.

Hannah braided Emma's hair to keep it out of her food. Jung Ki told stories in half-English, half-Korean, and I understood a decent chunk of what he said. Emma seemed to understand everything, and I was so proud. She did her best to reply in Korean and taught Reese several words too. I could tell Jung Ki was also proud. His granddaughter still worked on her Korean language with her white-ass dad. He slid more kimchi onto her plate when she wasn't looking.

I inspected Ronan as he watched Hyunji grandmother all over his son. His lips lifted at the corners but remained tight, hiding the rest of his emotions. I realized I didn't know about his, nor Reese's, relationships with his family or his in-laws.

I didn't know much about him and that made me sad.

"You okay?" I whispered as I placed my hand on his leg.

He turned to me with damp eyes. "I'm wonderful."

I removed my hand. "Good. Now eat."

"Yes, sir." He laughed and dug in.

I was not sure what I enjoyed more, the food itself or watching others loving the food I made for them. They showered me with compliments, causing an explosion of dopamine in my brain. A rose-tinted filter clouded my vision, and it was lovely and beautiful.

Vinny leaned into my ear. Mulled wine wafted off his breath. "Hey, proud of you, bud." He kissed the back of my hand. "You *sleigh*ed it."

I blinked a few times. "Thanks Vinny." I loaded my fork with mashed potatoes. "Merry Christ-*mash*."

"*Seasoning's* greetings." He shook the pepper shaker.

"It has been *dill*-i-tful to have you as my guest." I poked my pickles with my fork.

After dinner, Vinny and Katherine insisted I go sit and relax, and they cleaned the kitchen. I slouched on the couch and pulled a turkey-coma Emma onto my lap and gave her big cuddles. My heart burst when Reese joined us, climbing into my lap too. Although I lost him to Ronan's lap when Ronan joined us on the couch, that too made my heart burst. They struggled with life, but they were a fantastic father-son team.

Second round of gifts started. While Hannah opened the large bags of presents, Ronan shifted in his seat. My family showered Emma with gifts. Reese's eyes tracked the shiny box Vinny handed to her. Then, to his delight, Vinny handed him one, too. I had everyone bring a gift for him. Hyunji brought several.

Reese was ecstatic. It was mostly Pokémon toys and a few books.

"... and this is for Ronan." Vinny passed a box to Ronan while he wore the traditional ugly tie I got him every year. This year, it was a repeat pattern of the bass clef and read, "I'm All About That Bass."

Ronan had three presents, it turned out. A large bottle of cheap cheap wine from Katherine and Vinny, an assortment of chai tea from Emma, and my gift. I got him a baking book and his own terrycloth headband to keep his hair back while he baked. Purple with sequins. He put it on immediately. He held up the apron I bought him and unfurled it in front of everyone. It was black with bold white letters that read "Daddy."

The bewildered looks I earned from him, Vinny, Katherine, Hannah, and even Hyunji made me shrink back and hold Emma closer like a shield. "What?" I squeaked.

They exchanged looks.

Vinny broke the silence. "This is because Reese calls him Daddy, right?"

"Yeah? Of course? Why?"

He turned to Katherine. "He genuinely thinks this is for fathers."

"Of course it is," I said, "what else — Oh god!" They thought this was a kink thing. This was not a kink thing. Right? Oh my god, I got him a kink apron. He was going to think I was a weird pervert who gave their friends kinky stuff. Or I was trying to start a daddy kink with him. Or the truth, I was too stupid to know this was a kink apron. He might think super vanilla and boring in bed if I didn't make that connection. But honestly, I love a good scoop of vanilla. And other flavours occasionally. And why did I care what he thought my bedroom preferences were?

He gave me a sly grin, and everyone broke into fits of laughter. I blushed from my toes to my head and wanted to crawl under the Christmas tree and die.

The room stilled when Reese opened the last gift. It was from me. Emma helped him remove the paper and opened the box to find the bright orange headphones that Alex had given me. The icons of who I was. Or who I had been. I needed to move forward and rework who I was. And this was one way to start.

While I was glad no one was laughing at me anymore, a different uncomfortableness crept through me. It was both nice and sad to see them in his hands.

Emma stared at them, frozen in place, even her breathing stopped. The sinking feeling of "you done fucked up" crept in.

"They're noise-cancelling headphones," I said to Reese. "They crackle now, so they aren't good enough for my job, but they are fine if you're listening to music for fun." I cleared my throat and looked at Ronan. "I talked to the teacher, and she agreed noise-cancelling headphones may help him in class when it gets loud. And he could listen to calming music if he needed. She said she'd help him take care of them if he wanted to wear them in class."

Reese put them on, and I helped adjust the headband. I felt the judgement from others fill the room with a gooey thickness. Reese beamed and didn't notice the stares I got. Ronan noticed.

"Appa gave you those," Emma stated. Her voice was quiet, flat, cold, and her face scrunched in confusion, as if she couldn't understand why Reese was wearing my headphones.

"I know, love-bug. But I have others Appa gave me, and Reese could use these," I said.

"But Appa gave those to you." Her voice raised. "You can't give away Appa's gifts." Emotions flooded her speech. "You can't get rid of Appa!" Her wild eyes locked onto mine. Fuck.

"Love-bug, I'm not getting rid of Appa. No one could ever do that. These are just headphones. I can't use them for work anymore, and I think Appa would like to know they are helping someone."

"No. No, he wouldn't understand. He didn't know Reese. Why would he want Reese to have them? He got them for you. He loved you. But you're giving them away. Like he's nothing. You don't love him anymore!"

Tears and snot covered her face now.

"Emma, that's not true." I reached out to comfort her, but she flinched back. She tore the headphones from Reese's head and ran upstairs.

I jumped up to follow her, but all at once Reese started to wail; she screamed she hated me from the top of the stairs, and she slammed her door shut. I didn't know what to do. Everyone stared at me.

Reese started to make the high-pitched whirring noise he made before a meltdown. I turned to him. Ronan had gathered him into his arms and started to soothe him. "I'm so sorry, Reese." I smoothed his hair back. "I should have known she'd get upset. She didn't mean to hurt you. I will get you another pair. Promise."

The whirring got louder.

"I got him, you go take care of Emma," Ronan said.

I turned to head upstairs and made eye contact with Vinny. He glared at me. He had never directed so much anger and hatred towards me before.

"I'll be back," I muttered. As I walked by Vinny, he grabbed my wrist and yanked me down to his level. His breath was heavy with alcohol.

"He was my friend, too. Just because you have a new boyfriend doesn't mean you get to toss Alex to the side. I helped him buy you those. You have no idea how much trouble he went through to buy you the perfect set. He loved you, and you do this?"

"Vinny ...." I whimpered. Shame swallowed me whole. Everyone stared. I felt small, controlled, and like Alex had returned. I felt like shit for thinking that.

"Hey, Vinny." Ronan tried to intervene, but Reese bit him.

The harshness in Vinny's eyes faded and was replaced with confusion. Like he had registered he was squeezing my wrist. It took him a moment to loosen his grip.

His mouth gaped open in shock at his own actions. "Buddy, I —"

"Vincent. Let him go," Hyunji said over Reese's cries. I heard her stand behind me.

His hand dropped into his lap while he gave me a silent plea for forgiveness. I gave him the look of "we'll talk later."

"He was my son," Hyunji said, "and those are plastic headphones. Now you hurt my other son, because he wants his daughter's best friend to have a good Christmas?"

Hyunji lectured while I ran upstairs.

CHAPTER ELEVEN

I took a deep breath outside Emma's door. My heart pounded. Reese freaked out downstairs. It sounded like Ronan took him into the bathroom to calm down.

I knocked on Emma's door and opened it to find her sobbing on her bed, clutching the headphones. The bed dipped under me as I sat on the side and pet her hair.

"I messed up, didn't I?" I asked.

She nodded.

"Wouldn't be the first time I've messed up Christmas." I sighed. "Did I ever tell you about your first Christmas?" This got her attention. She sat up and smeared the snot on her face with the back of her hand. Gross.

"Your appa accidentally set the turkey on fire, and I used salt instead of sugar in the pie, so supper was potatoes, kimchi, and granola bars. But I wouldn't have traded it for the world. I had my amazing husband and the most beautiful baby in the world. And that made it perfect."

I pulled her into my lap. "There is no one in the world I love more than you. I don't know if there are words strong enough to explain how magnificent it feels to be your dad. Even my music can only express a fraction of how much I love you. Sometimes I cry because loving you is so great, it hurts."

"I love you too, Daddy," she said and hugged me.

"Sorry, I made a mistake. I thought Reese could use the headphones to help him, and I assumed you'd be okay with it. I was wrong. You can keep the headphones and we'll get new ones for Reese."

She wiped her nose on my shirt. Gross.

I rocked her back and forth while I sang her "Let It Go" from Disney's *Frozen*. She didn't stay on my lap long before she was up and belting along with me. Throwing imaginary ice into the air and twirling around in her dress made of ice crystals.

When the song ended, I kissed her on the forehead and dabbed away the salt of her tears. "Are you feeling good enough to go back downstairs? Can you apologize to Reese? While I understand why you acted that way, you hurt both his feelings and his head. And that's not okay."

She nodded and put the headphones in her bedside drawer, giving me the "I fucking dare you to touch them" look, then flounced downstairs. She got her dramatic flair from me.

I was a piece of shit.

I thought I did a good thing. I thought I was helping Reese, but instead, I hurt everyone. Big and scary thoughts and emotions poured over me. I rubbed my wrist. While Vinny didn't grab me *that* hard, it scared me. It sent me back to when my life wasn't so good. I tugged on my sleeves to hide the memories.

My intentions were to return downstairs, but I was swallowed by big feels. I stood at the top of the stairs. Reese was no longer crying, and I heard Emma apologize to him. He accepted her apology.

Vinny's voice slurred, asking where I was. His words echoed in my ears. Calling Ronan my boyfriend after I repeatedly told him we're just friends, accusing me of tossing aside Alex. All in front of Alex's family. Going downstairs was the last thing I wanted to do.

My chest grew tight. I'd worked so hard on Christmas, and I fucked it up with one gift. Tears welled in my eyes, and I shuffled into my bedroom for some time alone.

"I'm so sorry, Alex," I said over and over while I pressed the balls of my palms into my eyes. I repeated those words like I used to all the time. A pitiful mantra. My little hidey-hole of comfort was between the bed and the wall. It had been my safety space since I was a kid. I slid down the cream-coloured wall and let the grief I had been trying to hold back pour out. My throat tightened, and my mantra turned into a squeak.

A soft tap on the door sounded, and it opened. In came Ronan. He grabbed a tissue box off my dresser and parked next to me on the floor without a word. I took several tissues.

The body heat from Ronan was comforting. To have another human next to me was nice. I rested my head on his shoulder, and he pressed his cheek into the top of my head. My breathing calmed.

"Reese isn't mad at you or Emma." Ronan's voice was soft and soothing. "We talked about how special the present was. And how it was also special to other people, and you weren't aware of that. Reese said it's okay, he understands, and he feels loved that you tried to give him something that meaningful to him."

I hugged Ronan's arm tight and fought back tears.

"I'm touched," he said. "It means a lot to me you put so much care and effort into my son." His voice cracked. "No one not related to him has shown him how worthy he is of good things. Hell, I struggle to show him how much he means to me." He took my hand and held it tight. His eyes wandered to our hands clasped together. "He shouldn't have grabbed you like that."

It took me a moment to realize we were no longer talking about Reese.

"Did he hurt you?"

"It looks like Reese got you good. Are you okay?" There was a slight discolouring on his jaw.

"You're not changing the topic this time. Did he hurt you?"

I shrugged. "No."

"What about mentally? You look shook."

I shrugged and stared ahead at a loose thread on my bed. This time I stayed silent.

"What an asshole."

"He's usually not an asshole. I caught him off guard and he's drunk."

"That came out of your mouth a little too easily. Like it's been practiced."

I said nothing.

"Fuck, Wishes, is he the one who taught you that you deserved to be hit?"

There was a knock on the door frame. Vinny hovered in the doorway with his hands shoved in his pockets. His eyes were red.

I looked at him. My cheek cooled without Ronan's shoulder against it.

"He's right, buddy," Vinny said. "I was an asshole." His eyes shifted to Ronan. "But I certainly did not teach him he deserved to be hit. Quite the opposite."

Vinny sauntered over and flopped on the bed in front of us. "I'm so sorry." I watched him assess me and Ronan sitting the way we were. His eyes fell onto our hands. I flinched. "No, Wishes. Jesus. I'm being a dick. With the holidays and well, everything that happened last year has got me all moody. I'm not handling things well, but that's not an excuse for how I acted. I guess I'm struggling with the idea of you moving on."

"I'm not moving on," I protested.

He raised an eyebrow. "Right. Sure."

Ronan shifted next to me. "Why aren't you respecting what he's telling you?"

"He's *my* best friend. I know him better than you do, and that's who we are. I'm not being disrespectful."

"Oh? Is that so? Funny, I'd never grab my best friend the way you did. Or tease her as much as you tease Wishes. Or —"

"Ronan," I said, "you don't need to fight this battle for me. Vinny and I get each other in ways no one else will understand."

Ronan clenched his jaw. "Hurting you isn't understanding you."

Vinny's eyes welled with years. "Fuck. I'm so sorry, Wishes." He ran his fingers through his hair. "I should have been better." I watched his eyes glaze over as he chewed on his nails.

Ronan tensed and coiled next to me; he was ready to spring forward. Instinctively, I squeezed his hand in an effort to keep him calm.

"I've known you longer than everyone in this house," Vinny said. His voice was tight and shaky. "We graduated high school together; hell, we graduated Grade One Piano together. We've lived together several times. Remember when we accidentally set Alex's homework on fire? I still have no idea how we did that. He didn't believe us when we claimed spontaneous combustion."

I huffed a laugh. "He was so pissed. Luckily, his prof knew me and believed him when he said, 'My boyfriend set my homework on fire.' I had already accidentally thrown the flash drive for his last assignment into the dishwasher."

"You definitely have a habit of doing weird shit." He sighed and reached down. His fingers laced with my free hand. "I was your maid of honour, the witness for Emma's adoption, and I ...." He cleared his throat. "I was the first at your side when Alex died. When shit hit the fan, I helped you hold it together and take care of you and Emma. I was the one who found ...." His voice cracked. "I called the ambulance and waited for hours in the hospital for you to wake up and it was the worst day of my whole fucking life. And when the nurses were busy, I was the one who took care of you." His eyes flickered to Ronan. "Shit, does he know?"

"No," I muttered.

"Shit." He rubbed his hand over his face. "Sorry, buddy."

I shrugged dismissively.

He swallowed. "You mean the world to me, Wishes. You know me in ways that Katherine won't even be able to begin to understand. And I know you on a different level than Alex ever could have dreamed of. I know better than to touch you like the way I did. Better than anyone else." His face fell into memories. Vinny had saved my ass on so many occasions.

"I didn't realize how bad I was coping with Alex not being here this year until Katherine sat me down and forced me to e-mail my therapist."

"You didn't tell me that."

"Dude, you have enough going on. I'm supposed to be there for you. Let Katherine and my therapist take care of me." He swallowed and squeezed my hand. "I guess trying to hold it together to take care of you didn't let me process Alex's death enough. The headphones caught me off guard and I overreacted. I'm sorry I grabbed you. I'm an asshole. Especially since I was the one who helped you when Al —"

"Don't say it," I snapped.

His eyes wandered between Ronan and me. He was not helping his quest for forgiveness. "Man, you two are going to have several fun conversations one day."

"We've had a few already. Can't have all the fun at once. Gotta spread the fun and trauma out. Makes it more palatable." I was dry and sarcastic.

I caught Ronan staring at me. His eyes turned downcast when I looked at him. Frown lines creased around his lips, and he squeezed my hand. Leave it to me to make everyone miserable at Christmas. Again.

"Wishes," Vinny drew my attention back to him. He kissed the back of my hand. "I love you, my platonic husband. I'd do anything to make it up to you. You can spank me if you want to." He arched an eyebrow.

"Ew, Vinny. Don't make this gross." I pulled my hand away from him.

"Oh, that's right, you're the one who likes to be —"

"Vinny!" I pulled both hands to my face. The residual heat from Ronan's hand made my face burn hotter with embarrassment.

"Damn. I need to not talk while I drink." He laughed that rich laugh that pulled me through so many dark times.

"I've been trying to shut your mouth for years; I don't expect you to start now." I looked at him with playful exasperation.

"There's one way to stop me from talking." He made kissy faces at me.

I threw the tissue box at him. It bounced off his nose and back at me. Ronan was my knight in snappy vests and swatted it away before it could take my eye out.

He shrugged. "You got the dad jokes; I got the dad reflexes."

And like that, we were smiling again. Ronan unfolded himself from the tight space we were cramped into and held out his hand. "Shall we return downstairs?"

I took his hand, and he helped me to my feet. Pins and needles exploded over my legs, and it took an effort to not fall over. Vinny was at my side immediately, with his arm around my waist. "You good?"

"Yup, I'm just tripping over air."

He pulled me into a tight hug. "I'm so sorry."

My arms wrapped around him, and my cheek nestled into my place against his shoulder. A shoulder groove I was very familiar with. "I know," I said.

"I love you," he said.

"I know. I love you unduly."

"I feel like shit."

"You are." We laughed and hugged deeper.

Ronan muttered something as he slipped out of the room.

Vinny listened to Ronan's footsteps head downstairs. "He's pissed at me, isn't he?"

"I don't blame him. Dickhead."

"I have a lot of making up to do for both of you, don't I?"

"Yup."

"I like him. He's protective of you."

"You think?"

"Buddy, if he weren't holding a crying child, I am positive he would have dropped kicked my ass. Rightfully so."

"Is it wrong I think that would be hot?"

"Hell, I would find it hot. Him all sweaty on top of me, pinning me to the floor."

"You're gross."

"He has a nice ass."

"He does."

We disengaged, made our way downstairs, and I strode straight to the piano. My zen space. I was at home at the piano. After a warmup of scales and arpeggios, I was ready to bring on the Christmas carols. "Emma, you get first request."

"Jingle Bells!" she called out.

"Hold on, I'm getting in on this one." Vinny sat next to me on the bench and kissed my cheek. Making a show of us being okay.

"You're stealing the bench." I reclaimed space.

"You need a longer bench."

"You need a smaller a — bum."

"Oh look who's talking, Mr. Dad bod."

I clutched my invisible pearls. "I cannot say my retorts in front of children, but you know what I'm thinking."

He gasped. "Well, I never."

Katherine sighed. "Boys, are we going to sing or are you going to bicker?"

We did an improv duet for "Jingle Bells." We made a few mistakes, but it was fun. I caught Ronan's eye. Reese was curled in his lap, singing merrily along. Ronan watched me play, his big blue eyes not leaving me. I smiled so hard I could no longer sing.

We sang for at least an hour or more before my in-laws decided they needed to leave. It was late. Well past Emma's bedtime; it was a miracle she didn't have another meltdown. I gave my in-laws hugs.

Hyunji squished my cheeks. "Good night, son. This was perfect. And even though you don't need it, but knowing you, you are worried, but you have my blessing."

"What do you mean?"

She glanced towards the kitchen, where Ronan was giving the kids drinks and small snacks before bed.

"Oh, no. We're *friends*," I replied.

"Sure," she said.

"Why does everyone say that?"

"My stubborn boy. I love you." She ruffled my hair.

"I love you too."

And she left. I hated when she had to leave. She brought a sense of peace with her and took it when she left. For a split second, the sensation of being alone and grieving jolted me when the door clicked shut behind her. I forgot how much I needed her.

The kids raced by with their bedtime snacks and sat in front of the tree. I stood in the living room archway, watching them. They had become best of friends fast. Reese was spending the night in the guestroom. Emma's first sleepover in this house. And though they were in separate rooms, my guess was they would be mischievous goblins together if they thought we couldn't hear them.

Ronan stood next to me and leaned against the archway frame with his hands in his pockets. Silent while we watched the kids. My neck burned as he turned to me and looked up.

"Hey, it's mistletoe." He was quiet. I barely heard him.

"What?" My eyebrows contorted in confusion. I followed his gaze to the archway above us. "Dude, those are pine cones sprayed in gold paint. Remind me to spend extra time tutoring Reese when they get to the botany unit. I never use mistletoe. Too many horrible non-consensual moments." I walked over to the piano and played softer Christmas hymns, hoping to calm the kids and their sugar highs.

I played and sang Shubert's "Ave Maria" in my best classical tenor voice. It wasn't until halfway through that I realized that the mistletoe comment may have been Ronan's attempt to kiss me. I flushed. Hot goosebumps skittered along my skin. Luckily, I was a practiced performer, and I put myself into autopilot and didn't miss a beat.

When I finished, Vinny so eloquently said, "Fuck. I forgot you could sing like that. You need to do that more often."

"Language," I said. Reese gasped, and Emma giggled.

Ronan stared wide-eyed at me from the archway. Those hot goosebumps snaked along my neck again and followed into my cheeks. My neck hair stood straight like a meerkat searching for danger. I downed half a glass of wine and ran my hands through my hair. My curls flopped into my eyes.

Vinny waltzed to the piano. "Get up, you're singing 'Una Furtiva Lagrima.'"

"Really? Now?" He wanted me to sing an aria from the opera, *L'elisier D'amore* by Donizetti.

"Think of it as a Christmas gift. The gift of your voice." His smile was sweet, but there was mischief behind it. He struck the first few notes, cutting off any of my protests. I watched him as he conducted me, cueing me when to come in, when to hold, and when to change my volume.

But when I wasn't watching Vinny for cues, my eyes could not stop locking onto Ronan's. My little performance became only for him, and fuck, I couldn't look away. I hoped he didn't realize this was a love song, because I was totally singing him a love aria and I could not stop.

I tried to ignore the fact that the character who sang this song was smashed on wine and couldn't tell the difference between love and other emotions. Like. Me. Vinny knew what he was doing.

But damn, my pipes hit that round richness I didn't always achieve. My vibrato was on point. I emoted all over the place, and I kind of wished we recorded this.

The way Ronan looked at me made this experience breathtaking. Round, shining blue eyes filled with adoration and awe. Pink lips parted in a sincere, shy smile. His hair cascaded in an inky waterfall over his shoulders. I think he could tell it was a love song.

Fuck me.

Not "Ronan, fuck me" but more of fuck my life. I could not let this happen.

The piece ended. I took a bow and drowned myself in another large glass of wine. The room filled with applause and compliments. But I didn't want to be standing there with everyone staring at me. My self-saboteur told me they were being polite, and I wasn't good. *He doesn't like you like that. He doesn't want you like that. You don't deserve that, anyway.*

"You need to sing more and not only home karaoke," Vinny said. "One day, I'm going to persuade you to sing at our concert."

"You know I'm not comfortable singing in front of big audiences."

"When is your concert?" Ronan asked.

"We're aiming for the spring," Vinny said. "And I'm going to convince him to sing something."

"No, you're not," I snapped. "If you don't drop this, I'll stop singing for you all together."

"But you have such a gift. Yes, you're gifted at piano, but damn your voice. You'd put Josh Groban to shame." Vinny glared at me, daring me to argue.

"I'm not having this conversation right now, Vinny. You know why I don't." My shoulders slumped.

Vinny's eyes hardened. I assumed he was thinking about the argument I had with Alex. Alex said it was a waste of *his* money to pay for me to learn to sing songs no one liked. So, I quit my vocal training and only sang opera at home when he wasn't around, unless I sang Emma to sleep. He didn't mind that. Of course. With her asleep, he didn't feel as guilty for going out to the bar, leaving me alone.

"Okay kiddos, time for bed," Ronan said. I released a puff of air as I was saved from this thought spiral and turned my focus to the kids.

Thankfully, the kids went upstairs without protest. They changed into their pj's, and we piled into Emma's room so I could read them *How the Grinch Stole Christmas*.

Ronan carried a half-asleep Reese to his bed. But damn, I will not pretend it wasn't a great feeling to sit with him and the kids, reading bedtime stories.

"Did you have a good Christmas?" I asked Emma when we were alone. I tucked her into bed.

"This was both the bestest and the saddest. Thank you for letting me have Reese over." She yawned.

"No problem, love-bug. And thank you for making this an amazing Christmas. I couldn't have done it without you. Appa would be so proud of you. And jealous of those llama pyjamas."

I kissed her forehead and told her I loved her before stepping out of the room.

Ronan waited for me in the hallway. Electricity hit every nerve in my body and all at once, I wanted to run, puke, hit him, and kiss him. *Why am I weird?* This was not what I wanted. I took the route of nervous laughter and avoiding eye contact.

It was funny how one brief moment, like the pine cones, changed how you interact with someone. I guessed he was not straight, but I could have been wrong. I may have misinterpreted it; I wasn't good with this stuff. Alex had to take my face in his hands and say, "I find you attractive and want to date you" before I clued in.

"I don't think I'll get used to the idea that you sing so beautifully," he said.

"Th-thank you."

"Never feel pressured to sing in front of me though. I'd love to hear it, but I don't want you to feel uncomfortable."

Too late. I nodded. Uncomfortably.

"So, this." He stopped and took a breath. Oh, no. Serious talk. Sweat smeared my palms instantly. "This has been Reese's best Christmas. He babbled about how amazing today was when I tucked him in." He chewed on his nails. "I've never been able to do something this big for him. Not on my own. I mean, I do my best. But ... Even when his mom was around, Christmas was never magical. One year she was too strung out and missed most of Christmas. She yelled at him for making too much noise. He was four." He wrung his hands. "Thank you. You can't imagine how much this means to me."

"You're welcome." It touched me to hear I had such an impact on Reese's day, but sad that his best Christmas was at the house of someone he's only known a few weeks.

I had only known Ronan a few weeks and I had grown this fond of him. That thought scared me.

We became awkward and introverted with a million things we wanted to say but were too anxious to.

"C-can I hug you?" he asked.

"Sure?" I wasn't sure.

It was an awkward hug. Where did we put our hands? Which way did I tilt my head? I would venture he was at least five inches taller than me. Our stiff uncomfortable hug melted into something different. Fuck. I relaxed into him and pushed my face into his chest. He enveloped me and rested his cheek against my temple. At first, it was soft and timid. But after he sighed, he pulled me closer and held me tight in an intrepid grip. We lingered there longer than "just friends" would. Even longer than Vinny hugged me unless I was having a breakdown. I revelled in this, and it terrified me.

I pulled back to find him staring at my mouth. OhFuckDearGodNope. *That* was not happening. My brain would self-combust, and Alex's ghost would haunt me. "We should make sure Vinny doesn't finish all the alcohol. Including the bottle they gave you. Fair warning, it's not a great wine." I laughed inelegantly.

CHAPTER TWELVE

A lex's fingers ran through my hair. The sensation pulled me to the surface of consciousness. Still not awake enough to open my eyes but awake enough to know he was beside me. His hands in my hair felt sublime. I always loved how he twirled my curls around his fingers. Pulling me closer, trying to make us one human.

The sleep fog lifted a bit.

Alex was dead.

My stomach churned as I realized that these were not Alex's fingers. Who could it be? Vinny? We were touchy-feely, but this was a new level of weird. Right?

Oh right.

Ronan.

Maybe this was Ronan? God, he's gorgeous. Something about him made me want to do better in life, strip naked, or run away and ignore life. He was sweet, but this was ... was what? I did not want his fingers in my hair. Right?

ShitShitShit. *Did I fuck Ronan?*

I was going to vomit everywhere.

The fingers tangled in my curls and yanked. Sticky hands touched my face. Why were Ronan's hands sticky? And tiny. He's tall, so why were his hands so tiny?

I opened my eyes to see a hazy seven-year-old staring at me. "Hey, baby girl." My throat was raw.

"Hi, Daddy."

"Shouldn't you be in bed?" The sun blinded me. The smells of cheap wine, peppermint, and old upholstery filled my senses. I wasn't in my bed. Why wasn't I in my bed? The old couch sagged under me, trying to eat me alive, and a second-hand quilt laid over me. Still dressed in yesterday's clothes. Apparently, I passed out hard last night. "What time is it?"

"Ten-thirty. We let you sleep in."

"We?" Oh, my head hurt. The light pierced my eyeballs. Oh no. That stomach churning wasn't grief. I was so hungover. Did someone beat me with a baseball bat? Everything hurt as if I were in a bar fight last night.

"Uncle Vinny, Auntie Katherine, and Ronan." She continued to poke my face and attempted to stroke my cheek. I heard voices in the kitchen. She booped my nose. "You smell like Appa."

"What do you mean?"

"You smell like Appa did when he was drinking." Her face scrunched. "I don't like it."

"I'm sorry, love-bug. Last night, I did drink. But I was home safe and with others we love and trust. You know I don't drink as often as Appa did. Lord, I loved him, but man did he drink." Should not be saying this to my seven-year-old. Fuck, I had gross, boozy, donkey breath. "You know I will never drive while I've been drinking, right?"

"Pinky promise?"

"Pinky promise." We hooked our pinkies. "Come here, munchkin." I pulled her onto the couch, and she lay next to me. I wrapped my arms around her. Trying not to groan in pain and nausea as her bony child limbs jabbed into my churning tummy. My eyes roamed the room to find Ronan sitting in the corner reading a book, pretending not to listen.

And now he knew Alex had a drinking problem. Great.

Emma and I cuddled and talked about what we liked about yesterday, and what we'd like to keep for next year. She said she loved having Ronan and Reese over. I caught a small smile on Ronan's face. I watched his cheeks pink when I said, "Me too."

Emma poked at my fingers and snuggled in. I was in heaven.

Shamelessly, I stared at Ronan. Something itched in the back of my mind. There was a missing puzzle piece, and I had no idea what it was. "Are you wearing my pyjamas?"

Ronan looked at me. "Yeah, sorry. Vinny lent them to me."

"Where did you sleep?" My mouth tasted like ass.

"On the floor in Reese's room. Vinny found your sleeping bag."

"Huh." I gawked at the rat's nest on his head and scoffed a gravelly laugh, "Nice hair."

"Thanks, my stylist was drunk at the time." He arched an eyebrow at me. I stared blankly at him. His eyes flickered between me and Emma, looking like he wanted to say something, but not in front of Emma.

Katherine called Emma for breakfast from the kitchen. She took off from the couch hard enough that she kicked me in the stomach; I almost retched all over the floor. A simpering whine came from my voice.

Ronan laughed. "You that bad off?"

I didn't answer. I looked at him with pleading eyes. Hoping he could take away my hangover. "How much did I drink last night?"

"Probably too much. But Vinny and I made sure you and Katherine didn't hurt yourselves. We were sober enough if the kids needed us."

I stared at him. Unsure of how to respond to that. "What are you reading?"

He showed me the cover. It was *The Cruel Prince* by Holly Black. Vinny bought it for me for Christmas, along with the sequels. "Don't spoil anything for me. Maybe we should read it together?" Maybe I was still drunk.

"Like a book club? A single-dad book club reading young adult books?"

"Sounds like heaven to me." I had a stupid, dreamy look, and I couldn't stop it. Something was awry in my mind space. "Did I do that to your hair?"

His eyes widened. "You don't remember?"

I tried to shake my head, but it kept spinning when I stopped. "No," I mewled.

"Wow, I probably should have cut you off before I did. You obsessed over my hair last night. You would not stop playing with it."

I covered my face with a pillow. "Oh my god. I'm so sorry." The pillow muffled my apology. I looked at him again, and he grinned. A flash of a memory popped into my head; me sitting on the back of the couch behind him, braiding and unbraiding his hair. Running my fingers through it and raking my nails across his scalp. Him laughing and leaning into me with goosebumps raised on his long neck.

Vinny called out for us to come get breakfast. I smelled bacon. My stomach gurgled. Loud.

My smooth turtle-stuck-on-his-back moves sank me deeper into the couch instead of standing like I was aiming for. Ronan came to my rescue and pulled me off the couch. Everything both hurt and was numb. I shielded my eyes from sunlight with one hand, while Ronan held the other. Memories of holding his hands with him and laughing last night came in spurts. Oh, dear.

He led me down the hall with his hand on my back. I remembered he practically carried me to the bathroom last night. Panic struck my body, my stomach lurched. "Fuck." I stumbled to the bathroom and proceeded to vomit neon pink. Twice. What did I drink?

There was a gentle knock on the door. "Wishes? Are you okay?" Ronan asked.

Sweet crap on a cracker. He heard me puke. I wanted to crawl into a hole and disappear. "Yeah, I'll live."

"If it makes you feel better, Katherine vomited this morning too."

"I don't know if that makes this better." I luckily had a spare toothbrush in this bathroom and could brush my teeth. A sweaty dew clung to my skin. Emma was right. I stank like cheap booze and idiocy.

"Good?" Ronan asked as I opened the door.

I think I nodded. My head moved, but I wasn't sure what direction it moved in. He took my hand and walked me to the kitchen and helped me sit at the table. What was with all the hand holding? Did I miss something? Was he just taking care of my hungover ass?

Katherine set black coffee in front of me. I blinked. It smelled like burnt motor oil. The wave of neon pink whatever pounded the walls of my stomach. When she turned away, Vinny exchanged the coffee for a tea. Made just the way I liked it. Bless him. He winked at me, then drank the coffee. Katherine must have made it. Vinny shuddered as he swallowed.

Katherine did a slow once-over of me. "You look like shit."

Emma giggled. Reese gasped.

"What happened last night?" I asked.

"Hey kids, you want to watch TV while you eat?" Ronan asked. The kids happily took their food into the living room and turned on cartoons. I didn't care that Reese splashed orange juice on the floor as he toddled off.

Vinny waited for the sound of the TV to turn on. "You and Katherine got wasted. Do you remember anything?"

I shook my head. "Snippets. Did I seriously get black-out drunk?" I massaged my temples. Katherine, who shouldn't have even been standing if she drank like I did, set breakfast in front of me. I promptly pushed it away with thoughts of neon pink bacon. Nope. Not doing that.

Ronan stood behind me and combed his fingers through my hair. It was fucking amazing. I leaned back against him and made a strange, almost baa-ing sound. I'm not sure if it was in response to how extraordinary this felt or because I was worried I would puke again.

Part of me wanted to pull away from him. I mean, sure, friends do this kind of stuff. Vinny had done this to me. But this crossed the friend line, and I wanted to stay far away from that line. The other part of me wanted him to never fucking stop and carry me to bed and ravish me.

I leaned forward and put my elbows on the table, pulling out of his reach. Thinking about him ravishing me was not a thought I could handle.

Another flash of memory came to mind. "Did we do shots?"

"You and Katherine did," Vinny said.

"I have liquor?"

"Did. You had peppermint schnapps," Katherine said.

Oh no. No, no, no, no. I get super handsy when I do shots. I have gotten myself into many very awkward situations with shots. "Oh, oh no." I remembered climbing into Ronan's lap and wrapping my arms around him. My stomach glorped, and I sipped my tea. I remembered touching his cheeks and playing with his hair more. I remembered laughing hysterically with him, holding his hands, running my fingers over his lips, and burying my face in his neck. "Oh shit."

Whatever colour I had left in my skin drained out. I had asked him if he wanted to stand under the pine cones with me. I turned slowly to Ronan. "Did we make out?"

What colour I lost, he gained. He turned beet red. "No. You were very drunk. It wouldn't have been right if I let you kiss me."

"Thank fuck," I said before I realized how shitty that sounded. He looked away. "I mean. Not that. I didn't want. Fuck. Yes, making out while black-out drunk is bad. Thank you for not letting me do that."

"Sure." He crossed his arms.

"Did I miss something? I have a feeling there's something I'm not remembering. I mean, I'm remembering some things and I made a complete asshole of myself. But I have an inkling I'm forgetting something."

Vinny and Katherine slipped out of the kitchen.

Ronan's eyes watched them disappear out of sight, while his arms drew closer, and he stepped further back. That was the "fucking hell I hate this" stance.

I stood and stumbled like a baby giraffe learning to walk to him. "Ronan, I'm sorry I seem to have hurt you, and I honestly don't remember much. I mean. Apparently, I sat in your lap like an idiot. I'm really sorry. Did I say or do anything to offend you?"

"No. You weren't mean or anything." He still wouldn't look at me. "You asked me a question last night. Do you remember it?"

I covered my eyes. "If you wanted to stand under the pine cones with me."

He gave a short laugh. "Yeah, you did. But that wasn't what I'm talking about, and I think you were joking about the pine cones. More teasing me."

I searched my memory over and over. I think I told him Alex could be an asshole, but I don't remember what I said. Vinny shut down that conversation fast. The memory of sitting in his lap looped in my mind, but I didn't remember asking him anything. "I'm sorry. I don't remember."

"It's okay. It's nothing." His response was fast.

"Ronan." I put my hand on his arm. "If I upset you, please tell me. You're my friend, and I'd hate to ruin that. I'm pretty sure I got too handsy and I'm so sorry." My free hand rubbed my forehead, trying to scrub away the events. "I'm so fucking embarrassed. I promise I will not drink that much again. No idea why I did."

I knew why. I was trying not to hurt and to forget Alex for one fucking night. To loosen up and have fun. Hide from the truth and stay in denial.

"You didn't ruin anything. You listened when I said back off. Don't worry." He opened his mouth to say something but snapped it shut again. "Forget it. We're still friends."

Still avoiding eye contact, his brows furrowed. I was sure his eyes got watery. Fuck. What did I do? He shrugged me off and scurried to the living room.

CHAPTER THIRTEEN

I couldn't tell if things were awkward between Ronan and me or not. He took vacation days to spend time with Reese before he returned to school, so there were few excuses to see him. The kids had one playdate at his house between Christmas and New Year's. When I did the drop-off/pickup, everything seemed fine between us. We laughed, made awkward introverted conversations, I made a bad dad joke, and he hugged me goodbye. I held on probably too long. How long was the right amount? Should I have counted to three? He texted me daily. Being with a kiddo all day, every day was intense for him. I offered to take Reese for a few hours. Regardless of how exhausted he was, he wanted to spend every second with his son. It was sweet.

On the night of the 28th, he called me. No "hello" or "how are things?" he just started reading aloud his copy of *The Cruel Prince*. I almost died. How could this glorious bastard be this fucking glorious? It took me a moment to realize what he was doing, but once I understood, I grabbed my book and followed along. I read aloud when his voice grew strained. Mind you, the roughness made my insides heat.

He called the following night to read to me again.

"Hey," he said after finishing a chapter and closing the book. "So. Um. My best friend Maddie is having a New Year's Eve party, and...." He cleared his throat. "I was wondering if you'd like to come with me?"

I swallowed. "I don't know. I get really nervous in social situations with a bunch of strangers."

"I'll take care of you. Plus, you'll like Maddie; she's my Vinny."

There was silence as I thought over the idea of a party of strangers.

"I mean. I'm sure you have plans with Vinny and Katherine. So, it's okay to say 'no.'"

"We do have plans, but it's only watching a movie. Nothing special."

"Maddie has a piano, you could play "Auld Lang Syne" for us."

It was a valiant effort as a bargaining chip. "Technically, I can do that here."

"Okay. That's okay. Never mind." He talked fast. "I just thought since we ... like ... um ... I ... fuck." He took a deep breath. I've never heard him be so flustered. "I really enjoyed Christmas with you, even though you don't seem to remember some of it. I thought, maybe, we could try to party together again. Only this time have you remember it. Do you remember anything else from Christmas?"

There was a lot to unpack in his adorable, little nervous rant. "I have bits and pieces coming back to me, but I can't tell what is real and what I've imagined while trying to remember. Because I'm pretty sure there weren't any parrots, and I am remembering parrots."

"There were no parrots."

There was an awkward long silence while I weighed the pros and cons of staying home in my safety hole or venturing out into the world with Ronan. "Can I get back to you? I want to see if Vinny and Katherine are okay if I cancel on them."

"Y-yeah."

I texted Vinny immediately after we hung up.

Vinny the Great
Go! Dear lord Wishes, go be with your man! Tap that ass

Aloysius

There will be no tapping of asses. He is not "my man"
You sure I should go?
I hate crowds

Vinny the Great

Go, buddy. I love you. Have a great time. Text me if you need to bail
And if that ass consensually presents itself, tap it

Aloysius

Love you too

"Sure," I said when I called Ronan back. "Sounds fun. It'll be better than New Year's Eve in Times Square."

"I wouldn't say that," Ronan said. "People crammed into my friend's house with stale chips and a keg of cheap beer isn't as fancy as New York."

"Sounds perfect." Sounded hellish. "Besides, Times Square always drops the ball."

Ronan chuckled. "How long were you waiting to stuff that awkwardly into a conversation?"

"Too long."

"Good night, Wishes."

"Good night, Ronan."

Hyunji was next on my call list. She agreed to host a slumber party for both kids and was ecstatic to play grandmother to Reese.

Ronan read to me nightly until the party. This quickly became my favourite daily ritual. Hearing Ronan read gave me a sense of both fantasy from the story and grounding from his voice. Plus, being able to hold a conversation without thinking of what to say was an introvert's dream.

I lamented that our reading ritual was on hold for the party. But I looked forward to having adult time with him. Not adult adult time. Kid-free time. I wished it wasn't at a party with strangers. I'd rather sit together and read in person with hot chocolate.

The average-sized house had a good number of cars parked in the driveway and on the lawn. Classy. When Ronan parked, I knew we'd get blocked in, and I felt trapped. This was a bad idea. I shouldn't have come.

People on the front porch smoked pot and top '40s music blasted inside. My gut twisted. I was not cool like these people. I was the weirdo no one invited who sits in the corner and looks constipated.

Ronan turned to me on the walkway into the home. "You good?"

I stopped walking. "How many people will there be?"

"I don't know. But you'll fit in fine, don't worry."

My legs twitched, anticipating turning and leaving.

Ronan reached for my hand, and I gave it to him. Without hesitation and freak out. It terrified me I was this at ease with him. But his touch made me not as panicked about the crowd I was about to enter into. "Thank you for coming with me," he said. "It means a lot." He chewed on the tips of his hair. "Hey, Wishes, on Christmas you asked me something, but I don't think you remember. I've been thinking about it, a lot, and I was wondering … would you like to —"

The door opened and out stepped a stunning drag queen. Okay, these might be my people after all.

She was tall and dressed in a blue peacock-sequined dress. Her big hair brushed the arch of the doorframe as she stepped outside. The neon eye makeup popped against her dark skin. Her smile widened when her eyes fell on us. I may have gasped. Gorgeous.

"Ronan." The drag queen kissed Ronan on the cheek. "So nice to see you. And who's this cutie?"

She towered over Ronan. I looked like a goofy, grinning kid. "I'm Wishes."

"Witches?"

"Wishes. Like wish upon a star."

"So, are you the wish and he's the star?" She gestured to Ronan. "You know what I wish, Wishes? I wish synchronized blushing was a thing because you two would be world champions." I hid my face in Ronan's shoulder. "Anyway, lovies, I have to go. Another party needs crashing. Ronan, you need to call me and be more social. I miss you."

"Miss you, too," Ronan said as she sashayed away.

I watched her stuff herself in a compact car. "Who was that?" I asked.

"Barry. Also known as Blueberry Muffin Top." He tugged me along, dropping whatever he was talking about before. I laced my fingers tighter between his as we approached the door and my nerves started to get the best of me. *You can do this, Wishes.*

The house was disgustingly hot and fragrant with booze and perspiration. I took off my boots, and in introvert fashion, left them open for easy slip on and run. And I hung my coat in an easy-to-grab place. If I had a panic attack, the last thing I needed was to search for my coat and boots. Been there, done that. It was horrible.

Ronan took my hand again and led me further inside. I watched him from behind. He wore tight black jeans, a white shirt with little crow-shaped polka dots on it, and a blue vest that matched his eyes. Me? I wore a purple button-up shirt with cats playing pianos, a blue bowtie, and the pair of jeans that made my ass look marvellous. At least that's what Katherine said.

We wandered into a living room that held over two dozen people. My eyes went straight to the piano. It was an old upright, nothing fancy but acceptable. Alas, people sat on the bench. Jerks. Second thing I noticed was a large trans flag hanging on the wall. Nice.

A woman bounced over to us and hugged Ronan. "Hey, babe. I'm so glad you made it. This must be Wishes?"

I nodded and held out my hand. Those few seconds of letting go of Ronan made me tight-chested. In these kinds of social situations, I needed a friend to touch and ground me to reality. Otherwise, I might spin out into an anxious frenzy.

"Oh, I'm a hugger, is that okay?" I barely nodded before she scooped me into a loving hug. "I'm Maddie. Ronan's BFF. We grew up together." She had a beautiful, silky voice, and her brown, kinky hair flowed halfway down her golden-brown arms.

The desperate urge to know everything about Ronan's childhood vibrated through my veins. "What was he like as a kid?" I asked.

"As a teen, he was the most emo that ever emo-ed," she said.

I gawked at Ronan in his light blue vest. "You were emo?" I wanted to pull out his ponytail and smear black eyeliner on him. Oh. I needed to see him in black eyeliner. A heatwave ran through me.

"Goth, thank you. And this conversation is over," he scowled. "Let's find somewhere to sit."

Maddie led us over towards the piano and kicked the others off the seat. "Move, the pianist is here."

They "ooooo"ed as they left the bench.

I noticed a photograph of Maddie and Ronan hugging on the top of the piano, among other knickknacks. It was cozy. Made my fastidious pianist's heart pang, but cozy. The dusty keys told me it had remained silent for a period.

"Go on." Maddie gestured to the piano.

"What do you want me to play? Now?" It was weird to walk into a stranger's home and have them tell you to perform. Like a party trick. "I only know classical music from memory."

"Whatever you want, Wishes." Her eyes darted between me and the piano, and her excitement crackled around her.

I sat and played scales and arpeggios to familiarize myself with the instrument. A few sticky keys, but not awful, and predominantly in tune. The room stilled, and someone turned off the sound system. I guess I was playing. A hand rubbed my back.

Ronan smiled at me and tucked one of my curls out of my eyes. Of course, it bounced right back. My skin tingled where his fingers grazed. If I didn't pull myself together, I would melt all over this bench. "Play what you'd have fun playing. This isn't a concert, it's a party."

I chewed my lip in thought. I had an idea, and I wished Vinny was here. He loved this piece. As I played, I heard him singing in my head and I had to fight back laughter for the entire piece. Ronan must have thought me mad.

"That was cool," Maddie said. She seemed genuinely impressed. "What's it called?"

I turned brightly to her. "That was Mozart's 'Lich Mein Arse.'"

"What?"

"Yup. Mozart wrote a song called 'Lick My Ass.' It's sung in a magnificent six-part harmony. And it is about ass licking." I couldn't stop giggling. Vinny and I performed this piece for a show in high school. When the staff learned what the lyrics meant, they got so upset.

Ronan bust a gut. "Out of your entire repertoire, you chose that one? You are too perfect." Woah, he called me perfect? My eyes grew wide, and my brain stuttered. "I'm gonna hunt us down some drinks. Don't worry, I won't let you drink too much." He winked, kissed my cheek, and sauntered away.

I tried not to look stunned, giddy, and petrified. My body stiffened, and I was sure the tip of my tongue stuck out. What was going on? I think I liked this? *Was this a date!?!? No. He invited me as a friend. Right?*

Maddie's voice distracted me, and I looked at her. "Hm?" My tongue was absolutely sticking out. The second I drew it in, a giant grin took its place.

"Ronan told me you have a daughter?" Maddie asked.

"Yeah," I said exceptionally loud. *Wishes, calm yourself.* "Emma. She and Reese are classmates. That's how I met Ronan." I pulled out a phone and showed her a photo of Emma and Reese dancing around on Christmas Day.

"They are adorable," Maddie said. Then she broke the unspoken rule and swiped to the next image. It was a group shot of me, Ronan, and the kids dog-piled onto the couch and laughing. Ronan's hair flopped over my eyes, and Emma's hair choked Reese.

Maddie put her palm to her heart and looked at it as if she were Kristen Bell looking at a sloth. "You guys are so cute together." She squeaked, and I casually took my phone back.

My ears burned at "together," but she moved on to the next subject before I corrected her. But we were pretty cute. At least Ronan and the kids were. I'd be lying if I said I didn't look at these photos often.

It turned out I loved Maddie. She told me about emo Ronan and his obsession with *The Crow* and musicians like David Bowie, The Cure, and Joy Division. I leaned in and ate up everything Maddie said.

She told me he used to be a skilled artist. In high school, he wanted to go into interior design or illustration. I needed to see his art. It became a new goal of mine to get him to show me something.

Ronan's pretty laugh echoed over the crowd. He was talking with a beautiful woman. Short, perfect hair with pink tips, and perfect skin she was not afraid to show. Meanwhile, I wasn't comfortable enough to wear short sleeves, and the humidity in this house gave my hair a stylish alpaca perm. I worried I smelled like one too.

Maddie growled when the woman put her hand on Ronan's chest. He gave a nervous laugh and stepped aside so her hand fell.

Ronan returned with drinks and sat next to me. I don't know what came over me, but I glared at the beautiful lady as I linked my arm around his. She rolled her eyes and started texting someone. Shit. Did I stake claim to Ronan? No. That's not what I wanted. Perhaps?

As the night progressed, I primarily chatted with Ronan and Maddie and nursed my fruity wine beverage, not wanting a repeat of Christmas. Ronan knocked several back before he and Maddie made the rounds of talking to people. I attempted to chat with others, but my ass stayed on the piano bench. It was my safety net. Although I almost leapt off when the beautiful woman flirted with Ronan again. She stared at me and put her hand on his lower back, letting it slide to his ass. Ronan's body tensed, and he tried stepping away.

I pulled out my phone. "Hey, Ronan," I called out. He turned to me. Pale-faced. "Kids want to say goodnight." I held the phone in the air. He glided to me and took my phone. He frowned in confusion when he saw my lock screen of Emma. "They didn't call. They've been in bed for two hours now, but you looked super uncomfortable."

He sat next to me, "Thank you." A crease formed between his immaculate eyebrows.

"You okay?"

"That woman is ... was friends with Vanessa." He lowered his head. "It's a slap in the face to remember my old life."

I rested my chin on his shoulder. "I can empathize. Do you want to skedaddle?"

"No. I'm fine. Besides, it's almost midnight and you still need to get Auld Lang and shit." Strands of his hair had slipped out of his ponytail.

"You sure you're okay?" I tucked an escaped silky strand behind his ear. My fingertips lingered on his cheek as they pinked.

"Yeah. I'm great." The glow in his eyes told me what he thought of me, and it was terrifying.

I turned to Maddie and rambled about goats. I kid you not. "Did you know goats from France are considered more musical than goats from Canada? They have French horns that play in many keys, while ours are only in Eh sharp."

Ronan downed his drink.

When someone shouted it was almost midnight. I swivelled towards the piano keys. Ronan slid his arm around my waist, and we counted down, laughing, leaning into each other and evaluating each other's faces. His eyes moved to my lips, and I drew them in tight like I was sucking a lemon. Shit. New Year's Eve. Why didn't I think he'd want to kiss me? Fuck. I leaned on him, though, so I sent strong mixed signals. I'm an asshole like that.

As everyone shouted, "Happy New Year!" I played and sang "Auld Lang Syne."

Naturally, I dragged it out, and by the time I got to the third verse, Ronan tapped my leg. "No one knows these parts. I think you're good."

"But there are two more verses," I protested. I glanced behind me to see people laughing and kissing, and no one was singing anymore. I flourished out an ending and turned red. Alex used to make fun of me for wanting to sing all the verses, but Vinny belted it out with me.

"Sing them to me later," Ronan suggested and leaned in.

I hugged him before he readied his lips to kiss me and whispered, "Happy New Year, Ronan."

"Happy New Year, Wishes." His fingers wove through my hair, carefully holding my head against his shoulder.

I wanted to burrow in and hibernate forever against his smooth, hot skin. I felt safe there. Some dude ruined the moment by shouting "shots" and thrusting a shot glass into my hand. Christmas had wrecked me for shots. I looked between Ronan and the glass. He smirked, downed his and downed mine. My eyes tracked the glass from his hand to his lips. How much had he had?

Some nights Alex drank so much, he struggled to walk. Let alone drive.

My gut churned.

Ronan must have read my mind. "Hey babe, I won't drink anymore. Promise. We can cab home or sleep here. I always get first dibs on the guest room on party nights. Perks of being the bestest best friend." His speech slurred a bit.

Babe? Sleep here together?

The room grew energetic and vibrant. Someone turned the music back on and people danced. Flashes of brightly coloured clothes spun around the room. Ronan laced his fingers between mine and kissed the back of my hand. That I could handle. I turned into a tittering fool. His warm, bubbling chuckle was enough to get me drunk.

"Hey, Ronan." Someone new had arrived. "How are you, man? It's been ages." The man greeted Ronan with a giant smile, which didn't falter when he noticed our hands. Ronan tightened his grip on me. "Oh, I didn't know you're into guys. Introduce me to your boyfriend."

Boyfriend.

My lungs tightened. Things tilted sideways.

"No. We're not. I-I'm not." I stammered, yanked my hand from his and moved far enough away we weren't touching. "We're not boyfriends. I can't. No. We're just friends." My eyes bugged out, and I avoided looking at Ronan. Fear ripped through me. It tore my stomach to shreds and squeezed my lungs shut. "I need air."

No idea how I stumbled through the crowd. My legs were full of pins and needles from sitting and the panic-filled adrenaline made them shake. Before I turned the corner towards the front hallway, I glanced back. Ronan stared at me with the most painful, kicked-puppy expression I had ever seen. I hurt him. I really hurt him.

My feet slid into my boots and staggered outside. I couldn't believe I did that. For what? The word "boyfriend"? Why did it scare me so much? Handholding was one thing. But boyfriend?

Snow gathered in my boots as I paced the front lawn. I ignored the smokers on the porch, asking if I was okay or if I was tripping.

I shook my head and worked on breathing. It was tempting to call Vinny, to have him help me calm the fuck down. But I didn't want to start his new year off by taking care of my ass again. I ruined last year's New Year's Eve, and this year he deserved to celebrate. Plus, he'd drop everything to come get me, even if he'd been drinking. I couldn't take the risk of him being too dumb to not say, "No, I've been drinking."

Flashes of metal clattering across the pavement invaded my mind as I took in the cars owned by people currently drinking in the house. I swore I heard Alex laughing from inside the house. He'd have loved these people. They would have loved him.

What would I do if someone from this party crashed? What if Ronan crashed? What if he crashed, and I never kissed him? I hated how my brain worked.

Fuuuuuck. Breathe in and out. I shook from head to toe and gasped in air.

What would Alex think of Ronan? I didn't want Alex to be sad and think he was losing me. But Alex wasn't here anymore. How would I get that to stick in my head?

I wanted to know Ronan better, but I worried I might mess it up? Was it already over? I mean we weren't boyfriends. That guy was the only one saying that word. Ronan never said we're boyfriends. But we acted as if we were. Oh no.

I wanted to be his boyfriend.

I had to apologize and kiss him. Breathe, Wishes. I could do this. Tears froze to my eyelashes. I focused on the breathing techniques my therapist taught me and slowed my lungs. My hands stopped shaking, my shoulders relaxed, and I opened the door to the house.

Warm, sticky air hit me. I slipped out of my boots and jogged back to Ronan, but he wasn't on the bench where I left him. I met Maddie's eyes, who looked at me with horror. She glanced down the hall, towards the bathroom. I followed her gaze and found Ronan.

The beautiful woman's hands were in his hair, and her tongue was thoroughly inspecting his throat. I thought she pushed herself on him. But no. He kissed her back and grabbed her ass.

Air stopped entering my lungs, and I bolted. I shoved my feet back into my boots and I grabbed my coat. My quick escape plan came in handy.

"Ronan. Your boyfriend's running off," Maddie yelled.

"We're not boyfriends. We're just friends."

Yeah. That hurt.

"Fuck sakes," Maddie yelled. "Trish, go be skanky with someone else. Ronan, you can't let him —"

God bless Maddie.

I slammed the door and stalked to the sidewalk before I realized I had no way home. I zipped my puffy, black coat closed and opened the map app on my phone. Thirty-minute walk. In the dead of night in January. No problem. Tears burned my eyes, and I could barely see, but I walked away and pulled on my toque and gloves. My breath puffed out in front of me, obscuring my vision even more.

When I hit the first intersection, someone shouted my name. I turned to find Ronan running towards me. "Wishes, stop. Please."

I stopped, and he stumbled towards me.

"Don't come closer," I snapped.

"Wishes," he said. "I'm sorry."

"You made out with her. I was gone for ten minutes, having a massive panic attack, and you found someone else to smash faces with. Why? Because I'm too fucked in the head? I'm weird? I'm an ugly ginger potato?"

"Damn it, Wishes, you're not an ugly potato. And you're not fucked in the head." He pulled his arms around himself. "You were having a panic attack?"

"No, Ronan, I enjoy running into night during the dead of winter with no coat. It's fun." I looked him over. "Do your coat up. Do you have a hat or gloves?"

He searched his pockets and found nothing. I pulled my spare pair of gloves out of my pocket, stomped towards him, and shoved the gloves into his hands. Since I was there, I pulled his coat hood over his head, zippered up his coat, and fixed his hair.

I crumpled to the ground and bawled. Part of me cracked. A part I had been trying so hard to fix.

Ronan knelt beside me and reached out.

"Don't touch me," I screeched.

"Wishes, I —"

"Don't."

"Babe," he said and sighed. "I'm too fucking drunk for this conversation."

"Go back to skanky woman then." I sniffled.

"Don't. Don't call her that. And I will not leave you."

"You already have."

"*You* said we weren't boyfriends."

I took out my headphones and phone, threw on random music, and started walking. Salty tears flowed and froze, and I gave zero fucks. Ronan followed me.

Some drunk shithead in some shitbox of a car yelled at us as they drove by slowly. My music was too loud to make out what they said, but they knew Ronan. I turned to him to see him flip them off as they drove away, nearly crashing into a parked car.

Ronan walked closer to me after that and went all the way to my front door with me, which I slammed shut before he said anything. Welcome to sulky jerkface Wishes.

CHAPTER FOURTEEN

T he Sunday before the kids returned to school was the first time I interacted with Ronan since the party. I had spent the days leading to today pretending everything was fine in front of Emma, then pouting and crying at night. Pathetic. It served me right for turning my back on Alex.

My phone buzzed.

Ronan
Hey, is it still okay if Reese goes to your house after school?

Aloysius
Of course
He's always welcome at my house

Ronan
Am I?

I stared at the question and felt queasy.

Aloysius
I don't know yet

Monday morning, I played the glad dad, even though it terrified me to see Ronan. He knocked on the door. I guess he decided it wasn't appropriate to knock and walk in like before. Probably right.

Emma opened the door, and I greeted Reese with a big, genuine smile. I loved that kid. I handed him his new lunch bag Emma bought him with her Christmas money, along with a gift bag. His new set of noise-cancelling headphones. Emma decorated them with stickers and paint. He jumped around and wanted to put them on immediately, but I convinced him to wait until school. The kids ran outside to throw snowballs before Ronan could stop them.

I acknowledged Ronan's existence. He had big, blue, puppy-dog eyes. I wanted to hug him and tell him we were okay. Except he had hurt me, so I didn't. And I had hurt him, and I felt ashamed of myself. My lips tightened into a thin line, and I thrust his lunch bag at him. Emma picked out a She-Ra lunch bag for him, and damn right I put his lunch in it.

"You made me lunch?" He held the bag as if I gave him a delicate snow globe. "Thank you. You're amazing, Wishes, I —"

"Emma wanted to buy you a lunch bag. I guess she Adoras you." Even in anger, I couldn't let that pun go. I turned and walked three steps before I whirled around. "There's a muffin in there." Voice too loud for the morning. "Reese said you don't eat breakfast. And I made muffins. Don't think they're made for you. I was anger baking, so they're muffins made with anger." My fists balled at my side, and I threw a childish tantrum. "Because I'm angry. In case you couldn't tell."

Angry at him. Angry at myself for screwing up. Angry at Alex for making me feel guilty for wanting to be with Ronan.

"Wish —"

"ShutUpAndEatYourMuffin." I stormed into the kitchen and waited 'til I heard the door close to cry, leaving me alone with the smell of banana bread made with anger in the oven. I was going to gain some anger weight.

I hadn't told Vinny about New Year's Eve. I couldn't stomach it. I knew Vinny would call me out on my behaviour and force me to talk with Ronan. Like an "adult" or whatever. So, when Vinny came over to work, I acted cool as a cucumber. We recorded an unfinished piece he was writing so we could evaluate it or digitally experiment with it. We'd produced some amazing music using that method.

The concept of our concert and CD was coming together. The theme was "Healing." I loved what we had so far. This could become something fantastic. Focusing on music helped clear some of the Ronan-fiasco fog I had been in.

Both Vinny and I got the kids from school. We earned curious looks from other parents. I supposed a strange guy waiting outside an elementary school could be sketchy. The stares made me uncomfortable. I linked arms with Vinny to ground myself to him. My emotions were fragile, and I did not want to burst into tears. He thought nothing of it. This was normal for us. Clearly, it was not normal for some parents.

"It's okay, buddy," Vinny said. "I will not be offended if you pull away. Do what makes you comfortable."

This was why I loved this guy. I felt blessed to have a best friend like him. I didn't get time to choose what made me comfortable. The words "Uncle Vinny!" came screaming at us from both Emma and Reese. He gave each kid a big hug and hoisted Emma into the air and carried her side-saddle style.

Reese looked at me with imploring eyes. "Oh, hun, I'm not as strong as Vinny or your dad." Those gigantic blue eyes, like his father's. How could I say no? "I'll do my best." It was an awkward and clumsy hug-carry, but he seemed satisfied. We took the kids for hot chocolate, as a return-to-school treat.

Because of our hot chocolate detour, we were behind schedule. The kids were still doing their homework when Ronan arrived. He had to come inside to get Reese ready for home.

"Hey, Ronan." Vinny hugged him. "Good to see you, man."

"You too," he said and cocked an eyebrow at me.

I looked away. And as I did this morning, I thrust containers of homemade, salt-and-pepper chicken wings with peas and rice at him. As upset as I was, I still wanted to make sure he ate. "Vinny and I have work to do. You can't stay for supper."

"Can you look at me?"

I scowled at the floor.

"Fine." He took the bag. "And thank you."

Vinny looked between us. "Did you two break up?"

Neither of us answered. I continued to scowl at the floor, afraid I'd break into tears if I looked at him. I felt Ronan staring at me.

Reese was crestfallen and crushed. "Do you hate each other? I can't come back here?"

I knelt. "Oh, hun, you can always come here. We don't hate each other, friends fight sometimes." I may have considered adding sorbitol to Ronan's lunch, a sweetener that had laxative effects. But I hadn't. Yet.

He turned to his dad and yelled, "Why do you always ruin everything?"

"Reese," Ronan's voice was tired. He was at the end of his energy for the day. He looked like he was ready to meltdown himself.

"Hey," I said in a calm and soothing voice to Reese, "your dad didn't ruin anything, buddy. You know how sometimes you and Emma argue and say rude things you know you shouldn't and you don't really mean?"

He nodded and sniffled back tears.

"That's what's happening here."

"Then you should make up. You make Emma and me talk it out." He wasn't wrong.

"One day. Just not today." Now it was my time to get teary-eyed. I knew we both fucked up, but I hurt too damn much to talk about it. Every time I considered talking to Ronan, the memory of Trish pressed against him in the hallway played over and over to torture me. I deserved it.

Ronan took Reese into the living room for a father-son talk while I finished packing up Reese's stuff.

Vinny tried to talk to me about Ronan, but I was mature and pretended not to hear him while I hid my tears. He stood behind me and wrapped his arms around me. "Sorry you're hurting, Wishes. I'm always here for you, buddy."

Maybe because Vinny and I were touchy friends, I had trouble knowing the difference between friend touch and relationship touch with Ronan? I had no clue.

Emma hugged me, too. I was a sad, but loved, sandwich.

A few weeks later, I had a particularly rough night. That teenage garage band harassed me on social media and blamed me for their inability to get a record deal. Not my fault they couldn't sing. But trolls be trollin'. Emma was cranky and melted down in a large and dramatic way. I worried a neighbour would call Children's Aid.

And it was the anniversary of Alex's and my first date. I pulled a photo album out of a drawer. It smelled like old plastic. I flipped to the series of photos we took at the same restaurant for every anniversary. We changed so much over the years.

I was a goofy-looking university student with no sense of style, with fluffy, red, cotton-ball hair. Now I was a goofy-looking dad with no sense of style and floppy, defined curls.

Alex looked like a model. He was a gym bro. Well dressed with an amazing smile. To this day, I don't know why he fancied me.

Perhaps he found my music nerd life to be a fresh change from his frat-boy life.

God, I loved him.

I touched his face. "Alex *hyung*, I am still livid you left us. How could you be so stupid? It hurts every day. Emma still cries, I still cry, hell, Vinny cries." I wiped snot with the back of my hand.

"Emma yelled at me today. We had an epic fight, and I was a shit dad and snarled back. She screamed she wished it was me in the car and not you. I didn't argue. Some days I think the same thing.

"She hasn't apologized for saying it yet. And I don't think I'll ask her to." I was ugly sobbing. "Fuck you for getting wasted and driving. I would have picked you up." The photo album banged as I slammed it onto my dresser.

I wept until I could weep no longer. Grief sucked. I wanted Alex back, but I no longer had that choice.

I wanted Ronan back, that is, if I ever had him. And I had a choice here. But it was so fucking scary. Yes, he hurt me, but I was scared I hurt him too much and he'd never forgive me. I was scared if I admitted I fucked up too, he'd use it against me. I was scared he'd react like Alex did.

Fuck Alex, why did you have to fuck with my brain so much? Why did I still worry what you'd think of me?

Ronan wasn't Alex. Alex was gone, but Ronan was still here.

I grabbed my phone and texted Ronan.

Aloysius
Can we read?

Moments later my phone rang, and without a "hello," Ronan read from where we left off. The sound of his voice was comforting. And not having to talk made this effort to reconnect easier. Tears flowed and my breath turned staccato.

"Hey, Wishes, you okay?"

It took me a moment to realize Ronan had stopped reading and asked me something.

"Yeah. No, but I will be, I hope" was my confusing answer.

"I am so sorry. Can we talk about this?"

"This has nothing to do with us. You're helping just by being here. By being you." I cleared my throat. "Thank you."

There was a pregnant pause before he continued.

I fell asleep to his voice.

After a few more days of reading together, and being cordial in person, I decided I needed to fix this.

Aloysius
Can you stay for supper?

Ronan
I'd love to.

When he arrived, I was piss-my-pants nervous. I made that chilli he loved, put flowers on the table, and wore a nice, green dress shirt instead of my usual oversized sweater. The supper itself went fine. The chilli was spicier than planned because my hands shook when I added the spices.

After dinner, the kids played in the living room; I told them I was showing Ronan something in the studio and to use the camera if they needed us.

Ronan followed me into the studio and shut the door.

"I don't like this tension between us, but I don't know how to fix it," I said. My voice warbled with insecurity. "I'm confused about everything, and I don't know where to start. Something about that guy saying the word 'boyfriend' made my brain go static-y and I glitched. I'm still hurt you kissed her. But I also know I hate not hanging out with you. I miss you."

"I miss you, too. And I feel like an asshole for kissing her. I messed up. But I need you to understand I was hurting too. You dumped me in front of my friends."

"We were not boyfriends. Neither of us ever agreed to that. No one said that word." I tried not to raise my voice, but I wasn't quiet.

He smoothed his long hair back. "Sort of." He chewed on the tips of his hair, unable to make eye contact. "I know you don't remember this, but on Christmas, you asked me if I wanted to be your boyfriend."

"I did?" I did *not* remember this. My cheeks burned. "What did you say?"

He laughed. "My god, Wishes, I obviously said yes."

"Oh. Okay." I turned this over in my head.

"And at Maddie's, I had planned to ask you out, because you had already asked me out, but you didn't remember. So, I thought you'd want to. But we got interrupted, but then you held my hand and leaned on me, and you held me. It felt really good. I assumed we wanted the same thing. I mistakenly assumed we were some sort of a couple. Maybe not officially, but I thought something was there. Even Maddie told me we were a cute couple."

"There was something there. That wasn't a mistake, but I didn't understand what was happening. I'm not good with this stuff." I sighed. "So, it really looked like I dumped you. Fuck. I'm sorry."

"And that's not the best part of why it hurt." He slumped into one of my black rolling chairs. I sat in the other. "I wasn't out to anyone besides Maddie. And the guys and folks I fooled around with in college. My wife didn't know. We were married, so what did it matter? I shoved it to the back of the closet and buried it there.

"When we split, I didn't have it in me to date. She fucked me up bad. And you came along and that changed." He gave a breathy laugh. "I mean, I'm still fucked up, but now I wanted to date. Or, at least, I wanted to date *you*. You gave a fuck about me. Vanessa killed my ability to be myself, but with you, I've been reviving those parts of me I lost. It was nice."

I wiped tears from my cheeks. "I get that."

"I had several late-night conversations with Maddie about my sexuality. Honestly, I don't know what I am. Maybe I'm bi, or pan? I'm afraid to choose, because if I get it wrong, someone will call me out and say I'm faking it. And the bi versus pan arguments are intense." He shifted in his chair.

"It's insane, isn't it? I'm lucky I'm only gay."

He gave a soft huff of a laugh. "Yeah. It's something." He looked at me. "I was so happy I could be out with you holding my hand. Then it felt like you dumped me." His voice shook. "I was hurt, drunk, rejected at my own coming-out moment, and I got confused.

"While you had your panic attack outside, I panicked in the bathroom. Trish checked on me, and I thought, fuck it. She was like Vanessa. She was familiar, and she wanted to kiss me. Unlike you, who avoided kissing me. I knew kissing her was stupid, but I was pissed off and wanted to act dumb. Being dumb and doing stupid shit is who I am. I used to do heroin; I'm not exactly the best at making good choices."

"Ronan," I touched his arm, "you should have told me that was your coming-out moment. Especially since you planned on making me a part of it. I would have done things differently. First, I would have known it was an actual date and not had to guess." I mentally replayed the scene. "Wow, I'm a piece of shit." I had much worse coming-out moments, but I had better ones too.

"Why did you freak out? What's wrong with me? Am I too straight acting? Is that a thing?"

"It wasn't anything you did or anything about you. I'm broken." I rolled my chair closer to him and took his hand. He wouldn't look at me. "When... I... Alex —" I took a deep breath. This was a precarious topic and difficult to explain. "I freaked out because my brain isn't letting me process certain things. Especially when it comes to Alex, and apparently the concept of relationships.

"I've always been obtuse when people hit on me. I assumed they're being friendly. Part of my brain knew there was something between us; part of my brain believed you were just being polite because I'm ...." I drew back, made a self-deprecating gesture to myself, and tugged my sleeves.

"My brain freaked out, worrying about what Alex would say," I continued. "I want to move on. He would want me to. But I get stuck." My throat tightened. "It's like if I accept there's something between us, or kiss you, I'm forgetting about him. I'm closing that chapter like it never existed. And I know that's not true." I vibrated.

"I've never dealt with death like this before, and I worry he's going to fade from my memories if I build new ones. What if I forget his face, or his laugh, or him? It's like I'm betraying him, even though I'm not." I sobbed. "It's ridiculous."

Ronan slid off his chair, knelt in front of me, and wiped tears from my cheeks. "If you're not ready to date, you don't have to. I thought you wanted to."

"I do." It was true. All my brushing things aside and assuming he was only being friendly denied me my feelings. "I want to be yours, but I have to take it glacially slow. My brain needs time to process what we're doing."

"I'm fine with going slow. You set the pace, your boundaries, make the moves, and I'll follow. Tell me what you're comfortable or uncomfortable with. I need you to communicate with me, though. That okay?" He took my hand.

"Yeah. That sounds doable. Thank you." I squeezed his hand, and my tremble shifted from angst to joy.

He grinned. "Are we doing this?" God, I loved his dimples.

I grinned back with tight, salt-stained cheeks. "Yeah."

He stood, pulled me to my feet, and hugged me tight. If he didn't hug me this hard, I'd float away. This felt right. I buried my face in his neck and breathed him in. He smelled like a winter forest.

"What can I call you? Partner? Boyfriend? My Wishes?"

"Say them again." I giggled against his skin.

He swayed and laughed. "You are my partner. You are my boyfriend. You are my Wishes."

A content noise hummed from my throat, and I snuggled in deeper. "I like them all, but I like boyfriend the most. Even though it sounds like we're teenagers."

"Try them on me," he said.

I pulled back and locked eyes with him. "Ronan, you are my partner. You are my boyfriend. You are my Ronan."

His smile grew and his eyes glowed. He was beautiful.

"I like those too." Ronan brushed the back of his hand against my cheek. Goosebumps erupted on my neck. "Can I kiss you?"

My brain stuttered and my lungs stopped working.

"I'm taking the deer-in-the-headlights look as 'no.' And that's okay." His thumb rubbed my cheek. "Don't worry. However, you know you will have to kiss me first."

"Okay," I squeaked. Great, we would never kiss.

"Can I kiss your hand?"

I nodded, and he watched me as he held the back of my hand to his lips. I was going to die. His beautiful lips moved in an entrancing way. He drew out my fingers and kissed my palm. Slow and intense. The soft, wet inside of his lips dragged along my skin, followed by a light scraping of his teeth. When he pulled away, he smirked, and I deeply considered tearing his clothes off right then and there.

"Can I kiss your cheek?"

"Yes."

He grinned as he kissed my cheek, slowly and sensually. When he pulled back, I stood on my tiptoes and kissed his cheek. His skin moved under my lips as he smiled and hummed. My heart fluttered. I let my lips travel along his jaw. His hands gripped my waist so I wouldn't lose my balance. I left trail of kisses to his collarbone. His chest rose and fell.

With a faint moan, he leaned over me and kissed my neck. My fists clenched around his shirt, and I leaned into him as my knees wobbled. I tilted my neck to give him more space and questioned my need to take things slow.

"Woah," he tightened his grasp on me as my knees buckled. "You alright?"

"Yup. Yup. Yeah. I-I'm good."

He laughed. "Your eyes are glazed over. You high?"

"Feels like I am." I giggled. Ronan helped me sit. I grabbed his hand, needing to touch him. "Apparently, I like it when you kiss my neck. It makes me feel alive. You're a natural neck-romancer."

He groaned and played with my hair.

"Should we tell the kids?" I asked.

"Wait? For a little while."

"Yeah. I need time to adjust." I hoped Emma would be okay with us.

"Until then ...." He somehow made it onto my lap and kissed my neck again. I slipped into a kiss-drunk high.

CHAPTER FIFTEEN

I couldn't stop smiling as I texted Vinny.

Aloysius
I have a boyfriend!

Vinny the Great
It's about time you realized that!
I'm super happy for you buddy. You two are cute together!
And if he hurts you, I will fuck his shit up
I almost did after you told me about New Years, but I realized you two don't communicate well. And you need to. Don't hold back like you did with Alex. Speak your mind buddy. And you'll need to talk to him about … everything.
But next time he upsets you …
His ass is grass. No one hurts my side husband
I always have your back bud

Aloysius
Thank you
For everything
And we are adorable
Or at least he is

Vinny the Great
Aloysius Dermot O'Connor stop that nonsense
You're fucking adorable
I want a plushie of you so I can squish you all day

Aloysius
Yes Vincent Finn McDonald

Over the following weeks, Ronan and I snuck cuddles, held hands under the table, and touched each other's backs as we passed one another. I don't know if the children noticed; we tried to hide it. But I giggled and blushed enough to be sus.

Our Valentine's Day consisted of making valentines with the kids for their class the night before. He gave me a rose; I made him a pie, and we cuddled in my studio while the kids devoured said pie.

With fists on hips, I scolded their blueberry-covered faces. "I should have known batter than to crust you. But now you've done it. No more Mr. Nice Pie. You've hurt my fillings and I'm crustfallen. I love you both berry much, but for goodness bakes, this is the last slice."

Emma threw a tea towel at me and laughed. "You want a piece of me, you strawberry shortcake?"

Reese had a giggle fit, and I think Ronan questioned his choice to date me.

After the kids were asleep, we'd text, talk on the phone, or he'd read to me. It was amazing. We had moved to the next book in Holly Black's hot, Fae-prince series. His sexy villain voice was perfect. Deep, smooth, laissez-faire, and sultry. It gave me pleasant and confusing dreams. Ronan filled me with hope that I was worthy of attention. His attention. I still struggled to accept that. He was my Fae prince, and I was his potato.

"You know, Aloysius," he said to me one night, using his sexy voice, "you are gorgeous. And I hate when you say cruel things towards yourself. They are not true. Stop lying to my boyfriend."

"You are sweet, kind, amazing with my son, and you are my prince. Your sunset hair, emerald eyes, and freckles are the last things in my mind before I fall asleep."

"Thank you," I whispered into the phone. Even though I believed he'd change his mind if he ever saw me shirtless. "I think about you too." Only not just his hair and eyes.

Ronan was a brilliant father too. I saw a positive change between him and Reese now that he didn't have to scramble home for supper and do homework. Now they had the chance to talk, play, laugh, and help Reese with his behaviour. Which was improving.

I gave Ronan a copy of my lullaby music CD I used to play for Emma when she couldn't sleep or needed to relax. Ronan told me it helped Reese's anxieties; he also confessed that he listened to it to help him sleep too. The music itself was relaxing, but he said knowing it was me playing made him feel safe and cared for.

I learned amazing facts about Ronan while we got to know each other. He volunteered at the pet shelter before Reese was born. After university, he backpacked around Europe and spoke French and German at conversational levels. He attended protests with Maddie and knew first aid for pepper spray.

While Maddie transitioned, he supported her by going to doctor's appointments with her, taking her clothes shopping, and caring for her after chest surgery. At bars, he waited for her outside the bathrooms, ready to defend. And he did throw a few punches.

The more I learned, the more I was in awe of him. And in awe that he picked me. Although, maybe he had low standards after Vanessa. I tried avoiding those thoughts, but it was easy to slip into a negative mind frame. My therapist would be proud I was trying.

We arranged playdates on the weekend as often as we could, but sometimes it wasn't possible. He visited his parents for a weekend. I had clients who could only record on weekends. Some weekdays we couldn't hang out after dinner, as rehearsals ramped up for mine and Vinny's project. We had bit the bullet and hired other musicians; it was getting real.

Luckily, Ronan was delighted to watch Emma. They had bonfires in my backyard and roasted marshmallows, did facials and their nails, or he'd lay blankets on the deck and teach the kids star constellations. Emma rambled excitedly before bed whenever Ronan watched her.

Meanwhile, on those nights, Ronan on more than one occasion fell asleep on the phone while we talked. Emma could be exhausting.

We finally planned a weekend for the kids to have a slumber party. Alone time with Ronan after the kids went to bed was almost as exciting as Christmas. I was more excited than Emma was. Sleep evaded me the night before, and I had spent all morning cleaning. I knew I was being absurd. He knew the state of my house, but I wanted to clean for this occasion.

The afternoon was full of games. Ronan ordered delivery poutine, and we had "Decker family secret" sweet-and-salty popcorn while watching movies. The kids lay in a pillow fort while Ronan and I sat on the couch. The post-supper coma, and the lack of slumber, hit me like a ton of bricks.

I did the dad nod. The kind that dads do when they are trying not to drift off, so their head bobs and they startle themselves awake. I did that. I couldn't allow myself to snooze. This was mine and Ronan's first chance since New Year's to spend any decent amount of kid-free time together, and I did not want to sleep through it.

Wave after wave of exhaustion hit me.

Warm hands grabbed me before I faceplanted into the coffee table and pulled me back. My eyes fluttered open, and I was curled into Ronan's lap. He held me tight.

"Sleep. You deserve a nap," Ronan said.

And I did. I curled deeper into him and closed my eyes, safe in his arms. My dreams were of us cooking, taking the kids to the beach while we strolled arm in arm and watched them play, hosting parties together, and having games nights with the kids and our friends. My chest warmed with elation.

I opened my eyes and watched him as he snickered at the movie. My fingers combed through his hair, and he turned to me. So fucking pretty.

"Hey, everything okay?"

I touched his cheek and looked at him with adoration. His eyes shone and reflected my feelings back.

I kissed him.

It wasn't a passionate and lustful kiss that poets exalt. This was a kiss that said, "I'm happy. I am safe and comfortable with you. You make me feel cared for and appreciated. I trust you. I value you. I want you. I am home."

He kissed me back.

His kiss mirrored my statement, but with more lust and "I want you."

I pulled away, nestled into his neck, and fell asleep.

The next time I woke, Ronan was passed out. We were in an awkward, half off the couch, limbs tangled, stiff-necks position. Level nine of "dads can sleep anywhere in any position."

I looked at the TV screen to read "Are you still there?" The kids were gone. Hot panic flashed through my body.

"Ronan." I shook him as I tried to stand and possibly crushed his man jewels in my flail. "Where are the kids?"

The same wave of panic bolted him awake. He stood. "I'm sure they're upstairs."

We bolted up the stairs. I flew straight to Emma's room. She was fast asleep. She had tucked herself in bed for the first time. I searched the room, but Reese wasn't here. I followed Ronan to the guest room. The rumpled sheets lay empty.

Ronan became agitated and jittery.

I checked my bedroom, and Ronan checked the bathroom. He wasn't there. Ronan yelled Reese's name as we tumbled down the stairs. His boots were at the front door with his coat. Ronan checked the downstairs bathroom while I ran into my semi-finished basement. I couldn't see why he'd come here. "Reese," I yelled and looked in each dingy room and behind Alex's boxes. But nothing. Ronan joined me and he stared into the sub-pump foot-wide drain hole.

"Ronan, he's not in there. It's too small, and he's too smart." I tugged his hand to pull him away from that terrifying thought. Ronan checked my deep freezer. He grew frantic.

"What if she had him kidnapped?" His tone was high-pitched and panicking. "Those were her scumbag friends who drove past us on New Year's Eve. What if they broke in while we were asleep? They have my son, Wishes."

Fuck. I didn't think about that. "We would have heard something. He's fine. He's probably ...." What Wishes, he's probably what? The metallic tang of fear coated my mouth.

I had a thought. I dashed to my studio and shook the locked doorknob. My keys jingled when I grabbed them from the kitchen and opened the door.

There Reese sat, cheerful and oblivious, with headphones on, messing with my equipment. "Ronan! He's in here!"

Ronan dashed into the room and clutched his chest. "Thank fuck."

I sat in the chair next to Reese and tapped his shoulder. He took off his headphones with a start. He wore Emma's pink-kitty pyjamas.

Ronan was on the edge of losing his shit on Reese. I raised a hand to Ronan to hold him back.

"What are you doing, hun?" I asked Reese in a calm tone. Trying not to sound winded and rattled.

"I'm making music," he said hesitantly. He knew he shouldn't be doing what he was doing.

"Can you show me? I'd love to hear." I eyed my soundboard. The disarranged controls made me cringe. This would take time to sort out.

He handed me the headphones, pressed play, and I nearly cried.

A little voice sang in my ear. "I love my dad. My dad's the best. He is a super dad. If he were a dinosaur, he'd be a brachiosaurus."

"This is awesome, Reese," I said. "Can we let your dad hear?" I switched the system to speakers and hit play again.

Ronan's eye leaked. "I love you too, little dude."

Reese beamed.

"Why brachiosaurus?" he asked.

"Because you're tall and gentle," Reese said. "But if someone upsets you or tries to hurt me, you whack them with your tail!" He mimicked a dinosaur, whipping its tail around.

Ronan's bottom lip trembled. It was adorable.

I turned back to Reese. "I'm okay with you recording songs. But can we make some rules? Can you not record without me? I would be more than thrilled to explain how this works and show you how to use the equipment. But this stuff is expensive, and these buttons have places they need to be." So glad I was strict with documenting settings.

"I'm sorry." Reese hung his head.

"I'm not angry. Neither is your dad. We love you and we worried when we couldn't find you. Next time, tell us if you want to record music. Even if you have to wake us." He nodded and turned red. "Do you want me to teach you how to record music?"

"Yes." Reese glowed. "And piano? Like you."

My heart melted. "Absolutely dude. I'd love to teach you more piano and recording." I thought for a moment. "Hey, I have an idea. Why don't you and your dad go grab a bedtime snack, and I'm going to do something special to your recording."

He slid out of the chair and took off towards the kitchen. I stopped Ronan before he followed Reese out. "He's safe, he's creative, and he loves you. Don't freak out on him. I want him to know he won't be punished for making music."

"You're right. If I had lost it, I'd never hear his song, he'd have thrown a tantrum, and it would have been a disaster." He lifted my chin with two fingers and kissed me. "Thank you."

I tittered. Not giggled. Full-on tittering. "My pleasure. I'll be out in a few."

Once he left, I entered work mode. I may have been a classical musician, but I could get lit. I added a bass line, picked the cutest words to focus on and repeat, and threw in a few drop beats and electronic sounds. This was an adorable and happening forty-five-second techno.

I called them in, and we had a mini dance party. Reese was astonished this was his song. Something he did was "super cool." His eyes shone with euphoria, and he bounced and waved his hands with excitement.

He begged to listen to it ad nauseam, but we convinced him five times was enough. I took Ronan's phone while he tucked Reese into bed and uploaded both the original song and the remix to it so they could listen whenever they wanted.

I wandered into the kitchen and cleaned. When Ronan found me, he slid his arms around my waist and kissed me. Over and over. Our kisses started calm and sensual but escalated into harder, deeper kisses. His palms slid over my ass. I tensed.

"Don't worry." He lifted me onto the countertop, and I squeaked. My knees hugged his hips. And dear lord, I loved pushing kisses down onto him. I towered over him while he pressed me into the counter. I hadn't felt this sexy in years. Holding his face in my hands was like holding the most precious porcelain sculpture. I didn't dare let go in case it fell to the floor and shattered.

His fingers twitched, wanting to move around my body. Instead, he gripped my hips and his thumbs pushed through my belt loops to lock his hands in place. It made me feel like a prince, revered and respected.

"Hey," I panted. "A-are you spending the night?" My voice cracked.

"If you want me to."

"Y-yeah."

"I can sleep on the couch."

"N-n-no."

"No?"

"Unless you w-want to."

"I will sleep where you wish." He caressed my cheek and electricity hit every nerve in my body.

My heart pounded in my throat. Thoughts flooded my brain so fast I couldn't pick one out. It was white noise and static. My mouth was dry. I reminded myself to breathe. "M-my bed?"

"You sure?"

"Yeah. Sleep only, m-maybe cuddles and kisses, but nothing else."

He grinned. "I can do that. And if you change your mind, kick me out. I won't be offended." He ran his fingers through my hair and made me shiver.

"Okay." I was proud I stated my boundaries, and he accepted them. Hot AF.

"Thank you for inviting me."

I blushed and kissed him.

CHAPTER SIXTEEN

I lay there, watching him watch me. We exchanged thousands of words in those looks, and I was too obtuse to interpret them. I tugged the cuffs of my oversized sweatshirt, envious of his ability to wear a fitted tank top. More envious of his defined and strong arms. I pulled the cool bedspread tighter against me. Hiding my body from him.

I stared at a wisp of long hair that crossed his cheek. When I reached to move the hair, I realized how far apart we were. I was at the edge of the bed, afraid to be tempted past my comfort zone. He was at the other, cautious of my boundaries. It was just moving hair; I only touched his forehead and cheek; it wasn't a complex move. But it felt damned daunting.

His eyes closed. This tiny act showed me he trusted me. His throat bobbed as he swallowed. The soft curve of his mouth enraptured me.

Logically, I could trust him. Emotionally, I wanted to run screaming, buy a tub of cookie dough ice cream, and hide forever. But my trust was like a guitar pick. When you dropped your pick inside your guitar, the pick was still there. It didn't disappear, but you couldn't reach it. It rattled around. You saw the bastard when you peered in, but it took a good hard shake or two to get it out. I had to shake my guitar to get my pick out. Right now, it was trapped in a dark place. I was glad no one could hear my thoughts. That was such a stupid analogy.

Propping myself on my elbow, I shook that damn guitar. I moved closer to him. His eyes remained closed, but his smile deepened. Creating adorable little dimples. My fingers grazed those dimples. His cheeks were smooth and soft, with muscles taught in a grin.

I moved closer.

His smile widened, and the perfect lines of his teeth peeked between his pink lips. His hand pressed mine against his face. He slowly and sensually kissed my palm. My breath hitched, and I froze. The tickle of his mouth sent electricity pulsing through my arm. Hot AF.

"Too much?" he asked.

"No," I squeaked.

He kissed my palm and nuzzled his jaw against the heel of my hand. I watched with wild fascination. A small gasping whimper noise sounded in the room. It took me a moment to realize the noise came from me. The sound reflected my thoughts of "I'm unsure of what is happening, but I crave this."

Breath escaped me. He dragged his gaze along my arm, stopping at my neck for a moment, lingered on my mouth before meeting my eyes through his heavy eyelashes. My insides melted. The way he looked at me said, "I need you. I want to touch you and make you cry my name. I desire to make love to you. I want to fuck you." This, I believed, was what the poets called "smouldering eyes."

Mirroring my position, he inched closer and lifted himself onto one elbow. We were so close; we actively tried to avoid touching each other. And yet, the remaining gap between us bothered me. I wanted less gap. His winter-fresh scent wafted towards me, and I craved rubbing his smell all over me.

With him looking at me, everything seemed difficult. He saw when I made a mistake, got embarrassed, or worked through my anxieties. There was nowhere to hide. I had to believe he wouldn't hurt me.

Shake the damn guitar, Wishes.

I slid my hand under his ribcage and waited. What was I waiting for? For him to say no? For him to make the next move? I chewed on my lip, avoiding eye contact. Patiently, he let my brain sort itself out. I loved he could tell when I needed a moment to battle with myself. Right. I was waiting for myself to give myself permission. Okay. I could do this. I knew what I wanted, but my body hesitated.

Shake the fucking guitar, Wishes.

My free hand took his. Was this what I wanted? Sort of. Yes, I liked it, but it wasn't enough. He squeezed and reassured me everything was fine. His thumb drew circles on my skin. The movement was soothing and hypnotic, and the light pressure pulled my anxious mind into focus.

Smash the fucking guitar open. I could do this. I imagined myself holding a study pick with a good grip. Such a stupid analogy.

"I trust you," I whispered. It wasn't clear to me if I was talking to him, or myself, but it felt nice to say.

"I trust you too," he whispered back. Tilting his head to catch my eye, trying to read my mind.

I looked at him. There was soft concern in his expression. My lungs filled, and I slid my arm between him and my soft bedsheets. My back against the mattress, I looked up at him. I held his muscular hand against my stomach while I waited for signs of confusion, anger, discomfort. There was only compassion and lust. I dragged the hand on my stomach, past my shoulder, next to my head.

His eyebrows lifted in question before his body followed my directions. I pursed my lips, moments from losing my nerve and bolting if he didn't want this.

Imagining my guitar pick, I breathed in confidence and the fruity smell of his hair products.

The fingers on my free hand curled around his hip and guided him to straddle me. He hovered on all fours over me, and I was in heaven. Lacing his fingers in mine, he pinned my arm against the pillow as he got comfortable. I grew hot, wavering between fear and excitement. I gave him some control. Some.

He studied my face as if I were a masterpiece of art. Inspecting each brushstroke, each detail, each line. Absorbed into the finer points people missed when they stood back and adjudicated the canvas as one piece. When works of art contained hundreds of beautiful, soft, and dramatic moments. He leaned in, cautiously. Yearning to be close enough to touch the canvas, but afraid to trigger the proximity alarm.

He glanced at my lips, waiting for the signal to proceed. I closed my eyes, and with the softest smile, I tilted towards him. His hair tickled me, his nose touched mine, and I waited. My chest swelled, my toes wiggled, and I gripped his hand. The anticipation was going to make me lose my ever-loving mind, and I lived for it.

Lips contacted my cheek. Not what I expected. His second-long, intentional kiss to my cheek reminded me of him sexily kissing my palm. I flushed. My chest rose towards him, and my throat made that unfamiliar gasping whimper again. His mouth twisted into a grin, and he chuckled.

I expected to be embarrassed. Where was my embarrassment? He laughed at me for enjoying myself. Why was I not freaking out?

I had my guitar pick. I trusted him.

He wasn't laughing at me. He was happy I enjoyed this. And I was. I really fucking was.

I opened my eyes, searched for his lips, and kissed him. Despite brushing his teeth, he tasted like sugar and popcorn, and it filled me with joyful thoughts of being safe with him on the couch. We kissed over and over. A heavy lightness filled in my stomach. So desperate to be with him, it hurt. And being with him made me weightless and free.

My body tensed. He moved. He released me and shifted his weight.

I needed to trust him.

Twisting his body from side to side, he grinned. "I'm going to need to start yoga again," he laughed, and his back cracked. "You good, babe?" He eyed me.

"Yeah. We can stop if you need to." I opened a door for him to escape.

"I don't think I'm that out of shape." He drew a finger along my neck. Goosebumps pricked my skin. "I'd like to keep kissing you, if you wish." His finger brushed my lip.

In my mind, I said, "Yes. Please, sir, you may proceed." In reality, I produced a strange screeching noise, pulled him to me, and kissed him hard. He slammed his hands into the pillow on each side of my head to stop himself from falling into me face first. I nearly bit his lip. Perhaps I was too grabby. He didn't complain, though.

When his lips journeyed across my neck, I arched into him. I grabbed his hips and tugged at them. He didn't question or hesitate. Following my orders, he lowered his hips and pressed them into mine. Our worn flannel pyjama pants hid nothing from each other. We both enjoyed this immensely. And I meant immensely.

He swallowed a moan I let out.

"I love the sounds you make," he said.

"So make me make more." I flashed my most wicked of smiles.

He groaned and buried his head in my shoulder. "Oh my god, Wishes. I've hit my boundary wall though, haven't I?"

I thought for a moment. "As much as I want to, I-I-I —" *Shit, don't freak out now. You've got this. State what you need. Believe he will respect you. Breathe.* "I don't think I can go to the proverbial next base." With a coy smile, I said, "Consider this a challenge. You'll have to be creative if you want me to cry your name."

He turned red and shivered. "You're going to be the death of me, aren't you?"

"A little death." I bit my lip and writhed under him.

He inhaled sharply and looked away. "I am going to touch those boundary walls, just so you know."

"Don't cross them." I grinned.

He locked eyes with me. The hot-and-bothered expression shifted to a serious and caring one. "I won't. And tell me if I get too close for comfort. Promise me."

I nodded. "Promise."

He kissed me, binding a sacred contract between us.

I discovered that, with the right partner, hitting the edge of your boundaries was extremely hot when they didn't cross the line. I even allowed him to lift the frayed hem of my sweatshirt a few inches to kiss my hipbones. Dear lord, I was going to melt or explode or something.

I had forgotten the backs of my knees could be an erogenous zone for me. Hell, most of my body was an erogenous zone when Ronan touched me. He discovered my enjoyment of varying between light, ticklish touches and sharp claws and teeth. I learned Ronan kissing my neck was all I required to live, and I don't know how I lived without it before.

The best sensation that made me nearly weep was when he fell asleep on top of me. His head on my chest and my fingers twirling in his hair. Anchoring me to the world so I wouldn't run away. The muscles in my body melted to the point where moving was near impossible. This felt good. This was what I wanted. Ronan in my bed was what I wanted. Ronan in my life was what I needed.

And Ronan could indeed make me cry his name while fully clothed.

CHAPTER SEVENTEEN

When I woke, the sun peeked through my blinds, and I felt a peaceful bliss. Ronan lay on top of me, and I hadn't slept this well in ages. My bladder hadn't been this compressed for ages either. I petted Ronan's hair, hoping to wake him. No response. I rubbed my thumb along his cheek; he batted my hand aside, grumbled, and angled away. Adorable. My insides squeed and vibrated with how cute he was. I held back giggles, but I did a poor job at it.

He poked my side. "Pillows don't move," he muttered.

I hugged him tight and rocked him. He was grumpy in the mornings, apparently. Grumpy and adorable. He muttered in disapproval of being manhandled this early.

"Sweetheart, I have to pee," I said.

He lifted his head, hair flopped in one eye, while the other squinted at me. "What did you say?"

"That I have to pee?"

"No. The other part."

I pushed his mane out of his eyes. "Sweetheart?"

"Yeah that. I like that." He bear-hugged me and rolled me on top of him. "Say it again."

"Sweetheart." I laughed. "Hun. Hunny. Pumpkin." He frowned at that one. "Love-bug?" He shook his head. "Darling." He smiled. "My boyfriend."

He kissed me. His passion overflowed into me as he kissed me harder and harder.

"Ronan?" I pulled away. "I really have to pee."

"I don't want to let you go." He held me tight.

"I mean ... I never suspected your kink was water play, but if you want me to ...." I pretended to relax my muscles and he let me go. "Thank you." I bolted from the room.

After I used the facilities, I headed downstairs, and the smell of coffee greeted me. This was a make-or-break moment in our relationship. I didn't drink regular coffee, only basic bitch lattes. At home, I drank tea. I shuffled into the kitchen and found a cup of tea ready for me. I was going to marry this man. The fact I joked about that, even in my head, meant I took a gigantic leap in healing. I smiled and joined Ronan and the children in the living room.

Ronan jutted his chin at the tea. "I texted Vinny to find out how you drank it."

My cheeks hurt. I could not stop my foolish grin. "Morning, bug-a-boo." I ruffled Emma's hair. Her gaze never veered from the cartoons on TV. "Morning, whippersnapper," I greeted Reese, who waved and acknowledged my existence.

"Whippersnapper? Do you have Werther's hard candies?" Ronan jested. I sat on the couch, a hair's breadth away from him.

"I do. They are in the crystal candy dish on the shelf over there."

Ronan looked where I pointed and shook his head. "I'm dating an old man."

I coughed and nodded at the kids.

"Don't worry, Daddy, we already know," Emma said, still not turning from the TV. "We figured it out months ago."

"Are you okay with it?" I asked. My daughter likely knew I was dating Ronan before I did. Not sure if she was smart, or if I was daft.

Emma stood, took my hands, and with a deadpan expression, she said, "We coo."

"We've already told our teacher we're brother and sister," Reese added.

"L-let's not get ahead of ourselves," I sputtered.

"We're not. We're just ahead of you. As usual." My daughter threw serious shade at me. "He's a good guy, Daddy, don't f —" she cleared her throat, "mess it up." She turned to Ronan. "Welcome to the family, Dad-R." She shook his hand. "You're taking us out for breakfast."

Ronan and I stared at each other. He gave a lopsided shrug. My daughter called him Dad-R. Not sure what I thought about this.

"Well," Ronan said, "I guess we should get dressed. Where are we going?"

We walked to the diner to get fresh air. It was a nice enough day the kids didn't need snow pants, and I wore my not-quite-spring-but-not-freezing coat. I wanted to hold Ronan's hand, but as I reached for it, little fingers slid into mine and clasped shut. Reese's hand squeezed mine as he studied me with the facsimile of his father's eyes. "Can I call you Soda?"

My eyebrows raised. "Why Soda?"

"Emma is calling my dad Dad-R, and calling you Dad-W is too hard, and Dad-A sounds too much like daddy. So, we googled different dad words and found papa, but Emma doesn't like it because it sounds too close to appa. Which is Korean for dad. Did you know that? Then we saw pop, and it's okay, but hard to yell. Then I saw soda. It's easy to say, yell, and it doesn't sound like others."

Ah, thesauruses. I looked at Ronan, who was all sunshine and glee as he looked between me and Reese. "Sure. You know it's referring to the drink, right? Soda pop? Like cola? But you can call me Soda."

"Thanks! And yeah, I know, but Dad called you a tall drink of water to Aunt Maddie, so I think it works."

Ronan turned bright red.

"I'm the old man?" I smirked at him. "And I'm shorter than you."

"Just an expression." He was flustered, and I loved it.

I couldn't get over how much we acted like a family at breakfast. The kids took to calling us our new paternal names. I loved being called Soda. I was accustomed to having a weird name. Why quit now? The server took a "family" photo of us at Emma's insistence. And damn, we were cute together.

After breakfast, we took the kids to a park to run around. The benches were full, so we stood and watched the kids.

I took Ronan's hand. There was hesitation in his fingers. This may have been his first time holding a man's hands in public. His fingers flexed, then wrapped around mine in a vice grip.

"Well Soda, it seems our kids have decided we are a family." He chuckled and kissed my forehead.

"Seems so, Dad-R," I said.

"And I couldn't be happier with their choice."

I looked at Ronan and the immense amount he cared for me rolled off him. The waves of his adoration lapped at my ego, and I was wanted. Truly wanted. My skin warmed as if I were staring right into the sun and burning under Ronan's gaze. It was a good way to burn. Or melt. I was going to melt into him and never leave him.

Dear god. That was creepy imagery.

Yes, Alex loved me, but there had been layers of complexities I had to navigate to be appreciated. But Ronan wanted me with no conditions. I could be purely me again. For now, at least.

I pushed my forehead into his shoulder and breathed him in before I turned to watch the kids. Ronan slipped his arm around my shoulders. Someone familiar watched me and Ronan. It was what's-her-face. The parent who thought I was a sex worker. I waved. She ducked her head and furiously started texting. Ronan looked in her direction.

"I suppose we will have gossip to deal with." Ronan sighed but kept his arm around me. In fact, he pulled me tighter to him and fussed with my strands of frizzy curls.

"Soda Soda Soda Soda!" Reese ran to me.

"What's up?" I asked, unable to hide my giant, joyful smile.

"I found this for you." He gave me a little white-pink rock that sparkled in the sun.

"Thank you, Reese, that's so sweet of you." I spun the rock over in my hand and took the time to admire it before I placed it in my pocket. After he scampered off, I turned to Ronan. "Why are geologists great dates?"

"No."

"Because they ..."

"Stop."

"Make your bedrock."

"You have hit rock bottom."

"I sense a seismic shift in your dad humour."

"You're taking my patience for granite."

I laughed so hard I nearly peed.

We parted ways after the park, even though no one wanted to split up. Emma, overtired, fussed and protested before bed but was fast asleep after I read to her for ten minutes. I dragged my ass into my room and flopped onto my bed. My sheets still had Ronan's scent. I breathed in deep, not caring if it seemed creepy. No one could stop me, a grown-ass man, from suffocating myself in my bedsheets while sniffing Ronan's body odour if I wanted to. Yeah. Creepy.

The jagged edges of the rock in my pocket poked me, and I drew it out. I knew it wasn't a special fancy rock, and a dog or kid had probably peed on it. But how he yelled out "Soda" and ran to me with exuberance to share this gift he picked for me filled me with hope. And fear. I didn't want to let him down. I didn't want to let two kids down. I set the rock on my bedside table.

My phone buzzed from a text. Ronan asked if we could video chat. I opened my laptop and called him. He sat on his bed, shirtless. For all I knew, he was pants-less too. I couldn't see. There was something scandalous about staring at him without a shirt. I knew it was no big deal, but my cheeks flushed red anyway. When I noticed in my little video square how red I was, I grew redder.

"Hey." I set the laptop on the space next to me and lay on my side. My bedsheets were cool. It was weird seeing him through a screen. I tugged my bedsheets over my chest and hugged them, even though I was still in my clothes.

"Hello, darling. I had an amazing weekend."

If I had a fainting chair, I'd stand by it and swoon. I loved when he called me darling. "Me too."

"I wish it didn't have to end. I desperately want to be there with you."

"What would you do if you were here?" Those words surprised me as they came out of my mouth.

He gave me the smirk he made when he read the sexy villain voices to me. It was hot. My body shifted in anticipation of hearing what he had to say.

"I'd be there in bed with you. Curled up with you in my arms and we'd read together a bit. At the end of the chapter, I'd kiss you good night, roll over, and go to sleep."

"Oh. That all?"

"What? Reading to you and cuddling isn't enough?" There was a coy curve to his lips.

"No. They are perfect. But ..."

"But?"

I lost my nerve. This was ridiculous. I couldn't talk about kissing with him. It was so weird. I had never done cybering or sexting or whatever. Alex and I got married after university. I never used a dating app. Sure, I shared smut or naughty art, but nothing where I put myself out on the line like this. If Alex and I were horny, we'd fooled around in person. None of this through a screen thing. "Never mind." I looked elsewhere.

He went silent for a moment. "I'd also kiss your neck. Right there. And that soft part above your collarbone, I'd bite you there."

I bit my lip and inhaled. He described where and how he'd touch me, kiss me, bite me, claw me, touch me softly, and how he'd move me around and position himself over me, pinning my arms to my pillow. He'd undo my jeans with his teeth, and without thinking, I undid my jeans. With explicit detail, he told me exactly what he'd do with his hands and mouth on my body. My eyelashes fluttered as I touched myself and pictured his mouth on me.

"Are you jerking off?" he asked.

"No," I said and pulled my hand away. Afraid I was about to be struck blind by god. I almost slammed the laptop shut. Shame slapped me across the mouth. I should have asked him if it was okay first. I was a creepy pervert.

"Don't stop. Please, babe, don't stop. Me too."

I looked at him. His eyes were on fire, begging me to finish. I could do this. We locked eyes as we pleasured ourselves. He was powerfully stunning in the heat of passion, with his lips parted, his eyes heavily lidded, and pink bloomed over his skin. He looked at me as if he demanded to ravish me, fuck me, toy with me, or tear me to pieces, and I needed him to do all the above.

My back arched, the start of a deep cry coiled in my throat, and my eyes snapped tight shut.

"Look at me, darling. I want to see your face," Ronan directed.

I opened my eyes. He bit his lip and panted. The guttural cry broke free as I shook and spilled on myself. Moments later, I watched him make the most beautiful climax face, lips opened for his silent cry, eyes unguarded and wide, and forehead glowing with dew. I needed to see this in person. And soon.

We lay there, panting and laughing, before he read to me. We fell asleep with the video window still open.

CHAPTER EIGHTEEN

I had been flying on a Ronan high for the past few days. My high inspired me to compose a new song. On Friday afternoon, I planted my butt at my piano. Snippets of lyrics came to me, and I experimented with melodies on the piano and noodled around with my guitar. I hadn't written for a guitar for ages. It wasn't my forte, but I wasn't awful.

Ronan made me feel amazing, but I was ecstatic I found inspiration to write a new composition that wasn't broody and depressing. I recorded what I had to review later, but I mainly wanted to share it with Vinny. His reaction to hearing something like this coming from me would be golden. I knew it was weird, but I needed to make him proud of me. After everything he had done for me, I owed him that.

These moments of music and inspiration and fervour pushed me into a hyperfocused and electric mode. I felt alive and like the prodigy they foretold me I'd be. My pencil wrote feverishly, scribbling lyrics and notes, and dotting my blank music staff papers. I bounced with excitement.

The front door flung open. I startled and shot to my feet, knocking over my bench and spilling my music books to the floor. Ronan jogged breathlessly into the living room.

"Are you okay?" he panted.

"Yeah? What's going on?"

Ronan returned to the front door, giving me a look I couldn't read. "Come in kids. He's okay. Why don't you guys grab snacks and go upstairs and play." The kids shucked off their coats and kicked off their boots.

Emma, red and blotchy with her nose running, scuffed her feet to me. I stepped around the bench and hugged her.

"Are you alright, bug-a-boo?" I asked her.

She cried and nodded. "You're okay and safe."

Fear and uncertainty bloomed in my stomach.

Ronan ushered her upstairs, and I turned my bench upright.

"What is going on?" I asked again, stepping closer to Ronan.

"Do you know what time it is?" He was a mix of seething and worry.

I read the clock and gasped. Three forty-five.

"Where were you? You didn't pick the kids."

"I-I —" I looked at the work I accomplished today. "I must have time slipped. I'm so sorry. I didn't hear my alarms."

"The school called you several times before they phoned me. My boss is pissed I had to leave, the kids were terrified, and when the school said you weren't answering, I got scared. I called you over and over. It took me half an hour to get to the school. The kids waited for forty-five minutes for someone to come get them." His voice was unsteady.

"When I pulled up, Emma shrieked 'Daddy's dead,' and I nearly lost my shit. She said you almost died before? But here you were, playing around on your fucking piano while your daughter believed you were dead. Because that's what she needed after school, to believe she was alone in this world." His voice grew louder and angrier with every sentence.

"I-I didn't hear the phone ring." I searched around. Where was my phone? "I'm so sorry. I promise this is the first time I've done this. I'm so sorry."

"How dare you? Emma was scared to death something was wrong with you. I was scared to death something was wrong. I worried that Vanessa ...." He shook his head. "Reese flipped out and hit his head against a brick wall. If I had known you were this irresponsible ....” He didn't finish the sentence. He shook with fury. “You scared my child.” His yell echoed off my piano. I didn't blame him. Vanessa had neglected Reese and left him alone too many times.

I was as bad as Vanessa.

He seethed and was crimson red. I had never seen him this upset. Every muscle in my body screamed at me to run for cover. But my brain froze in place.

Images of my poor Emma crying flooded my mind. My carelessness triggered a trauma reaction in her. And poor Reese, not knowing how to deal with those emotions. I was a monster.

“Frig, Wishes, I worried you were dead. Why would Emma say you were dead?”

He stared at me intensely. Pleading for answers. I looked away and shook my head and pulled at my sleeves. I couldn't say it. Not now. Not yet. Maybe never.

Ronan made a noise in frustration at my silence. “Your shitty excuse of ‘time slipping’ isn't good enough here, Wishes. It has real consequences, and the kids were the ones who suffered it.”

The kids no doubt heard him from upstairs. I felt insignificant, worthless, a disgrace. I plummeted from my ultimate high ten minutes ago to thinking it would be better if I was lying bleeding on the floor. He wouldn't yell at me if I were. My head slumped forward, and my shoulders drooped. I tugged at my sleeves over and over in a nervous tic. I scared our kids. I scared him.

“Now I have to work extra hours next week to make up for lost time. Thanks for that. Our kids were beside themselves. How could you fuck this up?” He gestured wildly.

The rapid, grand movement made me flinch. Images of argument after argument with Alex strobed in my mind, disorienting and violent. The images lingered on the bigger arguments. The ones where he'd screamed at me while he was drunk because the baby didn't stop crying. Or I couldn't get baby puke out of his shirt.

"What kind of fucking housewife are you?" Alex had yelled. "I should have never married you. You're useless." I remembered the smell of whisky on his breath. He said didn't remember saying it the next day, but I think he did.

I remembered the fights that escalated so loud little Emma bellowed at him from the top of the stairs to stop being mean. I rarely yelled back. He was taller and stronger than me. While he was a shouting-and-argue person, I was a leave-the-room person. Sometimes, he'd let me walk away. Other times, he was so aggressive it terrified me to move.

Ronan's anger tangled with Alex's years of abuse, and my chest tightened. My wide, wild eyes stared at the floor while my lungs stopped functioning. I shook as my nerves danced and thrashed. Everything twisted sideways, then spun in the other direction. Ronan said something, but the roaring in my ears muffled his words. Each change in volume was a tsunami wave, one after another. Alex's speech carried on in the background, throwing daggers at me. I swayed back and forth, rubbed my wrists raw. My cuffs gave me red, raised welts.

Ronan reached for me. Slow and gentle. But I saw Alex's hand shooting out for me.

"Stop yelling at me, Alex. Let me go!" I yelled and crumpled to the ground and retreated into my cave.

Ronan wasn't touching me. Alex's hands gripped my wrists so tight they'd leave bruises.

"Wishes, darling," Ronan's tone was gentle, but Alex was so loud it drowned him out. "Wishes? It's me, Ronan."

I glanced at him. He sat on the floor, cross-legged, on his phone. My memories and my present transposed on top of each other. But I was off, out of reach in a cramped, dark cave protecting myself, while Alex threw a frying pan that missed my head by a few centimetres. It dented the cabinet and clattered to the floor. My arms flew over my head.

"Vinny?" Ronan said into his phone. "Something is going on with Wishes …." Their conversation was drowned out by Alex slamming the front door and yelling at me.

God bless Vinny. Alex was wasted and furious. I dumped every bottle of alcohol in the house. Including the ones he thought I didn't know about. Hundreds of dollars' worth. I was sick of broken promise after broken promise to get help. Drywall dust and blood mixed on his fist. I had texted 911 to Vinny, and he had burst into the house in time to pull Alex off me. I sputtered and vomited as I rubbed the handprints from my throat. Broken glass was strewn across the kitchen floor. Vinny had cut himself while helping.

It hurt to cough. My Adam's apple felt bruised. I had already decided what to wear to cover the bruises. My other hand slapped at the floor, trying to reach the shards. I couldn't let Emma step on them. "I'll clean it up," I repeatedly said to Alex. "Go watch the game, I'll deal with this."

A loud smack rang in my ear as Vinny punched Alex so hard, Alex stumbled dazed into the wall. I simultaneously felt vindication and feared life got worse.

I reached for a chunk of glass on our white-tile floors, but I hit nice, dark, hardwood floors instead. My hardwood floors. I was under the piano. Nausea in my body pulled me into the present and I was no longer off in a cave. Alex's voice grew distant and off to the side. The stench of whiskey wafted away as he moved to let Ronan in.

"I'm sorry I hurt you, baby," Alex said. His voice went silent. It was just me and Ronan now.

Ronan sat a foot away beside me, struggling to fit under the piano. I watched him and my eyes adjusted to the present moment.

"Hello, my darling, are you with me now?" he asked with a soft smile.

I nodded.

He handed me a cup of water. My hand shook as I tried to bring it to my lips. Gingerly, Ronan helped steady the glass, and I drank.

"I think we have to have a conversation," Ronan said. "Is that okay?"

"Yeah," I rasped.

"Can I hug you?"

I scooched towards him, and he drew me into him. I melted in his arms. My muscles stopped shaking. He petted my hair and kissed the top of my head.

"Was that a PTSD panic attack?"

I nodded against his chest. "It's been a while since I had one that rough. I'm sorry."

"Don't apologize," he said. "I'm the one who should be apologizing. I shouldn't have yelled. It was immature and reactive." He rested his cheek on my head. Silence filled the space. "Babe, was Alex abusive?"

My throat turned to rock. Men weren't supposed to be abused. Professionals laughed at me and brushed it off when I tried to seek help. Men were strong, defended themselves, and handled these situations with machismo. But I couldn't. I remembered when people made fun of male celebrities who claimed to be abused. My pain was a pathetic joke to them.

I craved curling into Ronan's lap, but the restriction of the piano overhead didn't let me. I nudged him to lie back, and I lay on top of him. Hiding my face in the crook of his neck.

"You're avoiding the question. Please answer me, Wishes." His fingers ran through my hair. His other hand pressed into the small of my back, pulling me closer.

"I guess so."

"How?"

"He yelled at me, called me names." I struggled to talk through my tight vocal cords.

"So emotional abuse." His chest rose and fell under me. He pressed his lips into my hair. "Did he physically hurt you?"

My hands tightened around the cloth of his shirt. "He grabbed my wrists or arms and yanked me around, pinned me to the wall, threw things at me; once, he choked me. But only once. And he only hurt me when he was drunk as a skunk."

Ronan's chest shuddered, the way mine did when I tried not to cry.

"Jesus Christ, babe. That's not okay. I don't care he only hurt you when he was drunk. He hurt you. Fuck. That's scary." He kissed the top of my head. "Did ... did he harm you ... in other ways? Like in the bedroom?" Ronan asked, barely audible.

I shrugged.

"Wishes? Please tell me. Please trust me with this. I don't want to do anything dumb that will upset you. I mean, I guess I already did that today. Fuck. I'm sorry. I don't want to be that ... I never want to hurt you."

"No, he didn't sexually assault me. Not really." My mouth went dry, and I wanted to return to my cave. I had refused to acknowledge what he had done to me for years. Vinny didn't even know this part. It wasn't a big deal, I had told myself. My stomach ached and my heartbeat staggered.

Why was I protecting Alex? He was dead, and I was the one living with the pain he caused me.

"What do you mean, not really?"

"I didn't tell him when I was uncomfortable or not in the mood."

"Wishes, we've made out a handful of times, and I know when you're uncomfortable or not in the mood. Did you say anything at all?"

"I used to. But he pressured me so often, I stopped caring." I shifted uncomfortably. "A sex-advice book I read said you had to give in to your partner's needs every once in a while, to keep the marriage happy, so I did. I caved, even when I didn't want to."

"That's fucking bullshit. I never want you to give in for the sake of pleasing me. I have hands, I can take care of myself. Please be honest if you don't want sex, or anything." He paused. "Why didn't you leave him?" It wasn't accusatory, the way he said it. It was curiosity with hurt.

"Because I loved him. I know it sounds stupid. Yes, he abused me, but there were more happy and loving times than not. We laughed more than we fought." And it was true. He hurt me, but I fucking loved him. My time with him gave me the happiest days I could ever imagine. "It's complicated."

It confused me how it worked. How could I love someone who hurt me?

"Plus, I was scared he'd get custody of Emma because he's closer to blood relations than I am." Well, I wasn't expecting that truth bomb that I had ignored for years. Denial sucked.

"Darling." He held me tight. "I don't know what to say." His voice cracked and his body betrayed him. He was crying, and I felt guilty for making him cry.

"You can't say anything Vinny and Katherine haven't already told me. The night he choked me, Vinny beat the crap out of him. Few days later, he found the escape bags Katherine packed for me and Emma at the back of Emma's closet. That was an awakening moment for him."

Ronan pressed his face into my curls.

"Things improved after that. Honestly. Not perfect, but better. He attended therapy, couples counselling, and an addictions group. I joined Al-Anon for family support. Life got better. Honest. He drank less, yelled less, pressured me less, and he mostly stopped physically hurting me. The months before the accident were pretty good. Not perfect, but a significant improvement. He worked so hard to fix things. He laughed more, and his health improved. Then he drove drunk and died." My voice caught on the rock in my throat.

"Did Emma know about the abuse?"

"Yeah. She'd yell at him to leave me alone. Threw her toys at him. Threaten to call his mom. But when it was truly bad, she hid."

"Did he ever hurt her?"

"No. God no. He was amazing with Emma. Except for *those* times, everything else was great."

"Except for the *abuse*."

I curled into him more.

"I can't guarantee I won't yell. Vanessa also yelled at me and called me names, and I bit back after a while. She didn't listen to me unless I raised my voice; otherwise, she pretended I didn't exist. But I promise you I will try not to. And I promise I will listen to you when you tell me you're uncomfortable. I need you to do it."

"Okay."

"Oh, my love, I'm sorry you went through that."

My ears burned at the "L" word, but I pretended he didn't say it. I'm sure it was a pet name, like darling. There was no sweeter sound than when he called me darling.

"I'm sorry Vanessa hurt you and Reese." I kissed his neck, and we cuddled in silence, processing my mental-break episode and all my baggage I threw at Ronan's feet.

He swallowed and made a noise as if he were trying to talk, but nothing came out. I remained silent to let him think. He rubbed my back. "Vanessa used to forget Reese or just leave him alone. She'd leave him at home when she went out while I was at work. She'd drop him off at her friend's house for 'an hour or two' and not go back. I'd have to go pick him up. Police were called when she left him in the car during the summer, twice. She forgot him at the mall once." His voice shook. "I don't know how well we can handle you forgetting him again."

I pulled back and looked at him. His cheeks were tear-stained. "Ronan, I'm so sorry. I'll do better. Promise." I pressed my face back into his chest, letting his dress shirt soak up my tears. My brain went into self-criticism mode, calling me every bad name I had ever heard.

"I know."

The front door opened. "Wishes? Ronan?" Vinny called out.

"Under the piano," Ronan replied.

Katherine went to check on the kids while Vinny slid under the piano next to Ronan. "Hey buddy," he said. "How you doing?"

"So-so."

"Ronan treat you right?"

"Yeah." I nuzzled my cheek against Ronan's collarbone.

"Good." Vinny leaned over Ronan and kissed my cheek.

Without a word, Ronan wrapped his arm around Vinny and pulled him in. I was thankful he at least tried to understand our strange relationship. Vinny cuddled into Ronan without a second thought.

"Thanks for coming," Ronan said.

"Anything for this weirdo." Vinny booped my nose.

The three of us lay there. The rhythm of Ronan's heart and the movement of his breath lulled me into sleep. PTSD attacks usually knocked me out for hours.

Vinny and Ronan chatted. Vinny was Vinny, lightening the mood and hinting he'd shank Ronan if he hurt me. Fingers combed through my hair, and hands rubbed my back. I both hated and was glad for Ronan to see how broken I was. Well, some of my broken pieces. I wanted to be with Ronan, and he needed to be aware of my history. I hazily kissed his neck before I drifted off while Vinny gave Ronan a Cole's Notes version of the "How to Care for Your Wishes" manual.

Footsteps entered the room. "Alright, dillberries." Katherine kicked the bottom of Vinny's foot. "Kids have calmed down. Homework is done. They are putting on their pyjamas. Reese is spending the night. I've ordered pizza for supper. Now get the fuck out from under the piano."

CHAPTER NINETEEN

T he rest of the evening, I wavered between sleepy and jittery from residual flashbacks. I kept it hidden from the kids the best I could. Emma and Reese clung to me, and I smothered them with cuddles. I apologized profoundly for scaring them. After everything they've been through during their brief lives, I didn't blame them for acting weird with me. Thankfully, they both had therapy appointments next week.

I decided I'd e-mail mine in the morning.

Ronan was a rock star. We played as one character in our post-pizza board game. I could excuse myself to "get water," and do breathing exercises in the kitchen without disrupting the game.

Ronan came to check on me and I showed him all my medications. My anti-depressants, my ADHD meds, and especially my fast-acting anxiety meds. I explained when I should take them.

"I am familiar with these," he said. "I used to take them too." With a soft smile, he poured me a glass of water and handed me a pill. "You look like you need one." He kissed my forehead as I swallowed the chalky, tiny, white pill.

We returned to the game, where he put his arm around me and provided his shoulder as a pillow. There was something magical about dozing off with the sounds of your loved ones laughing and having fun. Included but allowed to carry on as I needed to.

After the game, Ronan and the kids tucked me into bed. Emma held my hand as we went upstairs, Reese drew back the bedsheets, and they both pulled the covers over my shoulders. It was so sweet; I didn't care I was in my jeans still.

Reese declared sleepover time, and Emma and Reese snuggled into bed. Ronan gave me a big smile and slid into bed, too, sandwiching our kids in the middle. The kids took turns reading to me. Ronan helped with the bigger words, but they managed well on their own. Reese had come a long way since I first heard him read in December.

Ronan took over the bedtime stories for us all, and I fell asleep to his voice while cuddling my daughter. It was perfect.

When I woke, the kids had vacated the bed, and I had made my way on top of Ronan. My ear pressed into his belly, and I listened to him breathe as he read and played with my hair. I lifted my head and squinted against the morning sun.

"Good morning, darling." His thumb brushed saliva off my cheek.

"Good morning. Sorry I drooled on you."

"It's all good. Vinny and Katherine kidnapped the kids. There's a pet-and-play day at an animal sanctuary for exotic animals. The kids seemed excited. I warned Vinny Reese might get scared, but he thinks he can handle it."

"Exotic animals? Like ostriches and alligators?"

"Maybe? Vinny mentioned lizards and snakes. But Reese is afraid of snakes." He chewed on the inside of his cheek.

"Oh, are they the ones with the blind snake?"

"I dunno?"

"Yeah, they have a visually impaired snake. University students made it corrective lenses for a class project. Now it's a see serpent."

Ronan groaned and tried to push me off him, but I held tight until he relented and let me stay lounging on him.

"So, it's just us?" I asked.

"Just us. For a few hours. If we're lucky."

Holy shit. We had the house to ourselves, and we were already in bed. This was a rare opportunity. I became hyperaware of each curve of his body and how my body pressed into his groin. My nerves tingled, and a fire lit in my solar plexus. "Wanna make out like teenagers?" I waggled my eyebrows and wiggled my torso against his crotch.

"Always."

And we did. I devoured his kisses and flung my arms around his neck. I lifted the book from his grip and set it on the side table before I wrestled him on top of me. Our limbs knocked, and we laughed between kisses.

"Are you wearing my pyjamas?" I asked. "They're so short on you. Am I that short? Those are long on me."

"Should I remove them?" A sly grin spread across his mouth.

I simultaneously paled and blushed. I didn't know if he was joking or serious. But I wanted him to. An embarrassing amount. I wanted to touch his chest, his stomach, and yeah, I wanted to touch all of him.

"If you want. But I can't ... I'm not ...."

He kissed me. "I get it."

His hands gripped the hem of the tank top that rode high on him, and he lifted the shirt over his head and off. I stared. My fingertips ran along his ribcage. His skin was soft and smooth. I traced the muscle line down the middle of his abdomen, starting at his chest hair and continuing to his treasure trail. My pants rode low on him, exposing his hip bones and the valleys of his V lines. His skin was delicate and supple there. Those V lines made me salivate.

"Shall I remove the pants?" he asked.

"Only if you want to."

"I want to. Do you really want me to?"

"Yeah." I loved that he was careful with me, because let's be honest, I was pretty fragile.

He slipped off the bed and let the pants fall to the floor. Air rushed into my lungs. I raised myself to my knees, seized his hand, and pulled him to me. As we made out, my hands roamed his curves and bumps. He gasped against my lips as my hand caressed the top of his dick.

The power he gave me was immeasurable, and I wanted to do right by him. Many self-deprecating words tried to break into my mind, telling me I wasn't good enough, I wasn't capable of pleasuring him; he was using me. But Ronan's gasp and kiss shut all those thoughts out.

"You want this?" I nipped at his jaw. My heart pounded.

"Please, yes, Wishes," he moaned in my ear.

I teased him until he whimpered for more. My hand moved deliberately. His breathing grew ragged, and I watched him contort and shift in pleasured responses.

I stopped.

He looked at me with his eyebrows lowered and head stooped. "Something wrong?"

The fire in my chest spread across my body. I kissed him hard and unbridled. My fingers fumbled with my pants. "Touch me. Please?" I panted.

He licked his lips before his mouth pressed against mine and allowed me to guide his hand to my dick.

Goosebumps exploded across my skin, and my head lolled back. My skin was highly responsive to his touch. Muscles in my body repeatedly tightened, shuddered, wobbled, and weakened. I was at his mercy when he hit certain sensitive spots.

My hand returned to work and grasped his dick. His moans made me work harder. I focused on memorizing what movements gave this symphony of reactions.

His beautiful expression of ecstasy was more glorious and godly in person. I touched his cheeks and felt the muscles clench.

His mouth grew pinker, and his eyes glazed over as the explosion of dopamine hit him. Strands of his long, dark hair stuck to the sweat on his brow.

I hid my donkey-braying climax face and clung to him for support. My face pressed into his shoulder, and I bit him as I shuddered. Teeth-shaped bruises bloomed across his skin. He held me close and kept me from falling over. I was boneless and breathless. And really fucking happy.

We collapsed onto the bed on top of each other. Sticky and sweaty. It was magnificent. We basked in the afterglow and petted each other's hair and skin. My eyes hazily rested shut.

"Can I ask you a personal question?" he asked.

These questions were never good. Especially right after fooling around. "Sure." I propped myself up on my elbow.

"Are you afraid to take your shirt off because of your scars?"

My blood ran cold. "H-how did you know?"

He rubbed my jaw. "I'm obsessed with you and noticed them once when you pushed your sleeves back a bit to wash dishes."

Anxiety rose, and I drew back.

"No, no, no, no." He pulled me closer. "There is zero judgement. Please trust me. You don't have to tell me what happened. I find you hot no matter what. Promise. You're gorgeous." He kissed my cheek.

I tugged on my sleeves. Shame roiled in my stomach.

"Here" — he showed me his arms — "did you notice my scars? They are an everyday reminder of the shit I did, and that I'm grateful to be alive and healthy." Several small white lines were drawn near the inside of his elbow. "They're track marks."

"Oh." I touched them with a featherlight touch.

"While I am not proud of how I earned these scars, I'm proud of what I accomplished to get me from there"— he touched my chin — "to here."

He had learned so much about my disturbed life. But what if this was the breaking straw of the crazy mound? Dead abusive husband with a drinking problem whom I still loved irrevocably was one thing; this was another.

"You don't have to show me if you aren't ready. But you can trust me. And one day, I'll want to touch your ribs, your nipples, kiss your shoulders, and bite you back." One side of his lips curved upward. My teeth marked his shoulder in a clear, human-teeth pattern. Oops.

I tugged at my sleeves. My mind spun to every potential outcome and reason I should and why I shouldn't, but the answer that rang the loudest was "trust him."

My hands shook as I sat and pulled my sweatshirt off. I clasped my arms around myself, trying to hide the very thing I was attempting to show.

"Wishes, darling. You can put your shirt back on if you want. I don't want you to do anything you're not ready to." Ronan sat naked in front of me. Vulnerable and open.

I closed my eyes and turned my wrists to face him. A tight red scar from above my wrists to below my elbow ran up both forearms. Each thick angry line was decorated with dots from the staples that had held me together at one point. I opened my eyes to see Ronan's raised eyebrows as he looked at them.

"Those are bigger than I imagined." He ran his fingers over them. It took energy for me to not recoil. "Did … are…?" He swallowed. "What happened? No, wait. You do not have to tell me."

"You should know this. I think. It's not like I can hide it forever." I drew in a deep breath and let it out slowly. "After Alex died, I struggled. I quit working, stopped showering, and barely met Emma's basic needs. Children's services told me if something didn't change, I'd lose her. Vinny and Katherine moved in to help. But I had failed. I wasn't good enough to keep my husband alive, and I wasn't good enough to care for my daughter. And one day, I cut myself." I looked at my messed-up skin.

"You attempted suicide?"

"No. I completed suicide."

His breathing stopped and waited for me to continue.

"Vinny found me. Bleeding out in the tub. I had taken some benzos, so everything was foggy, but I remember him screaming, and I remember the water was so red. I have flashes of Vinny pulling me from the tub. Blood got all over him like a horror movie. I remember a paramedic putting a blanket on me, and I swear Alex was in the ambulance with me. But the world went dark, and I died."

My voice shook and my stomach convulsed as my soul tried to eject these memories. Phantom pain seared down my arms and I balled my fists so I wouldn't try to scratch away the sting. I concentrated on a small mole on Ronan's shoulder to keep my head here and not disassociate.

Ronan's tears dripped silently off his cheek.

"I woke a few days later. My ribs were broken here"— I touched below my heart — "where the paramedics did CPR. They had stapled my arms shut. Apparently, I needed a blood transfusion. I lost so much blood. Katherine hired a special cleaning service because there was a trail of red from the bathroom to the driveway.

"I don't remember how long I stayed in the ICU. Eventually, they moved me to a regular room for three or four days, then transferred me to psych for a month or more. That's why we missed Christmas last year. Vinny moved Emma in with her grandparents." I chewed on my lip and mindlessly traced my scars with my fingers.

"Emma didn't come home right after they released me. She stayed with my in-laws for a few months while Hyunji homeschooled her. That's why she's so smart. She had a private tutor for half the year last year.

"Vinny and Katherine moved in again and helped me get re-established. Children's services had a list of requirements before Emma could return. They punished me for having a dead husband and a mental breakdown. But Emma was almost an orphan. I did that to her. She nearly lost both dads within weeks of each other."

I lost my shit. That thought hurt the most. What I did to Emma would haunt me forever. Ronan shifted closer to me, kissed the top of my head, and held me as I sobbed relentlessly. He had no words of comfort. I think this broke his spirit. I hoped this didn't break us.

"Please don't do that again."

"I won't. Promise."

"Reese loves you."

"I know. I love him too."

"I —" Words caught in Ronan's throat. I knew what he was saying. I was not sure why he didn't. Perhaps he wasn't ready, perhaps he didn't know if I could handle it, or perhaps the first time you tell someone you love them shouldn't be when you're crying over their scars and pain.

"I know." I looked into his eyes, churning in an ocean of thoughts. "Me too." His lips were salty, but it didn't matter. I needed to taste them. To feel that he was still here after I showed him my scars. He didn't run away.

He laid me back against the pillows and comforters and curled himself around me, comforted me by holding me, rubbing the naked skin on my chest, and kissed my cheek. "I'm proud of you for going from here"— he touched my scars — "to here." He held my hand to his chest.

Vinny sent us a thirty-minute warning text. Ronan kissed me once more, helped me to my feet, and pulled me into the shower. After we showered and dressed, we flung ourselves onto the couch with enough time to pretend we had been watching ... What was this? *Kindergarten Cop*?

We turned it off when the kids ran to us. Reese had Katherine show us a photo of him holding a snake.

"Daddy, I was scared, but Katherine and Emma were there, and I did it because I'm brave like you. Can I get a pet snake?"

"No."

"Please, Daddy?" Reese whined.

Vinny sat on the arm of the couch while Ronan weaselled his way out of buying a snake. With an arm around my shoulders, Vinny whispered, "Nice T-shirt" and kissed the top of my head. "And wet hair. Both of you."

My lips tightened into a sharp line as he slunk into the kitchen.

The T-shirt itself wasn't remarkable. Plain, solid blue. However, it meant I had told Ronan about that day. The scars were hard for Vinny to see. Katherine had told me a cop grappled him away from me as they lifted me into the ambulance. He confided in me he felt me slip away while he held my hand and ran beside me to the ambulance. A scene of me embracing a shadow of Alex in the vehicle played in front of him, and he knew I was dead before they started CPR.

While they resuscitated me, I believe a part of me stayed with Alex that day. I feared I ripped a part of Vinny away with me when I died. Maybe I still have it.

Katherine noticed our subtle exchange. She gave me the look of "give him a moment."

I hauled Emma onto my lap and held her tight as she regaled me with the legend of Morris, the one-legged ostrich.

"Hey," I whispered and put my chin on Ronan's shoulder. "Did you hear the police arrested an ostrich that attacked a woman? They let him go because he wasn't a flight risk."

Ronan gave me the side-eye. "It's a good thing you're cute."

CHAPTER TWENTY

I wore more short sleeves. Emma and I talked about if it bothered her to see the scars. She claimed it didn't upset her. "All that matters is you're okay, but I will discuss this with my therapist." I loved this kid.

Ronan answered some of Reese's questions about the scars the best he could. He withheld the whole truth because he worried Reese wouldn't be able to handle it. He told Reese I was injured, and the doctors stapled me closed.

Reese poked at the scars one day after dinner. "Does it hurt?"

"Sometimes, but not as much now. Honestly, in some places, I feel nothing at all. See here?" I had him poke a spot on my arm. "I don't feel that." People neglected to tell me about nerve damage on scar tissue. It took a while to get used to the feeling of the tight spots when playing the piano. My physiotherapist was great at helping me regain most of my movement with no problem. Still felt weird occasionally.

Ronan watched our interaction, studying Reese's every reaction. Waiting to see if he got upset. I understood his desire to protect his son from everything. I wished I could have protected Emma from everything that had happened.

Reese hugged me before he wandered to the piano. He played "Twinkle Twinkle Little Star" for us.

I looked over my shoulder at Ronan with a big smile. He was checking his phone. When he looked up, he returned my smile, but there was something off. Distant. He sauntered over and ruffled Reese's hair. "That was fantastic, kiddo, but we need to head home. I have things to do tonight."

This didn't bother me. I knew he had things he needed to attend to, as did I. My laundry pile was ready to stage a coup. We both needed our own private space and alone time. I respected this.

It was the quick kiss to the cheek and sorrowful smile as he left that bothered me. When I texted him before bed, there was no response. Not a problem, we'd done that before. He could already be in bed, cleaning the bathroom, or working out as he said he did. I tried not to let it bother me, but my gut told me something was amiss.

Emma and I remained in Ronan's old, death-trap Corolla after a couple hours' drive. We waited outside his parents' home the following Saturday morning. It wasn't a planned excursion.

We were at the park with the kids last night when Ronan started acting weird. A couple of men, around our age, walked by us. They were drinking out of a paper bag and talking about us. Ronan demanded the kids return to us, and we left immediately. I mean, sure, they looked … not like the kind of people I would associate myself with, but Ronan had an overkill reaction.

After that, he insisted we get out of town for the day. He said it was a beautiful day for a road trip through the countryside to his parents, and he could stand to get away from the city for a day. So here we were. I was meeting his parents who he was not out to.

My poor sweater sleeves were going to come apart at the sleeves with how much I was tugging at them. He and Reese had been inside for at least ten minutes already. We had decided to wait until Ronan broke the ice. It was a nice, upper-middle-class house with a neat and manicured yard. Ronan was definitely raised without wanting. I could understand his frustration with struggling to give the same to Reese.

In the rear seat, Emma drank her juice box and kicked the back of my seat. Not to annoy me. It was nervous energy while we waited to see if we'd be invited in, or if I was in charge of cheering up the kids and Ronan.

"Do you really think Uncle Vinny and Auntie Katherine can handle getting tonight's party ready?" Emma asked. We had been planning a surprise coming-out party for Ronan.

"I'm sure." I hope. "You and I laid everything out perfectly for them to follow." I scrolled through Vinny's texts asking where things were, followed by Katherine reassuring me everything was under control.

The front door opened. I held my breath.

Ronan bounced down the stairs, beaming, and waved me out of the car. I was barely standing before he was on me with a big hug and kiss. "Mom can't wait to meet you and Emma." He kissed me again, giggled, and helped Emma out of the car. With Emma in one hand and me in his other, he walked us to the front door.

His mother was radiant and well coifed, as if she had expected a brunch with a group of luncheon ladies. She gave me a warm hug and a happy, buzzing sensation filled my stomach. She smelled of flowers and cookies.

"Nice to meet you, Aloysius. I'm Ellen." She turned to Emma. "And Emma, my, you are a beautiful child. Are you hungry? Do you want a snack before brunch?"

And bam, she became Gran-gran. She took Emma by the hand and led her further into the home.

Steve, Ronan's dad, gave me an uncertain once-over. I waited for my assessment to be approved. He clasped my shoulder and gave me a man-pat on the back. "Come on in, Al."

I was sure I hid my panic-freeze reaction to being called my dead husband's nickname.

"Wishes, Dad. He goes by Wishes," Ronan said while he rubbed my back.

"Right. Sorry. Whiskey? Whiskey for Wishes." He emphasized the "W"s. Steve had Ronan's eyes and mouth, yet Ronan somehow looked more like his mom.

"Sure," I said and followed him into the house. I hated whiskey, reminded me of Alex's drunken episodes, but I couldn't say no.

The house was stunning. Plastic on the furniture when there were no guests stunning. Strict no running indoors and "don't touch that" stunning. The formal living room was not meant for children. Beautiful antique furniture, art on the walls, and ceramics on shelves.

Images of young Ronan being told to behave and be quiet came to mind. Steve and Ellen seemed lovely, but I suspected they had many rules for their children. Ronan hesitated to sit, as if the years of being told to stay out of the formal living room had corrupted his ability to relax in the white-and-blue space. He stood awkwardly in the middle.

I had no problem occupying the navy, velour chaise lounge like I belonged on it.

Steve returned from the kitchen and handed me a whiskey on the rocks. He neglected to bring Ronan a drink. "Nothing for you. We don't want another incident." He scowled at Ronan.

Ronan stiffened and looked small. Steve was about to leave when Ronan stopped him. "Father? Could I have a word in private with you?" He fidgeted with the tips of his hair.

They disappeared into what looked like Steve's study. An ornate oak door shut with a loud thud. The desire to snoop and look at all these antiques was strong; the desire to eavesdrop was stronger.

I couldn't hear much through the thick door. There were raised voices, some yelling; I heard my name, and I heard Vanessa's name. A shiver ran down my spine at hearing her name. What were they talking about? Or, rather, yelling about?

Ellen turned up the music in the kitchen, like it was a practice she was well acquainted with.

When the fancy oak door finally opened up again, Ronan slunk out, looking defeated. Steve stepped out like he was moments from having a stroke due to stress and anger. When he saw me, it disappeared and shifted into a kind and welcoming smile. I had the desire to impress him.

Ah. He was a Jekyll and Hyde. Shifts his moods for what was needed. The art of manipulation. Dress you down until you see how unfit you are, then smile and build you back up the way he wants you to be and make you trust him again. A dizzying feat. And now so much more made sense with Ronan's struggles with addiction. It was hard to cope with that kind of emotional whiplash.

I would have to stay on my toes around him.

"I'm going to help the kids make lunch. You boys behave," Steve said with a glorious, model-esque smile.

"Yes, sir," Ronan responded on autopilot. He stilled until his father left the room before he looked at me. I patted the space beside me. Ronan stared at the spot, as if he was trying to gauge how much it would hurt him to sit on it.

"Ronan sweetheart, you're an adult. You deserve to feel how luscious this chaise lounge is."

His brain made a few calculations before he sat stiff and cautious. I rubbed his back until he relaxed.

The kids and his parents laughed in the kitchen.

"That's quite the photo." I nodded towards a large family portrait. A girl who looked identical to Ronan frowned in the front. Ronan looked like a morose teenager who was forced to cut his hair for the portrait. None of them smiled, and they all dressed in formal wear. The women perched on fancy, uncomfortable chairs, while Ronan and his father stood straight behind them. No one was touching.

"Yeah. It was quite the occasion. Father was promoted at work and wanted to let everyone know he was the country club kind of guy. He's relaxed now that he's retired. He is amazing with Reese. Mostly. He can get strict, but he's not too harsh anymore. Mostly." He tucked a strand of hair behind his ear. "I love him. I do. I just

....." He eyed my untouched whiskey, and I gave it to him. My years of living with an alcoholic told me not to, but I did anyway. He one-shotted it and gave me back the glass.

"He wasn't as fun and happy with you as he is with Reese?"

"Correct."

"Your mom?"

"Mom kept us together and as stable as she could. I mean, I ended up with an addiction and my sister moved to another province for a reason. Mom tried her best. Dad did too. We talked about it on family days at rehab. He apologized for putting such high pressure on me. But at the same time, he told me to man up and take responsibility for myself and I was a good-for-nothing brat. I was seventeen."

I wove my fingers between his. My stomach dropped hearing him say those horrid words. "You were in rehab?"

"Yeah, three months in-patient when I was seventeen. That was after I was arrested for public intoxication. And several months of out-patient when Vanessa was pregnant."

"Oh, I had no idea." Why did he hide this from me? I told him I was in the psych ward after dying from suicide. "Wait, you've been to jail? Not to visit?"

"Once. Just before my first stint in rehab, they held me in the drunk tank until my dad came for me. He made me spend the night as punishment. I paid the fees, and he had a lawyer strike it from my record as I was a minor and it wasn't a serious offence. I had to repay him for the lawyer, after rehab of course. He holds all the money he lent me over my head. Worse than a collection agency."

I remembered how upset he was before Christmas that he needed his parents to help pay the bills.

Steve coughed in the kitchen and Ronan sat at attention with perfect posture. I recognized that trauma reaction.

"Babe? Look at me."

His head jerked around to me. His brow crumpled and he held his breath.

I kissed him. "You're safe with me."

His kiss told me he believed it. I would protect him the best I could and never abandon him.

"Woah, you two. There are kids here." Steve laughed as he walked into the room. Half joking. Then he gave Ronan a disapproving look. His eyes trailed down to the chaise lounge under Ronan. Ronan immediately stood at attention, like he was caught red-handed breaking the law. I sprawled a bit more.

Emma took Steve's gigantic hand. "It's okay, Grandpa, we've seen them kiss before. It shows that they love each other, and it models a healthy relationship to us. That's what my therapist said."

"Oh. Okay. Hey, you called me Grandpa."

That won him over. He beamed like a child winning bingo.

When we entered the family dining area, in the room past the formal dining room, Reese was setting the table. Brownie points for me. Emma helped bring food out. Again, points for me. Reese helped seat Ellen to the best of his ability and placed a napkin on her lap.

Ellen stared at Ronan with enormous eyes. Ronan grinned and nodded to me. So many points my way.

The food was amazing. Steve served us eggs benedict with a side of yogurt and berries prepared by seven-year-olds. Reese poured us all juice with minimal spillage. Steve tsked as he blotted some juice off the tablecloth. Emma asked us if anyone needed anything else before we started eating.

"Everything is perfect, love-bug." I kissed her head. "Come sit."

"Reese, sit up straight and get your elbows off the table," Steve snipped. Reese sat at attention and his big, blue eyes looked at Ronan for help.

"Dad," Ronan started, but Steve cut him off.

"No. He needs to learn. Look at Emma, she's sitting properly," Steve said.

Emma beamed with pride at Steve. Then slowly slouched and put her elbows on the table. I managed not to snicker.

I survived the barrage of questions like how Ronan and I met, what my job was, what we did for fun, what was it like to take care of Reese, and were we satisfied with living in Ronan's neighbourhood. Steve made a snarky comment about it not being as safe as it appeared. Which was an odd thing to say.

As always, I was my charming and nervous self, who made awkward jokes and comments. But they seemed to find me amusing.

"Who was Cinderella's favourite musician?" I asked the table.

Ronan gave me the side-eye, wondering where this was going.

Emma played along. "I don't know, Daddy, who?"

"Mozart. What was Cinderella's favourite cheese?"

Emma's eyes squinted, struggling to figure out my joke. "Pumpkin?"

"Nope. It was Mozart-rella." I lifted a piece of mozzarella cheese onto my fork.

Ronan's head dropped while Steve howled with laughter. All the brownie points to me.

This wasn't a house for dance parties and pillow forts. But it seemed loving. At least it was now. My heart burst for Ronan. After Steve stopped criticizing Ronan and Reese, Ronan didn't stop smiling the remaining visit. It looked like Steve was making an effort to heal their relationship. I think. Maybe?

"Son," Steve said to Ronan as we were leaving, "be safe. Call us if you need to."

CHAPTER TWENTY-ONE

W e parked in my driveway a few hours later. Tired and cramped from the long drive. Ronan wanted to go home and nap, but I convinced him to come in. I struggled to not smile and reveal that I was being mischievous. I pretended to tie my shoe so he would open the door first.

"Surprise!" numerous voices shouted from inside.

Emma and I fist-bumped.

Inside, Vinny, Katherine, Maddie, and Barry the drag queen were dressed in pride colours. There were rainbow decorations everywhere and a banner that read "You're Here! You're Queer!" in gold and rainbows. On the coffee table was the six-layer rainbow cake with a chocolate unicorn horn and sprinkles that Emma and I baked. It had taken Emma and me weeks to plan this in secret when Ronan wasn't over.

Vinny put a pride necklace on him. I swooped in behind him and draped a flag I had poorly sewn together of half-bi flag and half-pan flag. Maddie, in her pink, white, and blue glory, stuck a pride flag stick-on tattoo on his cheek. And Barry put a lovely shade of red lipstick on him, by kissing him.

Ronan jumped on me, kissed me. "You are amazing," he said between kisses.

I giggled. "You deserve this." When I realized he wasn't going to stop kissing me with everyone watching, I pulled away. "Okay, okay, okay. Emma had a huge hand in this."

He turned to Emma, hoisted her in the air, and spun her in circles. She squealed with laughter. I tried not to wince as she barely cleared the ceiling light.

Katherine presented him with a "Queer AF" T-shirt. He whipped off his current shirt in front of everyone and put on his new one. Emma and Reese ran off to dress in their matching rainbow-striped tracksuits. I stepped away from others to put on the most splendid and hideous rainbow button-up with cats riding unicorns.

Emma started the karaoke machine and an incredible sing-along dance party broke out. I had never heard Ronan sing as loud as he did when Journey's "Don't Stop Believing" played. He was jubilant and in his glory. I took photos of him in this blissful state. Stunning. Like a beautiful god.

Emma jumped onto the couch and joined him/took over the mic, and he danced with her. I imagined little Ronan wasn't allowed to jump on the furniture and sing at the top of his lungs. It thrilled me to give him this experience. I helped Reese onto the couch to join them. The pure joy on their faces filled me with more love than my concern that the couch would break.

Vinny and I sang 4 Non Blondes' "What's Up?" more commonly known as "What's Going On?" Seriously, why not name it that? Maddie and Barry had to be taught to choose songs appropriate to sing in front of kids. They sang Bonnie Tyler's "Total Eclipse of the Heart." And Katherine sang Disney songs with the kids. It was a blast.

I relaxed on the floor, taking a butt ton of photos. This was better than any karaoke night at a bar. And we had proclaimed it a dry night. We were determined to avoid another drunken fiasco.

Ronan scrolled through the songs on the computer, produced a funny noise, and turned bright red. I arched an eyebrow at him.

When the kids' song ended, he politely asked them to sit in the sound studio for a few minutes because he wanted to sing an adult song. My curiosity peaked. When the door closed behind the kids, Ronan hit play.

A familiar piano chord rang out of the speakers.

Oh my.

Oh no.

"Take Me to Church" by Hozier.

I was doomed.

He knew the lyrics off by heart and changed the words "she" to "he" to make it personal. I felt like he was genuinely singing this to me from his heart. His blue eyes glowed, locked on me, and I came undone. I have no idea what I looked like, but I'm certain I was unable to hide how incredibly horny I was. I held my breath as he reached his hand out and dragged me to my feet. Giving Vinny the mic, he slid his hands around my waist. His nails raked through my hair, hard enough to tilt my head to the ceiling. My lip tugged with his fingers moving across my mouth, exposing the wet skin to the air. My body moved as he commanded it to. With insides on fire, my breathing grew shallow.

He dropped to his knees for the last chorus, and I watched him in complete awe. I almost believed that he worshipped me. Maybe he did. My god, the way he looked at me was fiercer than anyone had ever looked at me before. Pure hunger and reverence.

I whimpered.

"Jesus. Even I'm turned on, and I'm a lesbian," Maddie said in the corner. Vinny crossed his legs.

Ronan stood and kissed me as the last notes ended. He sucked my lower lip and lightly pulled on it as he drew his head backwards.

"Your face," he laughed. "Did I do something wrong?" That smirk.

"That's it." I grabbed the front of his shirt. "Vinny, let the kids out, we're going upstairs."

I hauled him to my room, and he giggled behind me. He closed the bedroom door behind him, and I pushed him against the wall.

His look of shock was as big of a turn-on as his singing. With a deep hunger, I yanked his mouth to mine and frantically kissed him. My fingers found the hem of his shirt and tore it off him, then my own. No hesitation. His skin burned against mine. My lips, tongue, and teeth explored his neck, chest, nipples, arms, and stomach. Goosebumps ran across his skin. He tried to touch me back, but I pinned his arms.

"No. This is for you. I don't want to be touched," I said.

My tongue traced his stomach, and I sank to my knees.

His hand ran through my hair. "Darling, you don't need to do anything. It was a fun song, not a suggestion."

We made eye contact as I undid his button with my teeth. With his pants and underwear tossed on the floor, I explored his hips and thighs with my mouth and fingers. Teasing, light caresses, and soft kisses. He relaxed and hummed. So, I bit his hip. He tensed and hissed. His glorious toothy smile beamed at me as he licked his lips, then morphed into an open-lipped gasp as I took him into my mouth. An involuntary moan vibrated in my throat as I sunk deep down on him.

It had been a while since I had done this; however, judging from the sounds he produced, I was doing pretty well. His moans drove me on to taunt, tease, and torture. Ronan bucked and arched. I pressed my palms into his hips and held him against the wall. My nails left little half-moon indentations. The power I had over him was immeasurable. I experimented with what movements caused him to react with intense pleasure. I made him whimper and beg, twitch and shake.

I forgot how much I enjoyed sucking dick.

He growled my proper name. "Aloysius."

I pressed my nails deeper into his skin, causing him to hiss. I moved deliberately and rhythmically until I took him to church. A guttural noise rumbled through his body, and his muscles twitched and pumped against my tongue. This was my favourite part, post-climax convulsions as my tongue happily played. He beat the wall and whimpered my name. He tapped on the top of my head and told me he couldn't stand it anymore.

I wiped my mouth off with my thumb and sat on my heels, and he slid to the floor. Panting and glistening. There was a sweaty ass-print above him. Beautiful art.

"Fuck, Wishes. That was something. Thank you."

I laughed.

We heard loud music downstairs. They had cranked the volume.

He keeled over on his side, laughing. I slid into a lounging position next to him. I leaned on one elbow and grinned stupidly at him. We giddily lay there, admiring each other.

"I can't believe you threw a party for me. How are you this incredible?"

"I'm not as great as you say but go ahead and praise me." I touched his chest. "We should return to your party."

"Oh, no you don't. I need to repay you."

"You don't need to. I'm perfectly happy. I very much enjoyed that too."

"What if I want to?" He lifted my chin to look at him. The fire in him had reignited. I swallowed. He pushed me onto my back and hovered over me, pinning my arms above my head. In his perfect, smooth, sexy villain voice, he said, "Wishes, my darling, there is nothing more in this moment that I desire than to make you squirm in my grip and come in my mouth."

"Okay." My voice cracked.

He lowered himself to my lips and kissed me. "You sure?"

"Yes."

One of his hands slid over my jeans and touched me. I lifted my hips and pressed my dick against him. He worked my pants and tossed them in a pile with his. If he hadn't taken my wrists, I would have covered myself as he regarded me. Self-consciousness rolled over me.

"You are gorgeous, and I'm going to take my sweet time."

And he did.

His tongue was warm and wet on me. I wasn't positive if he was intentionally taking his time or if he was nervous. His body tensed. I did the math and realized he probably hadn't done this in nearly ten years. I wasn't sure how many blowjobs he had given. If at all.

I ran my fingers through his hair. "Babe, this is amazing." I wanted to build his self-esteem and became more vocal and expressive. I usually am anyway, but I amped it up. Boy, the boost of confidence worked magic.

My head lulled back. "Yes, that. Fuck, Ronan." I moaned. My face scrunched and my body blushed from head to toe curl as I forgot to breathe. I panted as I gave him encouragement and directions. He pinned my legs with his elbows as the muscles in my thighs twitched involuntarily.

I watched him working me over. He looked like he was enjoying this more than I was. I moved his hair aside for a better view. His blue eyes flashed at me. Feral and electric. He paused and formed a smirk around my cock.

My chest swirled with emotions. Poetic words came to mind, about how handsome he was, how much I cared for him, how good he made me feel. But no. None of those words came out of my yap. Instead, I said, "I'd tell you a penis joke, but I don't want to seem cocky."

He sat straight. "All right, I'm done."

I sat and grabbed his hand. "No, I'm sorry. I couldn't help it." I couldn't stop smiling. Lucky for me, neither could he. I wiped spit off his chin and kissed him. "I'll behave. Promise."

"And why should I continue?"

"Because I'm adorable?"

"Good reason, but I want more. Convince me." His one-sided grin told me all I needed to know. He wanted his ego stroked more than I wanted my dick stroked.

"Because...." I pulled myself closer to him. "When I touch myself, all I can think of is you and those stunning blue eyes watching me. Because when I sleep, I feel your hands on me. And in the morning when I wake, I hear your voice whispering in my ear. I am always thinking about you, even if it's in the corner of my mind. You are there. I want you every moment of my life, whether it's by my side, or in my bed, I want you. I'm yours and you're mine.

Take me in your mouth and make my lips speak your name as if I were crying to the heavens." I paused a hair's width away from his lips. "Please?" I begged with a breathy whimper.

I was flat on my back with him feverishly working on me in seconds. No more taunting and teasing. Now it was determination and lust. My fists balled into my hair, and I tried not to move my hips. Intensity built in my body, my muscles tightened and pulsed, and my nerve endings lit on fire.

"Ronan," I gasped, "I'm coming."

Electricity shot through me. A dull roar filled my ears, and my body arched and toes curled. I stopped breathing and transformed into various shades of red. The world dimmed, and all I could feel was Ronan.

"Hey love, you okay?"

I opened my eyes to find Ronan over me. "Yeah," I panted.

"I seriously thought you were passing out."

"Yeah, I get like that sometimes. I'm seeing stars." I tried to slow my breathing. "That was something. Thank you." I reached to touch his cheek and missed, and my rubbery arm hit me in the stomach.

Ronan laughed and kissed my cheek before laying on the floor next to me. "We should probably give ourselves a few moments before going downstairs."

I agreed. "I think I have carpet burn on my ass."

Ronan helped roll me onto my side. "You totally do." He kissed my asscheeks. "There, all better."

"Thank you." Our fingers tangled, and we cuddled for a few minutes.

Once recovered, we begrudgingly dressed, tided ourselves, brushed our teeth, and headed downstairs. The music was loud. We walked hand-in-hand into the living room with big, goofy grins. The kids were singing with Katherine; Reese had his noise-cancelling headphones on.

Katherine turned the volume down. "That was some conversation."

"Ain't a coming-out party unless you're co —" Maddie said.

"Maddie," Ronan warned.

Perhaps I needed to soundproof the bedroom.

CHAPTER TWENTY-TWO

Monday morning, Ronan walked into my house to take Emma to school. He looked rough. He stood with a slight stoop, and dark circles under his eyes.

"Are you okay?" I kissed him as I brought over his lunch.

"I couldn't sleep, that's all." He took my chin and kissed me again, assuring me he was alright. I believed it. Mostly.

Emma faked a gag at our kissing. I threatened to kiss her, and she ran outside squealing with laughter. Ronan followed her at a slow pace, dragging a moody Reese behind him.

Partway through the day, Ronan texted me, saying he wasn't staying for supper tonight. Okay. That was fine. Although he forgot he was supposed to look after Emma. Vinny and I were rehearsing for our concert.

At evening pickup, a blurry-eyed Ronan forced a half-arsed smile. Again, he insisted nothing was wrong. He looked ragged; I didn't have it in me to be snarky that he left me high and dry with Emma.

Emma and I rushed out the door the moment we finished eating. This wouldn't be the first rehearsal I subjected her to. She joined us on the tambourine. You haven't heard Bach until you've heard it on a plastic tambourine. Very off-beat. I think our violinist was about to walk out on us.

The next day Ronan texted me partway through the morning, requesting I bring Reese to him after school. He wasn't feeling well and had left work to sleep and rest.

When I dropped Reese off with a thermos of chicken noodle soup, Ronan looked a right mess. "Oh, sweetheart." I touched his forehead. He seemed normal. Mind you, I was trash at checking temperatures. I combed his hair with my fingers. It was tangled and greasy. He smelled like layers of sweat and salt.

"I'm alright, darling." He kissed the inside of my wrist. It was strange to be kissed on my scars, but I didn't hate it. "I just need some rest."

The next day I brought Reese to school, and Ronan stayed home.

Something was wrong.

After I dropped the kids off, I marched to Ronan's. I made it to his door as he stepped out. Dressed in a burgundy fitted suit and heading out. When I questioned him, he smiled sweetly at me.

"I have an appointment. Don't worry, I'm fine. I'll talk to you later."

He didn't kiss me goodbye as he got into his beater car and drove away.

How sick was he? He was dressed nice for a doctor's appointment. Was it a specialist? Why would he need a specialist? Why didn't he kiss me? Was he preoccupied or pulling away? He hadn't been reading with me at night. He barely texted me lately. Did I do something wrong again? I wanted to vomit.

I stood alone on the sidewalk long after his car disappeared out of view; my head reeled. My eyes fell to a stain of hot pink spray paint on the sidewalk curb. White noise filled my head, and my vision went out of focus as I stared at the blight on the grey concrete. The whir of a drill pulled me out of near disassociation. There was a man on a ladder outside of Ronan's house, installing something on the wall. I couldn't tell what they were. Lights? Motion detectors? Cameras?

The man nodded at me when he saw me staring. I smiled and nodded before I turned to head back home.

At 2:43 p.m., every alarm in the house went off at full volume. I ran around and shut them all off and was at school at 3:01 p.m. Emma was in tears. Across the lot, Ronan was walking Reese to his car. He gave me a curt nod and opened the car door for Reese. Emma said Reese might not come over as much anymore. When I asked why, she shook her head and cried. Reese had no clue why either.

Stunned, I watched my boyfriend drive away without saying a word to me. I checked my phone to see if he had texted me to say he was getting Reese, but there was nothing. I wiped away Emma's tears and assured her things were fine. Hard to convince someone of that when I knew things were not fine.

The mother who thought I was a sex worker smirked at me with a condescending, homophobic, nose-in-the-air, Karen vibe.

It took all my power not to tell her to fuck off.

When we got home, Emma and I tried to relax and unwind, but I think we both felt we were losing the other half of our family and had no idea why.

Emma pouted and scowled at me. "You shouldn't have showed them the scars," she said. "Now they know how broken and reckless you are."

My mouth gaped. What do you say when your seven-year-old calls you broken and reckless? And she was right. "Hunny, they were bound to find out. I can't hide these scars forever."

"I wish you could."

"Me too."

I expected her to race off and slam her bedroom door. Instead, she curled up next to me on the couch, and we watched baking shows together. It was difficult to concentrate when all I could think was Emma was correct. I shouldn't have showed him the scars, or at least I should have hidden them from Reese. I had worried this would scare Ronan away, and I think it did. He had dealt with enough from his ex; he didn't need my crazy ass making his life more complicated.

Over and over in my head, I thought, I was losing him. I was losing Reese. I was losing the beautiful little family I had fallen in love with.

I sent Ronan a few texts, but there was no reply until after supper.

Ronan
Sorry. Busy.

I lost him. I felt it in my gut. My crazy ass broke our relationship. I suffered through abuse, PTSD, complex grief, suicide, almost had my daughter taken away, and now I was losing my sun, and my almost son. My heart raced.

Vinny was teaching piano all evening and couldn't respond to my spiral. Katherine did her best in soothing me, but she was no Vinny. She helped enough, though.

It wasn't until hours later I received Ronan's next text.

I miss you, darling.
I'll take the kids to school tomorrow.
Can we talk tomorrow evening?

I swallowed. He was dumping me. Wait. No. What if he was dying? What if he'd been really sick? He had looked like hell all week. A numbing prickle covered my body at this thought.

Aloysius
I miss you too, sweetheart
And yes. I'm always here to talk

When he came for Emma in the morning, he looked worse than the day before. Apparently, so did I.

"You alright?" he asked.

"Insomnia." I lied. I couldn't sleep because I was having wave after wave of panic that he was leaving me. How would Emma handle this? She already called Reese her brother. This would devastate her. Would they still be able to have playdates and be best friends? How was I going to handle this? I had decided to move on and fall for someone, and .... My heart ached.

And what if he was super sick and I lost another person I adored? What if tonight he asked me to sign as Reese's guardian in case he died? Emma couldn't handle another father (-esque person) dying.

Breathe, Wishes.

"Same."

He gave me coffee-and-vanilla kisses. Soft and sweet. Longer than our typical morning get-the-kids-out-the-door kisses. His hand lingered on my jaw, rubbing his thumb over my cheekbone. Even though I had spent the entire night building a mental wall preparing for the inevitable, I fell for him and dropped my guard. His eyes grew teary.

Oh fuck. He's dying, isn't he?

"See you tonight," he said as he left.

Emma grabbed his hand and peered at me over her shoulder. Her eyes said, "I am not letting him go."

"Wait," I called out. "Can I walk with you guys?"

Ronan bit his lip, and the wrinkle between his eyebrows deepened. "Sure," he answered, "I guess."

I slipped on my coat and shoes and ran outside. Reese took my hand.

The walk was full of awkward silences. I tried to get a read on Ronan's face, but I got nothing. Reese kicked rocks, flailed his arms, and grunted. I tried to distract him with songs and stories. But he told me to stop; he didn't want to hear stories. When we got to the school, he ripped out of my grasp and stormed off to the playground and kicked more rocks. Emma gave both Ronan and me hugs before she somberly walked over to Reese and hugged him.

Ronan looked gutted at his son's mood. I slipped my hand into his and squeezed it. Maybe there something was wrong with Reese? It couldn't be a custody battle, right? She was in jail. What if Reese was the one who was sick?

Ronan squeezed back and glanced around the drop-off area. A few parents watched us. He pulled away from me.

"I don't want to hold hands in front of other parents," he said in a hushed whisper. "And can you not walk me home? I need a moment to myself."

"Sure." Before I said anything else, he took off down the road, leaving me standing there alone.

Reese yelled and screamed on the playground. I walked towards him, but a teacher stopped me. Parents could not pass the magical yellow line that changed us from parents into kidnappers. Ridiculous. I wanted to cross the stupid yellow line to help him, not entice him with a van of candy and puppies.

I told them I wanted to help Reese, but they informed me I was not his father, so I couldn't. While the logic made sense, I hated it.

Reese's temper raised.

"Reese, hun," I called out around the teacher. "Look at me, Reese."

Reese glared at me with venom in his eyes. I had never seen him this angry. I reminded him to listen to his music and do breathing exercises, and that I loved him. He cried. The bell rang, and he ran off to line up for morning entrance. I couldn't do anything more. Emma shook her head with disappointment at me and slowly meandered to the line.

The same annoying mom who thought I was a sex worker sneered at me. "He's not your kid; you shouldn't say stuff like that."

I was done. "Sorry, what's your name again?"

"Samantha."

"Well, Sammy —"

"Samantha."

"Well, *Samantha*, it's none of your business what my relationship with him is. No, he's not my kid, but that doesn't mean I'm not allowed to love him and support him. Should I be coldhearted b-word like you and watch him meltdown when I know I can help? And you know what? Stop staring at me and Ronan. It's creepy. Stop being creepy and mind your dang business. If you get off on watching men hold hands, there're websites for that, *Samantha*."

I stormed off while Samantha tsked and clutched her pearls. I swear she muttered a slur under her breath, but I couldn't be sure. My blood boiled. Fucking neanderthals. I stormed off harder. Reese was upset. Emma was bitter. Ronan didn't want to be around me. And Samantha was a shitty excuse for a human. This was a horrible day.

CHAPTER TWENTY-THREE

A nd the day got worse. I ignored my client work and pounded out an angry improv piece on the piano. My body was fully engaged in it, and I was panting and sweating in minutes.

I stopped to catch my breath and grabbed my phone. I wanted to call Vinny, but he was busy teaching piano. Katherine rarely answered her texts while at work. Her and her work ethic. I stared at my phone, wondering who else I could call. Hyunji? That might be weird. Loneliness slinked in and my surroundings felt so big, and I was so small.

The phone rang in my hand. I jumped and almost dropped it. It was the school. There was an incident. The secretary refused to give me any more information than Emma was physically fine, but I needed to come talk to the principal. I heard crying and yelling in the background. I jogged to the school and didn't bother with my coat. My heart rate kept me warm enough.

Emma and Reese sat on a wooden bench in the office, while another kid — correction, the spawn named Joey who bullied Reese and Emma — sat across the office on an orange, plastic chair. Reese dashed to me and clung to my waist, sobbing. Emma was red-faced and glared at Joey. She greeted me but didn't get up. Joey had a bite mark on his arm and a dark bruise on his cheek. Dread crept through me.

I unhooked Reese from me, and I knelt down. "Hey, whippersnapper, you okay?"

Sobs were my answers. I picked him up to soothe him.

Principal Davis stepped out of her office and eyed me, holding the wrong child. "Mr. O'Connor, I assume you know Reese?"

"Yeah. Mr. Decker and I are in a relationship." Even though I was positive I was being dumped. "What happened?"

"Why don't we wait until the other parents arrive? You and Emma may have a seat in the conference room." She pointed to a dim room with a large table in it.

"Not Reese?"

"No, we need to wait for his dad," the principal said.

My heart sank. "I'll wait out here with Reese until he gets here."

Moments later, footsteps entered the office. I turned to see Samantha. Great. Let me guess, the other kid was her son. Sure enough, he ran to her and cried. She huffed at Principal Davis and didn't want to wait for Ronan. In her "I want to speak to the manager" voice, she demanded to be told what happened, and if she didn't get answers immediately, she would call her husband and he had an expensive lawyer. The principal calmly directed her to wait in the conference room and walked away. Davis was badass. It appeared I had misjudged her.

We waited another twenty minutes for Ronan. He came panting in with red cheeks. His eyes fell to me sitting on the bench, holding Reese, who slumped over my shoulder. Emma curled under my other arm.

Ronan ran his hands through Reese's hair. "Hey, what's going on?" Ronan asked. He moved to kiss my cheek but stopped midway.

"I don't know yet." I explained to him what the principal said. Ronan tried to take Reese from me, but he gripped me tighter. There was a pang of hurt in Ronan's eyes. The principal greeted Ronan, and we all ventured into the conference room. Ronan took Emma's hand and froze when he saw Samantha. They exchanged unhappy looks. We sat across the table from her. I set Reese on the chair next to Ronan. Emma sat between me and Reese. The kids held hands under the table. My stomach twisted one direction at how adorable and loving they were, then twisted the other direction as I dreaded what would happen if they lost their sibling bond.

"So," Principal Davis started, "their classroom teacher informed me that Reese was visibly upset but not quite disruptive. He wasn't mean to any students, and he didn't throw anything. Emma helped to calm him down. Apparently, they hugged and talked, and Reese was relaxing. When Joey made some highly inappropriate remarks intended to upset Reese, Reese flipped his desk but did not hurt Joey. Emma yelled at Joey, and he threw a book at her."

I noticed a red mark on Emma's cheek, below her eye.

Rage built inside me, and I had no release for it. The book narrowly missed her eye. If her injuries were worse, I did not know how I would have handled it. Little shit. It was unacceptable if I punched Samantha, right?

"Reese defended Emma, and Joey said something else highly inappropriate. Reese bit Joey, Joey punched Reese in the stomach and pulled his hair, so Emma punched Joey in the face."

"Why didn't the teacher stop this?" Ronan asked. Eyes wide and frantic.

"She tried," Principal Davis said. "However, she is pregnant, and Joey swung a chair at her stomach."

I gasped. "No way. That's monstrous." I ignored Samantha's scoff of offence.

"He missed, thankfully," Principal Davis said.

"That does not sound like my Joey," Samantha stated.

"It is in line with how he's been behaving this year at school." Principal Davis was not taking shit.

Samantha opened her mouth to talk, but I cut her off. "What were these highly inappropriate comments?"

The principal shifted in her chair. "There were comments suggesting incest, as Emma and Reese claim to be siblings. And there were several homophobic comments and slurs."

I went rigid and blood whooshed through my ears. Emma grabbed my hand. "Don't worry, Daddy, I told him he was wrong."

My daughter was amazing. I smiled at her. "Thank you, sweetheart."

"My son shouldn't have to be exposed to that at school. That kind of stuff shouldn't be near children. He was speaking his mind." Samantha gestured towards us.

"What stuff?" I barked.

"They were touching each other in front of the children."

"Holding hands is not 'touching each other.' How dare you blame your son's lousy behaviour on —"

"You must have seen wrong," Ronan interrupted me. "Wishes is just Reese's babysitter; we weren't holding hands."

Me, Emma, and Reese looked at him in shock. What the fuck did he say? I fought back tears. Emma didn't.

She yelled, "You lying SOB!"

"Emma," Ronan scolded.

"No. You don't get to tell me to be quiet."

"Love-bug." I placed a hand on Emma's leg. She went silent when she turned to me. I don't know how I looked, but I felt like a sand-filled weight with a gaping hole. My sand was dumping all over the floor.

The principal looked at me. She understood how bad this conversation was turning. Ronan refused to look at me. His jaw tightened and nostrils flared.

He'd dumped me. This was the worst breakup I had ever gone through. Samantha had a smug smirk. I understood why Emma punched Joey. He was a spitting image of Samantha, and she had a punchable face. My fists balled. But instead of punching her or Ronan, I retreated into myself. Running away from it all. My ears buzzed and a roaring noise grew louder and louder. I hardly heard what the principal was saying.

The principal hurried the meeting along before a domestic dispute broke out in her office. I struggled to concentrate. Since Joey was the instigator, he received a two-day suspension, and she forbade him to say those words at school again or face expulsion for hate speech. She suspended Reese and Emma for the rest of the day. I hoisted Emma into my arms and stormed out, ignoring the lying SOB.

The words "just Reese's babysitter" played over and over in my head. Ronan had texted me repeatedly to ask me to talk with him. But I couldn't. The audacity to ask me to talk after he did that to me. I was numb. He probably wanted to ask if I would *babysit* Reese, even though he'd dumped me like the douche canoe he was. Of course I would. I loved that boy. But I would not talk to Ronan anytime soon.

Alex had said a few times he shouldn't have married me, and now Ronan denied our relationship even existed. Was this payback for New Year's? I thought we had moved past that. I had worked so hard on my mental health and was open and honest with him. This was betrayal.

I wished he had dumped me earlier, instead of waiting for a parent-teacher conference. Maybe I should have dumped him and saved myself from this pain. This confirmed I was too broken to move on. I shouldn't have tried. I was fine being single. But no, I was naïve and fell for him. I should have quashed any hope I stupidly had. It wasn't worth it. I had Emma, which was all that mattered. She was the only person who mattered. Well, Vinny and Katherine too.

I hurt. My body numbed. My brain shut off. My bones ached. My soul was ripped out and stomped on.

Emma was full of emotions, too. She was in a fistfight with a douchey brat who said horrible things seven-year-olds should not know, and she witnessed Ronan and me fall apart.

"Screw him," Emma muttered while we sat on the couch and stared at whatever was on the TV.

I didn't bother to remind her about her language. She echoed my sentiments. "We've been through worse, bug-a-boo; we'll get through this too."

"I really thought he was going to be my stepdad," she said. "I loved him. Almost as much as I loved Appa. And he was much nicer than Appa. Why doesn't he love us back? Why doesn't he love me? What's wrong with me?"

My insides quaked and shattered. What horrid thoughts for my little angel to have. My stomach burned. How could Ronan do this to her? What fucking right did he have to upset my daughter? My breathing grew ragged, and the world tilted.

"Nothing is wrong with you, my love. You hear me? Nothing. You are the most important person in the world to me. You are amazing. He's a dick. Maybe he has some dark secret and hasn't told us about it yet." I said this more to comfort. We hugged, cried, and talked.

Vinny and Katherine came over after their work ended. Followed by a poor client who I had forgotten about. I pulled myself together and helped them record, but man was it awkward. The client, luckily, was someone I had known for months, and my gloomy state didn't bother them. They offered to leave, but I knew I could record for them. We worked for an hour, and honestly, my mood improved by the end of the session. Their songs were upbeat and fun. We got three songs done, and we were both happy with the recordings. The sweetheart gave me a hug before they left.

When the house door was closed behind them, Vinny's anger exploded like a volcano. Molten Vinny everywhere. While I was locked in my studio, Vinny paid a visit to Ronan. No fists were thrown, thankfully, but he made threats. They argued on the front lawn so Reese wouldn't hear. But Vinny caused a scene big enough for neighbours to poke their heads out. I bet Samantha watched. I loved Vinny, but I worried this made everything worse.

Katherine had taken Emma upstairs to talk and have a good cry.

"How dare he call you 'the babysitter'? You are more than that. Arrogant prick." Vinny hugged me.

"Whatever. It's probably best I stay single. Emma is heartbroken, and I can't do that to her again. I can't let her believe people will abandon her all the time. I'll wait until she's an adult to date again. It's only ten years."

"This is his loss. You are more than worth dating." Vinny looked me in the eye.

"I wasn't worth dating for you," I whispered. It was a low blow, and I knew it. It was a mutual decision for us to stop whatever we had in high school. Mostly. I had held a small candle for him for years after. Vinny's brow furrowed, and his eyes narrowed. I was a dick. "Sorry. I need some time to myself."

With a sad kiss to his cheek, I slipped away into the darkness of my bedroom. Full-on ugly cry episode in the nook between my bed and the wall. The buzzing in my ears rattled my brain. Katherine came to tell me they were leaving, and they had tucked Emma into bed. She kissed my forehead and told me not to lose hope. But it was hope that got me into this predicament.

Our weekend was glum and moody. Both Emma and I were pissy, and we snapped at each other. Sunday afternoon, we went out for food therapy. She picked a restaurant we couldn't go to if Reese was with us. Ninety percent of the menu had dairy in it. She ate deep-fried cheese sticks, chicken alfredo, and ice cream. She got eating her emotions from me. I had a giant cheeseburger and ice cream and pie for dessert.

On the way home, we bought a new video game. Momentarily, I wished Ronan was around to play, as he was better at video games than me. But he was a dick, so he didn't deserve to have fun with my baby anymore. We grabbed snacks and played until we were exhausted.

She read me a few chapters of *Charlotte's Web.* "Daddy," she said at the end of the chapter, "my tummy feels weird."

"Well, love-bug, we ate a lot of candy. You'll feel better in the morning." I kissed her forehead. "Seriously, I mint it."

"Stop sugarcoating the truth."

"Nothing will come be Twix us."

"You think you're a Smartie, but you're really a Ding Dong."

"Burn! That one stung. I'm proud of you. Good night, Tootsie Pop."

"Night, nougat."

CHAPTER TWENTY-FOUR

M onday morning, I knocked on Emma's door and stepped inside. "Hey love-bug, it's time to get ready for school."

She grumbled.

"Want me to read?"

She made a pitiful, wrong noise. I hit the lights. Her skin was pale and clammy. I felt her forehead; she was warm. But I was trash at taking temperatures. "How do you feel?"

She rolled onto her side and heaved. I grabbed the garbage can in time.

"I hurt, Daddy," she whimpered.

"Where do you hurt?"

"My tummy."

I took her to the bathroom, where she evacuated her system in horrible ways. She hugged the garbage can and sat on the toilet, crying.

"Okay, sweetheart," I tried not to panic. "You stay here. I'm making a phone call."

She vomited in response.

I dashed to my room and grabbed my cellphone. My heart thumped so loud I could barely hear it ring. My poor girl. What was wrong? What if she was so sick I lost her, too? Fuck.

The sweet voice I longed for answered. I set aside my anger. Anything for her.

"Something wrong?" Ronan answered.

"Emma's sick and I don't know what to do." My voice wavered.

"Breathe, darling. How is she sick?" Ronan asked.

"Diarrhea and vomiting."

"Does she have a fever?"

"The thermometer broke ages ago, and I forgot to buy a new one."

"We need to take her to the hospital. I'll be right over."

I waited for him in the bathroom with Emma. She wavered between falling asleep and clearing her system. I tied her hair back and wiped sweat and spit off with a damp cloth.

Ronan ran up the stairs. "Hey, Emma." He knelt beside her.

"You made us cry," she said, then spat in the garbage. She might have been ill, but she still had venom.

"I'm sorry. We'll talk about that later. But first, we need to get you better." Ronan caressed her forehead and moved strands of damp black hair out of her eyes. "I need to talk to your dad and make a few phone calls. We'll be in the hallway. Alright?"

Ronan guided me out of the bathroom and hugged me. "She'll be fine."

I fell into his arms. Curling into my safety zone.

"You get dressed." He rubbed my back. "I'll call the school, my work, and text Maddie. I'll have her meet us at the hospital to get Reese. But I'll stay with you. Okay?"

I nodded.

"She'll be fine." He kissed me. My body melted under his magic. He felt right against me. "I'm sorry for everything. It's complicated. Can we talk later?"

"Yeah."

I left the door ajar as I dressed so I could see Emma. Ronan informed the school of Emma's absence. He called his work next.

"Hi Abby, it's Ronan. I can't come in today. I need to take my boyfriend's daughter to the hospital." There was a pause. "Yeah, I'll check in later. Bye."

I stepped out of my room, dressed in whatever I grabbed. "You called me boyfriend." My chest was caught between exploding with joy, imploding with fear my daughter was dying, and peppered with shrapnel of confusion.

"Yeah, I guess I did." He ran his hands through his hair. "I'm sorry I'm making things difficult, but ...."

I heard Emma puke again. "We'll talk after." I kissed his cheek before I grabbed a bag with a change of clothes and blankets for Emma. Ronan bundled her into her coat and blanket. I brought more garbage bags, dumped the full ones in the outdoor trash bin, and tried not to barf. It was a struggle.

We loaded the kids into the car, and Ronan drove us to the hospital. Nothing gets you through triage faster than projectile vomiting. A nurse examined her once we were in an ER bed but said little. We didn't know how long we'd have to wait for the doctor. I wanted to scream at them. My baby was dying, and they needed to fucking hurry.

I stood at Emma's bedside and stroked her greasy hair. Her skin was green. I had assumed that was a hyperbole, but apparently not. She napped, and I was both thankful and scared. Was this a resting nap or a slipping-into-a-coma nap? Ronan wrapped his arms around my waist from behind. Reese sat in a blue vinyl chair and read Emma a book he had in his bookbag.

What if this was contagious, and we exposed Reese to it? What if both our kids died? Ronan would blame me and hate me forever. Vinny and Katherine would hate me for getting Emma ill, and everyone would see how useless I was.

Ronan hugged me tight and kissed my neck. "Hey," he whispered, "it's going to be okay. We are where we need to be."

Half the knots in my body eased a bit. He kissed my neck again, and a few more knots loosened.

The doctor still hadn't come, and if I weren't clinging to the bed rail, I'd have paced the ER, screaming for the doctor to get the fuck over here. The nurse changed the puke bucket several times. I never saw anyone vomit this much before. I ran her to the bathroom a few times, too. Poor kid. She was getting dehydrated.

"Did I tell you about the time I worked in a restaurant?" I said. "In walked one person with the flu, another person with pneumonia, and one with mono. I was like, what is this? Some sick joke?"

Emma laughed, coughed, and vomited. Alright, no more jokes.

Ronan's phone vibrated. "Maddie's here." He looked at Reese. "Come on, buddy, let's meet her out front. She's taking you to school."

"I wanna stay with Emma," Reese said.

"It's okay, Reese," Emma said. "You go. Daddy's here to keep me company. You can get my homework for me."

Reese gave her an awkward, too-short-to-reach hug before taking Ronan's hand.

"I'll only be a few minutes," Ronan said as he kissed my cheek.

Those were long-ass minutes. With no one to ground me, I paced. Emma spewed again and started crying. I flagged our nurse down. "Excuse me, any word on when we'll see the doctor? She's getting worse." I failed to hide the panic in my voice.

"I'm not sure, she's doing her best. There was an urgent situ—" The nurse turned to Emma and stepped aside, pulling me with her.

Emma made an epic mess of many kinds of bodily fluids all over the bed and herself.

"I'll get another nurse to help with the mess and tell the doctor to come here next."

The nurse handed me a mask and gloves so I could help Emma. By the time Ronan returned, they had ushered me out of Emma's little space, and the nurses took over.

"What is that smell?" Ronan's nose wrinkled.

"Emma," I said and tossed the mask and fouled gloves into a garbage bin. "She pulled an *Exorcist*; it just missed me." I hid my face in Ronan's chest. "What if something is seriously wrong? I can't lose her."

Emma wailed, and Ronan held me tight.

"We won't lose her."

A woman jogged towards Emma's space. "Are you her parents?" I nodded. I didn't have the energy to argue. We followed her behind the curtain. Emma had an IV in her arm and was lying back in clean bedding and gown.

"I'm Doctor Armstrong, and I see we have a girl who has a very unhappy stomach?" She smiled and checked Emma's chart before poking and prodding Emma and asking questions. "Well," she turned to me and Ronan, "I am ordering blood work as a precaution, but I believe we have food poisoning. It doesn't appear to be serious, especially since we have fluids going into her." She gestured to the IV bag. "We'll run the tests and continue to monitor her. If she evacuates her system at this rate for much longer, we may keep her overnight to ensure she doesn't get dehydrated. We'll have a better idea of what our next steps are in a few hours. Do either of you have questions?"

"How do you know it's food poisoning? Don't you need to order an ultrasound? Or an MRI?" I was being ridiculous, but damn it, I earned being ridiculous. Ronan hugged me from behind, and my pulse dropped a beat or two.

The doctor chuckled. "No, no MRIs for this. I have a *gut reaction* that this is food poisoning."

Did my doctor dad joke me?

"Anything else?" She asked.

I shrugged and looked at Ronan. He shook his head.

"Emma? Do you have questions?" she asked.

"Am I contingency?" Emma asked.

"Contagious? Not if it's food poisoning. What did you eat?"

"We've eaten the same thing together every day." I thought for a moment. "Except at the restaurant yesterday. She had chicken alfredo, and I had a cheeseburger." Bastard restaurant.

"So, we might be looking at salmonella. I'll make a note of that." She set Emma's chart into the holder at the end of the bed after writing in it. "Gentlemen, Emma, it was nice to meet you." And with that, she disappeared.

"We're boycotting that restaurant," Emma moaned.

"I'll make the signs." I smiled and petted her head. "Why don't you try to sleep, love-bug."

"Can you read to me?"

Ronan downloaded *Anne of Green Gables* onto his phone. He and I pulled our chairs close to the bed. He read to her, and I held her hand as she fell asleep.

"You okay?" he asked. We both sat back against the chairs and relaxed.

"I think so." I leaned on his shoulder. "Thank you for helping."

"Of course." He turned his body towards me.

I looked into his pretty blue eyes and bit my lip. "So, what's going on? Between us."

He held my hand to his mouth and glanced at Emma. Her chest raised and lowered in a deep rhythm of sleep. "Vanessa found out about us."

I wasn't sure why his ex in prison knowing about us was a big deal. "How did she find out?"

"Samantha apparently is an old friend of Vanessa's. They reconnected because Vanessa is in a church-run virtual rehabilitation program. The same church Samantha goes to."

"So, what does that mean? She can't stop you from dating me."

"I'm not sure. I've been talking to my lawyer. We can't find any legal actions she might take." He ran his hands through his rat's-nest hair he didn't brush before leaving the house. I was sure mine was worse. "Technically, no. She can't stop us."

Those knots in my stomach tightened.

"She's doing her best to make my life hell. I'm not sure if she's actually homophobic or transphobic, but last year she filed complaints I was exposing her son to a trans woman, only in transphobic terms. She didn't have issues with Maddie before we divorced, but she's desperate to hurt me. Nothing happened in the courts. Maddie is no threat to Reese. But Maddie was positive one of Vanessa's friends followed her home one night. No evidence though." Ronan chewed on his lip.

"Every complaint that involves lawyers involves me going further into debt or another fucking Children's Aid investigation. My lawyer said she filed a complaint that we are dating and I'm subjecting Reese to deviants and sinners. God will hurt Reese if I don't leave you. And it's her religious right to keep her son from you. She isn't even religious. It's all a big act." His voice dropped to a whisper. "But I don't think the threats are an act."

"Threats?"

"It's …." He swallowed and shook his head.

"If she's threatening you, you need to report it to the police."

"I already reported it and I —"

Emma moaned.

"This isn't a good time to talk about that," Ronan whispered. "But if I don't listen to her, things might get bad."

"This isn't fair." My voice cracked.

He brushed my hair aside and touched my cheek. "In the principal's office, I was scared. Seeing Samantha freaked me out. I didn't expect to see her. I didn't expect to hear what Joey said to my son." He hung his head. "Reese told me Joey called me a fag. Among other words a child shouldn't know. I don't need that kind of attention on my son. What if someone reports me as an unfit parent for exposing him to cruelty and takes him away?

"I hate that Vanessa got me wound tight. I can't believe she's fucking spying on me. She's vindictive and evil. I hate that Samantha outed me to her. She doesn't deserve to know about you. And I hate this hurts you and Emma too."

I pulled him close to me, wishing I could fix this for him. "Your appointment the other day was with your lawyer?"

"Yeah. And it was a dick move to get Reese from school without telling you. But I panicked. I thought maybe Samantha would say we weren't together if she saw that. I'm sorry. It was wrong."

"I understand panic." I rubbed his back.

"How do you do it?" His eyes brimmed with tears. "How do you deal with the shit people say? I've passed for straight my whole life. Hell, you thought I was straight. No one has said these horrid words to Reese before. I had to explain to him what those slurs meant, and he broke down." He swallowed. "What do you do when people say disgusting stuff to Emma? It hurts. How can I put him through that? Is it worth the pain?"

An icy chill ran down my spine. Maybe things weren't fixed between us. I tried not to take it as personal. This was an identity crisis many questioned. But fuck. This hurt to hear him ask if it was worth it. If I was worth it.

"People will always find shitty things to say," I said. "Even if I weren't gay, I'd be bullied. As a kid, I had water thrown on me as they shouted 'fire, fire' for having red hair. They made fun of me for being short, smart, for playing the piano. People beat me for fun. I had no clue what 'gay' meant back then. None of my childhood bullying came from being gay. And it was traumatic. Were you bullied as a kid?"

"Yeah. I was also the weird smart kid." He chewed on the tips of his hair. "But I don't want that for Reese."

"No one wants that for their kid. When we had Emma, I wanted to slap every motherfucker who said anything nasty. Most parents do. Queer or not. They bullied Reese before you came out. And it won't stop if you go back into the closet. Despite what your doctor has said, I'm pretty sure he's neurodivergent. And people can be dicks to people like us." I tugged at my sleeve. "We can't protect the kids forever."

"I know," he whispered. "But it hurts so much."

"It does. And I'm sorry." I licked my lips. "I can't tell you if being with me is worth the pain. That's your choice. But, pain will happen. No matter who you date. It's your choice how you want to be happy. Would you be happy in the closet? Or would you be causing yourself more difficulties? You have control over that part of your life."

I wrung my hands while he chewed his lip.

He lifted his head and looked at me. "Darling, I missed you this weekend. I was a wreck." He took my hands. "Maddie almost held an intervention. You and Emma mean so much to me, and I cannot imagine my life without you two. I want to be out and proud. To hold my head high and show off my amazing boyfriend. And Wishes, I need you to know I love you. I fucking love you."

My heart thudded against my ribcage as rainbows filled my vision and doves flew around me. Those beautiful words etched themselves onto my soul.

"I love you too." I worshipped this man, and yet, I still remembered Alex, and I loved him too. It did not erase him from my memories, as I had worried.

We kissed. Sweet and lovingly. I was home again.

"But…" he said as he pulled away. I wanted to steal the vomit bucket. "I can't risk being with you at this moment." He touched my cheek. "I don't want anyone to get hurt."

My lungs struggled to take in air. "What do you think you're doing now?"

"I know. But Vanessa is capable of worse. She doesn't care if she hurts me or Reese. Or you. And I'm not talking about broken hearts or bank accounts. Once, she set fire to my bed with me and Reese asleep in it because I gave Reese more attention than her. Reese was two."

"What the fuck?" My ears buzzed.

"That's who she is." His hand shook. "I love you, and I would die if you got hurt because of me. And I mean injured, or worse." His thumb ran along my jaw. "I need to figure this out. I'm working with my lawyer to look at our options. My uncle installed security cameras the other day in case someone comes to the house. It breaks my … everything to do this, but it'll keep us safe. I hope." He sniffled. "God, I hate this."

"So, you're still breaking up with me?" We were both wet-faced.

"Yes." With a kiss to my forehead, he whispered, "I love you. Please let Emma know I love her too. I'll message you later." He stood and left.

CHAPTER TWENTY-FIVE

H e did not message me later. Hours after Ronan left, Vinny drove Emma and me home from the hospital. Maddie texted me that night to let me know she was taking care of Reese after school for the rest of the week. Ronan wanted to make it visible that he and I were no longer together.

It hurt.

So much.

I kept Emma home from school for a few days. I wanted her well enough, physically and mentally, to be among people. There was a part of me that was terrified she and Reese wouldn't be friends with all this crap going on.

Emma, the strong being she was, went back to school after day three. She woke me in the morning. "Daddy, time to get ready for school. And you should work today. And shower. You stink." She climbed into my bed and read me a chapter of *Bunnicula*. Vampire bunnies who drink the juice from vegetables? Yes, please.

We stepped outside as Ronan pulled out of his driveway for work. We made a microsecond of eye contact, and my insides shuddered.

Emma tugged my hand and tore my attention away. "Come on, Daddy." We moped our way to school.

"Okay love-bug," I said when we arrived, "the teacher knows you might still not feel well, so you can call me whenever and I'll be right over to get you."

"Love you, Daddy." She gave me a big bear hug before wandering over to the playground. I watched her and Reese stare at each other before running into each other's arms. Laughing and whispering. It was like watching the sun beaming through the clouds and lighting the world with pure joy.

I released a slow breath that I didn't know I was holding. At least the kids would be okay.

As the school bell rang, and the kids lined up to go inside, a few of the other classroom parents gave me curious looks. Tracey, Jaxeon's mom, walked over and out of the blue gave me a hug. It was awkward. Cheap perfume wafted off her. The hug was a sweet and welcomed gesture.

"Sorry, Wishes," she said, "you two were so cute. It's a shame other people's hate got in your way. Screw Samantha. Jaxeon stopped going to Joey's house ages ago for a reason."

I guess the gossip had already spread. That was what Ronan wanted, right? For everyone to see how heartbroken and alone I was?

Amber, Everest's mom, squeezed my shoulder. "You're a good guy and an amazing dad. He doesn't deserve you if he's not willing to stand up to assholes for you. You deserve a knight in shining armour."

"Thank you," I said.

They walked away and left me standing in a brain fog. I turned to head home and noticed Samantha staring at me, chewing on her nails. Not a smudge of a smirk. She looked downright sick and ashen. She knew this was her fault. Guilt gnawed at her soul, and I hoped it ripped her to shreds.

Vinny sat at my piano, serenading me with goofy, lighthearted songs he knew would make me smile. And they did. I sang along, laughing and sprawled on the floor. Like we did when we were kids. Honestly, if I never dated again but kept Vinny as my best friend, I'd live a happy life. I had hands and toys for adult fun time.

He grabbed a bottle of wine and sat next to me. "I think he's going to come back to you when he gets his ducks in a row and he can assure you things are safe." He took a swig from the bottle.

"What if they never are?" I took a swig, too. "What if he's right and we'll think it's safe and Vanessa is some sort of psycho and has us murdered in our sleep? Did I tell you she lit his bed on fire?"

"You did."

"She lit his fucking bed on fire with him and *Reese* in it. On fire, Vinny." I took another swig. "What if she comes after me and Emma? If she hurts my baby girl, I will break into that prison and murder her."

"I'll seduce the guards to look the other way."

"I've been writing a song about him. Before all that mess. And I think I still want to keep it in our project. Regardless of how things work. It's still a moment in my life I'm capturing." I stared at the wall.

"Can't wait to hear it, buddy. Did you want to play it now?"

I shook my head. "Later. But now, a toast!" I cleared my throat and raised the wine bottle. "To Vanessa! May you never know kindness nor feel pleasure again. May your crotch forever smell like a seafood restaurant dumpster before garbage day. May you walk in the wake of people's vomit as your stench assaults them. May you forever be parched and never feel quenched. May you burp out your farts and never shit again. To you dear *Vanessa*, may your obituary be written in cat piss." I drank to that.

Vinny looked at me, stunned. "Jesus Murphy," he cursed. "Remind me not to cross you."

CHAPTER TWENTY-SIX

I knew it was a nightmare, but the panic was genuine. Police held me as I wailed and fell to my knees on the front yard. Alex was dead, and I was unmade. The lights and sirens of the cop cars split my head open and made it impossible to see. I stood at the scene of the crash. I had dreamt this a thousand times, even though I never saw it in reality. Crushed metal strewn everywhere. Blood poured from the car.

The sirens were so loud. Why were the sirens so loud?

"Alex." My voice was hoarse from yelling over the noise.

He slumped over the steering wheel, and I couldn't see his face. I ran to the car, but never got closer. My muscles burned as I tried to get to him. Smoke tinged my nose hairs.

Fire was new to my nightmare.

"I'm here, baby. Get up." I coughed as the smoke grew thicker.

A firefighter held me back. No matter how hard I fought against him, I couldn't break free. My body went limp in his arms, and lights from the trucks overtook my vision.

My phone rang, and I bolted awake. Two a.m. phone calls were never good. Drenched in sweat, I fumbled for my phone. Ronan. Please don't be dead. Please don't be dead. Please don't be dead. The police officer's voice telling me about Alex at 2 a.m. echoed in my head.

"What's wrong?" my voice shook.

"Can you come over?" His voice warbled. "Leave Emma asleep." He had been crying.

I tumbled down the stairs. "What happened?"

"They vandalized my house, Wishes. I need you to take Reese, please?"

"I'm on my way, my love." I grabbed my puffy coat and slid on my flip-flops. When I stepped outside, police, fire truck, and ambulance lights assaulted my eyes. Fuck. I ran. With ice in my veins, my brain went wild with what horror scene I might find.

Ronan stood in his pyjama pants talking to a police officer. His shoulders rounded over, his hair hung in a tangled mass in front of his face, and his arms hugged his bare torso.

The house, lit from the emergency lights, showed homophobic slurs graffitied all over the front of his house. Words that brought back an onslaught of painful memories. This was another one etched into my trauma bank.

Smoke billowed as firefighters sprayed water on a black smoking patch on the side of the house. A charred shape that was a bush smouldered under the patch. I coughed as I inhaled smoke.

Glass on the driveway and lawn glittered in time with the ambulance light. The glass was once the windows of his house and car. If it weren't so horrible, it would be beautiful.

There was screaming from the ambulance, and I took off towards it.

Reese was melting down and hitting himself in the head. The poor EMTs failed to calm him. I shouldered through them, ignoring their protests. "Hey, whippersnapper, it's me. It's Soda." I took my coat off and padded it around his head, leaving enough space for him to see me. "Look at me. I'm here. I've got you."

The EMTs told me, physically, he was fine, minus the self-inflicted bruises.

He screamed so loud my ears rang. His teeth clamped down on my bare arm. The EMTs almost intervened, but I shooed them off. I pushed my arm forward to open his mouth enough for me to pull my arm out and held him close against me. I got hit, but I didn't care. My safety was second to his mental health at this moment. I know that was not what most people would advise, but fuck it. He needed me, and I didn't care if I had bruises. I kissed the top of his head.

"It's okay, sweetheart. I've got you. You're safe with me. Soda's here." I repeated these over and over until he either calmed down or tired out. My boy slumped against me. "Are the lights too bright for you?" He nodded. I pulled the jacket up around his face. "Do you want to come home with me?" I felt him nod into my chest and I lifted him up.

"Sir, we can't let you take him without his father's permission," an EMT said.

Reese squeezed me tighter.

"So, let's go talk to Ronan." I turned and took in the scene of the crime. A rock formed in my throat. A slur was spray-painted in red across his front door. They'd covered the garage door with dicks and swears. His mailbox lay smashed open on the ground. They'd keyed his car with slurs and the tires were slashed. I couldn't move.

"You're the partner, huh?" the EMT said next to me.

This is my fault. This is my fault. This is my fault. This is my fault.

"No. Sort of? I don't know." My voice cracked.

My feet moved before I realized it, and I strode towards Ronan. Taking his face with my free hand, I pulled him to me, pressing our foreheads together. Our cold breaths danced around us. "Babe, are you okay?" The police gave us a moment of privacy.

"No." He looked like a fraction of the man I know him to be. Lifting the edge of my jacket, he peeked at Reese. "Hey, centre of my universe, are you going home with Wishes?"

"Yeah," a small voice squeaked.

Ronan ducked his head under the coat and kissed the top of Reese's head. I heard them whispering to each other.

"Whippersnapper, can you close your eyes?" I asked. He complied, and I lifted the jacket off him and handed it to Ronan. "You're freezing."

With a tight smile and damp eyes, he slid it on. It was baggy on him and not long enough, but it was warm. I managed to one-arm my shirt off and covered Reese's face. Not caring, I now stood shirtless in the middle of the street, at night, in the cold, in front of the police. Belly, scars, and pasty skin, bared for all to see. Because this fucking kid was worth it. This man was worth it.

"Darling, you'll freeze," Ronan protested.

"I'm going inside in a moment. I'll make some hot chocolate for me and Reese. How does that sound?" Reese hugged me tighter.

"Sir, can we get you to sign a release form saying you're letting him take your child?" The EMT held out a form to Ronan.

Ronan hastily signed it.

"I love you." I touched his face and tried to ignore the violence behind him. His muscles were tight, and his hair smelled of smoke.

He smiled and kissed my palm. "I know. I'll be along, soon enough."

It was hours later when Ronan crawled into bed with Reese and me.

CHAPTER TWENTY-SEVEN

I cleared my schedule for the day and kept the kids home from school. The school had already heard about vandalism. The entire office asked if we were okay when I called in the kids' absences. Principal Davis asked me to tell Ronan if there was anything the school could do for Reese to let her know. That was sweet of her.

I was glad they didn't question why I kept Emma home too. No matter what happened between Ronan and me, I wanted the kids to feel like they could be siblings. Found family is important. It warmed my heart to leave that option open for them to take if they wanted to.

All morning, I went back and forth between the kids at my house and checking on Ronan and bringing thermoses of coffee and food. His uncle, Tim, was over when dawn broke. They'd boarded over the broken windows and started spraying rattle-can paint over the graffiti.

Ronan hadn't let me inside yet. He had never let me inside. I tried not to take it personally, but it felt like there was a secret he was hiding from me. When I brought food and drinks, I stared at the charred and flaking siding. I shuddered, imagining the horrors if the firefighters were too late.

Now I paced my kitchen while preparing lunch for them. Ronan's parents were on their way, so it meant I was making an enormous lunch. Emma and Reese cleared toys from the living room to make space for company.

"Emma?" Reese asked. "Can I have a hug?"

I peeked into the living room to witness Emma hugging him so tight. His little, tear-stained face snotted on her shoulder. She didn't flinch.

"It was so scary," he said. "There was yelling and glass breaking, and I thought they were going to kill us. They said mean things. I didn't understand most of it, but I could tell it wasn't nice. Daddy made me hide in the closet. He grabbed the busted towel rod and ran downstairs. And all I could hear was shouting. And it was so scary."

I scooped them both into my arms, and we all cried.

"I love you Reese," Emma sobbed. "I'm sorry they scared you. I wish I was there to protect you."

Everything in my body numbed. I wish I was there too. It wasn't fair this kid dealt with that. He was the sweetest little boy, and I wasn't there for him or Ronan. This happened because Ronan was with me, and I couldn't protect them.

The front door opened and in walked Ronan and his uncle. Ronan immediately was at our sides. "We're okay, Reese. It's just damage to objects. You and I weren't harmed."

I pulled away to give Ronan and Reese space, then headed into the kitchen while I wiped my eyes off with my sweater sleeve. Leaving wet stains that matched the wet stains the kids had left. Heavy construction boots followed me in.

"Would you like a drink?" I asked Tim.

"Sure. Something hot?"

I put a fresh pot of coffee on and continued to make lunch. This was distraction cooking. My mind needed to be occupied to maintain a speck of calmness. My hands shook as I spread butter on the bread for cucumber finger sandwiches. Tim stole a sandwich, which they were for him. But it set off the symmetry of the plate I had arranged. I made another.

Tim watched me take cookies out of the oven. He reached for one, and I smacked his hand away. "They're hot."

"Yes Dad," he grinned as I set them down to cool. The aroma of chocolate chip cookies filled the kitchen and my urge to eat all the emotions grew.

"You know" — Tim drew a long breath — "I had never seen Ronan as happy as he was when he was with you. Growing up, he was a good kid. Weird, but good. It surprised me when he fell in with the bad kids. I thought he had more sense than that. But teenagers, right? And I mean, my brother wasn't exactly the warmest to Ronan. Steve could be a grade-A buttface. I almost had Ronan move in with me when he was a teen." He chomped on another sandwich, throwing off my symmetry once again. "You made Ronan that good kid again." Tim clasped my shoulder.

"He gained weight, which is great. I hated that he was underweight with the drugs, and then not having money for enough food. And I can see why he gained weight." He gestured to the numerous plates of sandwiches, baked goods, cheese cubes, and veggies. "When I visited him a few weeks ago, the joy that had been missing for years was back." He ruffled his hair. "So, I guess I'm saying, thanks kid, and I'm sorry he messed up with you."

I stared at my kitchen table. Too tired to care about symmetry anymore. "What happened last night was because of me."

"Now, don't you dare think that." Tim squared his shoulders at me. "That Vanessa is batshit crazy."

"Can you prove it was Vanessa?"

"Ronan saw the faces of the lowlifes and he knew them. My security camera caught all their faces clear as day. They were all friends of hers. She somehow orchestrated it from prison. Don't know how, but she did."

I looked at the floor. "Her son was in there. How could she?"

"She doesn't care. She had troubles but refused to get help. Once, some girl flirted with Ronan at a bar, and she slashed the poor girl's tires. Ronan didn't even flirt back. I told you, Vanessa is batshit crazy and we're all better off with her out of our lives. Now, if he can pull his head out of his ass and see he's ruining a great relationship, I'd be happy."

Ronan sheepishly entered the kitchen. "None of this is your fault. He's right. We knew she was planning something. I didn't think she would set our house on fire with us inside. And our poor basement-apartment neighbour." He was so pale. "Then again …." His eyes drifted to a memory.

There was a knock on the door.

"I'll get it," I said and headed for the front door.

I opened the door, expecting … not this. Samantha. A boiling rage fired in my stomach. I stepped outside and closed the door behind me. "What the fuck are you doing here?"

She stepped back, startled. "I brought squares." She held out a paper plate of Nanaimo squares. I didn't move. "I'm here to apologize. For any role I may have played in this."

"Such as?"

"Telling Vanessa about you." She cleared her throat. "I think she targeted my church for her support program because she hoped someone might know Ronan. Otherwise, it's weird, right? She didn't live in this area. Why else would she choose a church in his neighbourhood? I tried —"

Ronan opened the door. "You should not be here."

Samantha sighed and started from the beginning. "She used me for information. We went to high school together, and I remember her being a really nice girl who got caught up in bad things. I felt bad and thought I could help her. She seemed eager to be a better person. I thought it was genuine, but it was just a scam."

"You're not the only one who's fallen prey to her charm," Ronan said.

Samantha nodded. "She was charming. She knew exactly what to say to make me believe her. I thought I was helping her learn from her poor life choices. Then she said weird things about punishing sinners. Not what we teach. At all. She tried to manipulate me into running errands for her and calling strangers. When I said no, she swore at me and called me names."

"That sounds right." Ronan crossed his arms and looked at the ground.

"When I heard noise last night, I knew at once it was her doing. I called the police and scared one hooligan away. And he"— she cleared her throat — "had a Molotov cocktail. I chased him off before he lit it."

I maintained a calm expression, but the idea of tiny Samantha running outside in the cold in her nightgown with her hair in curlers to yell at thugs seemed hilarious to me.

Ronan, on the other hand, paled. "They tried to set more fires?" And I no longer found my visualization amusing.

"I reported it to the police. This morning, I spent hours at the station giving copies of all my interactions with Vanessa. E-mails and phone conversations. My church records our conversations with prisoners. And it came in handy."

She heaved a sigh. "I was wrong." She looked at me. "I watched how you comforted Reese last night. You're obviously a loving person. I was wrong. You two aren't the sinners, it's her." She swallowed. "And, it's me." Her jaw clenched like it was painful for her to say that. "I got swept up in her drama, and she manipulated me. I'm sorry." She lowered her head.

"Come in for a coffee," I said. Ronan opened the door for her.

CHAPTER TWENTY-EIGHT

"**W**hat is *she* doing here?" Emma glared at Samantha.

"She's come to apologize," I said.

"Is she going to tell her spawn of Satan to apologize?" Emma was not backing down.

"Pardon me?" Samantha gasped.

"Why? Did you fart?" Emma sassed back.

"Emma, this isn't how you have a meaningful discussion. Use your mature words," I said.

"Why should I? Joey says the meanest things to us." She listed off all the derogatory names, terms, and slurs Joey had used against them. "Some angel he is."

I turned in shock at Samantha. "How does a seven-year-old know the term 'muff muncher'?" I looked at the kids. "And don't either of you repeat that term until you're adults. And do NOT Google it. I will know if you do." I glared at the kids. "It's not a bad word, just not kid-friendly."

"I don't know what that means." Samantha's mouth opened and closed. "He's really said all that?"

Emma's fists were on her hips. "Yes. He also pulls at his eyelids and makes fun of me."

"Oh Emma, why didn't you tell me?" I knelt next to her.

She shrugged. "I can handle it. You have enough on your plate."

Oh no. My baby girl thought she needed to protect me. This was not good. Time for family therapy again. "No, love-bug, you can always come to me, no matter what. It's my job to listen and help you. I want to be there for you. Did you tell the teacher?"

She shook her head. "Reese was scared he'd get in trouble because he called Joey a neanderthal and an ignoramus."

"Well, he definitely got those insults from you." I heard a smile in Ronan's voice.

"I will talk to Joey. And I will also talk with my husband and my teenage son. They might be who Joey learned those words from." She knelt. "I am sorry for what my son and I have put you through. I plan on making amends, starting now. Do you forgive me?"

"No," Emma said. "In this house, you earn forgiveness. Not just make a promise to change. You have to make change."

"Wise," Samantha said.

I took the squares she brought, which smelled amazing and fueled my urge to emotionally binge, and led Samantha into the kitchen. Ronan made the kids' lunch plates. She eyed my wedding photos with curiosity. When she watched Ronan help Emma make hot chocolate for herself and Reese, a smile spread across her face. I gave Samantha her coffee in the gayest mug in the house, covered in rainbows and unicorns. Alex hated it. I loved it. But it was Emma's favourite.

Samantha smiled awkwardly at the mug but still drank from it. She was out of her element but was trying.

"Words cannot espresso how much it beans to me you're trying to make amends. It means a latte to me," I said, deadpanned to Samantha.

"Wishes," Ronan groaned.

"How did the hipster burn his mouth?" I pressed on. "Because he drank his coffee before it was cool."

It didn't take long for Samantha to laugh and join in the conversation.

Ronan's parents arrived shortly after. His mom was a mess. They drove by the disaster at Ronan's house, and she freaked out. She flung her arms around Ronan's shoulders and cried. "Oh, my baby. My sweet baby."

Even with Ronan standing a good foot taller than her, he became a child in her arms. He drew into his body and looked small and delicate. A boy needing his mama. She swayed him from side to side and whispered in his ear, and child Ronan gripped onto her and cried.

Steve clapped me on my shoulder. "Let's get some coffee in me. Shall we?"

I led him into the kitchen, where I spoiled him with coffee and food.

"Here, I brewed this espresso-ly for you." I handed Steve the biggest mug we had, full of coffee. He belly-laughed.

The kids bounced around him. Reese asked if he brought gifts.

"No time to get anything this visit, but you can have these." Steve produced two toonies. One for him, and one for Emma.

"Did you want to put those in your rooms for safekeeping?" I asked them. "I think Emma has a spare piggy bank you can borrow. We can get you your own later."

Emma grabbed Reese's hand, and they dashed upstairs.

"He has his own room?" Steve asked.

"Sort of. He claimed the guest room. Even decorated it with his artwork. He stays there when he sleeps over."

Tim and Steve exchanged a look, and I pretended not to notice.

"Does that lunch bag have Ronan's name on it?" Steve asked.

I looked at the collection of lunch bags on the counter and saw Ronan's She-Ra bag. "Yup. I make the kids' lunches, so I throw together one for him. Otherwise, he wouldn't eat."

They grinned at each other. I pulled on my sweater sleeves.

"Wishes makes them dinner every weeknight too," Tim said. I didn't tell him that. "That's why he's not wasting away anymore."

I didn't point out that had stopped.

"Reese is looking healthier too," Steve said.

I hated their silent brother speak where they grinned at each other. My cheeks turned red.

If I didn't know better, I would have sworn they robbed Ronan. His house was sparse. Besides the handful of toys, and the stack of bills on the table, you wouldn't know if someone lived here or if it was a low-budget Airbnb.

The old, worn couch had cigarette burns. The TV was cracked in the corner. His wooden dinner table had several notable repairs. The walls were bare except for a few photos.

A photo of him and Reese hung crookedly. Reese's school photos were held with push-pins. And there was a photo of me, him, and the kids. He had taken the selfie with us while we built snowmen in my backyard. A light dusting of snow covered his eyelashes. His cheeks were perfectly rosy. Magnificent. The kids and I were wet and snot-nosed. Great.

"That was the moment I realized I needed you and Emma in my life." Ronan said, standing a good few metres behind me with his arms crossed.

"This was before Christmas," I said.

We heard a crunch of glass and Samantha said, "Don't touch that. You'll hurt yourself."

Emma had reached for a glass shard from a broken window that was strewn across the floor.

"She's right. Why don't you and Reese go play while we clean?"

Reese bounded to me. "Soda, can I show you my room?"

"After we clean up. How does that sound?" I said. I supposed it sounded fine because he bounced away, yanking Emma with him.

Tim quirked an eyebrow. "You've never been here?"

"I preferred we go to his place. We help clean, so we're not a complete nuisance. There's more for the kids to do." Ronan shifted awkwardly, pulling his arms tighter around himself.

"For the kids. Right." Tim grabbed a broom and meandered away.

"You don't like me being here, do you?" I whispered to Ronan.

"It's not a nice place to be." He played with the tip of his ponytail. "The couch is uncomfortable, we don't have a lot of plates, what furniture we have is broken, and I sleep on a shitty twin mattress on the floor. Not a romantic setting. Reese has a proper bed, and toys though. And Emma is taken care of when she's here. We have a great sleeping bag for her that Reese got for Christmas."

I resisted reaching for him. "I know you're taking care of the kids. But who is taking care of you? You should have said something. I could help."

"You've helped enough." He looked small. Turning away, he grabbed a garbage bag and headed towards the mess. He and Samantha went to work throwing out the big shards of glass.

I casually glanced at the bills. Everything was past due. Some were one month, others a couple of months or more. One had five digits in red. That was his lawyer's bill. "Oh babe," I muttered.

He told me he struggled financially. Tim paid for Reese's swimming, and his parents paid for their therapy. But this was worse than I'd thought.

Steve wandered over. "Shit," he said. "He kept this from you, too?"

Ronan stormed over and grabbed the bills. "Do you mind?" He shoved them in a drawer.

"Son," Steve said. There was a sincere concern in his voice.

"No," he scolded us. "Don't start."

Steve bristled. "You don't talk to me like that."

"Steve," I said calmly, "timing. We're here to help. Let's just clean and you can talk about this stuff later when the neighbour isn't here."

They both stomped away in opposite directions to get back to cleaning.

Not being able to take care of Ronan left bill-shaped paper cuts on my heart.

I had brought my cordless vacuum over and searched outside for any remaining broken glass. I had already spent an hour sweeping, and the vacuum got the tiny, fiddly bits. I didn't care I was the crazy guy vacuuming outside in the winter. Nor did I care if my vacuum died. Like hell I'd let either of my boys hurt their tootsies.

I scanned for glass for the millionth time when my eyes fell on the car. My gut twisted. He couldn't afford a new car. Picturing him driving to work with those words around him tore me to pieces.

"I'm returning my vacuum," I yelled to no one. The door was closed. The door which the red slur still bled through the fresh paint.

I dumped the vacuum in my hall and grabbed my car keys. Returning to his house, I walked straight to him. Determined. Determined and sweaty.

"Hold out your hand," I demanded.

"What are you doing?" Ronan squinted at me.

"Do it."

He hesitated before opening his hand.

I dropped my keys in his palm. "It's not a great car, but you're not driving that." I nodded towards the driveway.

"Wishes, you need your car." He held the keys out for me to take back.

I crossed my arms, tucking my hands into my armpits like a child. "No. I work from home. I go out for swim class, therapy, and groceries. And we can taxi, or I drive you to work on those days. Vinny can drive me to rehearsals. He'd prefer that so he can make sure I'm on time."

Ronan opened his mouth to protest.

"No." I threw a tantrum, but I gave zero fucks. "I will not allow you to expose yourself to that depravity every day."

"I'll have it repainted."

Tim snorted. "Your shitbox isn't worth repainting. It would cost more than a new used car."

"I'll rattle can it myself then," Ronan protested, still holding out my keys.

"Really? You think you can do that?" Tim chided him. "It'll look like shit and the scratches will show through if you don't do it right. Besides, all your tires are ruined, that thing isn't moving. Your insurance probably won't cover that since you didn't go for the higher coverage. And if they do, they'll just write off the car and maybe give you a thousand dollars for a new one."

"You can let me buy you a new car," Steve added. It was a genuine offer, but Ronan would hate being more indebted to Steve.

"Or you take my car and deal with it," I said.

His head hung in defeat. "Thank you." He pocketed my keys.

"Wait," I said.

He raised an eyebrow.

"I need my house keys. And the rehearsal hall keys. And Vinny and Katherine's keys. My bike key is on there, but it's in the shed, and I lost the shed key."

His stupid grin made me warm inside.

CHAPTER TWENTY-NINE

It had been four days since the attack, and three days since I'd talked to Ronan. His parents had been in town, and they'd been taking care of Reese after school. So, when Ronan's phone number showed up on my screen after supper while I cleaned the kitchen, my heart jumped everywhere.

"Soda?" A boy sniffled into the phone.

"Reese, hunny, what's wrong?"

"Daddy and Grandpa are having a big fight and I'm scared."

I shoved my feet into my shoes. "On my way." I peeked into the living room. "Emma, I need to run to Ronan's. You stay here. Call me if you need me or call Auntie Katherine. I'll return as soon as I can."

"I want to come too," Emma said.

"Let me see what's going on first. I'll get you if it's a good idea." Before she argued with me, I headed out the door.

I heard yelling from outside, and I swallowed my trauma. With deep breaths, I breathed away the flashbacks of Alex screaming at me. Ronan. I needed to check on Ronan and Reese. No one answered the door when I knocked.

Steve berated Ronan, calling him irresponsible, childish, and falling short of his potential. Ronan yelled, "Shut the fuck up, Dad!"

"Don't you dare speak to me —"

I walked in. They turned to look at me. *Breathe, Wishes.* "Steve? If you'll excuse us, I'd like to talk with Ronan one-on-one, please."

"Al, we're busy," Steve said.

"It's Wishes. And the call I got from a scared little boy, means this conversation is over." I held out my phone that showed Ronan's caller ID, while Reese sniffled on the other end.

Ronan searched his pockets for his phone.

"He'll be fine," Steve said. "He needs to grow"— I covered the mic — "a backbone. Too soft like his dad."

Instead of arguing, Ronan turned and bolted upstairs. I didn't end the call until I heard Ronan soothing Reese.

I stepped closer and swallowed. "Steve, my daughter overheard my husband and me fighting often, and it does not make a kid grow a backbone. It makes them feel unsafe. And kids that have backbones and try to be perfect? It's because they want the adults to stop yelling.

"They cease being kids and become peacekeepers. When they can't keep the peace, they shut down or freak out. I've had this conversation many times with my therapist. Emma had to grow up too fast, and it's not fair. I'm the adult, I should do better. You and Ronan are adults, do better. Not tell him to grow a backbone so you can be a dick to his daddy." I held my head high.

"That's BS," Steve said. "Ronan is too easy on Reese. It's making him weak. My kids were told to behave, and they did."

"And your daughter lives in another province, and your son is recovering from an addiction and an abusive relationship." I couldn't believe I said that. "Ronan and Reese are amazing, and I don't appreciate how you're talking about them."

"This is none of your business, Al," Steve yelled at me and stepped closer. He towered over me. The Jekyll side of him was out in full force.

Keep it together, Wishes. In my calmest voice, I responded, "I care deeply for them, and it is my business." My breathing turned staccato, and my palms were sweaty. "And it's Wishes."

"This"— he gestured to the boarded-over windows — "is because of you, Wishes."

"No. It's not. And you know it. You're looking to blame your anger on someone else, and it won't work." My legs shook.

"If you think you're so perfect, why did he dump you?"

My gut retracted like someone punched me. "I never said I was perfect. I am far from it. We may not be together, but he turns to me when he needs help. I will always be here for him. Couple or not."

"That's what you think?" Steve scowled at me. I hated seeing him use the same eyes as Ronan's against me.

"I'm here, aren't I?"

"Are you so daft that you still love him?"

"Yes." I said with defiance. My stomach churned.

"He's using you as a free, glorified babysitter. You're a pushover and he's taking advantage —"

"Dad, that's enough," Ronan snapped behind me. How long had he been there? "You should go. We'll talk in the morning."

Steve said nothing as he grabbed his jacket and stormed out the door. Slamming it hard enough to make the remaining windows rattle.

Neither of us moved. I stared at Ronan, holding my breath.

"Babe, it's not true," he said. "You were never a glorified babysitter." He rushed to me and pulled me to him in a deep hug, and I buried my face in his shoulder. "I still love you too."

My hands tightened around the fabric of his shirt and clutched him against me. I looked at him and found his blue eyes staring at my lips. Our foreheads touched, and our mouths drew closer.

"I never stopped loving you," he said. His lips brushed against mine as he spoke. "I don't think I'm capable of not loving you."

It was a soft kiss. Full of hesitation. He drew back a hair's width, waiting for my reaction. My lips chased his. I melted into him, shaping my body to his. We were hungry for each other. Starved wolves finding an enormous meal after weeks of famine. Fingers tangled in my hair; his other hand pulled me in at the small of my back.

My hand was cool against his flushed cheek; my other hand found the softness of his skin at his waist. I felt him harden against me and I rocked my hips so he could feel how hard I was. He growled and grabbed my hips, directing my movements. If there wasn't a risk a child could walk in, I'd tear his pants off.

"We should go to your bedroom." I panted between kisses. "I want you to take me."

He ripped away and held me at arm's length. "No. Sorry. I can't." His chest heaved.

"That's okay. I thought you wanted to." My lips pulled tight in a grimace.

"I do, but ...." He stepped out of my reach with his eyes squeezed shut in pain. "I can't be with you."

"Why? I thought maybe ...." I didn't know what I thought.

"Wishes, please don't make this harder than it already is. It's not safe for us to be together. They set my house on fire. What if Vanessa went after you and Emma to punish me? I couldn't live with myself if she attacked you."

That thought had crossed my mind. "I'll get security cameras."

"They're only good if the police can find the bastards. Those assholes are still out there. And who knows what they'll plan next. It's better for us to end it." He stepped further backwards and crossed his arms.

I had had enough of this shit. "I'm not living my life in fear of some dimwitted fuck-ups." My spine straightened. "Fear ruled most of my life. I changed who I was to fit in and protect myself for years. And I'm tired of it. It took me a ton of work to be who I am today, and like fucking hell am I going back to living in fear. Those assholes do not get to take you from me." My fists clenched and unclenched, and my heart shifted into hummingbird mode.

"What if something happens? What if you die? Or Emma? You barely survived Alex dying, you wouldn't survive Emma dying. What makes you think I'd survive either of you dying?" He spat as he raised his voice. "I'm not strong enough for that. And if you died, it would be my fault." He was yelling, and it took everything in my power to not retreat.

"Babe, that will not happen."

"How do you know? You can't promise me that. Things happen. People die." His breathing grew ragged.

I stepped in to touch his arm, wanting to comfort him, but he flinched. His back hit the wall, and he chewed on his hair. Wild and feral, he looked for an escape. My shoulders drooped and I stepped aside, giving him space. I was too familiar with this look on me.

"You're right." My tone was calm and quiet. "I can't promise that. People die. I never expected Alex to die. And it shook my world. But we can't live in constant fear. It gets us nowhere, and it's exhausting. Please believe me when I say this, sweetheart. I'd rather be worried with you, than apart from you." I smiled at him.

A flash of understanding glittered in his eyes, but it switched into a storm. "And that's another thing. Alex. There's no space for me in your life when he's in every conversation."

"That's not true." It was my turn to yell. Why was he set on pushing me away?

"Really? You mentioned him several times tonight alone."

"You're talking about death. That's how I relate to conversations about death."

He crossed his arms again and jutted his hip out to one side. "I can never fit into your life. Alex takes too much space. You're obsessed with him, and I will never be as good as him. He was a dentist and made a ton of money. I'm an underpaid secretary who couldn't hack it as an engineer. He was a fun-loving dad. I work late hours and had to put my son in a shit afterschool program. Alex was this social person everyone loved. I'm a failure at life and people avoid me."

"Where is this coming from? It isn't true." I wiped away a tear. "If you're trying to hurt me, congratulations. Mission accomplished. Can you stop now?"

Silence lingered in the air while he played with the tips of his hair, and I tugged at my sleeves. This sucked.

"I'm sorry," he muttered. "Those were asshole things to say."

"Yeah," I said, "they were. And quit talking so badly about the man I love."

"I know, it's fucked of me to shit on Alex."

"I'm not talking about Alex. I'm talking about you. Stop shitting on you." I glared at him. His eyebrows furrowed and his mouth twitched. "No one gets to talk about you like that, not even you. I don't know what crawled up your ass and died, but this emo tantrum you're throwing has to stop." My head spun, and I sat on the couch. I breathed and looked around. Boxes were stacked at one end of the room. Moving boxes. "What's going on?"

He followed my gaze. "We're moving." His voice was soft and distant, like part of him had already left.

My stomach ached. Now I understood why he was pushing me away. It was easier to leave someone when they hated you.

"My uncle's insurance skyrocketed, and the basement tenant moved out. She's afraid for her life, and we understand. If they hadn't caught the fire in time, it would have trapped her. And neither I nor my uncle can afford me to stay here anymore. He can rent this place out and make decent money. With us, he'll lose money. So, we're moving."

"Where are you going?"

"To my parents'."

My eyebrows raised with my pitch, and my stomach knotted. "That's a couple hours away. What about school? Reese won't be able to finish the year here."

"I know. He's angry at me. I'm angry at me. But we don't have options." He ran his hands through his hair.

My fingers numbed. "When do you leave?"

"This weekend." He couldn't look me in the eye.

"So soon?" My voice cracked. "My concert is Saturday. I want you and Reese to be there. I need you to be there."

He sat next to me and took my hands; they vibrated in mine. "I'll do everything in my power to be there, but there's a lot to do before we take off Sunday morning. I'll make sure Reese is there."

"Please don't go," I begged.

All the anger and hostility melted away from his muscles, and he softened into my beautiful man. He wrapped his arms around me and pulled me into his lap. I breathed him in. He could be mine for a few more minutes. "I have no choice. I can't afford the apartments around here. This will save us money. I could go to college part-time for graphic design." Warm lips pressed into my temple while he rubbed my back. "Babe, I'm sorry."

"So you and I are done? There's no possibility of a compromise?"

He didn't answer. Didn't need to. Instead, he squeezed me tighter than he'd ever hugged me and pressed his face into my sweatshirt. That was my answer, and I hated it.

"Can we try long distance?" I quivered. "I could visit on weekends with Emma."

"My parents don't like having guests in their space all the time. They're not those kinds of people. And after I give you your car back, I won't have a way down."

"Train?"

"Wishes, I can't do long distance. It's going to hurt to not be able to touch you. And I don't want to keep you from moving on."

"I don't want anyone else. We can figure something out. Think about it?"

Tears dampened my sweater, and I knew it was truly over. Done. Finale.

The numbness in my fingers spread to the rest of my body.

We cuddled, covered in tears and snot, for a while. Emma opened the front door and snapped us out of our pity party.

"Love-bug, you okay?" I slid off Ronan's lap and went to her.

"I got worried."

Ronan got Reese, and we had a little family chat about the move. Emma did not take it well. I hadn't seen her cry that hard in months. We ordered food and watched movies until the kids' bedtime. It hurt to leave.

CHAPTER THIRTY

My ass was sore from sitting on the basement floor, staring at the boxes labelled "Alex's." There were big decisions to make, and I wasn't sure if I had the strength.

"I am lost, love. It's weird coming to my dead husband for relationship advice, but here I am. I wonder if you're listening, if you can listen, or maybe you don't want me to move on, and ...." I stared at the unfinished ceiling. "Fuck. I wish I could talk to you."

I closed my eyes and breathed in. Alex's spicy cologne filled my lungs.

What do you want, my prince? Alex's voice was smooth and soothing in my ear. It didn't startle me, rather I relaxed into it, like I did when I fit myself snugly in his arms.

"I want him to stay. To wake next to him and have Saturday morning breakfast with him and the kids. Kiss him in the morning as he takes the kids to school. I want to sleep with him curled around me while I nestle safely against him."

Did you feel safe with me?

"Most of the time, but not when you drank. But you knew that."

I'm sorry, baby. I fucked up. It hurts that I can never fix my mistakes or beg for forgiveness. I was the worst husband sometimes. You know I loved you, even when I was an asshole.

"I know. And I forgave you ages ago."

Does he ever hurt you? A shadow of cool fingers caressed my cheek.

"Not like you did. It's the denial of me that hurts. And telling me he loves me but can't be with me."

When you picture your life, five years down the road, what do you see?

"I see me and Ronan dealing with pre-teens together as a family." My head tingled as if Alex ran his fingers through my hair.

When you think about those boxes of mine, what do you feel?

"Sad. You had a lot of crap, and I can't bring myself to get rid of anything, I don't want to let you go."

You wouldn't be letting me go if you got rid of that Montreal Canadiens jersey. That was a gag gift from Vinny. Leafs forever, dude. Hell, if I could poltergeist myself, I'd burn it. There are things worth getting rid of. Things I should have Marie Kondoed ages ago. Nothing in those boxes is me. They don't make me more remembered or less dead. Wishes, you can create space for him in your world and still remember me. You know what you want. Do it. Take it from me, my dude. Don't squander your time because you're afraid to face your grief. I was afraid to face myself and look where it led me.

Emma won't hear me holler "that's my girl" at her graduation and embarrass her in front of her friends. I had signs planned and everything. Big neon orange ones. Amma and I planned to take out a full-page announcement in the local Korean newspaper.

You can be there for Reese's graduation if you let it happen.

I am giving you permission to move on. Live a beautiful life, my beautiful prince. That is what will bring me joy. I love you, and I am cheering for you.

A breeze blew across my lips. "I love you too."

Did I converse with Alex? Or was this a stress delusion? Mental breakdown? Regardless, it was fantastic to hear his voice. Even if it wasn't real. A powerful golden light flooded my heart.

I stood, walked to the boxes, and started sorting between keep, get rid of, and ask Emma if she wanted it. When I found the Montreal Canadiens hockey jersey, I made my way to the backyard with a metal pot and set the jersey on fire.

Suck it Habs! Go Leafs!

Aloysius

Hey, can we talk? Before you leave?
I have to run to rehearsal right now, but after the show?

Ronan

I'll see what I can do.

CHAPTER THIRTY-ONE

"Good evening, and thank you for coming," Vinny spoke into his microphone as the applause lowered. Vinny and I wore swallow-tail tuxes. My curly hair glowed almost as much as my face. Katherine had spread a layer of foundation on me that was a shade darker, so no one mistook me for the theatre's ghost under these lights. Vinny had slicked his hair back into a dapper swoop that felt like a helmet of hair gel.

We stood on the stage of a small concert hall. Behind us sat three accompanying musicians, two violinists, and a cellist, along with my acoustic guitar, and, most important, two sexy, black, grand pianos.

The bright lights obscured my vision and hid the few hundred people in the audience from me. In the front row, I saw the kids, Ronan's parents and uncle, my in-laws, Katherine, and Maddie. The seat I saved for Ronan remained empty. I ignored the pain in my gut and smiled.

"My name is Vincent MacDonald, and this is Aloysius O'Connor." I inclined my head. "And today we are proud to play for you a mix of traditional classical music, original classical pieces, as well as a few contemporary pieces. Which is a strange, unfamiliar territory for us." Vinny looked at me. "It's been a strange year."

"Many of you have followed Vincent and me for years," I continued into my mic. On stage, I was a natural. Not nervous. Not an introverted wreck. Confidence and ease rolled off me. "A few of you may even remember our first concert when we were in high school. Where we were awkward, nerdy, weirdos ...." I looked at Vinny and cleared my throat. "I guess some things never change." I got a few laughs.

Pause. Don't rush, Wishes. "I cannot impress upon you enough how honoured we are that you are here with us today. This concert, and album, have been a project of love and healing. As many here know, my husband passed away a year and a half ago, and this album played a major role in my recovery. Our recovery." I nodded at Vinny. "And it brings me great joy to return to the piano benches. I am incredibly proud and excited to share our new music with you. We truly believe this is our best work yet." I looked at Vinny.

"Yes," he continued, "thank you for choosing to support us on this special day. You, our audience, fans, family, and friends have been a blessing." He bowed to the audience in thanks. "And without further ado, let's get started."

I was about to announce our first piece when he cut me off.

"And what a start it is. We have a surprise guest to open the show for us." Vinny gave me a sly grin. I gave him the WTF look. "Our guest is a beginner musician. Since January, he has been secretly taking piano lessons from me in order to impress his special someone."

I stared wide-eyed at Vinny. What was he thinking doing this without consulting me first? We didn't do this kind of stuff. I had not included this in my fine-tuned time schedule.

Vinny winked at me. "Please give a warm welcome to Ronan Decker." He gestured to the side of the stage behind me.

I gasped and my hands clasped over my mouth while I turned to see Ronan step into the light with caution. The crowd clapped and awed. Ronan wore a tuxedo, eyeliner, and had his hair pulled back in a messy bun. Escaped strands framed his jawline. He was stunning. A fucking god.

Ronan gave me a little wave and stepped closer to the piano before he looked at the audience. The colour drained from his cheeks. Vinny walked over to him, took his hand, and led him to the piano while he whispered something in his ear. Vinny set out his sheet music for him while he sat.

His eyes flicked between me and the music. I stood at the curve of the piano and leaned on it to watch him. I don't think I stopped beaming. This was the most romantic thing anyone had ever done for me.

He raised his fingers to the keys, and the poor thing was shaking.

"That's my dad!" Reese shouted. "Go Dad!"

Ronan smiled and played a beginner version of Pachelbel's Canon. I decided it was no longer the piece I loathed as couples requested it for every wedding I had played at, but now it was my favourite. The crowd disappeared, and all I saw was him. And for the love of all beings sacred and horny, he was gorgeous and drove me to imagine many naughty acts. My loins felt things I shouldn't feel on stage in these tight pants.

With a frown of concentration, he hit the notes. I could see him counting the beats to himself. His fingers stumbled, and he hit two keys at once. He looked at me with terror.

I smiled in awe at him. "Sweetheart, you're doing amazing."

He blushed, and Vinny helped him recover. The piece was short. Maybe two minutes, but they were a beautiful two minutes. When the last notes ended, the audience cheered. They didn't care he was a beginner; they knew they had witnessed one of the sweetest gestures ever.

He stepped away from the piano, and I flung my arms around his shoulders. "That was fantastic. You did this for me?"

He kissed me, and my world got brighter. "I love you, and I wanted to show you how special you are to me. I want us to work and try long distance."

"Ronan, I love you too." We kissed again. "But I don't want to do long distance. Move in with me."

Ronan held me at arm's length. "What?"

"I'm serious. You're already packed. Move in with me."

He shifted nervously from foot to foot and glanced at the audience, who were muttering and waiting for an answer. "You're for real. What happened to taking things glacially slow?"

"If I take it too slow, I'd let you slip away, and I can't do that." My fists tightened around his tux jacket.

He gnawed on his lower lip in thought and searched my face for answers.

"Ask him to marry you!" Katherine shouted from the front row.

There were shouts of encouragement from the audience members and whisperings of "Oh my god, he's going to do it, he's going to propose!"

I shot Katherine a "seriously?" look. But when I turned to Ronan, he slid a foot behind him. His muscles tightened as he prepared to get on one knee. Internally, my organs freaked out; externally my eyebrows raised, and I wore a lopsided smile. Was this happening? I asked him to move in, and we were upping the ante? Was I ready for marriage? This was way too fast. Right? We hadn't even had sex. Not a requirement for marriage, but damn, I wanted Ronan to take me. Why was I thinking about sex now? He was proposing to me, and I was losing my mind.

He stepped forward and kissed my cheek. "We'll talk later," he said. "Knock 'em dead." He did a hard turn on his heel and sprinted off stage.

That was not a proposal. And I was genuinely disappointed. Wow, I was sad he didn't ask me to marry him and that was something interesting to note.

Vinny spoke into his mic. "Once again everyone, Ronan Decker." Another round of applause.

I leaned into my microphone and giggled. "I'm his special someone."

"I think they got that," Vinny said. But I couldn't stop stupid grinning. I watched Ronan take his seat. "Now we return to our program. That is if Aloysius can pull himself together."

I tittered into the mic as I blushed. The audience found it amusing, at least. "I'm good." My voice was high and squeaky. I cleared my throat. "I mean, I'm good," I said in a deeper, more masculine voice. Then tittered again. Damn it.

Vinny rolled his eyes and spun around to his piano. I followed suit and sat at my piano. The moment I sat, a still zen washed over me, and I was no longer a giggling fool. I took a deep breath, raised my fingers, and locked my gaze on Vinny. He silently counted us in, and we broke into the most complicated duet we'd ever composed or played.

Our fingers flew across a wide range of keys. Vinny and I watched each other, giving each other cues and silent directions. I understood why people thought Vinny and I were a couple. We were both animated players. The kind that didn't sit still and lifted off their bench when playing something grand and dramatic. When you stared at someone as we did each other while playing passionately, it looked like we were banging.

"Eye fucking," Katherine called it.

This composition swelled with cascades of emotions. Devastation, anger, hurt, and affection. It represented what Vinny and I went through together these past few years. Not focusing on events, but, specifically our relationship. Complicated and beautiful. This piece lasted ten minutes, and I was sweating by the end.

The crowd loved it. Ronan whooped. It was amazing to garner that kind of response. Releasing this song into the wilds gave me a sense of calm. People heard our story and appreciated it.

We stood and bowed. I moved to offstage to drink water while Vinny did a sonata with a violinist. A slow and flowing piece. It turned out to be Emma's favourite of tonight's concert. Of course, her favourite would be one I wasn't in.

Vinny and I performed solos, duets with each other or the other players, and ensemble pieces until the last number before intermission. I pulled out my acoustic guitar, double-checked its tuning, and approached the mic.

"Here's a pesky contemporary song we warned you about." I smiled. "Many people seem surprised to learn I play guitar. But I do, I'm not that pick-y of a musician." I held up my pick. Ronan facepalmed in embarrassment for me. That spurred me on. "I have several guitars in my studio. The one I struggle to play the most was one I got for free. It came with no strings attached." A small moan came from the audience. "But it's true I like to play guitar. They strike a chord with me."

"Wishes," Vinny warned me from behind. "Guitar-n with it."

"Fine. I didn't mean to o-Fender you."

"Stop it," Katherine yelled.

I smiled more. "Okay." I raised my palms to surrender. "I wrote this song a few months ago. It's about a guy." I cleared my throat. "I bet you'll never guess who he is." There were quiet chuckles from the audience. "Anyway. He doesn't know this song exists, so it's payback time." I glanced at Vinny, and he nodded, ready to back me up on piano.

Kid's plays and lazy days,
Gingerbread,
and books to be read
Your smile sets my world ablaze
I have become your awkward redhead

Ooo those big blue eyes looking at me.
Make me melt inside and yearn to be free,
of those chains inside my mind,
holding me back.
Holding me back.

But I know with you, day by day,
these chains will melt away.
In your arms, my heart mends.
So, I can be always yours.
Be always yours.

And when you're feeling alone,
I'll meet you under the pine cones.
With a basic latte and warm mittens,
I'll wait for you,
under the pine cones.

Ooo those big blue eyes looking at me.
Make me melt inside and yearn to be free,
of those chains inside my mind,
holding me back.
Holding me back.

They can't hold my back anymore.

Because
Kid's plays and lazy days
Gingerbread,
and books to be read.
Your smile sets my world ablaze.
And I'm yours.
I am yours.

I paused and waited for the guitar to stop ringing before I said "Thank you" into the mic. The audience clapped. But it was Ronan wiping away tears that made me proud of my song. He blew me a kiss. It took everything in my power to not mime catching it in the air and putting it on my cheek.

Vinny announced intermission, and I was grateful. I had to pee. Vinny and I bowed and disappeared backstage. I beelined for the bathroom. When I exited the washroom, Ronan was waiting for me.

Neither of us said a word. He cupped the back of my head and kissed me hard. His minty tongue slipped between my lips and tasted me. I grabbed his hand and yanked him into our small dressing room, where Vinny sat in a chair, drinking water.

"Should I leave?" He looked between us.

Desperation for each other radiated in our faces.

"Nope," I said. Ronan shot me a bewildered look. "We'll be in here." I opened the tiny, cedar-scented storage room and pulled Ronan in.

"You know I'll be able to hear everything," Vinny said. He was right. Stupid thin walls.

"Meh, don't care," I said. It was true. Vinny had heard it all from me and had done it all with me.

"You sure?" Ronan asked me.

"I'm okay if you are."

He pounced on me. Kissing me rough and hard. I fiddled with his pants, but he took my hands and pulled them away from his body. "No," he growled. "I'm going down on you. I want to eat you whole and suck you so hard, you won't be able to tell the difference between Brahms and Bach anymore." He nipped at my ear. "Plus, you turn red easily. I don't want you going on stage looking like you ate dick."

Valid point. "Shut up and blow."

A vicious smile spread, and his teeth glowed in the dim lights. He shoved me against a wall that curved under my weight. He followed through on his word. His hot mouth on me put me in an alternative dimension as I left my body. I tried to rein in my vocalizations, for Vinny's sake, but the moans did not want to be contained. That thing he did with his tongue? Dear lord have mercy. I flailed and knocked over a broom, and cried his name as I came in his beautiful mouth. For someone not experienced in this, he sure did a superb job. My legs were jelly, and he had to hold me. He petted my head as I regained my breath.

I had little time to recover before I needed to return to the performance. I re-dressed and stepped into the dressing room. Ronan came out, straightening his bowtie.

Vinny still sat in the chair, but now with his legs crossed. "Well. I feel awkward, aroused, and confused. Perfect combination for performing in a concert. Thanks." Vinny walked over to me and fixed my shirt and tie. "You good?"

I giggled.

"You're good." He kissed my cheek.

The second half of the show went amazing; our finale earned us a standing ovation. We took photos with fans and sold and autographed many CDs and prints of our cover. It was an artistic photo of Vinny and me that Katherine had arranged. I'll admit, we looked hot.

When the crowd cleared out, we could breathe. Hyunji hugged me. "I'm so proud of you, son. You did amazing."

"Thanks, Mom." I kissed her cheek.

"That was excellent." Ronan's mom hugged me. "Thank you for inviting us."

I shook Steve's hand. "Thank you both for coming. It means a lot to me to have you here." Ronan's dad smiled and nodded. I could see the guilt in his eyes over our last interaction.

I bit my lip and dropped my voice for only Steve to hear. "You'll notice my parents aren't here. There's no hope for my relationship with them to be fixed. I can tell you care about Ronan. You have the chance to fix things with him, and I think he'd like that. I know Reese would."

Steve pursed his lips in thought and looked over at his son, laughing with his grandson.

"You really love him, don't you?" Ellen asked me as she put a loving hand on my shoulder.

"I do." I blushed and looked at the floor.

"Ellen and I," Hyunji broke into our moment, "decided we should go out for dinner together before I take the kids home with us."

"That sounds great," I said.

"Vinny and Katherine, you are coming. And Maddie, you too. I have reservations, and they start in twenty minutes." Hyunji clapped and gave us orders.

Ronan stepped into my ear. "She's taking the kids?"

I smirked at my handsome man. "Yup. I got us an overnight babysitter." I leaned in closer and whispered, "I think we need to chat and continue what we were doing in the dressing room."

This time, Ronan squeaked.

Of course, Hyunji picked a fancy restaurant. But I didn't worry. The kids were on their best behaviour since they had grandparents, aunts, and uncles to dote on them. There was much cheers-ing of Vinny and me, and several congratulatory bouquets of flowers. Maddie had brought one for Ronan.

The success of this project got me excited about the future of my career. I already had ideas for my next project.

Hyunji got a server to take a group photo of everyone. She clutched her chest as she looked at it. "Such a beautiful family."

And we were.

CHAPTER THIRTY-TWO

W e stepped out of the shower, lips barely leaving each other. He chased me naked across the hall into my bedroom. I dived for the bed, expecting him to pounce on me, but he didn't. I flipped over to see him standing at the foot of the bed, licking his lips and looking me over. In an effort to be sexy, I sprawled like a woman reclining on a daybed in those old nude paintings. I pouted, and my red curls circled my head in a halo of fire. At least, that was how I imagined myself. I probably looked like an awkward potato with indigestion and a wet mop for hair. Regardless, he liked what he saw.

I liked what I saw. The curves where his waist met his hips drove me wild. I yearned to touch the valleys of his V lines. Soft and swooping. His arms and shoulders were strong and rippled as he moved. But what I loved the most about Ronan were his eyes and how they displayed his emotions. With a simple look, he showed me how much he cherished me, and that he wanted a future together. I saw him lusting after me, wanting me.

And his hair. I obsessed over his hair.

He knelt at the foot of the bed and rubbed my feet. I let my head drop back and grunted.

"Does this hurt?"

"No. It's amazing."

I closed my eyes and relaxed. His hands crept along my calves, rubbing the tendons as they journeyed to my thighs, and teasingly close to my sensitive bits. The heat of his hand hovering over me caused me to tingle. I wriggled in anticipation. Nothing.

"Flip over."

He allowed me space, and I obliged. He straddled my thighs and nipped my neck before reaching into the side drawer for my citrus-scented massage oil. Oh my. I was keen on where this was leading. His grip was firm on my neck muscles. I tried not to sound like a seal having an orgasm, but I'm pretty sure that was how I sounded.

"Your poor shoulders are tight."

"Pianist," I said into my pillow.

"Penis? How does your penis cause you shoulder pain? You know what? I don't want to know."

I lifted my head. "Pianist. Pi-AN-ist."

"Aww, my professional penis is grumpy."

I tried to buck him off, but his thighs held on tight, and I was too oily.

"Darling, are you trying to attack me?"

"No." I bucked again. "Yes."

He poured oil between my hips and his thighs. I had zero traction, and I smelled like an orange-juice factory. He roared with laughter as I wriggled pathetically.

"It's okay, my little pianist. You won't hurt me. Your Bach is worse than your bite."

I glanced over my shoulder. "I fucking love you."

"What else do you fucking love?" he slid his oiled hand between my thighs and explored my reactions to his touch.

I gave him big reactions. "That." I arched my spine.

He sat on his haunches. I turned to find an unfamiliar look on his face. Not a happy, sexy look. His brows furrowed, and he chewed on the inside of his cheeks.

"What's wrong?" I propped myself on one hand and rested the other on his hip. He was lost in thought. I allowed him time to figure it out, but after a few minutes, a chill crept under my skin. "Babe? You alright?"

"I think so." His voice was quiet.

I tucked his hair behind his ear. "What's going on?"

"I've never had sex with a guy before, and I'm afraid to make a mistake. What if I don't enjoy it?" His arms tightened around himself, and he leaned away.

Shuffling into a proper sit, I pulled him to me. "We don't have to if you're not ready. I'm happy cuddling with you. I'm the last person to judge needing time. Hell, if you never want to have sex, I'm fine with that."

"Darling, I want to. But I'm unsure about ... things. I've read articles and watched porn. A lot of porn. But that's different from real life. And we never talked about this." He turned scarlet from head to toe, and he couldn't look me in the eye.

I had never seen him so flustered, and it was adorable. I wanted to squish him. So I did. He laughed and relaxed into my arms. "So, let's talk, sweetheart. What are you wondering?"

He bit his lip, then took a deep breath. "Do you prefer top or bottom?" He pursed his lips, as if he'd get in trouble for asking.

"There's no need to worry about asking me those kinds of questions. I'm glad you asked." My knuckles grazed his stubble. "I'm a vers. I enjoy both. It depends on what my partner wants as well. What do you think you'd take delight in?"

He squirmed in my arms. "Both? But I'm nervous. No one has ... I haven't even touched my own ...." He hid in the crook of my neck. "I can't believe I'm acting this way."

I pressed my lips to his forehead and stroked his hair. "Tell you what, we'll remove sex from the table for this moment. We play, explore, and figure out how each other's bodies work. If you choose to have sex, then we will. And it's your decision if you top, or bottom, or both. And you can ask me to do something to you, or let you try something with me."

He lifted his head. "Okay."

"Ronan Decker, I adore you and I trust you. I promise to tell you if I'm uncomfortable with something. Vice versa. If you have to stop something, that's fine. We've got water and snacks if you need a break. I've got you, babe."

He kissed me, raw and passionate. I fell back against the mattress and latched my legs around his waist. One of his hands slid between my legs and explored. I moaned into his mouth. He pulled away to reveal a mischievous twinkle in his eye before his mouth went on a pilgrimage along my treasure trail.

Our mouths and fingers explored each other's bodies. Every nook and cranny. Exhilarating, relaxing, and one hundred percent fun. Making him quiver in my palms was my new favourite hobby. It surprised me how easily he directed me, and how much I enjoyed being directed.

"Use your teeth," he said when I played with his nipples. "Harder," he moaned, so I bit harder.

"Yes, that," he said when I massaged between his thighs.

And "please," he said as my tongue circled his asshole. "I need your fingers inside me."

I grabbed the lube and massaged the area to get his body to relax and let me in. This was the first time someone had done this for him, and I was honoured he was allowing me to do it. I showed him my devotion and care to pleasure him. I was cautious, used a superfluous amount of lube, and checked with him in often.

His muscles relaxed, and I introduced him to the world of the prostate. It was intoxicating touching him from the inside. A new intimate connection that he gave me the power over. He tightened and released around my fingers as I played with pressure and movement. "You're doing so good, babe," I said. I was near climaxing myself from watching him squirm, gasp, and jolt from my strokes.

My name on his lips while in ecstasy was a beautiful thing. His cries were sweeter than any song I had ever heard. Cum splattered his stomach. This moment etched itself into my memory, and I knew I would call upon it often at night.

I finished myself off on him, mixing our fluids.

With hazy vision full of stars and dopamine, his head lulled onto the pillow. "Why did I wait so long to try that? Wow." His smile was languid.

I gave him water and a cookie, washed us off with a damp cloth, and nestled next to him. My head rested on his chest and listened to his heart.

"Darling?" he asked.

"Yeah?" I ran my fingers over his stomach.

"Do you really want me to move in with you?"

I looked him in the eyes and said, "Absolutely. One hundred percent. I made room in the basement for you to store things as you unpack. We could finish the basement and build an office for you, or a playroom for the kids, or both. Maybe a new guest room." I scratched my arm. "I got rid of several boxes of Alex's things."

"You did?" He sat.

"I want you to live here and make space for you. This will be your home. Not Alex's. And I recognize you're worried about those assholes out there, so your uncle is installing a security system next week."

"For real?" There was a spark, followed by a cloud. "I can't contribute a ton to the mortgage."

"Ronan, stop. There is no mortgage. Alex's life insurance paid for the house outright. And I'm not charging you rent when there's no mortgage." I touched his jaw. "Reese won't have to change schools, the kids will have each other, you won't have to deal with your dad, and you'd have a cute boyfriend to kiss every day."

"I don't want to take advantage of you."

"Sweetheart, you won't be. Picture it: we'd start every day together, go on family outings on weekends. Have a shit ton of mind-blowing sex. And consider all the books we could read to each other."

He chewed his lip. "What about Emma?"

"She's on board. We talked. She would flip if you and Reese were to live with us, but you'd have to promise to be open and proud of us. It may take a while for you to convince her you won't leave her again."

He stared at the rumpled bedsheets. "I feel horrible about what I put her through during all this. I will make it up to her."

A match lit in my stomach.

"Are you planning on making it up to her while you're living with us?" My voice warbled.

His face made many slight changes as he thought things through. Concern, worry, hope. I saw hope. I was going to explode, yell, and cry while I waited for his answer. My fingers twitched to pull at my sleeves for comfort, but being naked I had no sleeves to tug. I touched my scars instead.

He looked at me. "Yes. I want to live with you."

I forgot how my body worked and my brain glitched into the blue screen of death and the system crash tone rang in my ears.

"Honestly, I feel safer knowing you'll be there for me and help me raise my son. Reese'll be ecstatic. He rambles on about how great you are all the time. And I couldn't ask for a better kid to add into my life than Emma. It would be an honour to be a part of her upbringing. Our own strange family."

There was that system crashing noise again.

"Darling? Are you alright? Are you sure you want me to move in?"

"Yes." I regained control of my body. "So much yes." My cheeks hurt from my giant grin.

He laughed. "How about tomorrow?"

"I believe I can clear my schedule." I threw myself into his arms and giggled. The lit match in my stomach grew into a glowing blaze.

I kissed him deep, sealing the deal. Our mouths grew frantic and impatient. His hands roamed my skin while I clung onto him. He pulled me into his lap and showed my body the attention it craved from him.

Ronan's voice softened. I stilled to give him my undivided attention. "I wish to touch you and give you carnal bliss. My body craves yours. I want your ass to grip onto me. I yearn to make you writhe under me and watch you come undone. Show me who you are, unrestrained, and abandon all your walls.

"I want to be greedy and elicit your body to vibrate against me over and over." His breath hitched. "I want to show you what it means for me to worship you."

"Show me," I choked out.

He grabbed lube and a condom off the nightstand and laid me on my back. His hand explored my genitals. I gasped and spread my knees apart automatically, being vulnerable to him. He kissed me feverishly, and I arched into him. I gave him all control, put my complete trust in him, and allowed him to take me.

My breathing became ragged as he touched me in ways that forced me to break into a cold sweat. I walked him through the steps of preparation. He was a diligent student, eager to please, and slid his fingers inside me and teased. He smirked when he discovered what movements caused me to gasp and twitch. I almost didn't want to stop this, almost.

Shifting his body, he positioned himself. He raised his eyebrows. "You sure?"

"Fuck me." I hooked my legs behind him and pulled him close.

His pupils dilated when he entered me, slow and careful, as my ass let him in deeper. I absorbed his high.

We kissed tenderly while he experimented with rhythm, movement, and position. He stayed close in kissing range. Our sweaty, oily stomachs stuck to each other and made funny noises. I tried not to giggle, but he did, so I lost it. My laughter gave way to a moan when an intense pulsation of pleasure hit me. I nipped at his shoulder. His concentration intensified. He was getting into his head. I broke him out by running my nails along his scalp, causing goosebumps to explode on his neck and chest.

He laced his fingers into mine and pressed them into to the pillow while he moved inside me. I wailed and screamed with elation. It was nice not to censor myself out of fear of traumatizing my child. Loud sex was an enormous turn-on for me. It amplified the eroticism. The louder I was, the more our sweet lovemaking turned into a good, hard fuck. He gave in to his urges and roared.

I definitely needed to soundproof this room.

Heat and static swelled in my body. "I love you." My ass tightened around him, and my nether regions pulsed. With curled toes, my legs pulled him closer to me. I closed my eyes tight and grunted. Not sexy, but I was no longer in control of the noises I produced.

"I love you too." He bit the soft skin of my neck while his hips rocked against me.

His name broke through my lips in a cracking cry out. "I'm —" I whimpered.

He watched me hit ecstasy and spill onto my stomach. I saw the fascination, lust, and affection in his eyes as he memorized this scene. My muscles pulsated, and I forgot to breathe. My fists gripped the bedsheets while body contorted, and I ripped the fitted sheet off the mattress. I arched like I was possessed.

His jaw clenched, and he turned beet red. With desperation, he pushed his mouth onto mine and wrapped his fingers in my red curls. Tugging and making me buck with enjoyment. My semen spread to his stomach with his undulations.

"Wishes," he groaned, and it was glorious. He watched me writhe as he pumped his final thrust.

With glazed-over eyes, he went off-kilter and lost strength. I grabbed him and held on. His breathing was rough. "Breathe, sweetheart. Slow it down." I said as I lowered him to lie on top of me.

"Was that acceptable?" His voice wavered.

"My love, that was amazing." I held him tight. "How was your first foray into anal sex?"

"Meh." He smirked at me. "I may require more practice."

"I offer you my services as a private tutor."

The post-coitus glow made my entire being tingle. Ronan nuzzled my neck and held me with worn-out, shaky arms. I ran my hands through his now sweat-damp hair and kissed the top of his head.

My room reeked of sex. It was awesome.

As mind-blowing as sex was with him, the one time we did it, it was these moments I craved. Raw intimacy, bearing the essence of who we are. My breath quivered and I willed myself not to cry.

In my mind, I felt him collect fragments of my broken mind and shattered heart and gently fit them back where they belonged. Using touch to glue the pieces in place and tie them together with brightly coloured ribbons that said, "I love you so fucking much."

I hoped I helped him heal and that he knew I would never abandon him, and I would always treat him with devotion and respect.

My little, former ass virgin passed out hard on me, and I was in heaven.

CHAPTER THIRTY-THREE

In the sleepy haze of the morning, with my eyes closed, Ronan wrapped his arms around me and curled into my back. His skin was warm against mine. I melted into him and hummed happily. Skin-to-skin contact helped quiet my mind. It had been a long time since I'd slept naked next to someone. In fact, I didn't sleep naked alone anymore. Not with Emma around. She still doesn't wait for a reply after she knocks on the door. Too many close calls for my comfort. Now I wanted to lie naked with Ronan every night. I would have to install a lock.

He kissed my shoulder, and a small smile crossed my lips.

"I knew you weren't asleep." Ronan's voice was gravelly. Dark hair tickled my arm as he loomed over me.

"Shh, sleeping," I mumbled, and my smile deepened. "We're kid-free. Sleep is needed."

"There are other things we can do to take advantage of being kid-free." I heard the sly grin in his voice. His fingers drew light pictures on my stomach, and I tried not to giggle. I failed.

"You're right," I said. "I could wash the windows in Emma's room. I swear she puts glue on her hands and touches the windows as a hobby."

"Well, if you want to wash windows, or doze, I won't stop you." He raised his fingers to my chin and turned it slightly.

I shifted my body and looked at him. The morning sun caused me to squint and blink away the sleep until he came into view clearly. He was so damn beautiful.

"Or I can offer another suggestion?" His voice was sultry and seductive. An aphrodisiac on its own.

"Get dressed and go to the moving van so we can move you into *our* house before your dad barges in on us to find you?"

"Oh shit. Right." He glanced at the clock. "We got thirty minutes." He kissed me and we had our first quickie.

After I called Hyunji and told her to let the kids sleep in and we would pick them up later in the day, we met Steve outside of Ronan's house. Old house. He looked grumpy and impatient. Tim, on the other hand, was clearly a morning person.

"Hello, you lovebirds," he said. "Are we making a two-second drive or a two-hour drive to your new abode?"

I watched Ronan with anticipation. I knew the answer, but I wanted to hear him tell the others. He smiled and took my hand. "It's a two-second drive."

My heart fluttered, and I beamed.

"Fantastic," Tim said. "Glad to keep you near me." He clapped Ronan on the shoulder.

"Alright," Steve said. "If that will make you happy, I'll start the van. Just remember, we're only a couple hours away if you need us." He gave me a look of "See, I'm trying."

Unloading the van didn't take long with Ronan, Steve, Tim, Ellen, and me all traipsing to and from the vehicle. There wasn't a lot of furniture, as Ronan deemed most of it garbage and had planned on using his parents' anyway. Ronan directed what boxes went where. I requested to be the one to bring the boxes for *our*

267

bedroom, which was currently a den of sin and stank of sex. And none of us needed his family to experience that.

By the end, we had neat little piles of boxes throughout *our* home and a few placed in the basement to deal with later. I suggested ordering delivery for lunch, but Steve muttered about "Hitting the road soon."

Tim said he needed to go, but he'd check on us later.

"Well Ronan," Ellen took his hands. "I guess we're leaving." Her eyes dampened. "I don't know why I'm so emotional. I was excited for you and Reese to live with us, but I'm happy you and Wishes are together again. And this is a lovely house. Perfect for a seven-year-old to run around in."

She kissed Ronan's cheek, then mine. "Take care of him."

"I will," I said.

We said our goodbyes. Once the door closed, Ronan turned to me.

"Welcome home," I said.

We became a mess of tears and kisses while we stood in the living room, surrounded by his boxes.

"Did I move in with you?"

"You did."

We started sorting through boxes, deciding what went where and making room for his belongings. I opened a box and found his art pads. Maddie had told me he was talented, and he was.

"These are amazing." I found a portrait of Reese in pencil crayon. It looked real. "Do you still want to register for a graphic design program?" I asked.

"I was hoping to. But since I quit my job because I was moving, I'm not sure I can afford it now."

"We aren't common-law yet, so if you hurry and apply for full-time student funding, you'll receive a decent loan because you're a single parent."

"That's genius." Under his breath, I heard him mutter about being common-law. My ears pinked.

I carefully leafed through his book and came across a portrait of me and Emma. We were throwing flour at each other while we made gingerbread houses. "Ronan, I can't believe you hid this talent from me. This is more than 'I like to draw'; this is gorgeous art. It's so realistic. I can hear Emma squealing in this."

The room fell silent, and I looked at him. He stared intensely at me. "What's wrong, babe?" It was too late to call Steve and pack it all in back in the van. He was stuck here now. And if he wanted to leave, he was on his own. I was tired and needed a nap.

"If I had asked, what would you have said?"

"Asked what?"

"If I had asked you to marry me. At the concert. Katherine yelled at me to ask you to marry me. I thought about it."

There was the system's shutdown sound. "You did?" My hands shook, and I set his sketchbook on a box.

"It crossed my mind. But moments before we weren't even a couple. Then we were back together, and you asked me to move in with you. This image of us married and happy flashed in my head. I chickened out because I worried if you said no, it would ruin your show. If you said yes, then it would have been a proposal worthy of a viral video. And all this zoomed around my brain in one moment, and before I processed it, I was leaving the stage." He caught his breath. "If I had asked, what would you have said?"

"Yes," I said, not taking any time to consider it. I wasn't even anxious about saying it. It was true. I remembered wishing he had asked me.

"Cool," he said. He bit his lip.

I tried to get a read on what he was thinking. "Do you wish you had asked?"

"Yeah," he blushed. "I mean I hadn't planned on it, but it feels like a missed opportunity." He chewed on his ponytail and stared off into space.

I pulled him into a hug, where he burrowed into my neck. With a sigh accompanied by a little, light, airy hum, I swayed him side to side and kissed his cheek. He relaxed and enveloped me.

As we swayed, I sang "Nessun Dorma" by Puccini as quiet as I could, so I didn't kill his hearing. And when I couldn't be quiet, I stepped back and serenaded him. Tears rolled down his cheeks as he watched in awe. I gathered my breath and built towards the climax of the aria, the part I loved singing the most, when something in my brain clicked and I stopped.

"Did we just get engaged?" I asked.

He wiped away tears. "Um. Maybe?"

We stared at each other.

"Do you want to be engaged?" he asked.

"I think so? Do you?"

"I think so." His brow furrowed. "I don't know what to say here, Wishes."

"Neither do I." I touched his cheek and sought answers in his eyes. "We should eat while we think."

He agreed.

I made waffles and put the coffee on, while he made whipped cream from scratch and sliced strawberries. Both of us switched between pensive thoughts, stealing glances, sharing kisses, and giggling.

We laced our fingers together while we ate and chatted about the kids' upcoming school show, then discussed building birdhouses for *our* backyard.

I started to clear the dishes when he took the plates from me and set them in the sink. He lifted me onto the countertop and kissed me with a wild fierceness. Over and over.

"Yes," he whispered against my lips.

I kissed him deep like he was the only thing keeping me alive. "Yes." I panted between kisses. "Yes." I pulled back. "With a few stipulations."

His eyes narrow. "Like?"

"The kids have a say. We'd be a family and I don't want to force them into it and be miserable."

"Sounds reasonable." He chewed his lip. Our kisses and bites left them chaffed and swollen. "If they say no?"

"We carry on like we are now, and one day they'll change their minds." I kissed his knuckles. He looked nervous. "I won't leave you. It means we wait. My second stipulation is we have a long engagement. We're not getting married this year. I need time for my brain to process. It was a rough ride to get my brain to be okay with asking you to move in."

"Don't overthink things like you usually do." He booped my nose.

"I'll try not to, but it'll happen. Be prepared for intense moments of crippling self-doubt."

"I'm always ready. I got you, darling." He cupped my cheek. "So ... are we engaged?" He looked like a shy, fair maiden, blushing as if I had asked him to accompany me to his first spring dance.

"As long as the kids agree."

"Let's go grab the kids."

"Should we buy them new toys?"

"You want us to bribe our kids into giving us their blessing?" he asked.

"Yes." I was so excited I needed to nervous-pee three times before we left.

CHAPTER THIRTY-FOUR

I held back a swear word as I entered the already dark, gym mat-scented auditorium ... audinasium? What was the correct word? I scanned the crowd, ignoring the scowls from other parents, judging my late ass. Ronan waved at me from front and centre. No matter how hard I tried to be quiet, my footsteps were as loud as cars backfiring.

I slid into the uncomfortable metal folding chair and kissed Ronan's cheek.

"All set?" he asked.

"Yup."

Vinny leaned around Ronan, and we shared a thumbs up.

Ronan took my hand. There was a tremor in his grip, and his palms were sweaty. It was endearing how nervous he was for the kids' spring talent show performance. His fingers fidgeted with my engagement ring.

We let the kids pick them out. Emma designed Ronan's: a lovely, white gold ring with his, mine, Emma's, and Reese's birthstones. She had the jeweller engrave "Stay or else ..." on the inside. My kid was low-key creepy.

I had orchestrated a grand proposal. But when I changed into my tux, I left the ring box on the table. Emma opened it and slipped the ring on Ronan's finger. Cute, but not what I wanted.

Reese had carefully designed my ring. It was ebony wood, to represent black piano keys, and a mother-of-pearl inlay of music notes, for the white piano keys. It arrived that morning. Ronan was running errands, and it was pure torture to wait for him to arrive home.

He rushed home with a dozen roses, knelt on one knee, and proposed to me in front of the kids. I had been giddy and tittering all day.

The weight of the ring felt strange on my finger. It was lighter than my wedding band from Alex, which sat safely in its box in front of a photo of him on my dresser. Ronan played with my new ring all evening. Maybe he was nervous, or he wanted to remember this was real. We were getting married.

We bought the kids simple, inexpensive, silver, Irish Claddagh rings. If they lost them, it wouldn't cost much to replace them. When they were older, we'd buy them higher-quality rings.

Principal Davis walked onto the stage and welcomed us to the end-of-the-year talent show. Ronan, Vinny, Katherine, Maddie, Tim, all the grandparents, and I whooped loud enough to warrant a teacher look from the principal.

The Christmas show had garnered a larger crowd, as the spring performance was for students who volunteered. I would say auditioned, but everyone got in. And because only a quarter of the students were performing, it was about a quarter of the Christmas audience. My crew managed to snag the entire front row.

They started with the youngest ones, which included the spunky kindergartner from the Christmas show. The one who had channelled Aretha Franklin. She was adorable.

My heart beat harder as each kid finished. Why were there so many grade ones? Ronan tapped my knee to stop me from bouncing it. When they announced grade twos, both Ronan and I sat straight. Joey came out first. He sang who knows what, quiet and off-key. Pffft. Amateur.

The teacher announced the Decker-Kim siblings. Hearing that made me lightheaded with joy. Vinny and Katherine cheered loudly. I chewed the nails on my free hand while Ronan squeezed my other. I hoped I did everything right.

Emma strutted to downstage centre in her red, poufy dress, red Mary Jane shoes, and drag queen–quality hair and makeup. Barry had done a remarkable job. It impressed me how well he'd curled her hair until he told me it was a wig. Still impressive.

She posed with one arm and face stretched to the sky, holding a mic, and the other on her hip. Barry helped Reese push the equipment cart onto the stage, turned on the DJ equipment, and checked the settings. He nodded at me before disappearing behind the curtain.

Reese hit a button, and my pre-recorded, shortened piano arrangement played. My little diva sang an acoustic ballad version of Lady Gaga's "Born This Way." She lowered her arm and faced the audience. Instead of singing "mama," she sang "daddy." My heart burst. She belted out her most grown-up-almost-eight-years-old voice and hit ninety-five percent of the notes.

It was tough to tear my eyes away from her, but I had to check on Reese. He had on my old, orange headphones. The ones that had caused drama at Christmas. Emma lent them to him because she wanted Alex there in his own way. She added that if he broke them, she knew where he lived. Reese didn't realize that was a threat. He responded with "We live in the same house, dummy."

He pushed a few buttons and nodded. We had practiced many times over the past couple of weeks. Live mixing was difficult, but he was determined. Halfway through the song was Reese's time to shine. He dropped a beat, as they say, and hit a rhythm track we had chosen. He had been sampling Emma's singing the entire time and made a dance mix.

The crowd went wild. Kids danced in the aisles. Emma broke into a choreography Katherine helped with. She switched from diva to dancing queen, and I loved it. Reese signalled to Emma to take charge. She brought the mic to her mouth. I'm not sure if I'd call it rapping, maybe rap-adjacent, but she did it. Whenever the song referred to being Asian, she pumped a fist in the air.

Hyunji and Jung Ki, and other Asian families, joined in when they realized what was happening. Whenever Emma sang about being Black, Barry stepped out and stretched his fist in the air, as did Maddie, and I saw movement from others in the auditorium.

My skin grew cold as my little audience participation approached.

When she sang "gay," I raised my fist high; "straight," Katherine raised her hand; "bi," Vinny and Ronan's hands shot up; "lesbian," Maddie raised one fist and the other on "transgender." There were cheers from the audience; some participated with their identities. Reese ended the song with amazing electronica sounds and echoed the word "queen" until it faded out. He undid a latch on the equipment cart and a progressive pride flag unfurled. Tears stung my eyes.

Standing ovation. Our little crew jumped out of our seats, and ninety-nine percent of the audience stood too. Our kids bowed and lived their best life. I didn't think I had ever seen Reese smile that big before.

Barry pulled the cart offstage, and Principal Davis thanked them for an "energetic and talented performance with a positive message of celebrating diversity." That woman had grown on me. A few moments later, she added, "Emma? Reese? Your performance is over, you must leave the stage. Thank you."

Barry ballet-lifted Emma and danced her offstage because she wouldn't stop bowing and blowing kisses. I predicted many singing competitions in my future. I mentally scrolled through a list of friends who were voice teachers.

The kids slipped into the audience and sat with the other students who had already performed. They waved boisterously at us. Our entire crew returned the wave. They whispered with other kids until a teacher shushed them.

Reese was a different child from the crying, biting, light-and-noise-sensitive kid I'd met in December. Now he was a musician, giggling, chatting with friends, and had tools for sensory overload.

Ronan watched his son ... our son? Too soon? He shone with pride and adoration. I had an intense need to kiss his cheek. So, I did. He grinned and kissed my knuckles. Barry sat next to me. He tried to fist-bump me, but I got confused and kissed his hand instead. *Can I die now?*

We had to clasp our hands over our mouths so we didn't bust a gut laughing.

The rest of the show was ... I don't remember. My brain was elsewhere, thinking of dinner, my strange little family, what I'd like to do with Ronan after the kids went to bed, and more dinner. I was hungry. If we wouldn't be taking a sizeable chunk of the audience with us, we would have snuck out. Plus, if I were the kid on stage, I'd be traumatized if the entire front row yeeted themselves out during my performance. So, we cheered on the other kids. Jaxeon had moves!

When Principal Davis closed the show, we meandered into the foyer with the kids, who chatted with everyone. Ronan laced his fingers with mine while he and Maddie laughed over something, and I made small talk with Tracy.

Samantha strode over to us with Joey in a firm grip. A teenage boy moped behind them. "That was amazing, you two," she said to Emma and Reese. "You put a lot of effort into that."

Reese stepped forward and offered her the pride pin from his lapel. His big blue eyes looked at her with hope and expectations. No one could refuse that look.

Samantha turned it over in her palm. Lips tight, brows furrowed. Big thoughts filled her brain. I held my breath. We all did. The teenager stared at her over her shoulder. His expression ran a gambit of emotions.

"Thank you," Samantha said. "Do you have another?"

I didn't expect that.

Maddie stepped forward. "Oh hunny, I have a ton. I give these out like candy on Halloween. Which one do you want? I've got the typical rainbow, the progressive rainbow, trans, lesbian, bi, pan, nonbinary, genderfluid, I have an ace in here somewhere. Oh, I found a poly. I thought I ran out of those." She fished through her purse.

"The regular rainbow is fine. That includes everyone, right?" Samantha was stepping out of her box. She swallowed while Maddie handed it to her. She turned to her older son and pinned one on him, and the other on herself. "There." She sighed in relief and stood tall.

Her son's bottom lip quivered, and he hugged her.

Joey muttered something rude, but Barry cleared his throat and threw him a look. "Sorry," Joey said and looked at the ground.

I tried to hold myself together, but Ronan cried, so I cried. Maddie cooed a sweet "aww" noise.

"We should give them space," Vinny whispered in my ear and tugged on my arm.

The best thing about all the attention the kids got today was that they fell asleep the moment we finished reading to them. I stretched out half-asleep in *our* bed in my pyjamas, and Ronan crawled under *our* sheets and lay on top of me. This was the love of my life.

"Hey, fiancé." He ran his fingers through my locks. I didn't know if I would ever not feel a lightning bolt in my stomach when I heard that. "Sleepy?"

With my eyelids half-closed, I murmured, "A bit."

His fingers traced a line along my forehead, my nose, and pulled on my lower lip. "I want to kiss all your freckles."

"You may try." I grinned. Then yawned.

"Darling, you are delightful when you're tired." He kissed my cheek. "Our kids did amazing today. I've never seen Reese come so alive." He buried his face in my shoulder.

I smoothed his hair out, both to be romantic and to avoid it going into my nose. I felt his body give a small shudder. "Are you okay?"

"I have good news." He lifted his head.

"What is it?" My nerves tingled as he hesitated. Was he accepted to a school in Montreal and was moving away?

"They caught them."

It took me a moment to understand. "The shitheads who vandalized your place? The police caught them?"

"Yeah. My lawyer called me while you were rehearsing with the kids. The police tracked them down and raided their apartments. There was enough evidence to arrest them for the vandalism, plus they found a meth lab and illegal weapons to add to the charges. My lawyer thinks the judge will lock them away for at least ten years."

"Babe, this is wonderful." I hugged him hard. The weight of a million bricks lifted off my chest. They couldn't get to him again.

"That's not the best part." He leaned backwards. "There was evidence to link Vanessa to the attack. They are adding charges to her already long list and restricting her contact with others. A judge signed an order, and she's not allowed to contact anyone I know. She can no longer file complaints against me because she is a known nuisance. And her lawyer blacklisted her, so she has no legal representation."

I stared at him while I let his words sink in. "Holy shit." I felt dizzy processing all this. "What does this mean?"

"She can't get me. She can't stop us from getting married. And..." he swallowed. "I had my lawyer look into something." He cleared his throat. "She can't stop you if you choose to adopt Reese."

The ocean crashed in my brain and the world glowed in beautiful gem tones as I registered what he said. I had not considered adopting Reese. I assumed I'd be his stepdad and that was enough. But now it was an option.

"Wow," I said.

"You're amazing with Reese." He fidgeted with my pyjama sleeve. "You have tremendous patience with him. You support his quirks and needs when I become frustrated and snap." Ronan looked away and frowned.

"You've been great with me, and I have similar quirks and needs. That's why I get him. You're working to understand, and he sees your efforts." I kissed his forehead.

"Thank you. I am trying." He smiled. "Now that I'm an unemployed, kept man, I've had time to read those books on PTSD and neurodivergence you recommended to me."

"I'm proud of you."

"Thanks." He blushed and ducked his head. His expression glazed over, and he chewed on his hair.

"Babe? What are you thinking?"

"What happens when she gets out?" His voice was quiet. "I know she has a restraining order, but who is going to stop her from driving by?"

"She'll have to get by your strapping husband who will defend you and Reese."

"Yeah, but where can I find a husband like that?" I heard the smirk in his voice.

I feigned offence and tickled him until he squealed for mercy, but I showed him none. He tried to break free, but I wrestled my legs around him so he couldn't escape. He laughed and gasped for air.

"Say I'm strapping!" I demanded as I tortured him.

"That sounds weird," he gasped.

"Say it."

"Fine! You're strapping!"

I stopped tickling him, and he pinned my hands by my head. Red-faced, he panted while he regained composure. His hair was a glorious mess. "You will be my beautiful, strapping husband, who will protect me from my prison-buff, drug-addled, ex and keep our family safe. Regardless of the fact that I can carry you, and you struggle to carry Reese."

I bit my lip. "How do you feel about guard dogs?"

"Deal."

"Seriously though, I will do whatever I can to protect you and Reese. Promise."

"I know, and I love you for it." He looked at me adoringly. "Plus, you have at least five years to get ripped." There was that smirk again. "And I wouldn't mind watching you work out topless."

"Me and my sexy noodly arms?"

"Sexy noodly arms that play beautiful music, hug our kids, and hold me while I sleep. I couldn't ask for anything sexier than that." He kissed me, loving and sweet. When he pulled away, I yawned again. "Want me to read to you?"

I nodded. We were on a T.J. Klune kick and were a couple chapters into *The House in the Cerulean Sea*. He rolled on his back, and I lay on top of him, listening to his heartbeat and hearing the low rumble of his voice reverberating through his body.

This. This was what I wanted for the rest of my life. And I was getting it. I was grateful for this man and glad I let him sit next to me six months ago. And, oddly enough, I was glad Reese bit Emma. It brought us together. And now we lay in bed, where we bit each other.

He helped me through my concoction of mental health issues, and I supported him with his trauma and self-doubt. We were a strong parenting duo. He set the boundaries for Emma that I couldn't, and I helped Reese cope with his brain glitches. I still mourned Alex, and I celebrated life with Ronan.

"I love you so fucking much," I said.

"I love you too." He kissed the top of my crown of curls.

A year ago, I never imagined finding love after Alex. I believed I would never love again. I'd raise Emma alone. Even with support from friends and family, the ache of loneliness was powerful.

Ronan gave me hope for the future. He was the light that shone through the mental fog I was trapped in. It hadn't faded completely, but it was clearer. Some days, it was barely there.

The pride I had for my new little family filled my chest. While I might not have fallen under the category of "strapping," I would fiercely protect them from anything.

I nuzzled my cheek against Ronan's chest. The sound of a book closing came from overhead, and I felt his muscles stretch as he set the book on the side table.

"Aloysius Dermot O'Connor ...." Ronan played with my curls. "Or perhaps one day Aloysius Decker? We may not be perfect, but we're perfect for each other. You're my perfect. It's a good thing you're a pianist because you crescendo into my life. It would blow if you played trumpet. Flautists push my buttons. And violinists are high-strung."

"Stop." I jabbed his ribcage.

He roared with laughter and held me tight.

Ronan was my perfect.

EPILOGUE

A Year and Some Later

Hyunji fussed with my bow tie. "You wear these all the time. Why can't you get this right?"

"The others are clip-ons," I admitted.

"Disgraceful." She grinned. "There." She spun me towards the full-length mirror in my hotel suite.

I looked good. I wore a tailored green suit that had a subtle, blue-floral print. Emma had spotted it at the store, and Vinny and Katherine approved.

"You're a handsome man, son," she said. "I've known you for many years, and while I've seen you happy before, I've never seen you this joyful. With Alex, you were happy, but, well, you know." Her smile wavered, and she cleared her throat. "With Ronan, I see not only joy, but this foundation. Like your soul knows you can build a solid life with him." We were both teary-eyed. "You chose right."

"Thank you." I kissed her cheek. "Wow, I'm getting married today." Cue the waterworks.

There was a knock on the door connected to a living-room space. We got a fancy honeymoon suite. Katherine peeked her head through.

"Can I come in?"

"Yeah." I wiped my eyes dry.

"I'm glad I haven't done your eyeliner yet. I knew you'd cry all day." She stepped into the room.

"You look amazing." I looked her over. The hairstylist had given her a poufy, Dutch braid. Her makeup was flawless. She wore a form-fitting, white, beaded gown. Since I wasn't wearing white, Ronan and I let her. This was far from a traditional wedding. Besides, her dress was identical to Emma's and Vinny's.

Vinny swaggered in and did a spin for me.

I gasped. "Stunning."

He curtsied. Well, he did an awkward bend at the knees.

When I first got married, Vinny wanted to wear a dress, but Alex wouldn't let him. But Ronan and I didn't care. Vinny's look of euphoria was priceless. He checked himself out in the mirror and made pouty lips.

Emma sashayed in and posed with Vinny. Barry had styled a wig for her with delicate braids, and she was my beautiful, sassy little angel.

"Love-bug, you are breathtaking. You ready to make Ronan and Reese officially family?" I asked.

"Yes," she squealed.

I looked my loved ones over. "Aren't Ronan and I supposed to be the centre of attention? You are all going to outshine us." I beamed as I hugged each of them.

Vinny clasped our fingers together. "No, buddy, you're hot." He sighed. "I want you to know how much I cherish you and —"

"Is this a long speech?" Katherine cut in. "Because you blabbed and cried all last night, and we're short on time." She was right. Vinny cried more than I did last night.

I glanced at the clock and wished I hadn't. Less than fifteen minutes before the wedding planner came to fetch me. My heart palpitated and my breathing grew shallow.

"Oh, no you don't." Katherine saw my panic and seized my hands. "Let's breathe." She led me through several breathing exercises. When I was calm enough, she put waterproof eyeliner on me and fixed my hair. "Perfect."

My curls were a delicate balance of ringlets and floppy. Our stylist had come early and rushed through my side of the wedding party before he dashed off to help Ronan. Rumours were, Ronan was doing something fancy.

Our wedding planner arrived exactly when she said she would and ushered us downstairs into a small room next to the hall. "Wait here until I come to get you. Get in order. Here are your flowers." She handed bouquets to everyone but me. I had something special planned.

The door closed behind her. I shifted from side to side, trying to shake my nerves. The music started in the wedding hall. Ronan was walking down the aisle first. I wished I could watch. We had a videographer, so I'd see it later, but it took strength for me not to run out and peek in.

It took me a moment to recognize the song. Ronan chose the music and kept it a secret. It was my voice echoing in the hall. He chose the song I wrote for him.

Katherine handed me a tissue. "Dab, don't wipe."

The wedding planner rushed us to stand outside the hall doors. Vinny and Katherine went first. They walked hand in hand and disappeared through the doorway.

"Oh my god, he's gorgeous," Katherine said.

When it was my turn, I linked arms with Hyunji, took Emma's hand, and we stepped into the hall. Fairy lights and flowers of all colours were everywhere. I stepped into a fairy tale, and my Fae prince waited for me. And wow. He was a gorgeous Fae prince.

Ronan wore a tailored white suit. The jacket had beautiful tatted-and-beaded flowers. They had sculpted his hair into an intricate 3D flower with a braid trailing down as the stem. Pure art. Silver dust highlighted the twists in the braids. He had smoky eyes, silver-dust highlights in his cheeks, and deep red, velvet lips. I couldn't wait to kiss them.

We were entranced with each other as I walked down the aisle. His blue eyes popped because of the makeup, but they glimmered because of me. He gave me a shy, subtle wave. My entire body blushed.

When I reached my mark on the carpet, we stopped. This was Hyunji's cue to give me away. I kissed her cheek, and she stood between Jung Ki and Hannah in the front row. Then, I kissed Emma's cheek, and she joined Vinny and Katherine on the dais. The rest of the way, I was on my own. I wanted to run to him.

"You're fucking gorgeous," I whispered when I got close enough for him to hear. Unfortunately, I was close enough for the mic to hear too. There were giggles from our guests. "It's true," I said louder.

"Hey, you're fucking gorgeous too," he said in a quiet, low purr.

He turned to an adorable Reese, who was dressed in a tiny white tux. Reese gave him a hairclip of white blossoms. Ronan clipped it into my curls. Emma handed me a clip of delicate, cascading flowers. Ronan had to squat so I could reach. It fit perfectly within his hair design. Clearly, the hairdresser was aware of the clip.

"So pretty." I giggled and fawned over him.

A throat cleared near me. It took a few throat clears for me to remember I was in front of an audience. I was blocking the officiant.

"R-right, s-sorry," I stuttered. Damn it. I stepped to where he directed.

There were laughs at my expense. I looked out at the moderately-sized audience, scarlet-faced. Most people were strangers to me. Ronan had way more friends and family than I did. I exchanged smiles with my musician friends.

Why did I agree to this many people?

My gaze moved around the room to the lights and decorations. The colourful flowers formed a rainbow, and I smiled. I looked at the ceiling and stared at the twinkling lights above us. It felt magical.

The most beautiful part of all of this was Ronan. Fine details polished his suit. And god, those exquisite eyes. I lost myself in them.

Maddie and Barry stood behind Ronan. Maddie wore the same dress as my party. That was all their doing: Ronan and I gave them free rein. Barry matched Reese's tux.

My green suit stood out.

My vision flickered around the audience. People laughed. The officiant was talking to me, and I hadn't realized. The enchanting setting distracted me, and I had spaced out.

Static crackled in my ears and my shoulders raised. The officiant laughed. My chest tightened, and I tugged at my sleeves. Why could I perform in front of hundreds but freak out here? This was something intimate and special, an occasion to savour between us and our closest people. Not power through in front of people I barely knew.

Ronan stepped close to me, pushed the mic aside, and took my hands. "Look at me, darling."

I obeyed, and my shoulders relaxed as I focused on him.

"There you are." His mouth curved in a gentle smile. The colour of his lips caused me to think of wonderful places they could kiss and smear across. "Stay with me, okay? This is our wedding, and I'd hate for you to disassociate and miss it." He touched my cheek.

I nodded. "That would suck. I don't appreciate people laughing at me. I was just enjoying the moment." My eyes burned with tears threatening to fall.

"Oh, babe." His thumb rubbed my cheekbone. "Do you still want to get married?"

I nodded vigorously.

"Good. Should I ask everyone to leave? Or we go somewhere?"

The officiant leaned forward. "I have another wedding soon; I don't have time to rearrange the room."

Ronan pursed his lips and looked at me. "Babe, I love you, and you are all that matters to me right now." He placed a hand on each of my cheeks and held me delicately. "Stay with me." He bit his lip. "We're getting married like this," Ronan said. He smelled of citrus.

"What? But —" the officiant started.

"Don't care. This is how we're doing it."

On Ronan's cue, the officiant continued. I breathed deep, and the world melted away. His touch sent beautiful lightning bolts through my body. It was only us and an omniscient voice saying beautiful words about devotion and building futures. I memorized Ronan's face and hair, my fists clung to his lapel, and I fell deeper in love. He fell deeper in love with me, too.

"Aloysius?" the officiant asked. I snapped to attention. "It's time to read your vows."

Ronan turned me away from the audience, and Vinny stood behind me. In case I freaked out and needed his support. I pulled my vows out of my pocket.

"You'd think I'd know how to write vows by my second wedding." I laughed nervously and glanced at my paper. "Ronan, my love, my number one promise to you is to be the best father to Reese I can be.

"I also promise to listen when you're stressed, keep music in your world, support you when you need it, and communicate with you to the best of my ability.

"When you're cold, I will have extra gloves to keep you warm. You will never have to order tea when everyone else has pizza. And with my strong, noodly arms, I will protect you. I do not promise, however, to protect you when the kids are coming at us with flour. It's every man for himself then.

"And as a symbol of my promises—" I gestured to Emma, who fished something out of her bouquet and passed it to me. "I present you this." It was two small gold pine cones on a ribbon. "I will always stand under the pine cones with you, but please excuse me when I'm too dense to understand what you're saying." The ribbon tied easily around his wrist.

"Oh, Wishes." Ronan lifted my chin and leaned in.

"No kissing," the officiant snapped.

Ronan's mouth puckered, and I swear he growled. But he backed away.

"Ronan?" the officiant asked.

He pulled a paper from his pocket and held my hand. "I promise you I had no help with this." He cleared his throat and smirked.

"I vow to you I will Handel whatever Mozarts our way. And when you are too Debussy with things, I will have your Bach and order a pizzicato. When life gives us treble and things are baroque, I will step up to the bar and search for alto-natives. I Wagner we will have many years of love and laughter together. And I will Tchaikovsky to be the best husband to you, the Pears to your Britten.

"I will try to be amuseing, be your *Entertainer*, and fill your life with *Midsummer Night's Dreams*. Even when you are a bit of a *Nutcracker*. I will love you fermata and hold you all nocturn. You better ballad I cantata legato you go. You are major in my world, and everything else, besides the kids, is minor. The key signature to my heart lies with you, and I symphony adagio you."

I lost it and howled with laughter. The amount of effort he must have put into that was so sweet. "I'm proud of you and your dad jokes."

I kissed him. Tradition be damned. I kissed him until I made it uncomfortable for the audience. I kissed him until the officiant relented and pronounced us husbands.

We glued one more fragment of my broken soul back into place.

Acknowledgments

There are so so so many amazing people that have helped me through this process, and I doubt I could ever thank everyone for their love and support. There is a handful of people who were extra amazing to me throughout this novel, and past manuscripts failed or were placed on the back-burner. These rocks in my life are Karel, Vicki, Amurlee, and Mercedes. All of who have put up with late-night messages, tears, crippling self-doubt, and gave me so much love and encouragement.

I want to acknowledge two special beta readers; Elizabeth and Emily, who were amazing and helped me out an incredible amount. You two rock. Seriously, you two caught plot holes, taught me about the music industry, built up my ego, and laughed at my jokes. I wish you all the best of luck in your projects.

And three cheers to my editing team! This tested "two below the median in spelling skills" author, never thought I'd be able to write something that made sense. My brain struggles to see the difference between wierd, wired, and weird. I received embarrassing comments growing up about my difficulties with spelling and reading, and it shut down my desire to write for years. But with the help of all of those above, and my amazing editing team, I got through this.

So here's to Ashely Rayner and Nikki Bell Morrison at Inkwell's Editorial Services (www.inkwellseditor.com) and Gillian Rodgerson (www.gillianrodgerson.com) who helped make my book better. Your support and skills mean the world to me.

And you, dear reader, thanks for sticking with me and kicking ass. You're awesome, and I appreciate you.

About the Author

C.J. Banks (*they/she/he*) hails from Canada and currently resides in Ontario with their spouse and several cats. C.J. writes LGBTQ romance, reads LGBTQ romance, and lives a pretty awesome LGBTQ romance. When not reading or writing, they are going for countryside drives, watching the waves, painting or gaming. They are an advocate for mental health, bad puns, and the creative arts.

If you liked this book, please consider giving it a review, or rating on whatever platform you prefer. Reviews and rates help indie authors tremendously.

- Website: https://cjbanks.ca
- Facebook: cj.banks.author
- Facebook Reader Group: C.J.'s Pine Cones
- Instagram: c.j._banks
- TikTok: c.j.banks
- Goodreads: C.J. Banks
- Discord Server: C.J's Banks' Pine Cones: https://discord.gg/ATqZuV3PDX
- Subscribe to my Newsletter: https://www.subscribepage.com/cjbanks

Made in United States
North Haven, CT
30 July 2022

22050855R00166